The Dragon's Test

By

Sam Ferguson

THE DRAGON'S TEST
Copyright © 2014 by Sam Ferguson
All Rights Reserved
ISBN:1943183023
ISBN-13:9781943183029

This book is for you. Without readers like you, Erik's story would never be told.

Other Books by Sam Ferguson

CHAPTER ONE

Erik and Braun exited an alley and turned right onto a narrow dirt street lined with squat, rectangular houses topped with cracked gray cedar shingles. A group of men stood in front of one of the houses, talking amongst themselves. As Braun and Erik walked by the men the three of them stopped talking and stared. Erik straightened his sword belt and glared back at the trio. One of them spat on the ground and grinned as his hand went to a knife at his belt. The other two stepped out into the street and pulled swords free from their scabbards. Erik fell back to his training at Kuldiga academy. He calculated the distance between him and the three men. Then he glanced around. "Anyone on the rooftops?" he asked Braun.

"No," Braun said quickly.

Then, another thought came to Erik. He called upon his power and used it to discern the trio's intent. He then put a hand out and steadied his companion. "These are not our enemies," he said confidently.

"That's isn't what I would guess," Braun quipped. His hand went down to his sword. Erik turned back and shook his head at Braun. Braun stiffened, and took a step back. "If they so much as breathe wrong…"

"Stay calm," Erik said. Then Erik turned and walked toward the trio. The man in the middle spat on the ground again and removed his hat, revealing a bald head encircled about with shaggy brown hair just below the scalp. He smiled wide, showing a pair of missing bottom teeth. The man at his left held a long sword out and abruptly set the point down atop his worn, faded black boot. The man at his right did likewise.

"You don't remember me?" the man in the middle asked with a gleam in his eye.

Erik shook his head. "My apologies," Erik said. "But, I meet a lot of people."

The bald man smiled and brought the tip of his dagger up to his mouth, pointing at the gap in his teeth. "How many of them did you take two teeth from?" the bald man asked.

Erik smirked. "As I said, I meet *a lot* of people," he repeated.

"I don't like this," Braun whispered from behind.

"Well," the bald man continued. "I remember you."

"I have urgent business," Erik said. "What is it you want?"

The bald man laughed and slapped the back of his hand into the man on his left. "What do *I* want?"

"You attacked the senate," the man on the left said. "There are a lot of people in this city that are looking for you."

"Some of the lower circles have put a price on your head," the man on the right said.

Erik nodded. "Well, I can tell that you are not here to collect the bounty, so what is it you seek?"

The bald man grinned wide and nodded his head once. "You are as perceptive as ever," he said. "I am here to make good on my debt to you." He slid his knife back into his belt. "When you took my teeth, you also spared my life. You may not remember, but you happened to catch me on the highway some years ago. At the time I was relieving a merchant of their coin."

The men flanking him laughed and nodded. "We were there too," they said in unison.

"You gave us a walloping to remember, Master Lepkin" the bald man said. "But, you found mercy in your heart and told us to change our ways." He gestured to his comrades. "Since then we have sought honest work where we can get it. Mostly as hired hands out in the nearby farms, but lately we have been here in the city. We work at the Singing Serpent as bouncers. We keep order in the place."

"Not exactly the most honest kind of work," Braun commented.

"Better than what we had done in the past," the bald man said as he peered around to Braun. Then he looked back to Erik. "In any case, we owe you a debt of gratitude for giving us a second chance."

"How did you know we would be here?" Braun asked.

"We knew you were in the area, but we weren't following you, if that is what you are asking," the man on the right said.

"This is my home," the bald man said, pointing behind him. "We were just deciding whether to go out and look for you when you came around the corner. It is as if the gods themselves brought you to me." The bald man pointed a finger to the sky. "It's a sign that they are pleased with my new life. They are giving me the chance to make good on my debt."

"We should go," Braun insisted.

"Master Lepkin, come inside. Allow me to repay the kindness you once showed me," the bald man said.

"Remind me of your names," Erik said.

"I am Lester," the bald man said. "This is Dax, and the man on my right is Korbin."

Erik nodded to each and then walked forward. "Alright, let's go inside."

"This is not wise," Braun said.

Erik turned and shot Braun a fierce look. "They mean us no harm."

"These are not our kind of people," Braun said.

Erik smiled. "Don't judge with your eyes," he said. Then he turned and followed Lester and the others into the house.

The brown door creaked and squeaked against Lester's push. A heavy scent of wood smoke wafted out from the opening that made Braun sneeze. Erik's eyes stung a bit as he walked into the main room. A crackling fire in the hearth spewed smoke around a large, black kettle. A long green sleeve hung over the side of the kettle.

"Had a run in with head-lice," Dax said as he pointed to the kettle.

"Wonderful," Braun said. The man nervously reached a hand up and scratched the back of his scalp.

"Wait here for a moment," Lester said as he disappeared behind a patchwork blanket hanging over a doorway that led to a room in the back. Dax and Korbin moved to a door on the right and opened it. Inside Erik saw a couple braids of garlic and some tobacco leaves dangling from a cast iron rack hanging by an old chain from the ceiling.

Lester returned a moment later with a pair of brown over cloaks. "Take off your clothes," he said.

"I beg your pardon," Braun retorted.

Lester eyed him with a grin and then tossed the robes over the back of a wooden rocking chair. "Don't worry, you aren't my type," Lester shot back. He pointed to Braun. "You look like you are employed by a noble house. You would do well to try to blend in a bit more until you get out of the city."

Erik nodded. "Even then we might do well to dress down a bit," he agreed. "No need to draw attention to ourselves."

"Exactly," Lester said. "If you are shy, you can change in the back." Lester disappeared through the doorway again for a few minutes and came back with an armload of clothes. "Here," he said as he plopped the pile on the rocking chair. Braun looked from the clothes on the chair to those in the boiling water over the fire. Lester noticed his gaze and laughed to himself. "That is a load of clothes from the neighboring family," he explained. "The lice didn't come to us."

Braun nodded, but he didn't look any more eager to put on the old clothes.

Erik stripped down to his undergarments and changed first.

"My clothes are plain," Braun said. "Changing won't make much of a difference."

"To the contrary," Lester said. "The people out there searching for you are looking for a well-dressed pair of men. Just because your clothes have a bit of dirt on them doesn't change the fact that you are dressed as a noble."

"None of my garments show my master's coat of arms," Braun argued.

"But they are of a very high quality," Lester countered. "Your black trousers are made of cotton, most of the commoners around here wear wool, which has a very different appearance. Beyond that, your sword belt is clasped with a steel buckle. A man in these parts would only be able to afford iron, and most of the time it would be much older. Your boots are highly polished, if a little scuffed, and your tunic is rimmed with a silk strip around the neckline and again on the sleeves. No one around here would wear anything like that unless we were invited to the king's table for dinner."

"He's right," Erik said. "Change your clothes."

Braun grumbled to himself and started undoing his sword belt. "We are wasting time," he gruffed.

"How much more time would you lose if you were being jumped by a gang of thugs around every other corner on your way out of the city?" Lester shot back.

Just then Dax and Korbin came back into the room, carrying a couple of old saddle bags. "It isn't much in the way of fine dining, but it will get you started," Dax said.

"Beans, bread, dried meat, and some walnuts," Korbin announced as he set the bags on a table nearby."

"Thank you," Erik said. He was pulling on the scratchy wool trousers and tying the drawstring tight when Dax took off his own shirt and grabbed Braun's clothes from the floor.

"What are you doing?" Braun asked.

"Decoys," Lester said flatly. "I will walk with you both to the west gate, and Dax and Korbin will go to the south gate."

"But the west gate is farther away," Braun said. "Besides, my horse is at the south gate."

"Exactly," Lester said. "And everyone looking to collect the bounty will be going to the south gate for that reason. I have a horse stabled outside the west gate that you may take."

"There are two of us," Braun said.

Lester grinned. "Then I suppose you will have to find another horse at the west gate."

"Thank you," Erik put in before Braun could say anything else. "You are going to a lot of trouble for us."

Lester looked to Erik and nodded. "You are a bit different," he said. Lester looked at Erik for a moment and then shrugged. "Perhaps that is what time does," he said. "Hurry and finish changing. We should get moving. Trade your sword belts with Dax and Korbin too."

Erik paused and looked to Master Lepkin's sword.

"Keep the sword," Lester said. "Just let us use the scabbard and sword belt. It won't do much good to change your clothes if everyone can see your sword hanging from your hip."

Erik nodded slowly. "I will be back for it," he said as he pulled the black sword out from the scabbard.

"Of course," Lester said.

Korbin approached and gave Erik his own scabbard while he took Erik's. Korbin slid his own, plain long sword into the black scabbard and clasped the belt around his waist after he had finished putting Erik's clothes on.

Within a matter of minutes the change was complete and Erik and Braun slung the saddle bags over their shoulders. "Thanks again," Erik said.

Lester shrugged, "Let's go."

The five of them walked out the front door. Dax and Korbin went to the left, toward the south gate while Lester led Braun and Erik out to the west gate.

Erik took in the scene as Lester led them through streets he had not seen before. Instead of luxurious houses and manors, there were stone and brick houses all smooshed together. If not for the occasional door it would be hard to tell where one dwelling ended and the next began. Several people were out, many of them going about their business as if nothing had happened. An older woman talked to herself as she hung out the day's wash on a line stretching from her window to a tree in front of her house. A pair of stray dogs were nipping at a bowl of bones someone tossed out onto the street. Smoke hung in the air in this part of the city, but not all of it was from wood.

"Even Drakei Glazei has a darker underbelly," Lester said flatly.

Erik nodded, but said nothing. He was not unsettled by the dirt. As a small child he had lived in similar areas before. He had stayed with a family once that didn't even have a door on their small, one room dwelling. They just hung a thick carpet over the entrance and placed a wooden crate behind it at night to keep prowlers out. Erik could tell he had changed over the years though, for now he knew that this was not the way men were meant to live. It was a strange feeling for him, as if he was caught in the middle of two worlds. Around him he could see the dirt, the toil, and the hardship to which he had been born and abandoned. Yet, as he looked to Braun he was reminded of his home at Lokton manor. A life with servants, guards, and more land and food than one family could use on its own.

Erik noticed something about Braun then that struck him. Braun kept looking left and right, as if he expected someone to jump out of the houses and strike. Even in the face of battle, Erik had not known Braun to appear as nervous as he now did. Could it be that Braun was so accustomed to his life in the manor that he was unnerved simply by walking among those poorer than him?

As if on cue, Braun turned and shot Erik a wary glance. "Keep your eyes peeled," he said.

"You are safe here," Lester said. "These people are too busy with living day to day. They have no time for politics."

"What about bounty money?" Braun asked.

Lester chuckled. "Most people in this quarter can barely afford a knife, let alone a sword or a mace. Relax."

Erik put a hand on Braun's shoulder. He was about to reassure the man that all would be well, but Braun turned and Erik caught sight of a ring dangling from a leather thong about Braun's neck. It was his father's emerald ring. Immediately a gnawing knot tore through Erik's stomach and he knew that it was not the location which had Braun on edge. Seeing the ring, and thinking of his father, brought back the dragon's warning. House Lokton was soon to be attacked.

"We'll get there in time," Erik said.

Braun nodded and reached a hand up to the ring. "I hope so," he said softly as he tucked the jewel back under his tunic.

The afternoon sun was just starting its descent as the three of them exited the dirt streets and found themselves only a few blocks away from the gate. The high, thick walls towered above the shops and houses in this district. As in the other part of the city they saw more people out in the streets, but these people were formed into various groups. Some of them were shouting about the murder of various senators, while others chanted their loyalty to King Mathias.

"Which side are you on?" someone shouted at Lester. Lester waved the man off hurriedly and tried not to answer. The man didn't give up. He ran up to them and stopped directly in front of Lester, placing a hand on his chest. "Do you support the king?" the man demanded.

"Move," Lester growled. He reached up in one swift move and grabbed the man's hand, turned it around and bent the wrist back. The man hunched over and hollered out in pain as Lester pushed him away.

"Hey!" the man protested as he stumbled to the ground.

"Today is not a good day to be out late," Lester commented dryly. The others who had been talking with the first man now stared at the three of them. "I am too busy feeding my family to cry over dead nobles," Lester said to the others.

The first man scrambled to his feet and walked away,

grumbling and rubbing his wrist.

"That was subtle," Braun commented wryly.

Lester shook his head and kept walking.

A group of guards came around the corner of the street on horseback just then. One of them stood in his saddle and blew his trumpet three times. Then, the guard at the front of the group halted his horse and addressed the groups on the street.

"By order of his majesty, King Mathias, all citizens are to return to their homes immediately."

The group of men shouted back at the guards, cursing them and throwing stones. "Go back to your castle!" someone said.

"The king sends us home when he should be arresting Lepkin for destroying the senate!" someone else bellowed.

The guard was unamused. "Go back to your homes now, or we will be forced to take action."

Several more groups of people poured into the wide street from nearby houses and alleys, all shouting and yelling angrily.

"This does not bode well," Braun said.

"Lester," Erik started. "Thank you for everything you have done, but now would be a good time to leave."

"No, I am with you until we get to the gate," Lester said.

Erik reached out and turned the man around. "You need to go, now." Erik looked into Lester's eyes. "Your debt is paid. Go home."

Lester nodded slowly and ducked into the nearest alley.

"What is it?" Braun asked

"None of these groups are friendly to the king," Erik said.

"How can you tell?" Braun asked.

Erik surveyed the growing crowd. "It is one of my gifts that I have been developing at Valtuu Temple. Just trust me."

"What is the plan?"

"There are only twenty guards, and well over a hundred people here," Erik said.

"You can't be thinking of stopping them ourselves," Braun commented. "That would be suicide. Besides, the whole point to going with Lester was to *avoid* being discovered by the people who want to cash in on our heads."

"Return to your homes!" the guard commanded again.

A man jumped up onto a nearby wagon and pointed to the

guards. "They would rather force us into a curfew than bring the murderer to justice! The king is no longer in charge of the throne, he is Lepkin's puppet, afraid of the Keeper and his sword!"

"I can't let them fight each other over me," Erik said.

"It *isn't* about *you*," Braun said. You know this as much as I do."

Erik scanned the crowd with his power, searching the men and looking into their hearts. "There are only a few that would fight me," Erik said. "The rest, though they are angry with the king, will not fight me if I reveal myself."

"And then what?" Braun asked. "We still have to make it to the gate."

Erik nodded. "If I can disperse the crowd, perhaps the guards can dissuade the rest and escort us to the gate."

"What if the guard would rather cash in on your head?" Braun pointed out. "These are men in the regular guard, not the king's personal guard. Their loyalty may not be as pure as you would hope."

Erik nodded and looked to the guards, quickly scanning them as well. "You are right," Erik said. There are two who would take the chance to attack."

"Let's just slip into the alley and be gone."

A large, middle-aged man emerged from the crowd holding a rolling pin in one hand and a fire poker in the other. "You go back to your homes!" he shouted at the guards. "You can't protect us, so we will protect ourselves."

The guards drew their swords and the captain leveled his blade at the man. "I will not ask again," the captain promised.

"No," Erik said. "I can't let this happen without trying to stop it." He stepped forward and drew back the hood of his cloak and pulled his sword from the scabbard. He let his power surge through him and the blade reacted instantly with hot flames that roared into life. "I am here," Erik shouted as loud as he could. "I am no murderer. The senate broke the law and would have put an innocent man to death in order to sate their own lust for power." Erik pointed his flaming sword at the man with the rolling pin. "The king is in control of this kingdom, and you would do well to mind your tongue."

The man glanced nervously from the mounted guards to Erik.

"Then he stabbed his fire poker into the ground in front of him. "You would draw sword against common citizens?" the man asked. The previous confidence with which he had berated the guards was now shaky, and unsure.

Erik stepped forward, glancing around him and watching the men back away from him. "Return to your homes, and trouble the streets no more with your anger." He scanned the crowd with his power, identifying a few men that intended to attack him. "I hold my sword out only in the hopes of saving you from disaster. I will strike none who do not attack me first."

"Why should we listen to him?" the man atop the wagon shouted. "He is the one who killed the senators!"

Erik flourished his sword before him, letting the flames crackle and roar before he extinguished the flames and returned the sword to the scabbard. "I attacked only those who sought to take an innocent man's life." He stepped forward, hands out in front of him. "Please, if you want peace, then return to your homes." He looked to the man with the rolling pin and stared into the man's eyes before continuing. "The guards are only trying to maintain the peace."

"Because you threw the city into chaos!" the man on the wagon shouted.

"Let's go," the man with the rolling pin said finally. "Let the nobles figure it out." He then turned and pushed his way through the crowd, leaving his fire poker in the dirt. Several others turned and followed him.

"Cowards!" the man on the wagon shouted. "You have the chance to bring the murderer to justice!"

Erik folded his arms and shouted over the man. "Is it justice you seek, or is it blood money offered by those who truly seek to undermine the law?"

The man bristled and his hand slid down to an axe hanging from his belt.

"If you want to cash in on my head, then come and try to take it from my shoulders," Erik challenged. "But I promise you will not succeed."

The captain of the guard pranced his horse toward the man on the wagon. "Choose now!" he commanded. "You may rest in your bed tonight, or in the dirt."

The man blanched and jumped down from the wagon to disappear into the receding crowd. A few of the others that Erik had identified as potential enemies lingered while the crowd quickly dispersed, but as the numbers around them dwindled, so did their courage and they all eventually left.

When only the guards remained Erik walked up to the two guards that wished him ill and looked them both in the eye. The captain of the guard trotted his horse up next to Erik to greet him, but Erik held a hand up and addressed the two.

"What say you?" Erik asked. "Is a bit of coin worth the blood of your own countrymen?" The captain glanced from Erik to the two guards and they nervously looked to each other before finally shaking their heads.

"We live only to serve our king," one of them said. The other nodded, albeit unconvincingly as he watched Erik with green, hungry eyes.

"Is something wrong, Master Lepkin?" the captain asked.

"I would not trust these two, if I were you," Erik replied bluntly.

"What have we done?" the guard with the hungry eyes asked.

"I will tell you exactly what you have done," Braun interrupted as he stepped up next to Erik. He pointed at the guard with the hungry eyes. "When I first came into town, you tried to buy my loyalty. You said you were forming a brotherhood that would ensure the proper heir would take control of the throne upon the king's demise."

"Preposterous!" the man shouted. "I have never seen you before in my life!"

"Desmon, we both know that isn't true," Braun said.

"Captain, he is making this up!" Desmon said.

"Then how does he know your name?" the captain asked sternly.

Braun then pointed to the other guard. "And what was your name?" he asked. "You were there too, playing cards."

"I don't know what you are talking about," the man said.

"Then you wouldn't remember me slapping the back of your head, would you?" Braun said coldly. The man clenched his jaw and his hand almost went toward a dagger at his belt. Braun smiled wryly. "Thought so," he said.

"Is this true?" the captain demanded.

"I have never known Braun to lie," Erik said.

Braun snapped his fingers and pointed to the other guard. "Miles," he said emphatically. "Desmon said your name was Miles!"

The captain gestured to his men and they instantly fanned out around the pair of guards. "Let's go," the captain said.

"They have no proof!" Desmon protested.

"Master Lepkin's word is good enough for me," the captain said grimly. "Even if it wasn't, the fact that this man knows both of you is also quite intriguing."

"There were others present," Braun said. "One they called Sweets, and another named Craver. Desmon here was sent to bribe me by another guard at the south gate named Jep."

The captain nodded and smiled to Erik. "Master Lepkin, you have done us a great service. You have prevented bloodshed, and helped us sniff out the rotten apples. You have my thanks."

"You can't do this!" Miles shouted. He pulled his dagger and lashed out at the captain, but the captain was quick to dodge. Then he followed in with a deft slice to Miles' shoulder, forcing the man's hand to jerk open and drop the dagger.

"Take them in!" the captain bellowed.

The other guards swarmed over Desmon and Miles faster than the other two could blink and stripped them of their swords before binding their hands behind their backs. Then the group of guards rode off. The captain remained behind just long enough to thank Erik again.

"The west gate has good men," the captain said. "If anyone gives you trouble, ask for Berven, he is my cousin, and as honest as they come."

Erik nodded. "Thank you," he said.

"Thank you," the captain said with a quick salute. Then he spurred his horse into a trot and followed after his men.

"That went a lot better than I thought it would," Braun commented.

"When did you recognize the two guards?" Erik asked.

"About the time you went to speak with them, but I wasn't going to say anything until I knew what you were going to do."

Erik nodded and looked past Braun to the horsemen,

watching them speed down the road. "I would not want to be those two," Erik commented.

"We should move," Braun said.

The two of them passed though the last couple of city blocks before they arrived at the gate. By that time they had both drawn their hoods back over their faces, though it probably didn't do any good by that point. A throng of people pressed the guards at the gate, forced into a bottleneck as a pair of city guards consulted with large books and lists before letting anyone pass through the gate and leave the city.

Luckily, Berven was one of the men with the lists and he let Erik and Braun through without much more than a cursory glance at Erik's face and a hasty note scribbled into the book. Then the two went to the stables and asked the stable boy where Lester's horse was. The boy took some convincing, but after a few minutes of negotiating they were able to procure both Lester's horse, and an additional mount so they could be on their way.

*****

Erik dropped his saddle bag onto the ground and slid his back down the chunky bark of the large pine tree behind him as he descended to sit next to his bag. He looked up to see Braun toss some deadwood into the center of the dirt clearing between the trees. The limbs and sticks bounced and kicked up a bit of dust.

"I'll get some rocks," Braun said.

Erik nodded and watched him disappear through the brush. He thought about getting up to help, but his legs wouldn't move. His right hand reflexively coursed over the stitched wounds in his shoulder and thigh before he finally crossed his arms and tilted his head back against the tree. Al had done a good job of dressing Erik's wounds after they fought with the Blacktongue's in Buktah, but they still ached and cramped from time to time. The dimming sunlight fought through the trees of the forest with its last rays of the day as a cool breeze whispered through the bushes to his right. His eyes were almost closed when a snapping twig brought him back to his senses. He saw Braun cradling a few hefty rocks in his arms. He unceremoniously dropped them onto the dirt a few feet from Erik.

"Think you can put these into a circle while I gather some more wood?" Braun asked.

Erik noted the tone was not the usual commanding voice that Braun had used with him before, but more of a pleading, entreating tone. "I can do that," Erik replied with a nod. He struggled against the burning in his thigh to get to his feet and walk over to the rocks. Each of them were easily the size of his head. He clicked and clacked the uneven surfaces together as he tried to fit them in like a large puzzle. He had barely slid that last rock into place when Braun returned with an armload of dead branches.

"I'll make a fire," Braun said.

"Do you think anyone will notice?" Erik asked.

Braun shrugged. "We are deep in the forest, so the light won't carry as far as if we were camping out on the plain. Either way, I expect it will get cold tonight and we didn't leave ourselves enough time to build a proper shelter."

Erik nodded. "I suppose some hot food would be good as well."

"It won't be anything fancy," Braun apologized as he went back to his saddle for the large pot and a waterskin. "I can put some beans in the pot to boil, and we have some dried meat and bread."

"That is enough," Erik said. "I am not overly hungry anyway."

Braun prepared the beans and then went to work building the fire. When he had set the pot in the flames he went over and knelt beside Erik. "I owe you an apology, but I have been unable to find the words."

Erik frowned and then looked over to see Braun staring into the flames, refusing to return Erik's gaze. He wanted to comfort Braun, but he didn't know what to say. So he turned and looked into the fire also, watching the wood crack and pop as the heat consumed it.

"I left him in the alley," Braun said after a few moments. "I thought he was safe. I had checked the alley before I left, and no one was there. I went ahead to scout the way. When I returned..." Braun couldn't bring himself to finish the sentence.

Erik turned and saw a tear sliding down Braun's dirt-streaked face. He put a hand on the man's shoulder. "It wasn't your fault."

"I should have been with him," Braun countered.

"So should I," Erik whispered. Erik closed his eyes momentarily and his head drooped down. "I should never have let you split from us. We should have stayed together."

Braun pulled the leather thong with his father's ring up over his head. "I know he would want you to have this," he said.

As Erik looked at the emerald ring, his eyes welled with tears. "Our family ring," he said. He reached out gingerly and took the necklace, twirling it in front of him. "When he came to adopt me I thought I was having a dream."

Braun smiled and nodded. "I was there," Braun said.

"He never treated me as anything other than blood kin," Erik said. He slipped the ring over his index finger for a moment before pulling it back off. "I will make you proud, father," Erik promised.

Braun laid a hand on Erik's back. "He was always proud of you," he said.

Erik shook his head. "But I failed him," he said. "Tukai was right. Maybe if I had died the night the warlock came, my father would still be alive."

Braun removed his hand from Erik's back and shook his head. "The warlock was wrong," he said firmly. "You didn't cause your father's death."

"I don't know," Erik said. "Maybe if I had done more, or if I had been faster…" he let his words trail off and the two stared at the fire a long while. Erik fumbled with the ring, turning it over between his fingers as he lost himself in his thoughts. After a few minutes he sniffed and choked back tears as he slipped the leather thong over his own head and let the ring hang around his neck. "I suppose I should keep it hidden for now," he said.

"At least until you figure out how to get your body back," Braun agreed.

Erik forced a slight grin. "It's too bad Lepkin isn't here with us." Erik sighed and let himself lay back in the dirt. He looked up to the trees above and watched as the last rays of sunlight winked out and gave way to the night. "Braun, could you wake me when the food is ready?"

"Of course," Braun promised.

Erik threw an arm over his eyes and let sleep take him.

*****

"I heard that Lepkin was making sounds," Dimwater said as she approached Marlin in the hall.

Marlin looked up at her and smiled. "He is improving, but it is slow," he responded. He raised a hand to stop her and then walked to her as he closed the door to Lepkin's room. "I am sorry, but I still can't allow you in with him. The situation is still delicate." Marlin noted the blue and red hues swirling through Dimwater's aura. "I know it is disheartening, but I have more reason to hope now than before."

A smile dashed across her face for a moment. "He will recover?"

Marlin nodded once. "I think he will. It will take some time yet, but I think he may well wake soon."

"Thank the heavens," Dimwater sighed. "I can't wait for this nightmare to end."

Marlin nodded and used his arm to turn her around and pull her along with him down the hall. "Will you follow me upstairs?" he asked.

"Of course," she responded. She threw him a sidelong glance. His smile had faded, replaced with a furrowed brow. "What is wrong?" she asked.

"I am not certain," Marlin responded with a shrug. "But something weighs upon my heart." He stopped abruptly and offered an unconvincing half-grin. "Perhaps I just need some rest."

The two of them then made their way up the several flights of stairs to the top-most level of the temple. They crossed a red carpet to a grouping of cherry wood chairs and a long, rectangular table covered with a mosaic of colored tiles. The image on the table was that of the ancient elvish rune for wisdom. The arcs and lines spanned the entire table. Unlike elsewhere in Valtuu Temple, there were no bookshelves here. Other than the table and chairs, there was little of anything in the room at all, save for a large brass gong at the far end of the room near a large sliding panel of lattice woodwork that could be opened to allow access to an overlook that stretched out from the north side of the temple.

"We were once on the balcony one level below this," Marlin said.

Dimwater nodded. "I remember," she said. "It is the spot

from which we launched into battle against the wizard Erthor.

"This level serves as a type of meditation room," Marlin explained. "It is where the senior members of our order can come together and discuss issues, and where initiates may undertake the Test of Arophim." Marlin turned and faced the table with a heavy sigh. "It has not been used for many years."

"Why not?" Lady Dimwater asked.

"The previous prelate ended the traditional councils some time ago, and we have not had any initiates take the test for quite some time now." Marlin sighed and ran a finger along the top of the table. "I have come up here on occasion, when I need to get away and find a quiet spot to think."

"Why have you brought me here?" Dimwater asked.

Marlin raised a brow and then turned to walk toward the overlook. "There is a sort of balcony here," he said. "From here you can see the entire span of the valley to the north. You can also see out to the mountains to the east, and to the forest out west."

"Marlin," Dimwater said flatly. "You didn't answer me."

He nodded and walked out onto the overlook. He reached out to the wooden handrail and pulled a parchment from the rail, tearing it free from a small nail that had held it in place. "I received this letter earlier today, before I went in for my shift with Lepkin."

Dimwater walked up to him and squeezed out onto the overlook with Marlin. She held her hand out expectantly. "What is it?"

"I could not read it," Marlin said. "It is not written with magic, like the books in our library. I had our chief messenger, a neophyte of two years, look at it."

"It is from the king," Dimwater said as she took it in hand and looked over its contents.

"The senate chamber has been laid to waste," Marlin said. "At least, that is what my messenger told me."

Dimwater nodded. "So, the seats of white have been destroyed," Dimwater said.

"The king's account is not overly detailed," Marlin continued. "But it is enough to see that Erik and Al are not esteemed as enemies of the king."

"That is good," Dimwater noted as she continued to read the letter. "King Mathias is asking for volunteers from the temple to prepare to be transferred to Drakei Glazei," she said as she neared the end of the letter.

Marlin nodded. "Specifically, he asks for half of my warriors."

"Do you intend to send them?"

Marlin sighed and leaned forward on the handrail. "Traditionally the warriors of Valtuu Temple do not engage in political conflicts. Since our foundation, we have let the nobles see to themselves while we take care of the temple. Our duties have ever been somewhat autonomous from the kingdom, as we serve the Ancients and distance ourselves from the affairs of men. However, it does not appear wise to deny the king his request. Before Erik destroyed the senate, perhaps we could have abstained, but not now."

"It would be seen as standing against the king," Dimwater noted with a decisive nod.

"It would," he agreed. "While we are certainly not against the king in any respect, we can't afford to allow others to think that Valtuu Temple would defy the king. I will send him more than what he has requested, just so others may see our overwhelming support."

"The temple will be more vulnerable then," Dimwater said.

"I know," Marlin replied. His shoulders slumped and he tapped his fingers on the rail in front of him. "To deny the king could spark a feud that we cannot afford, and to deliver what he asks is to invite those who seek the book to throw themselves at our walls until they break through."

"The letter did not mention what Al and Erik were doing now," Lady Dimwater said.

"Well, it wouldn't mention Erik," Marlin said with a finger up in the air. "The king believes it was Lepkin."

"Yes, but you know what I mean," Dimwater countered. Her tone conveyed she was not in the mood for pointless debate.

Marlin shrugged. "I had my chief messenger write back asking about them, but we have no response as of yet. I don't expect one for some time."

"Well, for our sakes I hope they are making the return journey," Dimwater said.

"As do I," Marlin agreed. "But we must plan as if they will not be back for some time. With Al going to get the scale from his brother, it may take quite a while yet before we see them emerge from the forest."

"Now I see what weighs upon your heart," Dimwater said. "I may not be able to see your aura, but the expression on your face is plain."

"I assume you will stay with us until Erik returns," Marlin said.

Dimwater smiled and looked back over her shoulder longingly. "I lost Lepkin once," she said. "I will not leave his side again in this life. I am here until Lepkin wakes and is recovered, no matter how long that may take."

"That lifts a bit of the burden from me," Marlin said. "It will be good to have you by my side if the demons come looking for the book."

"I will be here," she promised. "When do your warriors leave?"

"They leave at first light," Marlin said. "It is the soonest they could prepare for the journey. I want the kingdom to know that Valtuu Temple stands firmly with the king. A slow response would have been only marginally better than no response at all."

Dimwater nodded knowingly. "Then, knowing the Blacktongues, I should expect we will see them the day after tomorrow, just after your warriors are far enough away not to be recalled quickly."

Marlin nodded. "I thought the same thing." He turned and placed a hand on her shoulder. "We will still have some warriors here," he said. "And with you here it will not be so easy to overtake us."

CHAPTER TWO

Gondok'hr stepped into the room. The smell of charred wood and flesh assaulted his nose, but he didn't flinch. He walked by the bodies on the floor, searching each one as he passed. Occasionally he would point to a corpse and a little green kobold would scamper over and place a golden dot of paint on the body's forehead with his long, crooked thumb. The others were not disturbed.

The warlock stopped in front of one body and turned it over with his foot. A mangled, half-burnt face stared up at him with eyes frozen in horror. "This one too," he said. The kobold grunted and sauntered over, sloshing a bit of the gold paint out of the jar he held in his left hand. "Be careful, you fool!" Gondok'hr chided. A quick slap to the back of the kobold's bald head drove the point home.

"Sorry, master," the creature hissed.

"Your casualties were high," a low, dark voice grumbled from behind.

Gondok'hr turned to see a man standing in the doorway dressed in long, flowing blue robes. The robes bore no design at all, yet to call them plain wouldn't be accurate either. They were made of fine silk that shimmered with even the slightest of moves. The warlock knew at once who the visitor was, despite the low hanging cowl that covered the man's face. "Master Gilifan, my thanks for your quick response," Gondok'hr said.

"You left me little choice," Gilifan hissed. He reached up with bony, yet strong fingers and pulled back the cowl to reveal his long, narrow face under a thinning mass of neatly oiled gray hair. "Do you know how tiring it is to raise an army for you, only to have you carelessly waste my work?"

Gondok'hr folded his arms across his chest. "You are more than welcome to take control of the battles if you disagree with my strategy," he snarled.

Master Gilifan narrowed his eyes on Gondok'hr and wagged a bony finger at him. "Be mindful of what you say to me, or have you forgotten our arrangement?"

Gondok'hr bristled, but he relaxed his tone considerably. "I haven't forgotten."

"See to it that you don't," Gilifan warned. "I am willing to reward those who are faithful, but I will not suffer insolence."

"The fact remains," Gondok'hr began. "If you disapprove of my strategy, you are free to assume command of the army. It would allow me to concentrate on other avenues."

"Ah yes, you would go directly for the boy," Gilifan said with a smile. He pointed to the bodies on the floor. "You have already missed two opportunities." Gilifan strode into the room, stepping over a pair of bodies in his way. "I will raise the army once more, but do not expect me to rescue you if you should fail at Lokton manor."

"I will not fail," Gondok'hr said. "I have others joining in the assault. We shall prevail."

"Good," Gilifan said.

"Once the manor falls, and the boy is slain—" Gondok'hr was cut off by Gilifan's upraised hand.

"Yes, yes. Once you have delivered Erik's dead body then I will bring your family back from the dead."

Gondok'hr nodded.

Gilifan motioned for him to leave the room. "I have work to do, and you are only going to hinder it. I assume you want me to raise the bodies of those who challenged you as well?"

Gondok'hr nodded. "All with the golden dot."

"Very well," Gilifan said. "Now leave me to my work."

Gondok'hr walked to the doorway and stopped abruptly. He turned and stared directly at Gilifan. "I know Master Tul'uh favors you, but if you fail to uphold your end of our deal, I will destroy you. You are not the only one who has powers beyond the grave."

Gilifan stopped and regarded Gondok'hr for a moment. The two locked eyes, engaged in a wrestling contest of wills. Gilifan won. He watched the warlock disappear out the door and down the hall before turning back to a body at his feet. He placed a hand over the gold dot on a female's forehead. A small spark of lightning jumped from his hand to the dot. The dot burned and turned black.

The kobold squeaked nearby and turned to leave the room.

"Hold still," Gilifan commanded. The hunchbacked figure stopped dead in its tracks, visibly trembling. "I have no intention of hurting you," Gilifan promised. "Who is this person with the charred face? Why does he have a dot?"

"That is Master B'Dargen, he was loyal to Gondok'hr."

"B'Dargen," Gilifan repeated. He nodded his head. "Very well, you may leave." He sneered as he watched the kobold rush to scramble away from him. Then he rose to his feet and waved his hand over the female body with the black dot. The air in the room grew thicker and a silver light emerged from his downturned palm. It swirled in place like an upside-down tornado over the body until it became an orb roughly the size of a large egg.

Gilifan then waved his left hand, sending a shower of silver sparks into the air that hovered momentarily before darting down to find all of the golden dots of paint. Just as before, the dots turned black once a spark entered in. "Khosum-eh, blokch'ur-eh," Gilifan said. The silver orb responded by growing three times its size and spinning out and away from him. Small, black tendrils reached out from the black dots hissing as they connected with the silver orb. The orb sizzled and crackled and it too turned black. The walls creaked and groaned against the changing pressure in the room. Gilifan's robes waved violently with the churning air, but he stood still and calm amidst the spell's storm.

"Black death, I banish you for a season from these, my servants, on whom I have laid my claim under the rites passed down from Sandora, the first of our order. Take your cold grasp and be gone into the abyss!"

The black tendrils thickened, pulling out from the corpses' foreheads and joining with the spinning orb. After the span of several minutes the tendrils disappeared into the orb and the dots faded away, leaving a faint bruise on each corpses' forehead.

Gilifan moved quickly, pulling an amulet out from under his robes and holding the large emerald before him. "Khosum-eh, apres-ek," he said. The amulet hummed and gyrated back and forth on its golden chain. "Rise, my servants, and pledge your obedience to your new master."

Yellow and green flashes leapt from the emerald out to each corpse, igniting a flame no larger than that of a candle upon their foreheads. No sooner had each flame come to life than it would die and the corpse would gasp for air as if emerging from a deep pool. Gilifan smiled as the first few bodies extended their limbs and rose to their feet. Gaping wounds sealed themselves, repaired by the necromancer's magic. Burns and scars faded away to reveal new, living flesh so that each body was restored in full.

The woman nearest him cracked her knuckles and smoothed her hair away from her face. "How is this possible?" she said.

Gilifan's smile widened, stretching his lips thin over his crooked, ivory-colored teeth. "I am the master of death," he said. "I have given back the spark of your life."

The woman scrunched her brow. "And what do you ask in return?"

Gilifan bristled and his smile disappeared. He was never pleased when a soul was strong enough to regain its full consciousness. He preferred the bodies to be reanimated with just enough will to live, but not enough to question his authority over them. "I demand your undying loyalty and obedience," he said flatly. "Unless you prefer the darkness of death." The woman stumbled back, surveying the scene around her. Her eyes sparkled and Gilifan could see that her spirit was strong indeed. She was regaining her memory.

"Orres was right," she muttered. "This is madness..." she turned her gaze up to Gilifan.

"Pity," Gilifan said. He snapped his fingers and the green spark flew out from the woman's mouth and returned to the emerald. Her body fell limp to the floor and a black tendril reached out from the orb to connect with her again. "Resurm-eh, uzum-en," he said. He watched for a moment as death returned to the woman and seized her once more, then he turned to address the others.

"Does anyone else object?" he asked. Blank, undiscerning stares answered him. He nodded and smiled. "That is more like it," he said approvingly. "You are all to join the army in the courtyard. The warlock, Gondok'hr, will be your new master. To disobey him is to die." Gilifan pointed to the woman's lifeless body. "Lest there be any confusion, the second death is permanent." He stepped forward and patted one of the raised men on the shoulder. "However, to obey your master is to live forever. Even if a blade shall cut you down, I will bring you back so long as you are loyal. Now go and serve." The newly raised men and women began to exit the room.

Gilifan held out his hand and stopped B'Dargen. "You shall come with me," Gilifan said.

"As you command," B'dargen said.

"What do you remember from before?" Gilifan asked. The necromancer looked deeply into B'dargen's cloudy eyes, looking for any speck of recognition.

B'dargen put a hand to his head. He closed his eyes, obviously struggling to think. Finally he shook his head. "I don't know," he said. "It is a dark haze for me."

Gilifan nodded. "You remember nothing?" he asked.

"The name Gondok'hr is familiar, but I cannot place it," B'dargen replied.

"I see," Gilifan said with a slight smile creeping back onto his face. "You will be my servant. Come with me, there is much to be done."

"By your command," B'dargen answered.

Gilifan replaced the emerald amulet beneath his robes. Then, after all of the resurrected slaves were gone, he muttered a spell and summoned forth a shining yellow portal. The oblong, glowing disc grew until it stretched from floor to ceiling, then it widened as a great eye opening from sleep. A gust of wind swept into the room from the other side of the portal, carrying with it the scent of roasting pig and duck. "Ah, it is near time for dinner," Gilifan said. "First we shall feast, and then we shall march to gather more warriors for our cause."

B'dargen nodded.

"Come, let us depart," Gilifan instructed. He then walked through the portal. B'dargen followed him.

Neither one of them noticed the kobold sneak in behind them just before the portal winked closed.

*****

"My lord, we have located Janik's office," a large man announced.

Gondok'hr turned away from the painting in front of him. "Very well. What have you found?"

"If anything was ever there that could prove his connection to you, it is gone now," the man answered.

Gondok'hr nodded once and turned back to the painting. "Have them search Lady Dimwater's office next. Tell them to take Hobbs and Ferl, they will need to dispel her magical wards before they enter."

"By your command," the man said.

"One more thing," Gondok'hr added. The man stopped and turned back to him. "I want this painting saved." Gondok'hr held out his hand and touched the side of the frame. "The rescue of Lady Zana, daughter of Count Reginald," he said softly as he read the words from a brass plate in the bottom of the frame. "It appeals to me."

"My lord?" the man asked with a raise brow.

"It calls to me on a personal level," Gondok'hr replied with a shrug. "It embodies the truth that a man will do anything to save his family. Look at the way the hero advances against unsurmountable odds. He defies demons with an axe."

The man nodded blankly and looked at the image, but he said nothing.

"It also serves as a reminder of man's greed and selfishness," Gondok'hr added with a sneer.

"You see, the hero should have died that day, but instead he made a pact with those that had previously been his enemy." Gondok'hr chuckled. "An odd paradox we humans are. On the one hand we are filled with selfless love, and on the other we are consumed by our own selfishness. The legends depicting great battles between good and evil are really no more than varying shades of gray on the scale between these two principles that rule over our actions."

Gondok'hr stood for a moment more, staring at the painting. "My dear Janik," he said to the man in the painting. Then he backed away and turned down the hall, striding past his servant. "Take it to my carriage after it has been properly wrapped. I want it in pristine condition when I hang it on the wall of my home."

"Yes, my lord," the man promised.

Gondok'hr walked through the mess hall, where several men were standing around a platter of bread and fruits. One of them, a man with silky gray hair hanging over his shoulders, looked up and noticed the warlock's approach. They instantly bowed their heads as he walked by, quick to hide their food behind their backs or replace it on the platter.

"Eat," Gondok'hr commanded. "We have much work to do, and you will all need your strength." They all obeyed, shoving food into their mouths while continuing to nod at their master. Gondok'hr exited the mess hall and turned down a corridor to an office room he had commandeered as his own personal quarters.

The east wall was lined with book shelves, with books he recognized as treatises on the arcane. The wall opposite held several paintings of legendary wizards hanging over a credenza that held various jars of different animal parts preserved inside. The desk had been shoved up under the great windows to make room for the bed that he had ordered his men to bring inside. Next to the bed stood a short pedestal, about waist high and as large around as a small end table. Atop the pedestal sat an onyx bowl.

He approached the bowl slowly, staring into the empty basin. He placed his left hand on the pedestal and drummed his index finger for a moment. Then he pulled a vial of silvery liquid from a pocket with his right hand, pulled the cork out with his teeth and unceremoniously overturned the bottle, allowing the gurgling liquid to splatter down until the bowl was half filled. As the ripples ceased, the liquid turned dark. Godok'hr cast his right hand over the bowl and used his thoughts to reach through his scrying tool.

"Why do you disturb me?" a voice rumbled from the liquid.

"Master Tu'luh," Gondok'hr began. "I have taken Kuldiga Academy."

The voice growled low and the darkness parted to reveal Tu'luh's scaly red snout. "That is well. When do you march on the boy's family?"

"I want only two days to prepare before we set out. By the third day, the boy's family will be no more."

"He knows you are coming," Tu'luh said. "He contacted me from your home in Drakei Glazei."

Gondok'hr paused and pushed back from the pedestal. "What else does he know?" Gondok'hr asked.

The dragon hissed and plumes of smoke snaked out from his nostrils. "He knows that I exist, nothing more." The dragon sneered evilly. "Though I imagine he also found out about your family as well."

Gondok'hr stiffened. "That is of no importance to me," he

said.

"It should be," Tu'luh replied. "Know that if you fail, your family will remain as they are," Tu'luh cautioned.

"You promised to help me bring them back," Gondok'hr rebutted.

"I promised to help you *if* you help me destroy the boy. There is no reward for failure."

"I will not fail," Gondok'hr swore. "Swear to me that you will bring my family back," Gondok'hr said.

"Silence!" Tu'luh roared. The entire room shook at the dragon's voice. The glass in the windows creaked and a couple of panes cracked under the strain. "You do not command me, mortal! I am Tu'luh. I am as the Ancients. I have been ruling over the lands long before your great-grandfather's grandfather was even born. Your existence, and your family's future, depend solely upon *my* will. I have told you before that Gilifan will bring your family back once the boy is dead. Do not test my patience by making me swear an oath to you now."

Gondok'hr bowed his head. "Forgive me, my lord. It is only that Gilifan does not favor me. It is him I distrust. That is why I asked for your promise. An oath from you I trust, while a thousand promises from Gilifan I would not trust."

The dragon cocked his massive, horned head to the side. "My time is precious, do not interrupt me again until you have the boy's head in your hands."

The liquid clouded over and the image was gone.

Gondok'hr let out a sigh and tried to slow his beating heart. He stepped away from the pedestal and sat upon his bed. He reached into his left boot and tugged at a small leather coin purse stuffed in by his ankle. He opened the drawstring and dumped a pair of jacks into his hand. They were followed by a silver ring with an amethyst set in an exquisite mount. He smiled at the toys and ring as he turned them over in his hand. He looked back to the scrying bowl and sighed again.

"Djekk, are you around?" Gondok'hr asked.

A small, old kobold appeared cross-legged on top of the desk near the window. "I am here, master," the creature said.

Gondok'hr looked up and squinted at the kobold's wrinkly, green face. A series of scars stretched over the humanoid's left cheek and a patch covered the left eye. Long, stringy white hair hung loosely over the kobold's neck and back. Djekk wore his usual brown sleeveless leather tunic and black woolen trousers. His yellow, thick toenails protruded out from his stubby green toes enough that Gondok'hr could see them from the bed. "Where is your brother?" Gondok'hr said.

Djekk blinked slowly. "He is with Gilifan. He snuck through the portal after the wizard."

Gondok'hr nodded. "And B'dargen, where is he?"

Djekk sneered. "Gilifan took B'dargen through the portal, as you predicted."

The warlock closed his fist around the toys and ring in his hand. "The wizard seeks to double-cross me."

"What would you have me do?" Djekk asked. The kobold reached behind his back and pulled a pair of short, wickedly curved daggers. "Shall I follow and spill his blood?"

Gondok'hr raised a brow and thought for a moment. "Not yet," he said. He glanced back to the scrying bowl. "The dragon still favors Gilifan. If I move against him too early, I will gain nothing."

"So, then we strike after the boy is dead," Djekk offered.

Gondok'hr nodded silently. "That is a possibility." The warlock slipped the items back into the leather coin purse and stuffed them into his boot. "I have bought two days here. Go, follow your brother, but stay hidden."

"What would you have me do?" Djekk asked.

"I need Gilifan's necklace." Gondok'hr rose to his feet and walked toward the kobold. "But, I also need to know how it works."

Djekk raised a thin hand. "My brother was there when Gilifan cast his spell, he can tell you the words Gilifan spoke."

"No," Gondok'hr said with a shake of his head. "There is more to it than that. I need to know where his power comes from. Perhaps there is a book he has that explains it, or perhaps there is another artifact that gives him the power."

"I do not think so," Djekk objected.

"That is not enough for me," Gondok'hr said. "I need to *know* for sure. There will be no turning back after this. For my family's sake I need to be sure I know everything before I act."

Djekk nodded thoughtfully. "I understand, master." The kobold jumped up to his feet and stood atop the desk, almost eye to eye with Gondok'hr. "May I ask why the sudden change?"

Gondok'hr huffed. "Several years ago Gilifan met with me and offered to help me bring my family back if I could help locate and kill a boy. As time has progressed, and I have come closer to my goals, Gilifan has become withdrawn. He deals with me more in threats now, instead of appealing to my desires. I will not be barked at, nor will I stand being blackmailed by that blackguard. No one will stand between me and my family."

"So why not unite with the boy?" Djekk asked.

"Because the boy is of no use to me," Gondok'hr said quickly. "If it was his choice, all necromancy would be rooted out and destroyed." The warlock shook his head. "No, he stands in my way even more than Gilifan. The only difference is Gilifan would stab me in the back instead of facing me directly."

"So we will stab him first, eh?" Djekk sneered again and drew the back of his dagger across his throat.

"After I know how to use his magic," Gondok'hr said. "Only after."

"And what of the dragon?"

Gondok'hr shrugged. "The wizard cannot defeat the boy. If I deliver the boy's head, the dragon will not cry over Gilifan."

CHAPTER THREE

Another rush of water beat down upon Al from the hole above him. The cold, unforgiving liquid enveloped him as it fell to join the pool. Al blinked his eyes open as the waterfall ceased. His fingers still clung to the handhold in the rock, but he shifted his weight slightly. His legs dangled below him, half-submerged in the pool of water. The sides of this pit were too slick and sheer to climb. He had tried many times, only to fall into the pool.

He looked up to see the ledge above the pit. Torchlight played upon the ceiling of the hallway from which he had been thrown into the pit after he and Alferug were captured. The hallway was tauntingly close to him, merely three feet above his handhold, but it was too far away for him to reach. Beneath his handhold the walls sloped outward and away from his legs so that there was no way for him to hold himself up other than with his hands. His only other option was to let go and tread water, which is not something he, or any other dwarf, was especially good at.

Footsteps echoed in the hallway above.

Al waited patiently, watching the ledge above him. A shadow danced along the ceiling, mingling with the reflecting light from the torches. Finally a short, stocky figure appeared at the edge and peered down at Al.

"So you have come at last," Threnton said.

"I have no quarrel with you, Brother," Al said.

"Is that so?" Threnton replied. "Then why did you sneak into the mountain?"

Al gruffed. "Because your guards would not let me in the front door," Al quipped.

Threnton smiled and folded his thick arms across his round chest. "You turned your back upon your people. From what I hear you even shortened your name so that the tall folk could better speak with you."

"I didn't turn my back on anyone," Al said.

"How many times did father offer you the throne?"

Al sighed. "I never felt it was my calling to lead. I prefer to keep to my own dealings."

"Ah yes, you would trade your birthright for a smelly, hot forge." Threnton produced Al's hammer from under the folds of his red robes and twirled it over in his hand. "Sometimes I wonder if we had the same mother."

"Threnton," Al began. "Give me the scale and I will be on my way. I have not come for anything else."

"Don't lie to me, Brother," Threnton growled. "You have come for the throne. I know you returned with Alferug. He was also banished! The two of you came here to depose me, admit it!"

Al started to speak but a rush of water fell from above, burying him. It was all he could do to close his mouth before much of the water choked him. After it passed he could hear his brother laughing at him.

"You will not be able to hold onto the wall forever," Threnton said.

"Let me have the scale. I need it."

"For what?" Threnton asked.

"I have found the Champion of Truth," Al said. "I need the scale to help him and the Keeper of Secrets."

"Lies!" Threnton hissed. "The tales of the Ancients are nothing more than a method for the humans to hold us under foot. I will not suffer your ignorance, Brother."

"No!" Al yelled back. "You listen to me, without the scale, the Champion of Truth will not be able to defeat the dark one. He has returned. Those who follow him are upon us as well. We must do what we can to aid the Keeper of Secrets. Roegudok Hall has always pledged to—"

"Silence!" Threnton bellowed. "The Ancients abandoned us long ago. The humans now use their memory to control us. Roegudok Hall is now beholden to no one. As long as I am king, there will be no talk of the Keeper of Secrets or the supposed Champion of Truth."

"Then we shall all die, Brother," Al said.

Threnton thunked the hammer into his open palm and glared down at Al. "We all die someday," he said. "Either way, whatever danger the humans face is no concern of mine. Roegudok Hall will not intervene this time. Let the tall folk see to themselves."

"You will not be able to withstand the forces that will come if you stand idly by, Threnton," Al warned.

"Let the armies of man throw themselves at us. Our defenses have never been breached before."

"Our defenses will not stop Nagar's Blight," Al said solemnly. "Surely you must see the truth in my words."

Threnton shook his head. "Kingdoms rise and fall," he said. "If Tu'luh returns and seeks the power of Nagar's Blight to rule the lands of man, let him come. I am sure I can broker a truce between him and our kind. We offer him no resistance, and therefore we pose no threat."

"This is heresy," Al said. "You would throw in your lot with he who defied the Ancients and blasphemed their laws?"

"It matters little what I do," Threnton said. "You will not be able to hang there forever. In fact, I would wager that you don't last more than two days before your strength gives out and you sink to your death."

Al remained silent, watching his brother stare at him. How he wished he could jump up and strike his brother down. He knew it was the only way to get the scale. Another rush of water fell from above. This time his left hand slipped and he dipped into the pool for a moment before he managed to grab hold and pull himself up again.

"Perhaps you won't even last through the night," Threnton said.

"I challenge you," Al said. "By the right of my birth, and in the name of our father I challenge your right to rule. I claim the throne of Roegudok Hall."

Threnton let out a loud belly laugh that echoed throughout the hall. "You are pathetic," he said. "I will not accept your challenge."

"You cannot refuse it!" Al bellowed. "By our laws and customs you must accept it!"

"Ah, but there is no council here to hear your claim. In fact, no one even knows you are here except for a few guards who found you trespassing near my bedchamber. You will die here, in this pit. You are no more able to take the throne than your hammer is able to float." With that, Threnton tossed Al's hammer into the pool.

The hammer splashed down, immediately disappearing below the surface.

"You are right," Al said. "We are not of the same mother."

Threnton lifted his brow and his smile faded. "Oh?" he asked.

"My mother could never have given life to a dog like you."

"Insults are what someone results to when they know they have lost the argument," Threnton snipped. "Enjoy your final hours, Al. We shan't meet again."

"Yes we will," Al promised. "I will knock your head from your body before the fortnight is over."

Threnton laughed and shook his head as he turned and walked away. Al pulled up with all of his might and lurched for the ledge, but fell far short, sliding back down to splash in the water. He let out a yell and punched the water before swimming back to his handhold. As if to taunt his impotent rage, the chute above dropped another barrage of water down upon him.

*****

"How is he?" Master Wendal asked.

Lady Arkyn looked up and flipped her golden braid back around her shoulder. "He still sleeps. His fever has broken, though." She reached down and removed the wet rag from Master Orres' forehead and gently touched the back of her hand to his skin. It still felt warm, but not as hot as it had been before. "I will stay with him tonight."

Master Wendal shook his head. "I think it may be better for you to take watch over the camp tonight," he said. "I can watch him, but I can't see in the dark the way that you can."

Lady Arkyn nodded. "Alright." She glanced over her left shoulder. "The others have all eaten."

"Thanks to you," Wendal said.

Lady Arkyn shrugged. "I have been tracking deer since I was very young. It was not hard."

Wendal smiled. "Even still, without you to guide us, we would not have escaped."

Lady Arkyn laughed softly. "I think *you* are the one who enabled us to escape. That was quite a spell you cast back there. I had no idea you were capable of such power."

Wendal offered a half smile and shrugged. "It seemed our best option at the time."

Lady Arkyn nodded and rose to her feet. "Very well," she said. "See to it that you change the rag every ten or fifteen minutes. I have left the tea bags here in case he wakes. Otherwise his wounds have been dressed and there is nothing to do but wait and see if he wakes."

"He will," Wendal said.

Lady Arkyn smiled and slipped past Wendal. "Keep the fires low," she instructed. Then she darted off through the forest with her bow slung across her back.

She picked her way through the bushes and ferns until she came to a large, sturdy white oak tree. She glanced around, pausing to enjoy the crisp breeze rustling through the trees as she looked back toward the camp. From this distance, the trees covered the firelight well enough. Her keen, half-elf eyes could just barely make out the glow from the fire through the brush. She turned to the tree and ascended as gracefully as a squirrel until she sat perched atop a thick branch jutting out about forty feet above the ground. From this point, she could scan the grassy slope as it rose up and away from the forest.

If any foes had managed to pursue them this far, she would see them long before they could spot her. She let her left leg dangle over the branch as she brought her right knee close in to her chest. She adjusted her bow and leaned her shoulder against the tree.

Her ears twitched as something stumbled through the underbrush below. She looked down out of curiosity and found a small hare nibbling at plants and twigs as it hopped clumsily along the forest floor. She smiled and watched the animal for a few moments. Then she heard the whisper of wings on the night sky to her right. She looked up and saw an owl. The bird circled around above her and then dropped into a dive, silent as a falling leaf, but much more deadly.

The rabbit squealed as the owl's talons ripped into it and tore it from the ground. The owl then beat its wings ferociously to gain lift with its prize. It ascended only an arm's length away from Arkyn's perch as it made its way off into the night.

Lady Arkyn turned her attention back to the hill. As if on cue, two men on horseback crested the hill. A moment later a trio of men appeared, flanked by large hounds. Lady Arkyn reached behind her and readied her bow. She studied the large hounds as they kept their noses to the dirt and trotted around atop the hill. Their handlers stood with the horsemen, waiting for the hounds to signal.

The dogs stopped.

Up went their tails and they bellowed low and long. The dogs had caught onto the scent. The handlers pointed and ran off after the dogs. The horsemen galloped off a few yards to the side before descending down the hill.

Lady Arkyn breathed in deep. "I am no rabbit," she whispered to the night. "No one shall take our camp tonight."

She drew her bow back and let fly. The arrow flew straight and true, diving deep into the first hound's neck, just above the base where it connected to the body. The beast stumbled forward with little more than what can only be described as a gurgling yelp. By the time the hound stopped tumbling down the hill, the second arrow dropped the other hound.

"Back!" one of the handlers shouted. "We must get the others!"

"Too late for that," Arkyn said quietly. She let a pair of arrows fly at the mounted horsemen. Seconds later each of their lifeless bodies fell from the horses. The frightened steeds galloped off into the forest, one of them dragging its dead master, whose foot was caught in the stirrup.

The handlers died a few seconds later, each catching an arrow to the chest.

Arkyn waited in the tree until morning, keeping watch over the hill, but no one else came.

As the yellow sun peeked over the forest canopy to the east, Lady Arkyn descended from her perch and stalked out to where the slain men lay on the grass. To her dismay, she was only able to retrieve three arrows. The two in the hounds had snapped under the beasts when they tumbled on the ground and another was so deep inside of the horseman who had been dragged through the forest that the head did not come out with the shaft.

She cleaned the good arrows and slid them back into her quiver, quickly counting and making a mental note of her limited supply. She then looked along the ground for hoof prints and followed them until she found the pair of horses drinking from a spring near a moss-covered boulder.

She approached quietly, yet directly. She had no reason to sneak around the animals, and she didn't want to spook them. One of the beasts looked up from the stream and whinnied when he saw her coming.

"Easy, friend," she cooed softly. "Come with me," she said. Lady Arkyn reached out her hand and took the horse's bridle in her hand. The animal pawed at the ground twice and then relented, taking a step forward to nuzzle her shoulder with his nose. "There," she said as she stroked the horse's forehead between the eyes. She moved around and gracefully leapt up into the saddle. Then, she reached down and took the other horse's reins and made for the camp.

The scent of bacon and beans wafted through the trees as she came closer. The camp itself wasn't exactly bustling with activity, but a few people were up and moving around.

She spied Master Wendal right where she had left him, sitting next to Master Orres' cot. Wendal looked up and smiled when he saw her. She waved and dismounted. She tied the horses' reins around a young tree and then moved quickly to Wendal.

"How is he?" she asked.

"He mumbled a few times in his sleep," Wendal said.

"Did the fever return?" she asked.

The mage shook his head. "No, I think he was just dreaming."

Lady Arkyn nodded. "We should be moving along soon."

Wendal shrugged. "Most of us are wounded," he said. "It has been slow going just to rouse most of them this morning. We have only just barely begun preparing food, and I doubt that we have enough for everyone to actually eat their fill."

"All the more reason for us to move along quickly," Arkyn said. "There is a brook we can travel alongside. It will take us near House Lokton's estate."

Wendal pointed to Master Orres. "We are dragging him on a sled, I don't think walking next to a brook in the forest will be the easiest path."

Lady Arkyn bit her lip. "It isn't ideal, but I think we will need to carry him."

Wendal sighed and folded his arms across his chest while shaking his head.

"We can't go back to the road now. We would have to back

track, and even then we don't know how many patrols will be waiting for us. The forest is our best bet."

Wendal nodded. "And House Lokton is the nearest place we could find rest. At least you brought us a pair of horses to help carry him." Wendal looked back to the horses. "I assume the original owners didn't give you any trouble?"

Lady Arkyn smiled. "Well, I lost three arrows," she admitted. "But I suppose that is not a bad price for two horses."

Wendal laughed. "I will get a couple others to help me prepare Orres for travel. I'll have the rest of them break camp. You should get some rest."

"I'll be alright," Lady Arkyn said.

"You have been up all night," Wendal countered. "You may as well rest while we break camp."

Lady Arkyn nodded and looked down at Orres. "Very well, but let's not waste any more time than we must."

Wendal smiled and hurried off. Lady Arkyn moved to the small patch of fir branches that had been cut and placed on a level patch of ground for a bed. She removed her quiver and laid her things nearby as she allowed herself to lay down. A couple needles from the branches poked her leg, but overall it was softer than sleeping directly on the forest floor, and it smelled better too. She put one arm behind her head and crossed the other over her eyes.

CHAPTER FOUR

"Are you ready?" Merriam asked.

Eldrik smoothed out his maroon robes and nodded. "I think so," he said. "Is it on right?"

"Here, let me help," Silvi said softly. She moved in close to him and gently pulled at the collar, twisting the robe a bit to the right. "There," she said as she smoothed out the embroidered design of a dragon inside of a diamond. "The symbol should be over your heart."

Eldrik smiled dumbly. "Thanks," he said with a crack in his voice. Silvi winked and turned away, twirling her black, long hair behind her as she walked away. It took several moments for Eldrik's heart to stop pounding in his chest.

"Let's go, then," Merriam said flatly. Eldrik missed the disapproving glare Merriam shot the younger witch. In fact, he barely noticed Merriam at all. His eyes were fixed on Silvi. His feet moved more to follow her than in response to Merriam's invitation. He followed Silvi through a clean, brown tunnel until it opened into a chamber almost the size of the dining hall back at his family home.

"We do not have so many fine things, as a noble might like, but this is our banquet hall," Silvi said as she turned back to slip her arm under his.

Eldrik paused for a moment, not only taking in the room in front of him, but enjoying the company he found himself with. "It's beautiful," he said.

"It was carved out of the rock we found," Silvi explained as she pulled him into the room. "The middle was drilled through and the table in the center was carved out as the room was cleared. If you look at the base of the table you can still see the tool marks."

"It's impressive," Eldrik said.

"The walls were made smooth, of course, but the pillars on the side were also carved out from the existing stone."

"How long did it take to make?" Eldrik asked. "And who made it?"

"Come, let's eat," Silvi said softly with a smile. "The others are waiting."

Eldrik blushed a bit. He hadn't noticed that all but two of the chairs around the table were filled. He recognized some of the faces as people who had been in the other chamber during the ceremony with the dagger, but he didn't know any of the people by name. Each of them watched him intently, silently. No one said a word as Silvi showed him to a seat at the head of the table. To his left was Hairen, the oldest of the witches. Silvi uncoupled her arm from Eldrik and took the seat at his right.

Hairen stood. "The guest of honor has arrived," she said. "Raise your glasses." A glass rose into the air in front of each guest, except for Eldrik. He reached out and raised his own glass by hand. Hairen smiled, but it was not a warm smile. There was something in her eyes that felt cold and hard to Eldrik. He shifted in his chair a bit and looked away from Hairen. The old witch then continued. "Those of us with the gift, wish for you to partake of the gift as well." Hairen plucked her glass from the air in front of her and drank. Everyone at the table followed suit, including Eldrik. "Let us feast now. Many of you have travelled long to witness the induction of our newest brother."

The old witch sat down and motioned to the platters and trays on the table. The others wasted no time digging. Eldrik reached forward and tore a leg off of a roasted duck. As the skin cracked apart steam wafted up around his hand. He brought it up to his mouth and sunk his teeth into the meaty end. Immediately he regretted his hasty decision. He opened his mouth and tried to suck in a breath of air to cool the food in his mouth without drawing too much attention to himself.

"Take a drink," Silvi whispered.

Eldrik nodded and quickly swished the cool wine around in his mouth as he finished chewing the bite.

"Here, take some of the bread and fruits," Silvi offered.

Eldrik slid his plate close as she placed some other items down for him. A few of the other guests chatted amongst themselves, but for the majority of the meal everyone ate in silence. Eldrik might have excused himself, if not for the fact that Silvi sat at his side, occasionally rubbing his foot with hers. It was obvious that she was older than him, but that didn't bother him. There was something about her, something in her eyes that he felt drawn toward. He likely would have sat there in the hall all night if she had asked him to. However, it was soon obvious that there were other plans that night.

As the guests finished their food and pushed their plates to the center of the table Hairen and Merriam began cleaning the platters and other dishes away. Afterward, the other warlocks in attendance rose from their chairs and stood near the large pillars around the chamber.

"Should I move?" Eldrik asked Silvi.

"No," she said with a disarming smile. "You are the guest of honor. You must stay seated for the final course."

"The final course?" he asked. "I am already full."

Silvi giggled and dabbed the left corner of her mouth with her napkin.

Hairen moved to stand beside him and placed a hand on his right shoulder. Merriam stood on his left side and placed her hand on his other shoulder. Silvi withdrew her foot from near his and stood up from her seat.

"Bring it in," Hairen said. Eldrik turned to look at what was coming, but he couldn't see around Merriam. He tried to lean around, but Hairen gripped his shoulder tight. "Patience," she said.

A man in dark green robes set a silver goblet before him. Eldrik looked up to the black-haired man, but the man did not make eye contact. He simply slid the goblet so that it was centered in front of Eldrik and walked away.

Moments later four men approached the table carrying a large, golden tray covered with a black silken cloth. Eldrik studied the cloth intently as the men slid the tray onto the table. He felt a knot grow in his throat as they pulled the cloth back. Even before the pair of brown boots were revealed, he knew what they had set before him.

"I...I...no—I can't," he stammered.

Silvi stepped in behind him and gently laid her hands on either side of his neck. She bent down to his left ear and whispered, "It's alright. This will complete your initiation as the patriarch of our order."

Eldrik's stomach lurched. "No, I can't do this." He went to stand but Hairen and Merriam held him down with otherworldly strength.

"Take this," Hairen said as she placed his dagger in front of him.

Eldrik's chest began to burn as he looked down to the weapon. He shook his head. "I can't," he repeated.

"You can," Silvi said. Her soft, alluring voice did little to calm him this time. She reached around with her left hand and took Eldrik's chin between her thumb and forefinger. She turned his head to look into his eyes. "Do this for me," she said. She leaned in and kissed his cheek.

Eldrik's defenses melted away. He turned back to his dagger. "What do I do?" he asked.

Silvi stepped back and offered a nod to Hairen. The old witch returned the nod and motioned for Silvi to back away. The young witch flipped her raven hair over her should and went to stand near the wall.

Hairen eased her grip on Eldrik and pointed to his dagger. "Take your weapon," she said. "For you to fully realize your potential, you must consume another's power." She then gestured to the corpse on the platter. "This one has offered himself to you, so that you may lead us and restore House Cedreau to its former glory."

"Take your dagger," Merriam said. "Then take your goblet." Eldrik nodded and took his dagger in his right hand and scooped his left hand around the empty silver goblet.

Hairen began chanting. Her voice grew louder until it echoed through the small chamber and the walls vibrated and hummed. The torches dimmed, nearly dying out as the air grew thick and dark. Merriam started in as well, adding her voice to Hairen's. Eldrik felt the burning in his chest grow hot.

He stood and instinctively raised his dagger, holding the blade out over the corpse before him. The heat in his chest flowed out through his shoulder and down to his blade until the dagger glowed red-hot. He then lifted his goblet into the air and held it next to his dagger. A thin, smoky light emerged from the corpse's mouth, swirling up toward the dagger above the body. As the light ascended to the blade it whirled and coiled near the dagger's point.

"Take your blade and pierce the power," Hairen said.

Eldrik sliced into the glowing vapor. His dagger quivered and hissed as it cut through the essence.

"Hold your dagger inside until it is complete," Merriam shouted.

Eldrik fought to keep his dagger in the glowing mist as an unseen force began pushing against him, trying to eject the blade. Hairen and Merriam resumed their chanting and squeezed his shoulders tightly. More than once Eldrik heard a loud *pop* and his dagger would almost jerk free of the smoky light, but he managed to hold it in. With each passing second more of the essence drained from the body in front of him and fought against his dagger. His forearm stung not only from the heat of the spell he was under, but his muscles ached and quivered as well.

He grit his teeth and leaned his body forward, hoping his weight would help. If it did, he couldn't tell. It seemed for every ounce of effort he could muster, the essence grew harder and stronger. Then, the mist split in two and all resistance was gone. He would have fallen forward onto the table had Hairen and Merriam not been holding his shoulders.

"Now drink," Hairen commanded.

Eldrik brought the goblet to his mouth. As he did so, the essence flowed into the vessel as easily as if poured from a pitcher. The first taste of the warm, glowing mist was sweet as fresh nectar. After his second swallow the essence turned bitter and foul as if orange peels had been ground with rotting fish. Eldrik's stomach lurched and heaved, but he managed to hold down what he had drunk already.

"You must finish it," Merriam said.

Eldrik took a deep breath and held it as he opened his mouth wide and poured his goblet into the back of his gullet. He did his best to swallow without letting much of the essence touch his tongue, but it didn't matter. The foul taste filled his mouth and penetrated his nostrils as though he were drowning in a pool of the putrid gunk. As the last of it slimed down his throat he dropped his goblet and doubled over, clutching at his stomach.

Hairen deftly moved in and took Eldrik's dagger from him just before he started convulsing. "This next part might be a bit jarring," she said as she placed the dagger on the table. "Everyone out," she said. All of the guests filed out of the room in an orderly line, ignoring Eldrik as he fell into a fit of seizures on the floor.

"I will go and entertain our guests," Merriam said.

Hairen nodded. "Silvi, you wait here with Eldrik. If he lives through the night, then we will introduce him tomorrow morning as the new head of our order."

Silvi stepped forward and looked down to Eldrik. "No matter how many times you see it, it is never easy to watch."

"If we are to succeed, we need him to be more than a mere warlock," Hairen said.

"But can we control a shadowfiend?" Merriam asked.

"He will listen to me," Silvi said with a sly smile.

"Yes, your charms have been most effective," Hairen said. "Let's just make sure we keep his mother from finding out."

"Leave her to me," Merriam said. "I can take a few of our guests and pay her a visit."

"No," Hairen said quickly. "You don't know what she is capable of. She was dangerous before, but now she has nothing left to live for. To strike at her openly is suicide."

"We can't let her live," Merriam said. "Sooner or later she will find out what you have done."

"Perhaps," Hairen said. "But for now she has no reason to suspect we would do anything with Eldrik. As far as she knows the boy is still in Drakei Glazei."

"She won't have an easy time getting in there now with the recent incident at the senate chamber," Silvi put in.

"Come," Hairen said to Merriam. "Let's go entertain our guests."

*****

Hairen gently scooped a bit of water into her hand and brought it up to her face. The cool liquid helped wash away the rest of her fatigue from the late night. It was morning now. Time to check on the boy.

She pulled a brown wool over cloak from off a hook on her wall and wrapped it around her shoulders. Lately she found the mornings to be particularly cold in the coven. Whether it was from her age or perhaps a shift in the climate below the surface, she couldn't be certain. Either way, she needed the cloak to keep the chill out of her bones.

Hairen opened her door and walked down the corridor

toward the banquet hall.

"It is time then?" Merriam asked as Hairen rounded a corner, nearly bumping into her.

"It is," Hairen said. Everything was silent, except for the occasional snore that echoed through the halls.

"All of the guests stayed up late, and now they sleep heavily," Merriam noted.

"That is good," Hairen said. "Where is Silvi?"

"She waits for us at the banquet hall."

Hairen raised her brow and looked down her nose at Merriam. "How long has she been there?"

Merriam shrugged. "Several hours, I suppose."

The two of them quickened their pace. They found Silvi seated cross-legged on the floor near the entrance to the banquet hall. Her head was tilted back against the wall and her mouth was slack. Hairen could just hear Silvi's rhythmic breathing. The old witch walked over and nudged the young, raven-haired witch with her foot.

Silvi's eyes shot open and she jumped up to her feet. "I apologize," she said. "I must have dozed off."

Hairen shrugged and motioned for Silvi to stand next to Merriam. "I will go in alone." The old witch walked into the banquet hall, pausing at the entrance and peering inside. The room was dark. None of the torches burned inside. Hairen held out her palm and conjured a white orb of light to illuminate her path. She stepped into the room slowly.

"You have come to mock me," a voice hissed from the dark.

Hairen's heart skipped a beat. This was not the voice of the boy she had left lying on the floor last night. There was power here now. A dark power. Goosebumps ran along her forearms and she drew the cloak in tighter around herself. "I have not come to mock," she replied. With a nod of her head she commanded her orb of light to fly farther into the room.

The orb sailed in to hover over the head of the table. A spattering of dried blood dotted the slab floor and streaked across the front of the table, but Eldrik was not there. The light then moved onward, swerving left and right to chase away the shadows and allow Hairen to see the room.

"Why not come into the light?" Hairen asked. "Our guests

have travelled far to see you become the new patriarch."

"Patriarch?" the voice echoed. "I am no patriarch." Something hard scraped along the stone near the back of the room. Hairen held a hand to her ears, fighting off the piercing screech. "What have you done to me?" the voice hissed.

Hairen walked on the left of the table, keeping her eyes fixed on the small radius of light around the orb. "I have only helped you," Hairen answered. "I helped you unlock your potential."

The orb of light winked out. Hairen reached forward and attempted to conjure another light, but she stopped when a hot, fetid breath washed over the left side of her face. Something sharp dragged along the inside of her palm, almost splitting her skin. The old witch held still, not wanting to provoke him.

"You were as a caterpillar," Hairen said. "I have helped you make the transformation into your true nature."

The sharp claw pulled back from her hand and she heard a low growl from the left. "Very well then," the voice hissed. "Look upon me now, and tell me if I am the butterfly you expected."

Hairen conjured a light. This time she found the spell worked effortlessly and the entire room was washed in bright, white light. She looked to her left and almost stumbled over backward. Had it not been for the table, she most certainly would have fallen to the floor. "By Hammenfein's fires," she exclaimed with a hand clutching at her throat.

There, next to her stood not the boy, but a large beast. He stood easily head and shoulders taller than any man Hairen had ever seen. His young, supple skin replaced with gray, cracked scales almost resembling the look of a crocodile. His nose had fallen away, as had much of the flesh around his face, leaving only a skull with elongated, sharp fangs. A pair of leathery, pointy ears protruded out underneath a rim of bony bumps and miniature horns along the top of his head. Several long, slightly curved spikes protruded up from his shoulders. His arms bulged with muscles larger than a man's leg. His massive chest was crested with a mat of white fur over his leathery scales. His legs were as thick as tree trunks. His feet now had three pointed fore toes with a long claw protruding from the heel. The beast hissed and flexed a mighty pair of wings.

"Well, witch, what do you say now?" he growled.

Hairen slowly knelt before him and bowed her head. "The night has bestowed you with great power," she said. "I pledge the allegiance of my coven to you."

Merriam walked into the room next and knelt a few yards behind Hairen. "The master of the night has come," she said as she bowed her head.

The beast rushed forward reached down and snatched Hairen by the throat, jerking her up off the ground so that her feet dangled in front of him. "Change me back!" he howled.

Hairen, barely able to breathe, struggled and kicked her legs. Merriam fell back and scooted away on her rump. It was Silvi who ran into the room next.

"No, Eldrik, don't do it!" she pleaded. She ran up to the beast and put her hands on his arms. "Release her," Silvi said.

The beast looked down to Silvi. "Look what she has done," he said.

"You are beautiful," Silvi said as she reached up and caressed the side of his face. "Absolutely magnificent."

The beast slowly set Hairen down again and backed away. "You would want me to remain like this?"

Silvi shook her head. "You don't have to be like this all the time," she said. Silvi stepped in closer to him and smiled. "You decide when to take this form and when to take your human form. We will teach you how to control it."

"But first you will need a name," Hairen said, coughing and rubbing her throat.

"I have a name," he said.

"You have a human name," Silvi said. "But to use your new power you must take on a new name as well. A name that only you and Hairen shall know." Silvi gestured to the old witch. "This way she can use it to help you advance in your power."

The beast shook his head. "No," he said. "I will share this name only with you," he told Silvi. "If anyone here is to train me, it will be you." Silvi looked back to Hairen. The old witch folded her arms across her chest and glared at the young witch.

"Either that, or you change me back," the beast growled.

"Very well," Hairen said. "Come Merriam, let's go."

Silvi averted her eyes to the floor as the other two witches stormed out.

"I want to become myself again," the beast said.

Silvi stroked his arm. "As soon as you have a new name, you will have the ability to change back." She motioned for him to sit upon the table. He moved to the granite slab and sat upon it.

"All I need is a name?" he asked.

Silvi nodded. "It is a name that reflects your power, your innermost self."

"And what else will it do, besides allow me to change form?"

Silvi started to shrug. "It has a few other uses."

He reached out and grasped her forearm. "What other uses?" Silvi's eyes shot wide and she took a step back, pulling herself free from his talon-like claws.

"Whoever knows your name can summon you to them, or force you to change into this form."

"So, you will be able to control me?" he said.

"Only that much," Silvi said quickly. "You will retain your free will. Knowing your name does not allow anyone to control you, only to summon you or have you reveal your true form."

"Can you summon me from anywhere?" he asked.

"No, it has limits. We can discuss those later on." She stepped toward him again and put her arm back on his. "For now just know that this form gives you power. You now have the power you need to crush House Lokton, and all other enemies of House Cedreau." She smiled her disarming smile again and looked deep into his eyes. "You also have the power to lead this coven. You are the first shadowfiend to come to this coven in a long time. The other warlocks do not possess half of your potential. There will come a day when you could rival the Keeper of Secrets, and perhaps even a dragon someday."

The beast nodded. "Then, how do we choose a name?"

Silvi slid her hand up his arm and moved it over his rough, scaly skin to the patch of fur on his chest. There she flattened her palm and felt his heartbeat. She closed her eyes. "Your power is strong, and dark as the night." Silvi spread her fingers and then pulled away. "Your name shall be Lyvin'dechrn."

"Lyvin'dechrn," the beast repeated. As the name fell from his mouth the air grew heavy and thick. The gray, cracked skin regained its color and youthful firmness. The horns on his shoulders shrank back until they disappeared inside once more.

The tingling sensation that came over him felt as though thousands of live bees were crawling on his body, humming and buzzing as they restored his natural frame. There was no pain, only the loud humming as he transformed. Within a few moments he stood eye to eye with Silvi.

"From now on you do not need to speak your name to transform," Silvi said as she took his hand in hers. "You need only to concentrate on it in your mind."

Eldrik nodded. "Can't I use magic in this form?" he asked.

Silvi smiled and stroked his hand. "Of course," she said. "It's just that you will not be as strong in this form. To attain mastery would take several decades, which is time that we do not have."

"So, I drank the other man's power in order to progress faster?" he asked.

"Faster and better," Silvi responded. "Even after you have mastered the arcane in your human form, you will always be stronger in your true form. That is why you must always remember your name. It is the key by which you can unlock your true potential."

Eldrik sat silently for a moment. "Can I absorb more power?" he asked.

Silvi grinned wider. "Actually, you can," she said. "First you will need to learn the ritual spell, but after that you can absorb more power in your true form. I will teach you, if you like."

Eldrik nodded. "If I am to restore my father's house, then I want to be able to crush his enemies."

Silvi patted his hand. "Come, we must introduce you to the others now."

"But I have already met them," Eldrik said.

Silvi shook her head. "They met the boy last night who was aspiring to become a warlock. Now they will meet the shadowfiend, your true form. Then, and only then, will they swear allegiance to you."

"I will not tell them my name," Eldrik said. "I will not allow anyone else to summon me."

Silvi shook her head and moved her hand to his cheek. "Eldrik, I would not dream of it. Only I shall know your name, as I am the one who gave it to you. I will use it only to aid you in your training. No one else will ever hear me utter it."

Eldrik nodded. "Then what will the others call me?"

Silvi regarded him curiously. "What would you want them to call you?"

"I do not want them to call me Eldrik, for that is the name my father gave me. While I may align with the others to crush my enemies, I do not think it would be good for the world to know me by my real name."

Silvi nodded. "That is wise of you," she noted. "It would indeed be better to keep our alliance secret for the time being.

"I will be known as Aparen," he said decisively.

Silvi narrowed her eyes and cocked her head to the side. "Aparen?" she echoed.

He nodded. "In my studies there was a Tarthun warlord by that name. After Aparen's uncle murdered his father and took his mother as a slave, Aparen gathered several clans together and crushed his uncle, killing every last one of his descendants."

"I know the name," Silvi said softly.

"Aparen built a mighty empire," he continued. "One that still rules the lands east of the mountains today." He rose to his feet. "From this moment forward, no one shall ever utter the name Eldrik. I am now to be known as Aparen."

Silvi stood before him and kissed his cheek. "As you wish, Aparen."

CHAPTER FIVE

Erik slowed his horse as he and Braun emerged from the forest and entered onto Lokton lands. He leaned back in the saddle and watched the forest give way to the cottages and store houses that made up the small, nameless village that rested on Lokton lands. Erik smiled as they passed through the village. He knew that everyone here was a friend of House Lokton. Many of the families had lived on these lands for generations, each working for the Lokton family and proud to do so until they passed the tradition on to their own children. The village gave way to a vast field, enclosed with a wooden horse fence that Lord Lokton had helped his grandfather replace. Erik saw workers in the field afar off. A couple of them waved briefly and then returned to working the land.

A few minutes later the two of them passed through the wrought iron gate of the inner fence, a waist-high wall of stone covered in ivy and creeping, flowering trumpet vines. The large, gray stone manor stood tall anther hundred yards beyond the gate. Erik glanced to his left and saw the stables on the north east side of the inner yard, and noted the smoke billowing out through the chimney in Demetrius' forge behind the stables.

"We are home," Erik said.

"*I* am home," Braun said. "*You* are still Master Lepkin," he reminded him.

Erik looked down at his body, but it wasn't *his*. It was Master Lepkin's body. He sighed and closed his eyes. "Sometimes I forget," he admitted. "It is hard to keep up the charade."

"Well, do as you must," Braun said. "I imagine there are good reasons to keep the ruse going, even in your own home."

Erik shrugged. "Let's keep moving. We have a lot to get done."

Braun nodded and urged his horse forward. The two of them galloped up the gently sloping hill, kicking dust and small clots of dirt into the air as they went. Erik looked and saw a couple of guards standing about the entrance to the house. He waved to them and they rushed forward to meet him and Braun.

"What news of our master?" one of them asked.

Braun and Erik pulled back on their reins, slowing the horses to a halt and then Braun dismounted with a graceful jump. "The master is dead," he said flatly. "Master Erik is now in charge. We have sent word to him at Valtuu Temple."

Erik opened his mouth to add something, but hearing his father's death announced so bluntly, without apparent emotion or even a moment of reflection, took the breath out of him. He closed his mouth and swung his leg over his horse to dismount.

One of the guards pointed to him. "Were you there, Master Lepkin?"

Erik nodded.

"Wasn't there anything you could do?"

Braun clapped the guard on the shoulder. "Master Lepkin did all he could to save our lord. He tried every legal means to halt the preposterous trial. When all else failed, he fought alongside me to free Lord Lokton. We succeeded, but Lord Lokton was ambushed while he and I were making our escape. He was slain by an unknown assassin."

The two guards bowed their heads for a moment and then glanced to each other before looking back to the house.

"Who will tell Lady Lokton?" one of them asked.

"I will," Erik said. He pushed through the three of them. "Water my horse." He stopped abruptly and turned back to Braun. "You should prepare the men. There is much work to be done."

Braun cocked a brow and looked back at Erik. "What would you have me do, exactly?" he asked.

"We don't know who, or what, is coming. Call every able-bodied man we have to arms. And organize a caravan to get the women and children out."

"What is going on?" one of the guards asked.

"Lokton Manor will be under attack soon," Erik said. "Listen to Braun, he will instruct you."

Braun stepped forward and whispered to Erik, "How would you like me to prepare for a dragon?" he asked.

Erik shrugged. "I don't know," Erik said honestly. "I was hoping you would have an idea."

Braun leaned back and folded his arms. He looked at Erik for a moment and then he turned to address the two guards. "Boris, you go and tell Demetrius that we need to open the armory. It is time for our finest weapons and armor. Go now."

One of the guards nodded and sprinted off toward the blacksmith's workshop.

Braun then turned to the other. "Krill, I want you to go and tell Louis and his wife to prepare every carriage we have. I don't care who drives them, just so long as we are sure to get every woman and child off Lokton lands."

"Where shall they go?" Krill asked.

Braun turned back to Erik expectantly.

"We could send them to Drakei Glazei," Erik said.

Braun nodded his head to the side and stroked his chin. "You saw the riots in the streets. Drakei Glazei may not be the best place to send them."

Erik sighed. "Perhaps to Kuldiga Academy then. The journey would be quicker, and Orres should still be there."

Braun nodded. "That could work." Braun turned back to Krill. "Send them to Kuldiga Academy. Master Lepkin will draft a letter for Master Orres."

Krill saluted and turned away. He took only two steps when Erik asked him to wait.

"What is it?" Braun asked.

"We don't know what direction the enemy is coming from," Erik said.

Braun looked to the open field to the west and nodded. "King Mathias may also call the masters at the academy to Drakei Glazei to help quell the riots and solidify his forces," Braun added.

"What do we do?" Erik whispered. "To send them to Drakei Glazei is to send them to chaos. To send them to Kuldiga could be putting them in the dragon's path."

"Did the dragon not say where he was, or when he would come?" Braun asked.

Erik shook his head. He recalled the terrible image of the dragon's face in the scrying pool at the warlock's house in Drakei Glazei. "The dragon sneered at me and told me to 'come to Lokton manor' so he could give me a 'taste of things to come' and then challenged me to face my destiny," Erik said. The boy could almost feel the hot, red eyes upon him again as he thought of the dragon's threat. A shiver ran down his spine.

"He said nothing else?"

Erik shook his head again. "Nothing else." Erik looked to Braun sullenly. "After that he cast the fireball."

Braun put a hand on Erik's shoulder. "For now, we will have them prepare for a journey. We can decide the destination later, after they are ready to go."

Erik nodded. "I must go," he said.

Braun looked past Erik and his shoulders slumped. "She is coming out to us," he said.

Erik turned to see his mother, wearing a black dress and a dark veil, walking out to him.

"I see you have returned," she said.

A lump formed in Erik's throat and a gnawing pit opened in his stomach. He had nothing to say to her. He watched Braun step forward and begin to speak. Even the stoic warrior stumbled and stammered for words. Lady Lokton's tears fell freely over her cheeks, glistening in the sunlight behind the veil of lace. Her head drooped forward and she threw her arms around Braun's shoulders. Erik could not bear to watch as her shoulders convulsed up and down and she cried into Braun's chest. Erik turned and walked toward the stable, away from the sound of her agony.

He walked into an empty stall and collapsed atop the pile of straw inside. He buried his face in his hands and slumped against the wooden stall. A wave of emotion crashed over him. His stomach lurched, and then he retched onto the floor. His gut burned and his throat choked as his body convulsed over and over, until finally he gasped for air and laid back into the straw. He clumsily wiped his mouth and looked up to the rafters.

From outside, he could still hear his mother sobbing, but the sound was growing distant. When he could no longer hear her, he clambered to his feet, reaching a hand to the stall walls to steady himself. As soon as he was standing he leaned on a nearby post and coughed, expelling the last bit of vomit from his throat and spitting it onto the floor.

"You look pale," Braun said.

Erik looked up and saw the man coming toward him. "I..." was all Erik could say.

Braun held up a hand and shook his head. "No need to explain," he said. "I do, however, need you to think back to the dragon and tell me what you can about him."

Erik shrugged. "There is nothing to say. "All I could see was his head and neck. I can't tell you how large he is, where he is, or anything."

"Braun stopped and stroked his chin. "Was he alone?" he asked.

Erik shrugged again. "I could only see him, but I can't say if that meant he was alone. Certainly I would imagine all he could see was me, yet you were just a few feet away from the pedestal in the room. He could have an army, and I wouldn't know."

Braun smiled. "Then let's prepare for an army," he said.

Erik looked up, confused. "How will we slay a dragon?"

Braun's smile disappeared. "I will prepare the field for an army of men," he said. "We will dig pits, set up pikes and traps, and then we can try to set up something for the dragon."

"How long will that take?" Erik asked.

Braun shrugged. "We will dig trenches and pits around the manor's stone wall. Logically the manor is our best defensible position. I can have Demetrius work on something that could fire at the dragon, perhaps a bow of some kind."

"It would need to be a very large bow," Erik said.

Braun nodded and held a finger to the air. "I once heard of something, in an old legend my mother read to me as a boy," he said. "I think it was called a wind-lance."

"A wind-lance," Erik repeated.

Braun nodded. "I will go and speak with Demetrius. I don't know if it is possible to make it, or how long it would take, but he would know. I can also assign some men to help him build catapults."

"What should I do?" Erik asked.

"You should grab a shovel and help the others dig the trench," Braun said.

"I have never done anything like that before," he said.

"It's alright," Braun said. "Just make sure the trench mimics the stone wall and is half a man deep and four feet wide. I will have other men cut down the lumber to prepare the pikes. By the time you are done with that, I will be back and I can direct the men further."

Erik nodded. "Alright. I'll go get a shovel."

CHAPTER SIX

Gilifan sat at the head of a long, rectangular mahogany table, laying back in a high-backed chair with his feet up on the table next to a plate that held the remnants of what used to be a trout. He swirled the red wine in his goblet lazily and drank the last mouthful of the liquid. He set the cup down and rubbed a hand over his weary eyes. Out of his peripheral, he caught sight of someone in the doorway. He turned to his right to see one of his soldiers standing there patiently.

"Come in," Gilifan ordered. The soldier obeyed immediately, walking up to the side of the table and resting his forearm on the back of the chair to Gilifan's right.

"We are ready," the soldier said.

Gilifan nodded. "The men hold the king's banner?" Gilifan asked.

The soldier nodded affirmatively. "We standby to march on Spiekery."

"B'dargen," Gilifan called out.

The resurrected mage stepped through the doorway. "Yes, master?"

"You will ride at the head of the troop. Make sure to announce yourself exactly as I told you."

B'dargen bowed his head. "Of course," he said.

"And be sure to let a few of the villagers escape," Gilifan added. "It will not serve our purpose unless some live to tell of the attack."

"I understand," B'dargen replied.

Gilifan kicked his feet down to the floor and stood. "Well then, let's be off." He dismissed the others before him with a wave. He walked to the back of the room and opened a curio cabinet. He pulled out Lord Hischurn's ring and turned it over in his hand. "Too bad you did not live to see this day, old friend," he said as he put the ring back into the cabinet.

His ears twitched, picking up a noise from inside the room. It was like a scrape against the floor, but when he turned, there was nothing there. Gilifan lifted his brow and scanned the room more intently. The light from the chandelier above threw shadows behind the chairs and under the table, but there was still adequate light to see the entire area. He was alone. Not even a mouse would have gone unnoticed under his careful eye, and yet he could feel that he was being watched.

The thought came to him to cast a dispelling enchantment on the room to uncover his stalker. A slight sneer stretched his lips over his pointed chin. He need not uncover the intruder, not yet. What fun would it be to ruin the intrigue? Gilifan cleared his throat and exited the dining room. As he walked down the hall the hairs on the back of his neck prickled and began to stand. His intuition told him that his follower was close behind.

I do enjoy these shadow-games, he thought to himself.

He put the thought out of his mind and continued about his work. He exited the main keep to see a troop of fifty-five men on horseback assembled in the courtyard. B'dargen sat atop a chestnut colored horse, with another soldier next to him holding the king's banner.

"How ironic that the flag of the dragon shall be the image the villagers will see before their doom," Gilifan said to himself. "They will run from one made of cloth only to find a serpent of fire lying in wait." He reached up with his left hand and jerked his chin to the right, cracking his neck. He took in a deep breath and rolled his head around before descending the stairs and saluting his men. "Go, and deliver the king's justice," Gilifan said tongue-in-cheek.

Gilifan's smile faded against the men's silence. None of the men laughed at his jest. The mindless servants never laughed. Gilifan waved them off dismissively. "Follow B'dargen's commands until we meet again," he instructed.

The silent group turned their steeds in unison and walked the horses out through the front gate, with B'dargen in the lead. Gilifan was not far behind the last rank. He jumped atop a paint horse and followed just fifty yards back. He had no interest in leading the fight, but he did have a duty to see that his plan was executed flawlessly.

The journey was not long, the island itself was only large enough for a couple of settlements. Spiekery was the largest of those, except for Hischurn's keep. Hischurn himself, along with another of Gondok'hr's order had been slain only a few weeks back by Lady Dimwater. A most unfortunate event in which Tul'uh lost one of his noble supporters. Had Gilifan been present that day, the sorceress would not have triumphed. The wizard gripped the reins tight at the thought of her. If only he had been warned of her meddling in time.

No matter now, he knew. Her interference in Spiekery actually provided him with a pretext to attack the village and enslave the people. In the end he would get what he wanted, an island from which to stage his assault and people willing to stand against the king.

After the space of two hours a fork in the road appeared. The army took the left path. It went north and around the rolling hills of the island, Gilifan knew. The wizard took the right road. It was narrow, and overgrown with weeds cluttered with leaves from the nearby trees. It led south by southeast, directly into the foothills. He guided his horse over the forgotten road for slightly longer than an hour before he crested the final hill leading into the valley where the others were waiting for him. A troop of twenty men on horseback waited under the yellow banners adorned with the face of the wolf, the banner of Lord Hischurn. Gilifan grinned and approached the group.

"Are we prepared?" Gilifan asked as he pulled his horse to a stop next to the lieutenant.

"Yes, sir, we are ready," the lieutenant answered.

"Good," Gilifan commented. "Follow me, and remember nobody moves in until I give the command."

"As you wish," the lieutenant said.

Gilifan kicked his horse into a run and the group sped off after him. The sound of hooves beating the ground was not unlike the march of drums of the armies of old. The clanking armor, and the grunting, snorting horses added their own beats to the cadence of death.

By the time they crossed the last of the rolling hills and bore down on Spiekery, the town was already under attack from the others. A tall barn just outside the town was ablaze, spewing thick, black smoke into the sky. The screams and shrieks of dying townsfolk hung in the air, ringing out over the land. Gilifan spied a group of corpses near the burning barn.

"Not much for fighting," he commented to his lieutenant as

he signaled for the group to halt. "I do them a favor by bringing them into our fold," he said.

"Yes, sir," the lieutenant agreed.

Gilifan looked to his mindless officer and snorted. "Not that you would disagree with me anyway," he said. The officer remained silent and looked back to the fight. Gilifan sat atop his horse, patiently. He wanted to time his entrance at precisely the right moment. He listened to the screams for help and the pleas for mercy, and watched intently whenever a townsperson managed to escape the battle. He would watch, gauging whether the person would make it to the nearby forest on the eastern side of the town. He was not surprised when they were cut down by one of his other riders, however. He had given specific instructions. In the first few minutes of battle, B'dargen was to allow a few to escape, but after that all were to be culled.

On the other hand, neither B'dargen nor the other riders knew of Gilifan's second group. That way, the ruse would be intact. Gilifan raised his hand and turned back to the men behind him. "Ride now. Charge hard and fast, leave no enemy alive and spare every townsman you can."

Instantly the riders obeyed. Their horses tore off, briefly enveloping Gilifan as the riders galloped around him toward the town. Their war cries drowned out the suffering screams momentarily, only to be replaced by the sound of steel ringing against steel and the agonizing cry of warriors meeting their death. Gilifan moved his hands quickly, calling down enchantments for the group he chose to be victorious. Their blows were stronger, quicker, and more accurate. At the same time, he cursed the group under the king's banner. Some he made slow, others he struck blind, and some he simply willed to die. B'dargen was among those from whom he took the breath of life. As Gilifan had been the source of his resurrection, it was a simple matter to reverse the spell and drop the lifeless corpse back on the ground.

Within a matter of minutes, Gilifan could hear the cheers and shouts of victory. The deed was done. He urged his horse forward and pranced nobly through the carnage. He feigned disgust and turned his nose as he passed by a pair of women who had been run through with a single lance. He stopped near a broken fence, where a group of survivors had gathered inside the protective perimeter of the men riding under Lord Hischurn's banner.

"I am Gilifan," the wizard declared. "I am the new lord at Hischurn keep."

A couple of people in the group stole glances at each other, but no one spoke. The shock and terror was plainly written across their pale faces and their wide eyes locked upon him, waiting for him to announce his intentions.

"You have been betrayed," he continued. He pointed to a slain soldier at his feet. "This man fights under the king's banner, but what have you done to stir the king's wrath?"

He waited silently for a moment, but no one dared to speak.

Gilifan descended from his horse and walked to B'dargen's body. The man's eyes were still open, frozen from the moment his soul was ripped from him. The wizard nudged him with a foot. "This man was from Kuldiga Academy," he said. "He was sent to kill all of you."

"Why would the king want us dead?" a middle-aged woman cried out. "We have done nothing to anybody!"

Gilifan raised an accusing finger. "But, didn't you harbor the shadowfiend, Be'alt the Black?" he asked. "That is why the king has sent these men against you."

"But we didn't know," another shouted. "He had us all bewitched!"

Gilifan nodded. "I believe you," he reassured the man as he patted the air with his hands. "Trust me, I know you didn't intend for the demon to walk among you. However, the king is unforgiving. After he sent the sorceress to slay the demon, he had her murder Lord Hischurn. As if that was not enough, he vowed to wipe this island clean of life."

Gilifan walked back to his horse and jumped up. "I say we cannot allow ourselves to live in fear of a tyrant who is impotent to control his own kingdom without waging war upon our women and children."

"What should we do?" someone shouted from the back of the group.

Gilifan made a point of looking at the dead soldiers with the king's banner. "We declare ourselves independent," he said after a long pause. "Join with me. I will not levy any taxes beyond what Lord Hischurn has already laid upon you. I will rebuild your town, and I will protect you from future attacks."

"How can you protect us against the king?" the first woman shouted.

"The king is old," Gilifan said. "His kingdom is fracturing. Have any of you heard about the senate?" He paused. No one answered him. "The senate has been destroyed."

Gasps rippled through the group.

"The Keeper of Secrets himself murdered several senators and laid waste to the senate chamber."

Again people gasped and murmured amongst themselves.

Gilifan whistled above the din to get their attention. "I say again, we cannot live under the threat of a tyrant. The king would wipe our island off the map for no other reason than to show he is in control. You are naught but pawns to him. I will protect you."

A young man stepped forward. "But you have only seventeen men, how can you offer us protection from the whole of the king's army?"

Gilifan nodded and looked directly at the young man. "I came with twenty today and we defeated more than twice our number and only lost three," he countered. "Besides this, I have a much larger army at Hischurn Keep. We are simply one of the patrols that roam the island to keep invaders and petty, manipulative nobles off the island." He sat back in his saddle and turned to address the whole crowd. "I would be honored to have those of you who are able-bodied join my men. Together we can keep this island free."

"And what if we don't want to join?" someone shouted from the back.

Gilifan looked into the crowd, searching for the one who asked the question. People stepped out of his gaze until at last he saw a man, roughly in his mid-thirties standing with a large warhammer in hand. Gilifan kept his face neutral, showing no emotion. "If you will not pledge to join in protecting the island, then you are free to leave." He then shrugged and addressed everyone with a great outstretching of his arms. "Only those who are willing to labor with us, for the common good, should stay on the island. However, I bear no ill will toward those who would prefer to pursue their interests elsewhere."

"You are saying that unless I join your army, I can't stay in my home?" the man retorted. "Sounds like we are trading one tyrant for another."

"You are bold, I will give you that," Gilifan said. "But you are foolish and blind. I am not evicting you from your home, the king's men have already done that. They laid waste to your people and burned your buildings. I am offering to rebuild it, but I cannot have detractors in our midst. Why should I offer my protection to you, and allow you a place at our table if you are not willing to work for it? So my offer is either stay and be one of us, or leave and do as you please. The choice is yours."

"My ma and pa raised me here, and their blood waters the ground this day. I will not be run out by you or anyone else," the man replied.

Gilifan smiled. "What is your name?"

"I am Malek, son of Dorin."

"Malek, son of Dorin, I would not dream of running you off your homeland," Gilifan said confidently. "But I would be honored if you would accept a position as captain of the garrison that I assign to this town. I would send ten men that you may order and command as you see fit. Why not help me protect the home you obviously love so dearly?"

"I am not bought with honors," Malek shouted back.

"I do not esteem your character so little," Gilifan replied. "What say you? It is obvious the townsfolk look up to you. They would also trust you with the command of the garrison. Any men from this town who wish to join could also become a member of your garrison. It will be a force of your own. You will be watched over by your own people. This way you need not wonder whether I will turn on you like the rabid king. My men can help yours train, and then you may lead them all."

"Take the offer, Malek," another young man said. "It would be good to have you at our head."

Malek stood there silently for a moment before finally nodding. "Alright. I'll do it."

A cheer went through the crowd.

"Good," Gilifan said. "The offer still stands, however." He looked to the rest of the people. "Any who wish to leave the island may do so. The king's men came by boats, which are docked to the west of here. We will take their dead back to the boats and bury them at sea. Those of you who wish to leave the island may use the left over boats." Gilifan waited as some of the gathered people chattered amongst themselves. Then he cleared his throat. "Those who wish to stay, if any of you are able to assist my men with cleaning the ground, I would appreciate it. However, I understand it has been a tragic day, and if you would prefer to go and rest, please feel free to do so." He turned to one of his men. "Put the king's dead men on their horses so we can take them back to the boats. We will also help the townsfolk bury their dead. Send a rider back to the keep and get a covered wagon. We will take the dead townsfolk to the hills to the south and give them a proper burial."

"We have a cemetery here," someone called out.

"Yes, but I intend to erect a monument to the fallen of the day," Gilifan said gallantly. "Let all those who look upon it know of the tragedy that has befallen our island, and the catalyst for our independence from the king." He turned back to his officer. "Go and see that it is done."

The officer nodded and began shouting orders to the others under Hischurn's banner.

A woman came up and grabbed Gilifan's leg. "Thank you, kind sir, thank you," she said.

Gilifan forced a smile onto his face. "But of course, my dear woman, don't mention it." He looked out to the appeased crowd one last time and then pulled the reins out to his right and trotted his horse out toward the south. As soon as he was out of the town his smile disappeared. "Oh the things I do to make them happy," he grumbled to himself. "Then again, a willing crone is better than a mindless zombie." He kicked his horse into a run. He would meet his men in the south.

It was some time before he saw the banners of his men. The sun hung low in the sky. A cool, gentle breeze wafted over the waving grass on the hills. Gilifan knew there was not enough daylight left to bury the fallen townspeople, but that had never been his intent anyway. He pulled his amulet out from under his clothing and kissed the warm, buzzing stone. His men drew the wagon in close and uncovered it before the necromancer. The others halted their horses behind the wagon.

"What of the others?" Gilifan asked.

The lieutenant rode forward and clapped a fist over his heart.

"We have taken the other dead and laid them in the barges as planned, master."

Gilifan nodded. "Did any townsfolk go with you?" he asked.

"Yes," the lieutenant said with a nod. There were slightly more than a score who wished to return to the mainland."

"And?" Gilifan pressed.

"As you instructed us yesterday, we led them to the barges, killed them on site, and laid their bodies in the barges with the others. Six of my men are steering the barges back around the island toward the docks near Hischurn Keep."

"And what of B'dargen?" the necromancer asked.

"The men have orders to drop his body into the sea, as you instructed me," the lieutenant said with a slight bow of the head.

"Good," Gilifan said. "He has served his purpose. Did you bring the monument?"

The lieutenant nodded. "It is already in the wagon, underneath the bodies."

Gilifan slipped his amulet up over his head and held it out in his right hand. "Well then, let's bring our new brethren back from the dead. Take the others now and set the monument up on the hill over there. After it is erected and these new recruits are raised, we will go back to the keep."

Somewhere behind him, Gilifan sensed movement. He turned around, but could only faintly see a depression in the grass. He narrowed his eyes, trying to scan the area for his stalker, but he could find no discernable trace.

"What are you after?" Gilifan mumbled.

*****

Gondok'hr exited the courtyard, leaving his assembled army standing in the cold, evening rain. He wrung his hands and shook the water from his robes. He reached up and wiped a pesky droplet from his brow and stormed through the halls until he reached his chamber. He looked to the scrying pool and went straightway to it. He waved a hand over it and whispered a name into the water. "Djekk, can you hear me?"

The pool reflected his confused, glistening face against the dark liquid. No answer came.

"Where is he?" Gondok'hr grumbled. He reached his left hand into a pocket and pulled out an old, warped copper coin. He tossed it into the scrying pool.

The coin *plitted* into the water and sank, swaying side to side until it vanished in the dark liquid. A few bubbles rose to the top and disrupted the surface. A purple glow emanated from the bottom of the bowl and fine, white bubbles rapidly formed around the light and then sailed to the top of the liquid. Soon the whole bowl was alive with bubbles sizzling up and bursting as they tore through the turbulent surface. The purple haze turned gray and then a silver mist rose from the depths of the scrying pool. The mist ascended up a few inches out of the bowl and then formed an oblong sphere, roughly the size of a man's head.

"You have need of me?" a voice asked from within the mist.

"I do," Gondok'hr replied sternly. "Are you free to appear?"

"I am," the voice replied softly.

Gondok'hr waved his hand and the door to his room slammed shut and the bolt slid into place. Then he looked back to the mist. "Hairen, come now," he said simply. He uttered a few arcane words and the mist floated out to the side of the scrying table. It grew and took the form of an old, slightly hunch-backed woman.

"What can I do for you?" Hairen asked as the mist dissipated to reveal her full form.

"How is our prodigy?" Gondok'hr asked.

Hairen scoffed. "He is proud, and I fear that Silvi's hypnotism may not be enough to hold him."

Gondok'hr gestured for the old witch to take a seat in a chair next to the desk against the wall. She nodded her thanks and went to the chair. "But she holds him for now?" Gondok'hr asked.

Hairen nodded. "She does," the old witch said. "He wishes to dissociate himself from his house. He fears what his mother would think."

Gondok'hr folded his arms. "Do you?"

Hairen shrugged. "She was always powerful," she said. "But I think I could handle her if she presents a problem."

Gondok'hr raised a hand. "No, she must not be hurt. If she is harmed then Eldrik will not go along with us no matter what kind of spells Silvi uses."

"His name is *Aparen* now," Hairen put in sarcastically.

Gondok'hr sniggered. "Interesting choice," he said. "In any case, for our plan to work he must be known for who he is. House Cedreau must join forces with Senator Bracken. It won't take long for word to spread about the senate hall. Soon, all of the noble houses will know of it, and they will start choosing sides. It is vital that all know House Cedreau aligned itself with Senator Bracken."

"Will that be enough?" Hairen asked.

Gondok'hr nodded, though he wasn't sure it was. "So long as Erik Lokton dies, I only need the nobles to fear the name Bracken. That should help stir the pot a bit while I make my exit."

"But, master, what of the coven?"

Gondok'hr sneered. "The coven can see to itself," he said. "You existed long before I came along."

"True, but it was you who had the prophecy about Leanor and Lord Cedreau. Without your foresight, we may have missed our chance to protect ourselves."

"Given the family's past with the coven, I am sure you would have thought of it," Gondok'hr said.

Hairen shrugged. "Perhaps," she admitted. "Either way, we have always needed a warlock to lead us. It is the way our order functions. Without the additional ability to see into the future, we will be weakened."

Gondok'hr waved the notion off. "Then train your new master, Eldrik."

"He has potential, it's true," she started. "But he does not have your capacity."

"I told you long ago what my goals were," Gondok'hr reminded her. "I have no care to remain with the coven. I never have. Besides, you have turned the boy into a shadowfiend. That has potential greater than that of a mere warlock."

Hairen nodded sullenly. "I suppose it matters little, if Tul'uh is coming."

Gondok'hr nodded. "He will subject all to his rule," he said.

"When you came to us, you were not unlike Eldrik," Hairen commented. "Older, of course, but still driven in much the same way."

"Family is a powerful motivator," Gondok'hr said. "That is why you should not meddle with Eldrik's mother."

"What would you have me do, as your final command?"

"Get the boy to openly commit House Cedreau to Senator Bracken. Tell him that Bracken orders Lokton manor destroyed, as the family has been declared traitors to the crown. Ply him with promises of glory and prosperity."

"If he doesn't want to go along with it?" Hairen asked.

"Convince him," Gondok'hr said. "Just get him there. After Erik is dead, then place him up as the true head of the order."

"The other warlocks may not like that," she put in. "They have gone along with the ruse so far, because you ordered it, but to truly pledge themselves to his service is another matter. I doubt that they will feel comfortable telling their true names to an unseasoned boy who can barely shave."

"Tell them I command it, as my final wish. If any object, then inform me of their names and I will deal with them personally."

Hairen stiffened. "I understand," she said.

"One more thing," Gondok'hr said with a raised finger. "I doubt his mother would take kindly to our interference. So, make sure Eldrik does not speak of the coven."

"How should he convince his house to march against House Lokton so soon after their defeat?"

"Just have him say that while in Drakei Glazei he was proclaimed a hero after he helped me apprehend Lord Lokton. I will create an official letter with my personal thanks, in Bracken's name of course. Then it should be simple for him to convince his house to ally with a senator and go to war with House Lokton."

"His mother may see through it," Hairen pointed out.

Gondok'hr nodded. "It is the best option we have at our disposal."

"Agreed," she said. "It was fortuitous, you sending Merriam to tell Eldrik where to find Lord Lokton."

"It would have been fortuitous if I could have foreseen the attack at the senate," Gondok'hr growled. "But I suppose we may yet turn this to our advantage."

"Why didn't you see it?" Hairen asked.

Gondok'hr bristled. "Those of my order have not ever been able to decipher the future regarding the Keeper of Secrets. Somehow it is hidden from our sight." The warlock kept silent about the fact that it was actually Erik who had attacked.

"But you have been able to see events with Erik, the boy who we are to kill?"

"In the past," Gondok'hr said with a nod. "That is how Tukai was able to stir up turmoil in House Lokton."

"What about now?" she asked.

Gondok'hr turned a keen eye on her. "As I said, deciphering events with the Keeper has been beyond our grasp." He was not about to disclose the truth that none of his order had ever been able to see Erik's future accurately. He would prefer she think it was some magical barrier around Lepkin, rather than risk her losing the courage to go after Erik.

"And he travels with the Keeper," Hairen said with a sigh. "Well then, the sooner I go, the better we can prepare."

Gondok'hr nodded. "You are released," he said with a wave of his hand.

Another ball of mist emerged from the scrying bowl and moved toward the old witch. It grew in size and opened, as if it were a great beast swallowing the lady whole. As it closed around her body she vanished into the mist and the silver haze shrank away into nothing, leaving only a copper coin on the chair she had been sitting in.

Gondok'hr stood there, staring at the copper coin silently. He replayed the conversation in his head. Hairen would handle the boy. That much he was sure of. It was that which he couldn't see that plagued him now. He went to the center of the room and sat cross-legged on the floor. He snapped his fingers and produced a stick of green chalk from thin air. He took the chalk and drew three runes on the floor in front of him. They were arcane symbols, from a tongue almost as old as the language of the elves. The rune on his left was the symbol for the past. The rune in front of him was the symbol for the present. The symbol on his right represented the future. Upon completing the last line of the third rune he quickly turned back to draw the symbol of an eye enclosed by a triangle over the middle symbol. Then he took the chalk and pressed it to the center of his forehead. He dragged the chalk straight down to the end of his nose. He could smell the bit of dust that fell as he pulled the chalk away.

Gondok'hr closed his eyes and dropped the chalk on the floor in front of him. He then extended his hands out over the symbols for the past and the future. He sat silently, focusing hard on the moment he wanted to see. He used his mind's eye to cover the distance between Kuldiga Academy and Lokton manor. He had been there before, so it was easy to conjure the image in his mind. He recalled his most recent memory, when he arrested Lord Lokton. His left hand grew warm as an invisible conduit connected him the symbol on his left.

The warlock groaned as the warmth passed through his body, inviting him to step into the memory and relive the past, but that is not what he was here for today. He wanted to see that which was yet to come. He shifted his thoughts, concentrating on the manor and propelling time forward in his mind. As he did so, the warmth shifted to his right arm and emerged through his right hand until it connected with the symbol of the future drawn on the floor.

He could feel the inviting pull. In his mind the manor became hazy, as if covered by a sheet of murky water. His body, on the other hand, felt the gravitational pull of the rune. Gondok'hr took a deep breath and allowed the spell to pull him in. A sudden rush of wind encircled him and he felt as though he were falling down into a cool, damp shaft leading deep into the ground. Then, as quickly as it had begun, the sensation was gone and he found himself standing in an open field in front of Lokton Manor.

He was not really there, he knew. He had looked into the future enough times to know that the spell only transported his consciousness, leaving his body behind with the symbols on the floor while the essence of his soul was free to wander in a world that had not yet taken form in the present. Yet, despite this, everything felt as real as anything he had ever experienced. The flowers in the field bowed and swayed in the gentle breeze as their sweet scent wafted up into the air. A pair of swallows chased each other overhead, diving and circling this way and that until they disappeared from view over the trees to the east. There were many men about the manor.

Gondok'hr walked forward to get a better look. Many men labored in the afternoon sun. He could tell they had been working for some time. None of them wore their shirts anymore, and their glistening skin was caked with dirt. He examined the trenches they dug with interest. "So you are preparing well," Gondok'hr commented. He walked along the trench, noting that several wooden pikes had been set in place as an additional barrier. "This will not protect you from magic," he promised. One of the workers slung a shovelful of dirt right at the warlock. The dirt passed harmlessly through him and spread onto the ground beyond.

Unimpressed, the warlock walked back to the front of the manor. He passed through a waist-high stone wall and walked toward the main house looking for other signs of defense preparations. Suddenly the front door opened and Master Lepkin and Braun emerged. Only, Gondok'hr knew it wasn't Master Lepkin. He didn't know how, but he knew it was really the boy inside of Lepkin's body. He froze in place, afraid to disturb the spell. This was the closest he had ever seen a future event that included Erik. All of his previous attempts had been unsuccessful.

"I told them to be ready," Braun shouted.

"Then why are there no wagons?" Erik retorted.

Gondok'hr looked around and saw that except for the men preparing the trench, there was no one else about. Who could Erik be talking about?

"I instructed them to prepare to evacuate, but they don't want to leave. They want to stay and fight," Braun said.

Erik wheeled around and thunked Braun in the chest with an angry finger. "The *women* and *children* cannot fight!" he hissed. "They need to leave before the enemy arrives."

"I can't force them to go," Braun quipped. "This is their home."

"You can!" Erik snipped.

"I have too much else to do preparing the field for battle," Braun said. The big man crossed his arms over his chest and shook his head with an exasperated sigh."

"We can't fight with them here," Erik said. "We don't have the capacity to protect everyone."

Gondok'hr sneered and he knew what he had to do. He turned back to face the field. He broke off the spell and pulled himself back in between the future and the present. As before a rush of wind came upon him, but he didn't allow himself to fully return to his body. He kept himself in that space between reality and the future, just long enough to peer into an alternate future. He wanted to know what would happen if he left immediately.

The wind stopped and he found himself back in front of the

manor. Erik and Braun were not outside. The warlock turned to see the men working as before. The distant pair of sparrows dashing through the sky overhead. He turned and waited patiently. Everything played out as it had previously. The front door opened and Erik and Braun stepped outside again.

"I told them to be ready," Braun shouted exactly as he had before.

"Then why are there no wagons?" Erik yelled.

"Braun!" one of the men shouted from the trenches. "In the field!"

Erik and Braun ran out toward the field and stopped just a few paces short of where Gondok'hr watched the alternate scene unfold.

"By the gods!" Braun said. "That is him!" he said. "That's Senator Bracken!"

"And he has an army with him," Erik said. "Tell the men that he is not a senator. He is a warlock."

"His army rides under the king's banner," Braun said.

"They are not the king's men," Erik said. "Come, we must sound the alarm."

"We aren't ready," Braun said.

Gondok'hr turned and glanced back. He saw his future self, riding at the head of his army. He nodded his head. He turned back to see Erik and Braun running to the manor and shouting frantically. The men in the trenches abandoned their tasks and scrambled for their weapons. He would have remained and watched the battle unfold, but something blocked him. The scene stopped, as if it were a play frozen in a block of ice. The colors faded, replaced by a gray and blue haze. The warlock tried to fight it, but he was unable to push the spell forward. Something ripped him from his spell and he found himself gasping for breath on the floor in the room.

He coughed and sputtered, rolling over to his knees and pushing himself up to stand in the room. His head throbbed and a stabbing pain assaulted the back of his neck. If only he could have seen the battle! No matter, he had seen enough to get an advantage. He waved his hand and the runes disappeared as if they had never been drawn. Gondok'hr grabbed the copper coin and bolted for the door. There was no time to waste. He would lead his army out now and catch the boy unprepared.

CHAPTER SEVEN

Al's fingers ached deep in the bones. His arms barely could muster the strength to hold onto his handhold anymore. He released his grip and floated back into the pool, relying on his stubby legs to keep him afloat as he gave his arms a break. He took in a deep breath and tilted back, trying to bring his belly up to the surface. He managed to float on his back for several minutes, but as sleep took over his body fell under the water and he woke sharply. He sputtered and coughed water out from his mouth as his arms flailed about, splashing and smacking the water. His feet began kicking furiously to keep him above the surface.

"It won't be long now," a voice shouted from above.

Al wiped the water from his eyes and saw his brother peering at him over the ledge. "Have you no decency?" Al asked. "Where is your compassion? I am your brother."

"No," Threnton said with a shrug. "You are a thief. You broke into my home to usurp my throne. I have no brother."

"Be gone then, dog," Al grumbled. "Isn't it enough to let me die, or must you taunt me also?"

Threnton frowned and held up a small parchment. He turned slightly and angled the paper in the torchlight to read it. After a moment his mouth dropped open and he gasped. "Oh, dear brother your friend is in dire straits!" he shouted. "Someone by the name of Erik, do you know him?"

Al ignored his brother's feigned concern. "What does it say?"

"It says that Erik expects a dragon to attack Lokton manor!" Threnton clasped a hand over his mouth and gasped again. His wide eyes looked down to the pool at Al briefly before he pulled his hand away from his mouth to reveal a sickening sneer. "I suppose you will not be alone in the afterlife after all," Threnton said. "Where do you suppose traitorous dwarves go when they die?"

"You don't know what you are doing," Al said. "Leave me here if you will, but send the cavedogs out to help him. The dragon will come for Roegudok Hall also!"

"Enough!" Threnton bellowed. "I only came to tell you so

you may die knowing that you could not save your friends. They are as doomed as you."

"I promise you this," Al said determinedly. "Send the cavedogs or I will crush your life from you."

"How do you propose to do that?" Threnton said. "You only remain alive because you are too stubborn to admit defeat."

"Perhaps so," Al conceded. "But mark my words. I will fulfill my promise, whether in the flesh or as a ghastly spirit from the beyond. I will punish you unless you send the cavedogs to help him."

Threnton tossed the parchment into the air above the pit and watched it flitter down as a leaf on the wind. "I think not," he said simply. "You will die here, and no one shall ever hear from you again."

"If I am too stubborn to drown in your pit, then perhaps I am stubborn enough to strangle you as a specter," Al threatened.

Threnton drew his head back and looked long and hard at Al before finally whirling around and storming off through the hall.

Al felt his heart sink with each echoing step his brother took. If a dragon came for Erik at Lokton manor, there was little that could save him. Al could only hope that Erik had sent a message to Lady Dimwater as well, for there was no way he could help his friend. He had failed.

The dwarf swam back to the side of the pit and groped along the walls for some sort of handhold. The only one he found was the one he had been holding onto since being cast into the pit. He pulled himself up on it and reached out, hoping to find some sort of crack or crevice, anything to pull up farther. There was nothing there. He let himself bob down to his arms' full extent and then yanked himself up as hard and fast as he could. He let go of the handhold and reached out for the ledge, but it was still beyond his reach. He splashed back down into the pool and let out a feral yell, cursing the pit. In answer, the chute above opened and another blast of cold water rained down upon him, knocking him under the surface for a few seconds until he managed to swim to the far side of the pit.

"I'm sorry, Erik," Al sputtered. He turned his head up to the ledge and his eyes welled with tears. "I'm sorry." He shook his head and wiped his eyes. As he looked down he caught a faint glimmer beneath the water. At first Al thought perhaps it was a shiny rock reflecting the torchlight from above, but that couldn't be it. The torches above barely threw shadows onto the wall of the pit, and hardly any light at all reached the water's surface. This was something else.

The light grew, ever so slightly, until Al could just make out the outline of his hammer. The dwarf laughed aloud. "Now you mock me too," he said to his hammer. "Ha! If only my father were here to see that!" Al punched the water before him. He laughed twice more and then his smile faded. "Oh father, what have I done?" He looked back to his hammer. "Had I not chosen the hammer in the first place, then I would be able to help my friends. If I had honored your wish and become king, then I could protect our people." Al sighed. "I have failed so many."

He let himself fall beneath the surface of the water. He was ready to meet his fate. He fell down toward the hammer, reaching out for it with his hand as he descended in the pool. He didn't bother to look up again. The darkness closed in around him and the water grew colder as he neared his hammer. The silvery light about the tool grew brighter and then a voice echoed through the pool.

"Don't you remember the fishing hole?" the voice called out.

Al startled and turned about but no one was there. The light around his hammer faded and winked out. Al plucked the hammer up into his hand and then the voice returned.

"Don't you remember the fishing hole?" it asked again.

Al's thoughts raced through the years of his memories. Centuries back, when he was only a small child, he had gone fishing with his cousin after his father had told him not to. He had fallen into a pool of water not unlike this one, and almost drowned except...

Al burst into action. He held his stinging lungs in check and tightened his mouth and nose to keep the water out. He swam down beyond where the hammer had been and groped around with his other hand. His hand went down through a small shaft in the bottom. The pull of the water exiting the pool was only slight, for the hole was barely large enough for him to stick his hand through.

His lungs burned and started to spasm. He turned and put his feet to the solid rock and pushed off. As his head and mouth burst out through the surface he exhaled quickly and gasped for air. He still clung to his hammer in one hand. The instrument began to glow again. He took in a deep breath and dove down to the hole in the bottom of the pool.

He thrust his hand into the shaft once more and felt around. It was then that he knew what to do. The stone underneath the pool was not solid granite. The floor was shale, thick yet brittle. He was able to even chip a small piece off with his hand inside the hole.

His hammer glowed brighter, allowing him to see the floor of the pool. He grinned when he saw the gray stone around the hole. It was obvious to him now that the chute above, which dropped water periodically, had managed to erode this hole in the pit. Though it wasn't large now, the shale would be no match for his hammer. With any luck, perhaps there was a larger chute on the other side of the thin hole.

Al steadied himself and gave a mighty swing. The water restricted his strength and slowed his strike, but it mattered not. The hammer struck the stone and sent shards of brittle, thin shale all around. A crack ripped through and a bit of rock fell away. The force of the water draining out grew, and Al's beard swayed toward the drain. The dwarf took another swing, aiming for the end of the crack. A large area, the size of a wine barrel, shifted and rumbled as the crack ripped around and loosed it from the floor.

With the third swing, a large section of the shale floor shattered and was sucked into the hole below. Al was drawn into the chute after the rocks. He brought his arms up to protect his face as he slid side to side through a winding chute. Once he got stuck as the chute narrowed and caught him around the belly, but the crushing pressure from the water above forced him through and sent him shooting through the rest of the chute.

Finally the chute turned and angled sideways. Al flew out through an opening the size of a normal dwarven doorway. He briefly flew through the air before crashing down into a new pool of still water.

He slid his hammer into his belt and clumsily pulled himself above the surface and looked around. He looked to his left and saw a berm of dirt behind an outcropping of rock. He swam to it with the last of his strength and pulled himself up to lie on the hard, black stone.

Al laughed a couple of times and turned over to kiss the rock beneath him. "My weary bones thank you for the respite," he said to the rock.

"And my weary soul thanks you for returning," a voice said.

Al sat up erect and looked out over the pool he had just left. There, above the water, he saw the glowing figure of his father. "It was you in the pit?" Al asked.

His father nodded his head and moved forward. He did not walk so much as float toward Al. "You remembered the fishing hole," Al's father said with a slight smile on his face.

Al nodded. "This wasn't exactly the same," Al said. "I didn't have to dig my way out last time."

"No," his father said. "But the principle was the same."

Al smirked and rubbed a nervous thumb over his hammer. "I'm sorry father," he said. "I never meant for any of this to happen."

The ghost held up a hand and smiled wide. "Apologize not," he said. "After all, it was your hammer that enabled you to escape. It is your past that makes you who you are today. You will be a better king for it, and a better ally to the humans as well. You know them and their ways more intimately than I ever could."

Al looked to his feet. "I would have been happy to take the scale," he said. "I did not want to challenge my brother."

The ghost nodded and his smile disappeared. "It brings me no joy to see this day. A father can never rejoice when his sons fight. Your brother has grown hard in his ways, and he will not see the truth. You must press on. It is the only way to save your friends, and our people."

Al nodded. He fumbled for something else to say, but no other words came to him. He looked up at his father and smiled. "Stay with me father," he said. "Guide me. I am still not wise in the way of kings."

His father's smile returned and the ghost looked upon him with loving eyes. "Be not a king," he said. "Be a friend, be a protector, and be a helper. These things are better than a king, and will give you true power as you wear the crown. Now, you must go. The guards are coming for the patrol. The two that you will see are friendly to you. It is Timmin and Brinon, your old, dear cousins.

Tell them that you have seen me here, and that you are to gather the council and restore Roegudok Hall to the ancient ways. They will help you."

Al stood and reached out to his father, but the apparition faded away over the water as dust in the wind.

"Halt!" a voice shouted from behind.

Al wheeled around to see a short, stout dwarf with a thick chest, bald head, and a neatly braided black beard. Al smiled. "Hello Timmin," he said. "Where's Brinon?"

A second dwarf emerged from a tunnel off to the side and his jaw dropped open. "Al?" Brinon said.

"Hello cousins," Al said.

"Stonebubbles, Al! How did you ever end up in here?"

Al patted the air and stepped over the berm to the stone path in front of the tunnel his cousins had just exited. "You boys might want to sit down. It is quite a tale."

The two of them exchanged grins. "It doesn't have anything to do with your pa does it?" Timmin asked with a crooked smile on his face.

Al smiled wide and nodded his head. "He told me you would help me restore the hall."

"Well, it's about time!" Brinon shouted. "We've been doing patrol here for years after that brother of yours threw us out of our homes. We'll help you throw the old lout out on his backside!"

Al chuckled. "Well then, let's go and get the council."

Timmin held up a hand. "Nope, nothin' doin'!" he said quickly. Al shot him a confused look but Timmin walked over and threw his arms around him in an embrace. As he pulled back he patted Al's shoulder. "You were exiled long ago. Anyone sees you and it will be off to the dungeon with you."

Al shrugged and laughed. "Actually I just escaped from a pit that Threnton threw me into."

Timmin and Brinon looked to each other. "Really?" Brinon asked. "No one has heard of your return."

Al gestured to himself. "Why do you think I am all wet?" he asked. "I only escaped the pit by swimming through a chute of water that brought me here."

Brinon frowned. "Then that is all the more reason for you to wait here. We will go and get the council and bring them to you. If the whole council is with you, no one will dare intervene."

"Alferug is here as well," Al said.

"Where is he?" Timmin asked.

Al shrugged. "I am not sure, we were separated when my brother's guards arrested us."

"Alright," Timmin said. "I will check the dungeon for Alferug." Timmin thumbed at his brother. "Brinon will go and get the council."

"Thank you," Al said.

Timmin nodded and bounded off into the tunnel from which he had come. Brinon dug into his pocket and pulled out a small cloth bundle. He smiled and tossed it to Al. Al opened it and found a hunk of sourdough bread inside.

"Thanks," Al said.

Brinon shrugged. "It isn't much, but it's all I have on me." Then he turned and left.

Al turned and looked for a place to sit down while he tore a hunk out of the bread. He wasn't sure he had ever tasted bread that was so good before in his life. His stomach roared with hunger as he chewed. He had forgotten how hungry he had become, trapped in that pit his brother had thrown him into. It was good to sit and eat.

As he licked the last crumb from his fingers he laid back against the rock and let his eyes close. Sleep was upon him before he could take another breath. He slept heavy and sound next to the pool of water.

CHAPTER EIGHT

Hairen moved into the room and set a scroll down upon the table. "I have the map, Aparen," she said.

Aparen looked down at the table. "Where is Silvi?" he asked.

"She is busy," Hairen said.

Aparen smirked. He noted the contempt in her voice, but he ignored it. He reached out and unrolled the map. "So Senator Bracken is attacking from the west?" he asked.

"He has a small army under his command," Hairen started. "He will be leaving from Kuldiga Academy and striking Lokton manor from the west." She moved her gnarled, wrinkled finger over the map and pointed to their position. "We will come south from here and strike the manor from the north."

"If Senator Bracken has an army, why would he need us?" Aparen asked.

"Have you not heard of Master Lepkin's victory at Gelleirt Monastery?" Hairen asked. She turned a condescending eye on him. "If he could defeat three hundred Tarthun raiders single-handedly, surely you can see why Senator Bracken might need assistance?"

"But why would he trust us?" Aparen asked. "A senator working with a coven of witches and warlocks would be strung up in the center of Drakei Glaei."

Hairen smiled her crooked, sly smile and cackled. "Don't you worry about that. Senator Bracken can take care of himself. Besides, his official report will say that House Cedreau came to his aid."

"But I told Silvi that I don't want anyone to call me by my given name. I am Aparen now, not Eldrik."

Hairen turned on him and pushed him back to the wall with an unseen spell. "Do not talk to me with such contempt," she warned. "I am still witch enough to handle the likes of you." She flicked her wrist and dispelled the force pinning him against the wall.

"The others have already pledged their allegiance to me," Aparen said as he rubbed his chest.

"Make no mistake that I am the matriarch of the coven. You may have the warlocks behind you, but they still listen to me."

"So you wish to control me?" Aparen guessed.

Hairen smirked again. "No, I have no use for you long term."

Aparen moved up and looked at the map again. "So you need Lokton manor destroyed as well?"

"The manor means nothing to me. That prize is for you. However, I do need the Keeper of Secrets dead. Kill him, and you will have me as an ally until the end of your days."

"And he will be at the manor?" Aparen asked.

Hairen nodded. "He will. I will send Merriam and Silvi with you. They will offer you whatever assistance you require."

"And the warlocks are mine after the battle?"

"If you wish." Hairen sighed and tapped her yellow fingernail on the map. "But you must defeat the Keeper. Lepkin must die."

"I would still prefer not to use my name," Aparen said.

"For this battle, it will help your family more if you are known by your birth name. Think of it, would you rather have 'Aparen' steal the glory from House Cedreau? Or would you prefer that King Mathias knows you and your family helped his senate?" Hairen folded her arms in front of her. "In fact, it would be best if you return to your manor and collect as many able-bodied men as your house can spare for the fight."

"My mother will not like being associated with warlocks," Aparen said.

"Then take this," Hairen said. She produced a sealed letter from the folds of her robe and slid it across the table. "It is a direct summons from Senator Bracken to House Cedreau for help."

He took the envelope in hand and slid his finger under the purple wax seal. He pulled the letter out and read through its contents briefly. "This might work," he said with a nod of his head. "How do I explain to her where I have been?"

"Just tell her the truth. Tell her you went to Drakei Glazei to see Lord Lokton sentenced for your father's murder."

"I cannot lie to her," he said. "She will know."

Hairen shrugged. "Then tell her you stabbed him when he attacked the senate and escaped. Tell her you are considered a hero for the feat, and that is why Senator Bracken is calling upon you for additional support. Surely the news of the attack has reached your home by now. The story will make sense if you explain that Lepkin and another from House Lokton are fugitives on their way to Lokton manor to raise troops."

He nodded. "Alright. Can Silvi come with me?"

Hairen shook her head. "No, you should go alone. Silvi and Merriam will take the warlocks separately. Just collect your retinue and then explain that Senator Bracken has sent additional aid for you to meet with before assaulting Lokton manor." Hairen straightened her stiff, creaky back and looked into his eyes. "For now, you must still be known as Eldrik. After this battle, you may do as you wish."

"Alright," Eldrik said. "I will do it your way, for now."

*****

Marlin stopped when he saw Lady Dimwater resting on the bench outside the room where Lepkin lay. She was leaned back against the wall, mouth open slightly as she breathed peacefully. Her head was tilted down a bit over her left shoulder and a few strands of her dark hair had fallen over her face as she slept. The prelate walked over to her and gently placed a hand on her shoulder.

"Have you been here all night?" Marlin asked.

Dimwater stirred and looked up to him. "Is it morning?" she asked.

Marlin nodded. "You really should rest in your room. This can't be half as comfortable as your bed."

She smiled and rubbed her shoulders with her hands. "I can't sleep there," she said. "I just lie awake in my bed thinking of Lepkin."

"You know I will come for you as soon as he wakes," Marlin said. "Go, you should get some rest."

"Can't I go in and see him?" she pleaded.

Marlin shook his head. "You know I would let you, if I could," he said. "We need to have only the purest of energies around him while he recovers. I don't want to take any chances."

"What if he never wakes?" she asked sullenly.

Marlin knelt down before her, noting the sorrow swirling through her aura. "He will wake," he said confidently.

"You sound so sure," Dimwater replied.

Marllin nodded. "Lepkin is strong, he would not abandon us now. He will return to us." Marlin could see the doubt flowing through Dimwater's spirit. He reached over and gently turned her chin to look directly at him. "I may be blind by normal standards," he began. "But there are many things that I can still see. His spirit is strong, and he gains strength every day. He may not be awake yet, but the gods will not take him from us before his mission is complete. He is the best of all the Keepers that have lived. If you have no faith of your own, then lean on mine when I tell you that he will wake again."

Dimwater nodded and a sprout of hope blossomed within her heart. "Isn't there anything I can do to help?" she asked.

Marlin nodded. "I have given Tatev the task of researching a lead on where Allun'rha's book, The Illumination, might be. I am sure he could use some additional help with the research."

She nodded and rose to her feet, looking briefly over her shoulder at the door behind her. "You will come for me if there is any change in him, right?" she asked.

"Of course," Marlin promised.

"Alright, then I will go and help Tatev."

Marlin watched her leave and then he turned to the door and pushed it open. Four healers stood in the early morning sun, passing their green, healing energy into Erik's body in the hopes of waking Lepkin from his sleep. The prelate closed the door behind him and stepped up to the foot of the bed. He examined Lepkin's aura carefully, studying the myriad colors that intertwined and vibrated through his spirit. The healers' energy flowed in steadily, mixing and pushing into the blue, red, purple, and orange hues. The golden light in the center was growing, but it was still bound and constrained by thick black cords.

"Has he spoken?" Marlin asked.

"No, prelate," one of the other healers replied. "But he has moaned a couple of times during the night."

Marlin sighed. "Why won't you wake, my friend?" he asked Lepkin. The healers ceased adding their energy and slowly pulled away. Their shift was done and Marlin could see the exhaustion in their auras. "Go and rest," Marlin said.

"Shouldn't we wait for the others?" one of them asked.

As if on cue, the door opened and in walked five fresh healers. Upon seeing their replacements, the tired healers exited the room and closed the door behind them.

Marlin moved around to stand at Lepkin's head. He placed a hand on either side of Lepkin's head and began to focus his own energy.

The others fanned out around Marlin, but they waited for him to say when it was time to begin.

The prelate concentrated, building his restorative energy within his chest and then bringing it up to his hands. He could feel its warmth in his palms as the pressure started to build. "Join with me," Marlin said. Two more priests came up and placed their hands directly over Lepkin's chest. Green energy started to flow from the three, starting in their chests and coursing down their arms to their hands and finally mixing with Lepkin's aura. Once the connection was made, another priest came up and placed his hands on Marlin's shoulders, augmenting Marlin's efforts by sending his own energy through Marlin. Two additional priests augmented the other two healers.

No one spoke. The only sound in the room was the warm, vibrant hum of the healers' energy as it flowed into Lepkin. Their energy spread through Lepkin's aura. It strengthened the golden light in the center of the sleeping man's soul and weakened the black cords that bound it. For hours they stood, continuously giving their energy to Lepkin and trying to chase out the impurities in the man's aura. Lepkin groaned a couple of times, but he showed no sign of actually regaining his consciousness.

After a total of six hours, Marlin sent the last amount of healing energy into Lepkin that he had. The priest behind him removed his hands from his shoulders and the others simultaneously broke connection with Lepkin. Marlin exhaled wearily and slid his hands down to the bed as he leaned over and took in a few breaths.

"He looks the same," one of the healers noted.

Marlin scanned Lepkin's aura and his heart grew heavy as he watched the black cords thicken again around the golden light in the man's soul. "That he does," Marlin agreed.

"What shall we do?" another priest asked. "If we can't heal him, then we must choose a new Keeper."

The prelate shook his head. "No, we continue on as we have been. Lepkin will wake." He turned and looked to the others. "Go down to the library and see if there is anything that might help us with this."

"With respect, prelate, we have already searched the library," a priest replied.

"Twice," another one added.

"Then look again!" Marlin shouted. He backed away from the bed and used the back of his sleeve to wipe the sweat from his brow. "Get some food and then go down to the library. There has to be *something* that we missed." The others relented and walked out of the room. Marlin could see the doubt in their auras, but at least none of them continued to argue with him. As they left, another group of six healers came in, ready to start their shift.

"Any change?" one of them asked Marlin.

Marlin shook his head. "None," he said. He gestured for the others to take their positions around Lepkin. They did so and immediately began pouring their own energy into Lepkin. Marlin watched for a few minutes and then he walked to the far end of the room and stood in the window, letting the afternoon sun warm his skin. He looked out to the distant trees, scanning the energies of the forest and wondering what more he could do to help his friend.

The rumbling in his stomach pulled him from his meditation and reminded him that his body needed sustenance. He sighed and left the room as quietly as possible so as not to disturb the others. He went down several flights of stairs as he made his way to the dining hall. By the time he arrived, only one of the other five healers that had been with him was still eating.

"The others have already gone to the library," the priest said as soon as he noticed Marlin enter the hall.

Marlin nodded quietly and sat at a far table, alone. He put his elbows on the table and propped his hands up against his forehead as he closed his eyes. A few moments later he heard soft footsteps approaching and then something *clunked* down on the table in front of him and the footsteps then walked away. The prelate slowly opened his eyes and reached down to take the spoon and shovel the first bite of stew into his mouth. The food was piping hot, and burned his tongue just a bit, but he chewed and swallowed it anyway. Then he set to stirring the contents of his bowl and blowing gently over the top as he waited for it to cool.

Another set of footsteps entered the hall from the left. They came closer to him, so he turned away from his food and looked up to see Dimwater approaching.

"The other healers told me that there appears to be no change," she said.

Marlin nodded. "We are doing our best," he said.

The sorceress sat next to him quietly and looked down at his food. "Stew again," she noted.

"We are a simple order," Marlin explained. "We don't often have larger feasts the way that nobles might."

A cook came out from a room to the right and placed a bowl of stew in front of Lady Dimwater. She thanked him and waved her hand over the steaming bowl to cool it down enough for her to eat. She took a bite and then conjured a glass of absinthe and took a small sip. "Do you mind?" she asked Marlin.

He shrugged. "If Lepkin doesn't wake soon, then perhaps you can start conjuring a bit of the stuff for me too," he said.

Lady Dimwater chuckled to herself quietly and took another bite of stew. "What of your faith?" she asked. She didn't mean to sound insulting, but she could tell by the way Marlin sighed that the comment didn't quite sit right with him. "I'm sorry," she said. "I didn't mean to mock. It's just that I don't know how much longer I can remain sane while Lepkin lies in a bed, helpless."

Marlin nodded knowingly. "My faith is still there, but that doesn't mean that I don't have any doubts. Sometimes it is hard to walk forward in the darkness, hoping for a ray of light to come and end the black night."

Lady Dimwater nodded and took another sip of her absinthe. "Perhaps they will find something in the library," she said with feigned hope.

Marlin leaned back and dropped his hands into his lap. "How about you conjure me up a small shot of your favorite drink," he stated dryly.

CHAPTER NINE

"I sent the messages," Braun said.

Erik pushed back from the table. His plate of half-eaten eggs and bacon sat before him. "Thanks," he offered.

"You should finish your breakfast," Braun insisted.

"I am not hungry," Erik replied. He stood up from the table and went to the open window. "The men have been working tirelessly, but we still have a long way to go to prepare the field."

"All the more reason you should eat," Braun said.

Erik turned back to Braun and shook his head. "Where do our preparations stand?"

"We have set the pikes," Braun replied. "We have assembled a pair of catapults, and amassed a decent arsenal to use with those."

"Has Demetrius finished the wind-lance?" Erik asked.

"No," Braun said flatly. "He is working as quickly as possible, but he has to design it from scratch. As it is a weapon only found in legend, there are no plans or schematics to use."

"Is it really so complicated?" Erik asked. "There are ballista schematics he could use."

Braun shook his head. "No, a ballista fires a large projectile horizontally at ground troops. A wind-lance is a type of launcher that must be able to maneuver freely to follow a dragon's flight. It is not simple at all."

Erik nodded, as if he understood, but he didn't. He turned back to the window and let it go. Surely Demetrius was doing his best, and questioning him about it would only halt any progress he was making. "Is the trench around the manor finished?"

"No, but we are close. Another two or three hours and we should have the circle completed. We have managed to set the tar-balls."

Erik smiled, those had been his idea. "And we have selected the archers who will fire the flaming arrows?"

"Yes," Braun said. "As you suggested, we placed a tar-ball at the base of each hay stack in the field. Our archers will be able to hit them from the roof. They are there now, waiting for any sign of the enemy."

"Good," Erik said.

"I would caution one thing, however," Braun said. "When the time comes to use the tar-balls, we should take note of which way the wind is blowing. I would advise to use the devices only if there is no wind, or if it is blowing away from the manor. If it is blowing toward the manor, the smoke screen will hinder us."

Erik raised his brows. "Of course," he said. "I assume you have already instructed the archers to act accordingly?"

"I have, but I still wanted to inform you of my decisions."

"I appreciate that, but you are more experienced," Erik said. "I will not question you."

"Except for when I tell you to eat your breakfast?" Braun quipped.

Erik smiled. "Alright, I'll finish the food." He reached over and picked the plate up in his left hand. He tossed the cold bacon into his mouth, folding the strips over to make them fit. He chewed half-heartedly and then tipped the plate to allow the over-easy egg to slip off and into his waiting gullet. He barely chewed it more than twice before swallowing and washing it down with the last bit of his apple juice. "Happy?" Erik asked with a bit of yolk dribbling out the left corner of his mouth.

"Not exactly what I had in mind," Braun said.

Erik shrugged and the two walked out of the dining hall and into the front foyer of the manor. Their steps echoed through the halls. The front door opened, throwing the early morning light into the foyer. Erik looked up to see a tall woman with golden, braided hair laid casually over her right shoulder. A bow was slung over her back and a sleek, curved scimitar hung from her hip. She wore a forest green tunic and brown trouser, with black boots that had long ago lost their sheen under a film of dust and dirt.

A Lotkon guard walked in after her. "Presenting Lady Arkyn," he said officially to Braun.

"Yes," she said coyly. "We have met before," she told the guard.

He waited for Braun's signal, and then the guard bowed his head and backed out through the front door, closing it after him.

"What can House Lokton do for you?" Braun asked.

She looked to Erik for a moment and smiled faintly. "I come seeking refuge for the wounded, and to add my blade to yours,"

Lady Arkyn said with a slight bow.

"The wounded?" Erik said confused.

Lady Arkyn straightened up and nodded her head. "We were attacked at Kuldiga Academy. Some of us managed to escape, but we also carry wounded along with us."

"Braun, why have you not called for me?" Lady Lokton asked from the top of the stairs.

Erik caught Braun blush just before bowing in deference to Lady Lokton. "My apologies, our guest has only just arrived. I was about to call for you."

"I heard the guard say your name was Lady Arkyn, is that correct?" Lady Lokton asked. She started down the stairs, using the hand rail to guide her.

Even before she was near, Erik could see his mother's puffy, red eyes behind the black veil of lace. He looked to the floor and stepped aside to let her talk with Lady Arkyn.

"That is correct," Lady Arkyn said. "I am one of the instructors at Kuldiga Academy.

"Who attacked you?" Lady Lokton asked.

"It was Senator Bracken," Lady Arkyn said.

Erik and Braun exchanged glances. "Senator Bracken?" Braun asked.

Lady Arkyn nodded, staring firmly into his eyes. "It was him," she said.

"Why would he attack Kuldiga Academy?" Lady Lokton asked.

"Because I attacked him," Erik said truthfully. Lady Lokton turned on him and stared into his eyes. He was certain she would be able to see who he was. It had to be obvious to her then, as they stood silently, locked in a gaze that seemed to last a lifetime. Would she hate him? Would she strike him? Would she be able to forgive him for failing to rescue his father?

"Master Lepkin nearly killed him," Braun put in. His interruption disrupted the stare and Lady Lokton looked to Braun expectantly.

"*Nearly* killed him?" she said questioningly. "What does that mean?"

"It means he uses powerful magic," Braun replied. "He was able to escape." He didn't offer any more of an explanation than that, for which Erik was grateful.

"I see," she said. "Well, don't just stand there. The lady said they have wounded. Go and get them and give them beds."

"My lady, it would be better to move them with the evacuation," Braun said.

Lady Lokton snorted, not in a haughty, condescending way, but out of resignation. "Do whatever suits you, then," she said. Her eyes looked off to some distant point and she slowly made her way back to the stairs.

Braun bowed his head briefly and then turned back to Lady Arkyn. "The wounded who cannot travel may stay with us, but I cannot guarantee their safety."

"We are all staying," Lady Arkyn countered. "We have lost friends already, and we'll not be put out of the fight now."

Braun leaned back and glanced to Erik. A grin crept across his face and he nodded his approval. "We could always use the extra help," he said.

"Was a dragon with him?" Erik asked.

Lady Arkyn turned and knit her brow. "Are you expecting one?" she asked.

Erik nodded his head. "We went to Senator Backen's house. We were met by a servant he had trapped there. It turns out that he is actually a warlock who has assumed the form of Senator Bracken."

"By the Ancients," Lady Arkyn muttered.

"That isn't the worst part," Erik continued. "The warlock is allied with a dragon."

Lady Arkyn sucked in a breath. "Then, there is no time to waste. I will bring everyone inside. With your permission, we could use a bit of food before we join the others outside in preparing the house."

Braun nodded. "Anyone who raises a blade with me is my brother, or sister as it were," he said. "Feel free to help yourselves and ask the kitchen staff for what you need."

The front door opened again and in walked a man with long black robes, propping Orres up with Orres' thick arm draped over his shoulders.

"Lepkin," Orres said gruffly. "We don't have much time."

Erik sucked in a breath. At once he felt both relieved, and

angered by Orres' presence. He wasn't sure whether to welcome him into his home, or to expel him for what he had seen in his journal. Orres noted Erik's silence and studied him. Erik looked to the bandages, each stained dark with dried blood.

"Master Orres, welcome," Braun said, breaking the silence.

"I may not be much for fighting, but I am here to offer whatever is left of me," Orres said.

"Master Lepkin asked whether we saw a dragon," Lady Arkyn put in.

Orres shook his head. "No, but the senator obviously has something else up his sleeve." He turned to the man holding him up. "Tell him, Wendal."

"I think the senator is working with a necromancer," Wendal said softly. "Or, perhaps he is one himself." Erik turned to look at Braun for a moment. Braun cocked a brow and nodded.

"That would fit with what I found at the senator's home," Erik said. "I stumbled upon some personal effects at the senator's home that might help us understand our enemy."

"First," Lady Arkyn cut in. "You should know that the senator is dead, and we were attacked by a warlock that is impersonating him."

Orres and Wendal glanced to her and then back to Erik for confirmation.

"It's true," Erik said.

"A copy of Aikur's War was found along with some mementos of a family that has long been dead," Braun added. "Actually it is my belief that the warlock is Master Pemo."

"Pemo," Wendal repeated solemnly. "If that is true, then we are in a lot of trouble."

"Who is Pemo?" Orres asked. "I don't recognize that name."

Braun nodded. "We found a letter from a Governor Randal that informed Pemo that his wife son had been slain by a band of Tarthun raiders while Master Pemo was in service at the border."

"Governor Randal," Orres said under his breath as a wave of recognition washed over him. "I know that story. About thirty years ago Governor Randal was killed by a wizard that served in his court. Governor Randal had the duty of overseeing part of the border to the east and protecting the kingdom from Tarthun invaders."

"Exactly," Wendal said. "Except he failed because he spent more time trying to romance his wizard's wife while he sent the wizard on dangerous assignments."

Erik nodded. "We think the warlock who impersonates Senator Bracken, is this rogue wizard. We found numerous books on necromancy in the warlock's library as well."

"So he want to bring his family back from the dead," Orres said.

"That's what we think," Erik confirmed.

Wendal nodded and put a finger to his chin. "That would explain why he was working with necromancy."

"We don't know if he is Master Pemo," Orres said. "A letter and a few books found in a man's home doesn't tell us everything."

"True," Erik said. "It would have been better if we had found his journal, then we could have learned all of his secrets." He looked hard at Orres.

The big man returned the stare for several moments, as if the two were locked in a silent argument which could only be lost by blinking or turning away. Erik forgot all others in the foyer then, as he recalled how the journal detailed Orres underhanded dealings to win Lady Dimwater away from Lepkin.

"Well," Orres said after a minute. "I suppose it matters little now. He is likely not far behind. If he is working with necromancy, then the only way to win the battle will be to get to him and kill him."

Erik shook his head and turned away. "I did find your journal, Master Orres." Erik blurted over his shoulder. "When this is over, we have something else to settle," he said as he walked away.

"She never loved me," Orres called out.

Erik froze in his steps, but kept his back to Orres. "Then why interfere?" he asked.

"Because I never loved anyone else," Orres replied. "I only ever had eyes for her."

Erik turned around and walked back to the group. "You say this now?" Erik chided.

Orres slid his arm off of Wendal and struggled to stand on his own. The grimace on his face showed that he was hardly fit to be moving, let alone fighting. "I never claimed to be a perfect man," he said. His shoulders slumped, and there seemed to be very little of Master Orres left in this hulking body before Erik. The fire was gone from his eyes, and the strength that had always been evident in his booming voice, had been stripped from him.

Erik thought back to Lepkin's lessons. What good would it do to rebuke Orres here, now? Why break the man down? It wasn't even *Erik* that Orres had wronged, so why was Erik making it so personal? He sighed and hung his head low for a moment. He had to think beyond himself. He looked back up to Orres and offered a smile. "Let us focus on the task at hand," Erik said. "Let us fight side by side when the enemy comes."

"Can you so easily forget?" Orres asked.

Erik folded his arms. "Relinquish your claim," Erik said. "You and I both know it is not just. Let it go and I will not only forget, but I will forgive as well."

Orres' mouth turned up into a half smile and he nodded. "I am not likely going to live through the battle," he said. "But, whether I live or die, I hereby swear that I have no claim to Lady Dimwater's hand, and I release her to marry whomever she chooses." He turned to Wendal. "You are my witness." He turned to Lady Arkyn and said, "Lady Arkyn, you are also a witness. Whatever becomes of me, Lady Dimwater is released from our engagement."

Braun stood uncomfortably silent and shifted his weight. Wendal and Arkyn both nodded and looked to Erik. Orres stretched his hand out to seal the promise.

"Braun, you are also a witness to this," Erik said. "Let all here today say that Orres and Lepkin are brothers, inseparable from this point on." Erik reached out and took Master Orres' hand and gave it two hearty shakes before pulling his hand back. He was proud to have finally ended the feud, and yet he felt a twinge of guilt. He knew that the real Lepkin had no idea what had happened. In fact, the last time Erik had spoken with Lepkin, he had sworn to challenge Orres.

"We should get back to preparing the field," Braun said. "We are wasting time."

Erik nodded. "Go and get yourselves fed. Where are the others?"

"They are waiting in the forest to the southeast," Lady Arkyn said. "We three came alone to test your hospitality before we brought everyone else."

"How many more are there?" Braun asked.

"Seventeen," Wendal said. "Including us, that is."

"That is not a lot," Braun replied. "Go, get some food and we will go and get the others out from the forest."

"It will be good to fight alongside you once again," Orres said to Erik. "Let's hope you have a few more tricks in that sly head of yours." Then Orres reached up to steady himself by grabbing onto Wendal's shoulder and they slowly made their way to the dining hall. Lady Arkyn walked behind them.

Erik watched the trio go for a moment and sighed. "We should go out and check on the men," Erik after a moment.

"Then we can get the others that came with Orres. Any extra pair of hands would help tremendously," Braun noted.

Erik nodded. He turned and looked up the stairs. "Can I count on you to make her leave?"

"Lady Lokton is not easily dissuaded once she has made up her mind," Braun said sourly. "I don't know if I can make her leave or not. As it is, no one else has actually prepared to leave either."

"What do you mean?" Erik said hotly. "I told you that they needed to leave. Everyone who is not going to fight should be gone." Erik sighed and pulled the front door open. "Why didn't you listen to me?" Erik yelled as he stepped out into the late morning sun.

Braun was only half a step behind him. "I told them to be ready," Braun shouted back at Erik.

"Then why are there no wagons?" Erik yelled. He pointed to the space in front of the manor where he had instructed Braun to assemble the wagons. Nothing was there. He turned back and sent a cold glare toward Braun, but he was unable to say anything else.

"Braun!" one of the men shouted from the trenches nearby "In the field!"

Erik and Braun ran out toward the field and stopped abruptly when they saw it.

"By the gods!" Braun said. "That is him!" he said. "That's Senator Bracken!"

Erik noted the banners high on poles, carried by a sizeable troop of mounted warriors. On their flanks were ranks of footmen. "And he has an army with him," Erik said. "Tell the men that he is not a senator. He is a warlock."

"His army rides under the king's banner," Braun said.

"They are not the king's men," Erik said. "Come, we must sound the alarm."

"We aren't ready," Braun said.

"Move!" Erik shouted as he slapped Braun's arm. "Get the catapults out now!" Erik took off running back to the manor. "I'll have Lady Arkyn get the others they brought."

Braun broke into a dead sprint for the blacksmith shop. He shouted up to the rooftop, "Archers prepare for battle!" He looked back over his shoulder at the men in the trenches. "Shovels down men! To arms!" The men in the trenches abandoned their tasks and scrambled for their weapons.

CHAPTER TEN

Gondok'hr motioned for his lieutenant to come up to him. The officer galloped up beside and pulled his horse in close. The warlock grinned and pointed to the north side of the manor. "Send the first group of footmen there. The enemy has not yet finished their moat."

The officer nodded and reached for his bugle. He gave a single, long blow and then shouted at the top of his lungs. "First squad, advance!" The lieutenant then broke off and galloped out to the first squad of footmen.

Gondok'hr didn't halt the rest of his army, he kept them moving along with him at a slower pace to allow his footmen to advance ahead of the group. He still had much of the field to cross, but he had already seen Braun and Erik run away as they had in his vision. A feeling of triumph washed over him. "I will have your head, boy," he promised. "Then I shall trade it for what I seek."

The footmen sprinted out ahead of the main army, their armor clanking and causing a horrible ruckus. As they pulled about sixty yards ahead of the main army their captain halted them.

"Archers!" someone shouted.

Gondok'hr held up his hand and halted the army.

Several men fired bows from the roof of the manor. The arrows rained down onto the footmen's shields. A couple men were caught by arrows that found gaps, but most of the men survived. The captain gave the order and they began running forward again, only to stop and take cover under a second barrage of arrows. This time, however, the arrows were aflame and they were aimed behind the footmen. Each arrow struck near a pile of hay and instantly burst into a roaring fire. Smoke billowed up from the field, reaching for the heavens above the manor.

The warlock sniggered. "Clever boy," he said. Then his ears picked up the sound of squeaking wheels coming around the manor. He guessed at what the sound heralded long before he saw the catapults launch their black projectiles through the air. His stoic grin was wiped from his face when he noted that each projectile was dripping with dark liquid.

"Back!" Gondok'hr shouted. "Everyone back!" It was too late. The missiles slammed into the ground as if the god of thunder were attacking. Hulking, boulder-like globs of rock and oil pulverized several groups of warriors unfortunate enough to not get out of the way in time. Oil and tar splattered out onto anything near enough to get caught. Next came more fire arrows, and the catapults threw clay pots of flaming oil out.

The smoke from the burning hay was too thick to see the group of footmen anymore. It also veiled the battlefield as though a curtain of fathomless night had descended between him and the manor. What's worse, it covered the sky so much that he could not see when the catapults fired next. Sizzling clay balls rained down around him, erupting in fire as they broke on the ground. Horses and men shrieked in horror as flames lashed out and engulfed many of them.

Gondok'hr looked to the sky just in time to see a clay ball descending out of the smoke. Its trajectory would have plopped it directly in his lap, but he cast a spell with a wave of his hand. A blue, bubble-like shield encircled him and a few warriors lucky enough to be within ten feet of where he sat atop his horse. The clay ball shattered against the shield and flames washed over it as the oil inside ignited and slid across the surface of the magical ward.

"Back!" Gondok'hr shouted again. A bugle blew three times and the army quickly moved into a retreat. He didn't halt his army until they all stood at the far edge of the field, just out of range of the catapults, and far from the archers' reach.

The warlock's lieutenant rode up next to him and saluted. Gondok'hr noted that the lieutenant's armor was scorched on the left side. The man's left hand was charred, but the officer didn't make any mention of it. Then again, none of the warriors raised by Gilifan's magic ever complained. That was one of their better traits.

"Take fifty men and go around to the south, through the woods," Gondok'hr commanded.

The lieutenant nodded and galloped away, shouting orders to a group of footmen nearby. They broke into a run after him, making for the southern edge of the field.

Gondok'hr looked to the thick blanket of smoke and smiled. He could clear it, if he wanted to, but he had an idea of how to use it to his advantage. The smoke was drifting, covering the field, and slithering through the trees to the south.

*****

Lady Arkyn raced through the trees and bushes. She bent over slightly, keeping her head just below the thick, black smoke as it stretched into the forest. She found the others exactly where she had left them, huddled together in a small clearing edged with a large fallen oak on the north side.

"What is happening?" Master Gorin asked. The large, hulking man had his steel warhammer slung over his left shoulder.

Lady Arkyn noted the look on his face and nodded to him. "They are here," she said. "Master Lepkin is inside with Wendal and Orres. All of House Lokton has been called to arms, but I fear we are in for a long, hard fight."

"Well then, let's go and give them a warm welcome," Gorin said as he brought his hammer down to rest in his other hand.

Lady Arkyn held up a hand. "We have wounded," she reminded him.

"Then send them to the house for respite, Gorin and I can move to the defenses," Master Peren said.

"The enemy is sending men this way," Lady Arkyn said quickly. "I need both of you to escort the wounded to the house."

"Better we should stay with you and cover our friends," Gorin said. "How many are coming?"

Arkyn shook her head. "Two score, perhaps a few more, it was hard to count through the smoke. I only caught a couple of glimpses on my way out to you."

"I can handle that," Gorin said. "I already proved as much back at Kuldiga Academy.

"Let's not waste time arguing," Arkyn said finally. "Let's move." She pointed to a couple fellow archers. "You see to it that everyone gets to the manor. Orres and Lepkin are expecting you. Peren, Gorin, and I will delay the enemy."

The archers nodded and started moving quickly. Lady Arkyn took a mental note. Not counting Orres, herself, Wendal, Peren, and Gorin, there were twelve masters, most of whom were in decent enough shape, but some could use fresh bandages at the very least. Any time they could rest while House Lokton fought would be a welcome respite as well.

"Leave the horses with us," Peren said. He smiled at Arkyn. "It will help even the odds a bit. She regarded him curiously but nodded her consent. Peren walked to the horses and grabbed their reins. "This is going to be fun," he promised them.

The three went toward the enemy, keeping their pace slow enough to stay just inside the thickening smoke where they could remain hidden. They could hear the clanking armor coming closer. Sticks snapped under foot and men shouted at each other as they made their way.

Lady Arkyn gave a soft whistle to Gorin and gestured that she was going to kneel in a copse of young saplings. She pulled several arrows from her quiver and stuck them in the ground in front of her. Gorin nodded and walked out several yards to the left, hiding next to a large, leaning oak. He pulled his knife loose and twirled his hammer in front of him before jerking his head to the side and cracking his neck.

Peren walked ahead, to the edge of the smoke. Arkyn could see all but the back of his head as the smoke there was beginning to descend lower under the push of a breeze. The horses stood, flanking him. One of them nickered and pawed at the ground with its hoof. The other snorted and struggled to keep its nose below the smoke. Peren released the reins and started weaving his hands in front of him.

The clanking armor came closer. The steady, heavy footsteps were almost in synch with each other, as though they marched to drums. Lady Arkyn squinted and looked under the curtain of smoke, just making out the first glints of armor through the forest. Someone in the oncoming group let out a shout and then the footsteps broke rhythm. She could tell that each soldier was running forward separately. They had seen Peren.

She set an arrow to the string and went to pull back but she stopped as a column of orange and red fire encircled Peren, ripping through the smoke. Lady Arkyn raised a hand to shield her eyes from the intense light. Even with her keen sight, she could not see beyond to the enemy, but their frantic cries told her that something awful had stopped them in their tracks. The light and fire disappeared and there, where Peren and the horses had stood, were a pair of beasts the like of which she had never seen before.

Each monster stood upon hind legs as thick as tree trunks, with sharp talons stretching out from their scaled feet. Long, barbed tails swished back and forth behind them and their arms were tipped with sharp, curved claws instead of hands. The enemy stood before them, petrified and unmoving. The beasts emitted low growls from behind their massive, fur covered heads.

"This should be good," Peren whispered as he appeared next to Lady Arkyn.

"What did you do?" she asked. He winked and pointed back to the beasts. She turned back to see a man on horseback charging forward with his sword drawn.

The beast on the left moved impossibly fast. Despite its massive size it weaved in between the trees and lashed out with its right claw, severing the horseman in half. Then it brought its left claw down from above, drilling the horse through its neck and pinning it to the ground. The beast on the right launched forward, jumping over the first two lines of warriors and crushing several men under its talons. The enemy erupted into action. They descended upon the beast, swinging and hacking at it with swords and axes. The beast lashed out with its claws, sending men flying into nearby trees with such force that they broke through the lower branches and then bounced off the ground.

Lady Arkyn sucked in a breath and averted her eyes. "What are those things?" she asked. Peren didn't answer her, he was busy weaving his fingers in the air and muttering arcane words that she did not recognize. She looked back to the enemy and watched as the two beasts tore through their ranks. It seemed that they were unstoppable. Within a mere couple of moments the entire group of warriors lay broken on the ground and the beasts snorted and howled their triumph.

"We should be good to go now," Peren said. "I will send them to greet our enemy."

Lady Arkyn nodded and whistled for Gorin. The large man nodded and cast one more glance at the beasts before joining them.

"Remind me to pay you the four copper pieces I owe you," Gorin told Peren. "Don't want you to send those things to collect the debt."

Peren snorted. "Four copper pieces wouldn't cover the

trouble," Peren said.

"Why didn't you do that at the academy?" Lady Arkyn asked.

Peren shrugged. "I have to be standing with the animal I am going to change," he said. "At the academy I was inside with no animals nearby."

"Couldn't you turn the enemy soldiers?" she asked.

Peren shook his head. "No, I can only change animals. Besides that, I have to be able to get the animal to assent to my spell for it to work. It may have looked easy, but that is the biggest change I have ever been able to create successfully."

"What happens if you don't succeed?" Gorin asked as they started back for the manor.

"You don't want to know," Peren said honestly.

*****

Gondok'hr turned his horse to the side and trotted out to the southern side of the field. The screams and shouts that erupted from the trees let him know that something had caught his men, and they had met a horrible fate. He halted his horse and waited. As the shouting and screaming died down, a pair of sharp howls assaulted his ears. The hairs on the back of his neck stood on end. Whatever it was, it was big.

Suddenly the smoke parted and warped away from a pair of hideous beasts. They had long snouts filled with fangs and their arms ended in sharp, bloody hooks. They ran forward at the speed of the fastest horses. A lesser man would have soiled himself and cowered in fear. Gondok'hr sniggered and cast a hand before him, muttering an ancient incantation. A ball of blue fire appeared before him and he sent it flying for the pair of beasts. As it tore through the air, sizzling and dripping blue liquid fire, it doubled, then tripled in size until it slammed into the first beast and laid it low on the ground in an instant. The second beast jumped to the side, avoiding the blue death and then resumed its charge.

Gondok'hr smiled and pointed at the beast with his left hand. "Kazhur, mo himbei," he said. A bolt of green energy streaked from his hand and stung the beast in the left eye. The beast twirled around and slammed to the ground, twitching and howling terribly.

"Archers," Gondok'hr called out. "Finish them off," he said.

A rank of twenty archers ran to him and aimed their bows at the beasts. They let their arrows fly just as the second beast started to rise to its feet again. The warlock waved his hand again and each of the arrows glowed white with fire and magically turned in the air to descend on the second beast, raining a searing hot death down upon its head. The beast groaned and fell back to the dirt, never again to rise.

Gondok'hr turned to the smoke and sighed. "Enough games," he said. He stood in the stirrups and waved his hand at the smoke in the field. The thick blanket moved to obey his command, lifting from the forest and the field to descend upon the manor, allowing him to see his way to the house and covering his approach. Next he summoned a raincloud and extinguished the flames in the field. "March forward," he told his men. "Archers remain with me, the rest of you march forth and raze the manor to the ground!" The men instantly obeyed, marching forward in lockstep through the field as the fires sizzled and protested against the rain.

*****

"Curse this smoke!" Braun bellowed as the thick cloud dropped down around the manor. "To arms men, to arms!"

Erik looked around and saw just under three hundred men, all of whom had recently fought alongside his father, in full battle-dress. The men closest to him wore grim, sober expressions and seemed to care little about the smoke.

"Shall we ride out?" one of the men shouted to Braun.

"Wait!" someone called out from around the corner of the house. Erik and Braun turned to see Lady Arkyn running toward them, with a couple of others trailing close behind. One of the men was a mountain of a man, arm's thick and muscled, carrying a great war hammer as he ran. The other was tall, but thin and wiry, with a tuft of scraggly hair jutting out from the bottom of his chin.

"Master Lepkin," the wiry man called out. "We should wait until the enemy gets close."

"But our archers cannot see where to aim," Braun argued. "We should march out from the screen so we can see our foe."

"Please, listen," Lady Arkyn said as they closed in. "Master Peren can weave a spell that will allow us to see out of the smoke.

When the enemy is within range, I will help the archers fire upon the enemy. The rest of the men should wait here until the enemy is upon our moat. Then Master Peren will push the smoke back around the enemy so as to cut them off from their commander's view."

"And then I will gladly charge out with you and bash their skulls together," the large man said.

Braun walked up to the man with the war hammer. "I don't believe we have been introduced, but unless I am mistaken, you are Gorin, son of Duaordin, and hero of Rororke."

Gorin stood tall and nodded. "I would not call myself a hero, but I was there," he said.

"They call him Boneshatter," Master Peren said. The wiry man gestured to Gorin's hammer. "I suppose the reason why is obvious."

Braun nodded. "Go and weave your spell, Master Peren," Braun said. "If you can do as you claim, then it will give us the advantage."

"He can do that, and more, I assure you," Lady Arkyn said.

Master Peren walked forward and worked his finger in the air in front of him, drawing ancient runes that only he could see. Then he muttered something Erik couldn't quite make out, but after Peren's words ended the very air itself seemed to expand near the manor. The smoke was pushed away from the men and formed a thin line around the moat, as if a large opaque bowl had been placed around them by some unseen giant. "Can you see, Lady Arkyn?"

"Perfectly," the half-elf said. "Give me a moment." She ran to the manor and ascended the ladder leading to the roof. Once she was with the other archers she waved down to Peren. "Hold it exactly like this, we can see everything."

"How many come for us?" Braun shouted.

"Maybe five hundred," Lady Arkyn replied. "But we are about to even the odds a little." She walked among the archers and pointed to the field.

Erik could see the archers nodding and moving into position. "Can the enemy see us?" Erik asked.

"No, Master Lepkin," Peren said. "To the enemy the smoke looks as thick as it was before. It is only altered for us."

Erik nodded and waved to the men. "Hold ranks behind the wall. Prepare to jump over it and charge through the gap in the moat only on Braun's command," he said.

Braun leaned in close. "Perhaps you should stay here, next to the manor," he said.

"You would have Lepkin stay off the field of battle?" Peren said shocked. "That would be like not using your queen in chess."

Braun sighed and looked to Erik for support. Erik shrugged. "I will fight with the others," he said. "It will not be the first time I have raised my blade." He patted Braun on the shoulder and walked past him to Gorin. "Stay by Braun," he said.

Gorin looked to Braun and then nodded his head. "As you command, Master Lepkin," Gorin said.

Braun walked back to his waiting horse and jumped up into the saddle. "On my mark," he told the waiting troops. Then he looked back to Master Peren, "I wait for your word, mage."

Peren nodded and kept his eye on the field. "We'll let the archers whittle them down and then just as they start to climb over your wall we'll go."

Erik could see shifting shapes through the smoke. He couldn't see them clearly, but he could hear their march. Their armor and weapons rattled in synch with their steps, as if someone played a great set of drums and was rolling forward. Erik slid Master Lepkin's sword out of the sheath and looked down at the black, Telarian steel. The weapon felt cool to the touch, but he could already feel the fire inside, yearning to be set free again. It matched the angry blaze growing inside Erik's heart.

Bowstrings snapped into place above and a whoosh of arrows tore out through the bowl of smoke. Erik listened to the whistling missiles until the shouts and yells of men assaulted his ears. The drumming marching stopped as men clambered under shields and the arrows rained down upon them. Unable to see the result, Erik strained his ears, tying to discern the effect. Many cried out in pain or short, gurgling yells. Surely some of the arrows had struck their marks. Then followed a sound like pebbles falling upon plates of metal. Erik guessed that many of the opposing army were able to find cover in time.

Someone shouted from beyond the smoke and the marching resumed. This time the cacophonous thunder of steel boots assaulted the ground with a quickened pace. The enemy was running toward them.

Another round of arrows was set free. The running didn't stop this time. Instead, the foe ran quicker. Many were taken down by the arrows, shouting and yelling out as the deadly shafts disrupted their sprint, but many others were still able to effectively cover themselves as arrows *plitted* and *pinged* off their armor and shields.

"They are close to the moat," Peren said.

Braun raised his arm to ready the men. Erik swallowed hard and wrapped his fingers tighter around Master Lepkin's sword.

A third round of arrows flew. This time the whistling lasted only for a brief second or two before the arrows sank into the enemy force. There were only a few shouts this time, most of the arrows bounced off harmlessly.

Master Peren slowly raised his hand, index finger pointing to Braun. He kept his eyes trained forward, on the enemy. Shining breastplates could be seen now beyond the waist-high wall. The first couple of ranks reached the wall and dropped their shields to climb over. "Now!" he shouted.

"HUZZZAAH!" Braun yelled with all of his might. The three hundred men at his back answered in kind and the force tore off at full charge toward the enemy. Erik couldn't see Peren, but he knew the mage had already gone into casting another spell for the bowl of smoke disappeared entirely, only to reform a moment later behind a sea of shimmering armor and grisly faces.

Erik's stomach squirmed as if a nest of baby snakes had suddenly hatched inside. Until now, the reality had not sunk in. Now, faced with an army, he felt small and insignificant. Both armies clashed over the wall and mixed with each other violently. Soldiers rushed around him, eager to get at the front line of the oncoming enemy. Erik stood motionless for what seemed like an eternity. Everything around him moved slower somehow, as if he were no longer in the moment, but watching from afar. It was then, amidst the storm of shouts and the clanking armor that he felt a calm come to him. Something slid against his chest. He reached up and grabbed the leather thong out from under his shirt. He looked down to the jewel and all became clear again. "For you, my father," Erik said as he raised his father's ring to his lips and kissed it. Then he charged forward. The sword in his hands absorbed energy from Erik's rage and a white hot blaze of flame erupted around the blade. He ran forward, his feet carrying him almost effortlessly. The enemy rolled at them like a great wave of the sea, moving together and running directly into the moat and clambering up the other side, picking their way through the large wooden pikes only to be slowed by the waist-high wall.

"Fire the moat!" Braun shouted. A slew of flaming arrows zipped down into the moat from the roof and a great *whoosh* of flames engulfed the enemy. Erik's eyes went wide as a pair of men struggled to get through the pikes. They were wrapped in yellow fire, but on they came. Erik deftly hopped over the wall and rushed to meet them. He raised his sword and ran at them, but a pair of arrows put them down, dropping their bodies back into the fiery moat. Erik looked up and saw Lady Arkyn. She waved to him briefly and then went back to stringing her bow.

Master Gorin and Braun drove into the breach, where the moat had not been finished. The main body of the enemy was funneling into the clear space as well, coughing and gasping for air. Gorin raised his mighty hammer and came down in a sweeping arc that took three men to the ground. As he brought his hammer back above his head a warrior yelled and ran for him. The mountainous Gorin lashed out with a savage left kick, denting the warrior's breastplate and dropping him back to the ground.

Braun was equally as savage. He slashed his sword down through the gap between a man's helmet and hauberk, sliding his blade deep down into the man's body and pulling it back just in time to remove the head of an angry axe-wielder running at his right side. Then the main throng of the enemy slammed in through the breach and Braun's horse was closed in as efficiently as if it had been trapped in a great, writhing vice. Braun leapt from atop his horse and took two enemy warriors down to the ground under him. He quickly ended them with a slice of his blade across their necks and rose to his feet. He looked up to see the blade of an axe streaking for his face.

Gorin let out a mighty roar and his hammer slammed first into the axe, and then into the axeman that had been poised to slay Braun. The man's body flew back, knocking several others into the fiery moat.

"Many thanks," Braun said as he engaged the next nearest foe.

"Try to keep up," Gorin teased as he continued sweeping his way through the enemy, laying several foes low with each swing of his mighty hammer.

Erik joined them then, fighting his way through a group of swordsmen with the help of his other warriors. As the bodies began to fall, Gorin, Braun, and Erik led House Lokton's men through the breach, fighting off all who tried to come through the bottleneck.

As the main body of House Lokton's army pushed forward, Peren ran back to the catapults. He kept close to the manor at first, so as to avoid the throng of eager warriors rushing to the battle. He found a group of six men loading tar and oil into ceramic containers and hailed them. "Do you have any cats?" The men looked to each other and shrugged. A large man stepped forward from the group wearing leather greaves and a breastplate of bronze. His hands were thick and sturdy, covered in soot and dirt.

"What are you about?" the man said with a hand resting on his heavy broadsword.

Peren waved the man off. "I need cats, or maybe small dogs," he said.

The large man raised an eyebrow and stopped Peren from reaching the catapults with a strong palm against the wiry man's chest. "I am Demetrius," he said. "I am in charge of the catapults, so you will either explain yourself or I will throw you to the front lines."

Peren took a step back and looked at Demetrius' thick body and nodded. "I bet you could do it too," he said.

"If I can't, I could set you in the basket," Demetrius said half-jokingly as he pointed to the nearest catapult.

Peren put a hand in the air. "I have an idea, but I need cats."

Demetrius folded his arms, unimpressed.

"I can cast a spell to change a cat into a wyvern. The problem is that cats are stubborn and they only ascent to changing form if they are in great danger."

Demetrius looked back to his men. "Back to work men," he said. He glanced back to Peren. "I am busy, I don't have time to suffer fools."

Peren let out an exasperated sigh and started for the catapult again. Demetrius quickly reached out with a hand and snatched Peren by the collar of his robes. The thin mage weaved his fingers and Demetrius stood motionless, as if turned to stone.

"I have tricks of my own," Peren said. The men each drew their weapons, but Peren cast another spell and held them motionless as well. Then he went to the catapult and checked the levers and triggering mechanisms. He nodded to himself, pleased with what he saw and then ran to the stable, leaving the statue-like men where they stood.

Once he got to the stable he looked in each of the stalls. Near the back of the second stall he found an extremely furry white cat with a gray tail fighting a packrat in the straw on the ground. The packrat was almost as large as the cat, but the cat was obviously toying with its prey, batting it across the side of the head whenever it tried to attack.

"What luck!" Peren exclaimed. He sprang into action and seized the packrat and cat at the same time, pulling them apart before the cat could finish the packrat. The rat shrieked and gnashed its teeth, but Peren held it firmly around the neck, nearly choking it. Its claws tore into his hand, but he paid that no mind. The cat was equally as agitated, growling in a low, menacing rumble, but Peren held onto the scruff of the cat's neck, being careful to point all of its feet as far away from him as possible.

Peren looked to the rat first and whispered an incantation. He couldn't hear the rat's thoughts of course, but he knew the rat was succumbing to his will when the rodent ceased fighting and hung limp in his hand. The cat, on the other hand, wanted nothing of it. Peren swore the cat was angry enough to rip its own hide out from its neck to break free if it could. Its body was rigid and poised, yielding to Peren's grip only inasmuch as it was unable to retaliate. The animal was not willing to subjugate itself to the mage.

He turned and ran back to the catapults, holding his catch out from him as he sprinted. When he got close to the first catapult, he set the rat down into the basket. "This will be a bit jarring," he told the rat. The animal curled into a ball in the bottom of the basket and waited. Peren yanked the lever and the rat flew up into the air, spinning and sprawling around with flailing claws. Peren pointed his left hand at the rodent and muttered, "Wyve'ne lesun'be."

A flash of light erupted from the rat and it sprouted a pair of leathery wings, followed by a wickedly long, barbed tail. Its snout elongated and emitted a high, piercing shriek that was so loud the group of soldiers directly underneath stopped and grabbed their heads for a moment. Then, in an instant the wyvern swooped down and started attacking the enemy.

"Alright, do you believe me now?" Peren asked the still motionless Demetrius. The mage walked over and touched his left index finger to Demetrius' forehead and broke the spell.

"I misjudged you," Demetrius said as he looked out to the wyvern swooping and looping through the air above the enemy ranks. "Still, I will probably knock your teeth out for what you did to me."

Peren smiled. "I knew we'd become good friends." He then motioned to the growling cat in his right hand. "Lend me a hand with this one?"

Demetrius chuckled and nodded. The two went back to the catapult and Demetrius worked the winch to reset the basket. Once it clicked into place, Demetrius nodded and went to the lever. "I assume you want me to fire once you let go?"

Peren nodded. "One instant too late or too soon will result in failure, and I am not going to try to catch this one again."

"Couldn't you freeze him like you did me and my men?"

Peren shook his head. "I'd have to touch him to break the spell. It's easier to drop him into the basket." Demetrius shrugged and nodded that he was ready. Peren held the cat over the basket at arm's length. "One, two…THREE!"

Down the cat went, hissing and growling. Just as its paws made contact with the basket Demetrius pulled the lever and the cat was flung into the air, yowling and flailing about. Peren held out his right hand and muttered, "Wyve'ne lesun'be." Nothing happened.

"It didn't work," Demetrius said.

Peren repeated the phrase, ignoring Demetrius. Still nothing happened. The cat reached the apex of its trajectory and started its descent toward the front line of the enemy. Peren repeated the spell again, and then again.

"Perhaps it thinks it can still land on its feet and get away," Demetrius jabbed.

Peren shouted the spell at the top of his lungs. A crack of

thunder rumbled through the sky and a dark, metallic orb appeared around the sprawling cat. A bolt of blue lightning struck the orb. It exploded, showering sparks and flame on the men below.

"Oh no," Peren said.

"What is it?" Demetrius asked.

"I didn't do this," the mage whispered. "We're in trouble."

A great roar sounded through the sky and where the metallic orb had been was now a firedrake. Black scales reflected the hot flames from the moat as it beat its wings and climbed up above the smoke. It disappeared for a moment and then it streaked down as fast as a lightning bolt, slamming into a group of four soldiers only a dozen yards away from where Peren and Demetrius stood. The ground shook beneath them and they fell to their knees.

"What have you done?!" Demetrius shouted.

"It wasn't me!" Peren protested. "It was someone else!"

"Release my men, now!" Demetrius shouted.

Peren scrambled to his feet and ran for the others. "Where are you going?" he shouted at Demetrius when he saw the man running for a large building.

"I am going to get the wind-lance!" the large man shouted.

"Wind lance?" Peren repeated. Something snarled behind him and his insides froze in terror. Hot, fetid breath seared the skin on the back of his neck and the ground vibrated and trembled nearby. The mage didn't have to turn to see what was behind him.

"Master Peren!"

The mage turned in time to see a pair of arrows *plink* off the firedrake's scales harmlessly. He could see Lady Arkyn firing franticly from the roof, but he knew it was too late.

"I suppose you are a bit upset?" Peren asked the firedrake. The beast opened its fang filled maw. Deep in the back of its throat the mage saw a spark, then a wave of flame washed over him and he was no more.

CHAPTER ELEVEN

Al opened his eyes and sat up, stretching his arms out wide to the side. He heard footsteps coming from the cave nearby. The dwarf shifted to his knees and then pressed himself up, arching his back and sticking his hips out in front of him. His clothes were still wet in places, and they were uncomfortable, but he put that out of his mind for now. He walked forward to the cavern opening and smiled when he saw Brinon and Timmin emerge.

"Thought you might still be sleeping," Timmin said. "We came by earlier, but you were passed out on that rock over there, so we decided to leave you alone for a bit."

"Are the others assembled?" Al asked.

"The others are here," Alferug called out as a handful of dwarves stepped out from the cave. "The entire council is here."

A silver haired dwarf with a long, thick gray beard pushed his way forward. His bushy brows hovered only slightly above his dark brown eyes that rested narrowly on either side of his large nose. "I want to know one thing," he said in a gruff voice. "If you beat your brother, will you reopen the mines?"

Al regarded him curiously. "Are the mines closed, Dvek?" he asked him. "I could not imagine the minister of commerce allowing that to happen."

"I wasn't given a choice," Dvek huffed. "I was simply told that we had all we needed and that since we no longer would deal with outsiders, there was no need to dig anymore."

"You closed off all trade?" Al asked.

Dvek nodded. "We were to rely only upon the king for everything. At first everything went well. There was plenty of gold to go around, but soon we ran out of things to buy. The men lost their will to work hard because everything was given away. Then, when the food shortages started a couple weeks ago I sought to reopen the mines and reestablish trade, but your brother said that until the humans finished their war, we could not afford to trade with them."

"That is nonsense," Al said.

Dvek nodded.

Alferug then placed a hand on Dvek's shoulder and addressed Al. "Will you also see us return to our old ways?"

Al nodded. "I don't know all of the wrongs that have been done," he said. "But, if I am successful in my challenge, then I would see the mines opened. I would allow trade and free commerce again with the outside world, and by the Ancients I will give us back our religion." Al eyed each of the dwarves for a few moments and then sighed. "I know I am not my father, but I will do my best to restore Roegudok Hall to its former glory, and reestablish our traditions from when he sat upon the throne."

"Then I bow to you," Dvek said as he bent down to take a knee before him.

"As do I," Alferug said as he bent down quickly.

Timmin and Brinon knelt as well as all of the others save for one dwarf. He was a large, thick dwarf with a beard of fire, braided into a double plait stretching from his chin to his round belly. A pair of axes hung from a harness on his back and his chest was covered by an old, yet expertly crafted, shirt of mithril mail. He stepped forward, locking his deep blue eyes on Al's, and thunked a meaty index finger into Al's chest.

"And what of the soldiers," he asked. "I have heard rumors of war beyond our mountain. Would you send the sons of Roegudok Hall out to fight and die for the humans?"

Al was silent for a moment. "Faengoril the Bull," Al said with a tone of respect. "I remember you from the days of my father. You have ever been a faithful warrior, and a keen minister. I would value your counsel on all matters to do with battle." Al reached out and offered his hand to Faengoril. "I will not lie or pretend not to have war on my mind."

Faengoril shook his head. "I would not easily agree to order our warriors to fight outside of the mountain."

Al nodded. "I know," he said. "Nor would I ask you to do so, except in great need. This war you have heard of stretches not only across the human realm beyond our mountain. It will come to us."

"Our mountain will protect us," Faengoril said stubbornly. "We have never lost a war at home. Even when the orcs roamed the forests beyond, before the humans and elves came, we drove the beasts back. Time and time again they assaulted, but the dwarves of Roegudok Hall never faltered."

"This war is not a war of races, nor is it a war for land," Al said solemnly. "It is a war for the hearts and minds of every soul in the middle kingdom. Our foe is not flesh and blood, but a perverse magic that would warp us into mindless servants. The Ancients did not put us here to cower in the mountain. They created us from the stone so we could dash our enemies out from our lands, and serve as protectors of the realm. The humans, though different, are still our kin in that we all hail from the same mother. The dirt gives life to them as the mountain grants us breath. To abstain from battle will not save our kinfolk, in fact it will only bring our foe into our homes."

Faengoril arched a brow and took in a deep breath. "A king knows not to waste his countrymen in battle," he said. "However, a true king also knows when to issue the order to march." He pulled a parchment out from his pocket and held it out for Al. "I received another letter from Lokton Manor. Fortunately, I was able to read this as the message came directly to me. I gather there have been other letters, but your brother would not share them with me."

Al took the letter and quickly scanned through its contents. He looked back to Faengoril. "Do I have your support?"

"Who is Erik Lokton?" Faengoril asked.

"He is the Champion of Truth, and the only one who can ultimately stop the impending doom," Al replied.

"Are you sure?" Faengoril asked.

"I have seen him wield the white flame, and he has taken the form of a dragon before my very eyes," Al replied evenly. "He is green yet, but I believe he is the one."

Faengoril fell to a knee. "My king, I live to serve you. May your days be long and bright in the golden hall under the mountain."

The others repeated, "May your days be long and bright in Roegudok Hall!"

Al reached down and took Faengoril by the forearm. "Let us go and see my brother."

"First, we thought you might like some dry clothes," Timmin said quickly as he jumped up and slung a backpack around to drop it at Al's feet. "Some of our pa's old clothes, but we think they'll fit you."

Al nodded. "Thank you." The others all went to the cave and

waited while Al changed into a dry set of clothes. The musty, earthen smell was pleasant to him as he slipped the hooded shirt on. It brought back memories of running into the deeper tunnels as a young dwarf. An old monogram on the loose sleeve had the initials 'A' and 'S' sewn above the wrist. Al smiled. He remembered then that he had been named after his uncle. A warm feeling came over him, like he had finally returned to his home, where he had always belonged. He had no idea how much he had missed his birthplace, until this moment as he looked at the letters on his sleeve.

"Time to set things right," Al said. He slid his hammer into the belt and walked into the cave. The councilors all swarmed around him as Timmin and Brinon led the group through the tunnels. Al slipped the hood up and over his head as they walked through the main areas.

The once bustling market area was now a shell of its former self. A couple of wooden tables displayed some older trinkets, but it was nothing like what he remembered from before he left. In place of heaping fruits and roasting meat he saw only small wagons with shriveled blood-roots and potatoes.

"Where is all the food?" he said.

"I told you," Dvek replied. "We started having shortages a couple of weeks ago."

"Things were better even when the Keeper came to call on your brother," Alferug said. "But after he left, your brother severed all ties with the outside world. Since then we have been trying to live off of our own stores. Only a handful of guards are allowed to go out for game, and no one is farming on the mountainside anymore."

"This is not right," Al said.

Al looked up at the vaulted ceilings which almost disappeared well over two hundred feet above his head. The plated gold and platinum that reflected the light of the torches and oil lamps which hung over them all was a testament of the dwarves' ingenuity and wealth. Each supporting column had been hewn from a unique, pink granite quarry deep in the mountain and was smoothed to perfection. Even the simpler stone buildings set against the wall of the western side of the great hall bore engravings that displayed expert craftsmanship.

As he walked through the marketplace, which had once been the most renowned market in all of the Middle Kingdom, his heart sank at the sight of so many vacant shops. Instead of hammers ringing on workbenches amidst the roar of kilns and open forges, the hall was quiet. Long, tired faces looked at him from behind barren tables and empty market stalls.

After crossing the market the group wound its way up a spiraling staircase cut right into the stone of the eastern wall. The way was long, and would be tiring to all but the dwarf folk, who were built for climbing up and down long tunnels in the mountain. The staircase was twenty feet wide, adorned with stone engravings and murals along either wall. Some depicted historical events, battles, coronations, deaths and births of kings. Others were simply ornamental designs created by the greatest of dwarven masters. The stairs themselves were hewn right out of the black mountain stone, polished to a high sheen and inlaid with gold that crisscrossed diagonally and glittered under foot as the great chandeliers above burned bright and cast their light down.

Thirty minutes passed before Al and the council reached the top landing in front of the throne room. The landing itself was forty feet long and flanked with sets of armor on display atop pedestals of solid gold. Each pedestal had the name of a great hero carved into it. One of those heroes was Misgerahh'tanah Sit'marihu, Al's grandfather. Al went to the set of armor and gently brushed the left pauldron.

"I wish you were still here with us," Al said.

Alferug moved to stand next to Al and put a hand on his shoulder. "Come, we should go inside."

Al turned and looked to the two guards standing in front of the golden double doors that separated the stairs from the throne room. Diamonds, emeralds, and sapphires sparkled and shimmered as Al approached.

"Open the doors," Alferug commanded the guards.

"You can't be here," one of the guards hissed. "You have been banished!"

Faengoril stepped forward. "Open the doors," he bellowed. The two guards blanched and snapped into action and pulled one of the great, heavy doors open.

Al could hear laughter and clanking dishes coming from the

throne room. "Sounds like we are about to interrupt a party," he said.

The group entered the throne room and stopped briefly just inside. Al spied his brother sitting lazily in the throne with one leg over the side and his head back over the other side as a female dwarf dropped a bite of meat into his mouth. None of them seemed to notice that they were no longer alone until one of the guards near the throne went up behind Threnton and whispered into his ear. Threnton rose to stand in front of his throne and planted his hands on the large table in front of him.

"What is the meaning of this?" he bellowed.

Al stepped forward and threw his hood back. "Brother!" his voice boomed, echoing off the shiny marble walls.

Threnton blanched and fell back into the throne, but he said nothing. The woman at his side shakily set the platter of meat back on the table and moved to stand behind the throne.

"I see you have plenty of food on your table," Al noted. He walked over to the platters of fruits and nuts and put a hand on the table. "You call yourself king, yet you would let your brother die in a pit while you allow our kinfolk to starve in their own homes. All the while you sit up here, fat and happy." Al took a walnut, still in the shell, and threw it at Threnton.

Threnton deftly caught the nut, crushed it in his hand, and let the small pieces fall to the ground. "I am king," he said. "Seize him, and any who are with him!" Threnton commanded.

The guards moved forward but Al held up a hand. "I am invoking my right to challenge you for the throne," Al said. "I do so in the presence of the entire council. To deny my challenge is to break the one law that even the king is bound by." The guards froze in place and looked to Faengoril, who was now holding his axes and staring directly at them.

"Very well," Threnton said. "You may have the scale. That is all you wanted anyway. Take it and be gone." Threnton went to undo his belt, as the scale was his belt buckle.

"No," Al said. "It is too late for that."

"Take the scale and be gone, you never wanted the throne anyway," Threnton hissed. He pulled his belt free and tossed it onto the table in front of Al. "Take it and go!"

Al stood firm. "No more will I trade what is right for that

which is convenient. Your reign ends today, and I shall shake your dark cloud from our father's throne."

Threnton stepped forward and shrugged off the red velvet cloak, revealing round, solid shoulders and thick arms. "You will not find me so easy to dismiss," Threnton promised. He held a hand out to a guard. "Give me your axe," he commanded. The guard quickly gave Threnton his axe and backed away.

The council members fanned out around Al, forming a semi-circle near the entrance. Al took his hammer in hand and walked forward. "Nor will I find you so difficult," Al replied grimly.

Threnton scoffed and shrugged his shoulders. He glanced to the councilors then and threatened, "You will have your reward as soon as I deal with my squabbling brother!" Threnton flipped the table over, flinging the platters and bowls of food through the air and forcing Al to back away quickly or be squished under the table.

The king then lunged forward over the table, sprinting on his short, stout legs toward Al. Al deftly somersaulted to the left, just under Threnton's swing. As Al came up he lashed out behind him at the back of Threnton's right leg, but Threnton was quick to jump out of reach.

Al jumped up to his feet and turned to face his brother. Threnton started slowly circling to the left. Al reciprocated for a moment, while letting his brother size him up. Then he suddenly stopped and lurched forward with his hammer. Threnton, caught off guard by the sudden move, back pedaled and threw his axe up to deflect the blow. The hammer connected with the side of the axe blade and a mighty ring echoed through the throne room. Threnton answered the assault by coming in low and straight with the spike atop the axe like a spear thrust. Al turned to the side and sucked his stomach in while pushing out with his left palm, moving the spike far from harm. His right arm swung out fast and hard. The hammer connected with Threnton's chest and threw the dwarf king back several feet, but he managed to keep his footing.

Threnton reached up and rubbed his chest while glaring at Al. "You'll have to do better than that," he said. "It appears life outside the mountain has made you weak." The dwarf king jumped forward, feinting a swing of the axe just until Al raised his hammer to block, and then he lashed out with a savage front kick, driving the heel of his boot into Al's ribs.

Al flew back and landed on his side several yards away. Hearing his brother's footsteps he rolled away after he hit the ground, just narrowly missing his brother's axe as it came down to bite the stone floor, spewing chips and shards of rock all about. Al pushed up to his knees and managed to block his brother's next swing with the top of his hammer catching the axe's shaft, just a few inches above Threnton's fingers. Al then slid his hammer down, aiming for his brother's hands, but Threnton pulled away in time, laughing as he took an extra pair of steps back.

"Get up, Al," Threnton said. "It is too late to grovel on your knees for forgiveness."

Al rose to his feet and smirked. He cocked his head to the side a bit and studied his brother. Then he loosed his hammer with a furious throw. It spun end over end blindingly fast. Threnton just barely managed to raise his axe to block, but it did little good. The hammer splintered the axe-shaft and slammed into Threnton's chest. This time the dwarf king flipped over backward to land face down on the stone floor at the base of the throne.

"I would rather fight from my knees than live on my belly," Al chided.

Threnton growled and pushed himself up. The two locked eyes and each let out a feral yell as they charged toward each other. Their bodies slammed together with such force that each of the onlookers gasped. The two brothers pulled and yanked, each trying to topple the other to the ground first. Al sent a slurry of right punches to Threnton's left ribs while the dwarf king retaliated by slamming his forehead down into Al's nose. Al's head whipped back and a splatter of blood hit the stone floor. His eyes watered, but he didn't let it slow him down. He sent a strong uppercut into Threnton's jaw, stealing the dwarf king's smile and shattering his four front teeth on impact.

The dwarf king came back with a right hook, but Al shot his left forearm up and blocked the punch while he came down with his right hand in a back-fisted strike that connected with Threnton's bottom lip, tearing it and Al's knuckles on the jagged stumps of Threnton's broken teeth.

Threnton staggered back, but he regained his composure quicker than Al had anticipated. He rushed forward, bending low and grabbing Al around the waist. Threnton lifted up while driving his feet forward, ripping Al from the ground and slamming him into the far wall. Al absorbed the hit and steadied himself by grabbing Threnton's hair with his left hand. He jerked his brother's head back and slammed his right fist down several times. Almost in rhythm with the punches, Threnton would arch back and slam Al into the wall again and again.

Al poured his entire strength into one last punch. A gash opened under Threnton's left eye. The dwarf king hollered out and wound back to slam Al into the wall again. This time Al twisted and kicked his legs up to catch the wall as Threnton tried to slam him. As his feet pressed against the wall Al let his brother expend his energy and then he thrust forward with his legs, using the wall for leverage. Threnton toppled over backward and lost his grip on Al. Al tucked and rolled away, going for his hammer while his brother was dazed. He grabbed his weapon, turned and let fly his mighty hammer.

Threnton smiled and a great flash of white light erupted around him. The hammer blasted into the light and a deafening thunder ripped through the hall. The white light expanded quickly, sending a shockwave through the room and knocking everyone to the ground.

The dwarf king rose to his feet, holding Al's hammer in his hand. Blood slid down his left cheek and dripped out of his mouth. "I told you I would not be easy to put down," Threnton growled. He wiped his bloody mouth, smearing the red liquid into his now gray beard.

Al eyed his brother. "Aye, but now you are without any more magic tricks. That spell can only be used once." He stood up and pointed to his brother's beard. "I like what you have done with your beard. Gray becomes you."

"You have the same gray in your hair and beard," Threnton said. "I am still younger than you."

"But not wiser," Al said as he walked forward.

Threnton raised Al's hammer and lunged forward with a yell. The hammer came down in a great chop, but Al reached up and caught Threnton's wrist with his left hand. He squeezed his brother's wrist and twisted it. Threnton fell to his knees, gasping for air. Al ripped his hammer out of Threnton's hand with his right hand and then held it over his head while still keeping his grip on the dwarf king's wrist.

"The Stone Shell is not something that you can use in the middle of a fight," Al said. "It leaves you weak, and vulnerable." Threnton growled and struck out with a weak punch that barely made Al flinch as he absorbed the hit in his thigh. "Yield the throne," Al said.

"Never," Threnton growled. "It's mine."

Al took in a breath and shook his head. "Yield the throne, and I will let you live."

"You would banish me," Threnton said.

Al nodded. "I would," he affirmed. "But, I would let you live. Perhaps some future day you will rediscover your honor."

"May Khefir take you," Threnton spat. "As long as there is breath in my body, I will not yield the throne. It is mine!"

Al raised his hammer high above his head. "The wrongs you have done cannot go unanswered," he said solemnly. Threnton looked up to the hammer briefly and then turned his eyes back to Al's.

"Go on," he said. "You know what I would do if the situation were reversed."

Al nodded. Quick as lightning he released his brother's wrist and came down hard with a left hook to Threnton's temple. The dwarf king's head snapped out to the right and Threnton toppled over and landed face-first on the stone.

"I am not you," Al said. He looked up to the guards and then turned back to the council members. "The king has lost the challenge," Al declared.

Alferug stepped forward. "The rightful king has won," he said. The council members each bowed low. Al turned and saw the female drop to her knees as well. Then he looked to the guards. They also went to bow but Al motioned for them to come closer.

"I recognize you," Al said.

The guards glanced to each other nervously.

"You were the pair of guards standing outside the hall when I first came."

The guards quickly dropped to their knees. "Mercy, good king, we beg for mercy!" they cried in unison.

Al bridged the gap between him and them in two steps and then held his boot up to the first guard's face. "I told you that when I was king you would lick the bottom of my boot. I aim to keep *all* of my promises." The guard tentatively leaned forward and stuck his tongue out. His face turned sour and he quickly pulled away after licking the boot. "The two of you will now report to Faengoril for reassignment," Al said.

The guards rose and went to Faengoril, who promptly sent them away with orders to hunt in the forest until they had enough meat to fill a wagon. Then Al went to the overturned table, picked it up with one hand and reached underneath to retrieve the belt with the scale. He turned the scale over in his hand. The golden, concave scale was hard as stone, and brighter than gold.

"I must go," Al said.

"You are needed here, sire," Alferug said. "There is much that needs to be done.

Al turned a quizzical look at Alferug. "I must save Erik," he said bluntly. "It is the only way to save us all."

"But you don't have to leave to save Erik," Faengoril said. "You are king now, and our kinfolk need your guidance now more than ever. I will take the army out to House Lokton. I would personally ensure that Erik lives."

"And I can take the scale," Alferug said. "I know the ways of the Ancients as well as you, my king."

Al nodded. "You know them much better than I," Al commented. He held out the belt and Alferug came forward to take it. "There is something you should know, if you are going to take this."

Alferug arched his right brow and looked into Al's eyes quizzically. "What is it?"

"Erik, the Champion of Truth, is stuck inside Lepkin's body, and Lepkin is stuck inside Erik's body. So, although it is Erik who is in peril at Lokton Manor, you will see Lepkin's body. Lepkin is currently unconscious and lying inside Erik's body at Valtuu Temple."

"By the Ancients," Alferug muttered. "How in Hammenfein did that happen?"

Al sighed. "Marlin could likely explain it better than I. The important thing though, is that Erik and Lepkin must be changed back to their natural bodies. This scale is the only artifact I know of that is capable of performing such magic."

"I will get him to the temple alive," Faengoril swore.

"And I will see order restored to your friends," Alferug promised. "You should remain here and set things right for our kin."

Al nodded. "When order is restored, I will come to the temple," he promised.

Alferug smiled. "I expected nothing less. Reopen the mines, acquire food, and send word to King Mathias that a new day is dawning over Roegudok Hall. I suspect King Mathias may have a request of you before you may join us at the temple, but I will expect to see you soon."

"As soon as I can," Al said. He turned to Faengoril. "Take the cavedogs with you," he said.

"What of our infantry?" Faengoril asked.

Al shook his head. "They would slow your pace. I want our forces to be there as swiftly as possible. Take every cavedog we have and make your journey in haste." Al then turned to Alferug. "Also, I want you to take the sacred banner."

"My king?" Alferug asked.

"Erik will need it," he explained.

"But I thought you said he had already made the transformation?" Alferug asked.

Al nodded. "He did, but I don't think he will be able to do it again without help."

Alferug nodded. "As you command. I will carry it personally."

Al nodded with a grateful smile and then turned back to Faengoril. "King Mathias may likely ask tribute of our infantry forces, so I will march to Drakei Glazei with a company after I have resolved the issues here."

"What of him?" Faengoril asked as he pointed toward Threnton.

Al looked down upon his unconscious brother. A small pool of blood had gathered around his smooshed face. "The Stone Shell is extremely draining. He will sleep for at least a couple of days. I will have him taken to the mountains and released. Let him live out his days as he chooses, away from Roegudok Hall and never to return."

Faengoril nodded once.

Brinon and Timmin stepped forward. "We can take him,"

they said.

"Take a bag of food for him," Al said. "Give him a knife, but nothing else. Take him into the mountains and then leave him before he wakes. Just make sure he is left in a safe place, so no beast or vagabond can get to him."

"As you command," Timmin said.

"Farewell, Threnton," Al said as he turned back to his brother. "I wish you a long life, but so help me, I do hope we shall never meet again."

CHAPTER TWELVE

"What in the four hells is that?" Braun shouted above the din of battle. Men pressed past him and clashing weapons and shields sounded all around.

Gorin dropped two more enemies with one swing of his hammer and then turned around, briefly standing on his toes to look over the men. "It's a firedrake," he said. "Come!" The gargantuan man tucked his hammer behind him and ran through the men, roughly shoving them aside and clearing a path. "Lepkin, you are needed at the rear!" Gorin shouted.

Braun picked and weaved his way through the throng, grabbing Erik by the shoulder. "We need you in the back," he shouted.

Erik turned and his eyes went wide.

"Is that the one you saw?" Braun asked as he pulled him along after Gorin.

"No," Erik said. "This is much smaller, like a cat compared to a horse."

Braun shrugged. "Either way, we need that sword of yours!" They ran hard and fast. The closer they got to the rear the more shouting they could hear. The men's faces turned from aggressive determination to fright. A beast like this had never been faced before on Lokton lands.

A pair of bodies flew up into the sky, one aflame and flailing about in agony. The firedrake spun and lashed out with its forked tail, skewering another soldier through the chest and flinging his body aside. Soldiers ran away, clearing a wide swath around the beast. Its shiny scales dripped with blood. Plumes of smoke emanated out from its narrow nostrils above a snout filled with fangs as large as knives. The beast emitted a low growl and coiled its tail around its rear, not unlike a cat as it crouches down before springing upon its prey.

Gorin never stopped. He ran straight at the beast, hefting his hammer high. The firedrake spewed fire out at the mountainous man, but Gorin deftly skipped out to the side, as graceful as a stag might leap over a brook.

"He is agile, I'll give him that," Braun commented.

Erik nodded and looked for an opening. Gorin was going in on the beast's right side, so he motioned for Braun to go in from the left as soon as the firedrake turned its head to snap its jaws at Gorin. The two of them sprinted as fast as their legs could carry them. Erik hoped Gorin could keep the monster's attention. He saw Gorin connect with a blow of his hammer into the beast's side, but it didn't look as though the firedrake was phased any more than if a fly had lighted upon a horse. The firedrake lashed out with his front talons, nearly catching Gorin across the chest, but the warrior was able to backpedal out of the way.

"Look out!" Braun shouted suddenly. Erik heard a *clank* and then watched helplessly as Braun flew backward, flipping end over end through the air to land in the midst of some of his men. Then Erik heard the horrendous hiss from his left. He looked just in time to see a great wall of writhing flames coming for him. Instinctively he held his sword out as if to block. To his surprise, the white flames from the sword grew larger, creating a small shield and splitting the firedrake's fire. The heat licked and singed Erik's shoulders and hair, but the majority of the blast went by harmlessly.

Something smashed into his back and knocked him face first to the ground. A clump of dirt flew up into Erik's eyes and mouth and he gasped for breath. The sword flew out of his grip. Something heavy pinned his neck to the ground. He struggled against it, but there was no force he could muster that would save him. He opened his mouth to shout, but the thing atop him ground his face into the dirt even more so the words were lost. He struggled to find his inner power. Perhaps if he could turn into a dragon, then he could finish the battle.

Nothing happened. There was no transformation. He found no power inside ready to be unleashed. Whatever it was that had allowed him to use Lepkin's dragon form before, he could not unlock it now. He panicked. He thrashed and kicked. He clawed at the solid mass of scale over his neck. He screamed into the dirt. The firedrake drove its tail farther into the dirt, choking the life out of Erik. He could not hear the ferocious fighting around him. He could not see how many troops had rallied to his plight, or if they had all run away. This was the end. He had failed.

*****

Lady Arkyn loosed another arrow at the beast. Again the projectile *plitted* off the scales harmlessly. She ran to the other side of the roof, getting as close to the firedrake as possible. She had only three arrows left, and the other archers were busy holding off the main enemy force.

She strung another arrow and waited for an opening. Gorin danced around the firedrake, swinging his hammer whenever the opportunity arose. Braun was just getting back into the fight after being thrown like a rag doll. She looked to the firedrake's tail. The forked spikes had pinned Lepkin to the ground and the beast was effectively crushing him. She knew he was not long for this world if they could not save him. Braun went to work hacking at the tail, but the scales were impervious to his blade.

The beast roared and hissed, spewing fire out at any before it. Gorin was obviously tiring, he was moving much slower now than at first. Lepkin's thrashing was getting weaker too. She had to do something. Lady Arkyn pulled a second arrow free from her quiver and slid it into her teeth. She had an idea, but speed was of the essence. She aimed carefully for the space just under the firedrake's tail on its rump. She let her arrow fly and moved to string the next arrow before the first found its mark. Her hope was rewarded. The first arrow sunk into a soft spot and the beast twisted its head around with a mighty hiss to see what had struck it.

She sent the second arrow and then she pulled the third and put it to the string and took aim. The second arrow glanced off the narrow ridge above the firedrake's left eye. The beast jerked its head aside and then looked up directly at her. Lady Arkyn let the third arrow loose and uttered a quiet prayer. The arrow sailed fast as lightning and drove home into the beast's eye. The firedrake hissed and bellowed as it stumbled backward. It ripped its tail from the ground and took to the sky in a fit of growling.

"Get up, Lepkin," Lady Arkyn said. He was still. A shadow fell over her as the beast climbed into the air. It looked down to her and its chest glowed from within. The firedrake opened its mouth to reveal a crimson glow in the back of its throat. Lady Arkyn reached back for another arrow, and then realized she had no more.

Just before the beast threw its fire, a great spear-like arrow burst through its neck. The beast gurgled and the fire shot out around the great arrow and harmlessly into the sky above before the firedrake fell to the ground. Lady Arkyn shouted a warning, but Gorin and Braun had already picked Lepkin up and were moving him out of the way. The firedrake crashed mightily, shaking the ground and sputtering gasps of fire and smoke across the dirt. Another great arrow pierced the firedrake in the body and the beast let go of its final breath. A silvery column of smoke rose from its mouth and it laid still.

A large, thickly muscled man stood behind a great contraption. He was loading a third projectile into a socket and working a large windlass to pull the four strings back into place.

"A wind-lance," she said softly. As if on cue, the man working the great weapon looked up to her and gave a salute. She waved back. Then she ran back to the other side of the house where the other archers were working their bows as fast as they could.

Lokton's forces were winning. She could see them driving the enemy farther and farther back from the moat. The heaps of corpses now formed additional obstacles for the enemy to navigate, a task they were willing, but ultimately unable to do without getting bogged down.

Lady Arkyn reached into a comrade's quiver and pulled a handful of arrows out for herself. She quickly set to work, picking off any enemy she could see clearly enough to fire upon without hitting her own forces. Five arrows later there were five additional slain enemies on the field.

She took heart when she saw Gorin, Braun, and even Lepkin back at the front lines. The men below cheered their heroes on and the three of them led a great charge into the enemy's middle. A few moments later the enemy lines broke and she watched as they fled.

The main army did not pursue, but Lepkin, Gorin, and Braun gave chase, cutting down a few more foes before stopping and returning to the safety behind the moat. Lady Arkyn quickly went down the ladder to greet them.

When she got close she saw that all three were smattered with blood, but none appeared to be heavily wounded. Gorin had an open gash across his left shoulder, along with what appeared to be scorch-marks across his armor. Braun was walking stiffly, obviously trying to hide the fact that his back had been hurt in battle, but his face was emotionless as stone. Lepkin was breathing heavily, and walking slower than the others. His neck dripped with blood from one side. He looked at her and noticed her stare.

"The firedrake's tail," he explained. "He had me good."

Gorin elbowed him in the side. "How does it feel for the mighty Lepkin to be saved by a woman?"

"I seem to recall rescuing you a time or two," Lady Arkyn said.

Gorin smiled and folded his arms. "You can't prove that," he said with a wink. Then he patted him on the back. "It's alright," he said. "I won't tell anyone."

"You are an amazing shot," Braun said.

"I owe you my thanks," Erik said. "I…" his words trailed off and he looked beyond her. She turned around and the four of them straightened. "Demetrius," Erik said. "It appears you were able to finish the wind-lance."

Demetrius smiled slightly and nodded. "It isn't exactly as I had hoped, but it works, and that is what matters."

"Where did the beast come from?" Braun asked.

"Your wizard friend made him," Demetrius said.

"Peren?" Gorin asked. "That doesn't make sense. If Peren made the beast, then why would it attack us?"

Demetrius shrugged. "I am a smith. I leave magic to the wizards. All I know is he made a wyvern out of a rat and used my catapult to throw it at the enemy. He then stuck a cat in the catapult and threw it too. There seemed to be a problem with the spell. He said he couldn't change the animal and then it became a firedrake and turned on us."

Lady Arkyn sucked in a breath. "The cat didn't submit," she said with a slight nod. "That could explain it, especially if the warlock on the other side was somehow able to see the animal and use his own spell."

"Nah," Gorin said with a shrug. "Peren had the smoke screen up. The warlock couldn't see." He turned back to Demetrius. "Where is Peren? He'll tell us what happened."

"I'm afraid he won't," Demetrius said. "The beast got him, along with my catapult crews. All that I found was a scorched shoe."

Gorin's smile faded and his shoulders slumped. The big man silently walked away from them. Lady Arkyn watched him go and kept her head bowed for a time.

"Perhaps while Peren was struggling with the spell the warlock could see through the smoke?" Erik put in. The others nodded.

"It's possible," Lady Arkyn said. She looked to the sun, it was starting its decent and dusk was creeping in over the field. "What do we do now?" she asked.

"The fighting has ceased for now," Braun said. "We should get back to our preparations, they will likely attack in the morning."

"Our archers will need more arrows," Lady Arkyn added.

"And we will need to reclaim our dead," Braun said.

"We have more arrows," Demetrius said. "Have the archers come and see me at my forge, our reserves are there." The large blacksmith turned to Braun. "Anyone who needs their armor repaired or replaced, send them to me. I can't promise a miracle, but I will do what I can." He started to turn away and then stopped suddenly and turned back to Erik. "Lepkin, I heard that my master died in an alley, by an assassin's blade." Demetrius' lips tightened as he struggled to choke back his emotion. "If we live through this fight, I want you to tell Erik that I apologize for doubting him. I should never have listened to that fool warlock's prophecy. Erik is a good, strong lad, one of the best House Lokton has ever produced. Would you tell him that for me?"

Erik nodded and watched as Demetrius spun away and made haste for his forge.

Braun patted Erik on the shoulder and sighed as he looked around. "By the ancients, this is a dark day," he said.

CHAPTER THIRTEEN

"I know you are there," Gilifan said confidently. He turned his head and looked to the doorway. "Why do you persist in staying in the shadows? Come and step into the light." Nothing moved. No one answered. Gilifan arched a thin eyebrow and sighed. "I grow tired of our game." He waved his hand and a blue orb expanded through the room like a wave of water, casting a silvery film on everything it passed over. A form near the doorway held its hands up in front of itself, examining the silvery residue the spell left behind. Another form sat in a high-backed wooden chair by the hearth. Gilifan smiled, pleased with himself.

"Now that you know I can see you, perhaps we can dispense with the shadows. Come, let us discuss this like gentlemen," the necromancer said.

The seated form was the first to appear. It was the cowardly kobold from Kuldiga Academy. "We have already met," he said.

Gilifan nodded. "Though the last time I saw you, you were not so bold. I thought you a spineless underling." The kobold grinned, pulling its thin lips tight against its sharp, jagged teeth. Gilifan turned to the doorway, and the other form was gone. The wizard recast the spell and the blue orb expanded quicker than the first, casting its shine over everything in the room.

"He is gone," the seated kobold said. "As is your amulet."

Gilifan reached up to his neck, and his face soured when he discovered the jewel was in fact missing. "Stay still," he told the kobold. He pointed a finger and sent a black bolt at the creature but the kobold was quick to counteract the spell with one of his own. A dark mist filled the room. The necromancer snapped his fingers, summoning a white orb of light in the midst of the darkness. Pain flashed across the necromancer's left leg as a blade tore through his hamstring. He fell backward onto the floor, calling out in agony.

He heard the coming footsteps and uttered another spell. A shell of fire encircled him, catching the would-be assassin and lighting him aflame as easily as though he had been covered in oil. The kobold squealed and shrieked as it ran away. Gilifan put a hand to his leg and closed the wound with a quick healing spell. After his leg was whole, the blood was dried in the heat of the fire-shell. He looked down to his brownish-red hand and stood again. His left leg protested with a couple of spasms, but the healing spell had done its job.

The necromancer extinguished the fire-shell and then dispelled the heavy mist in the room. As the last of the black particles dissipated, he saw a smoldering, smoking hulk in the far corner. "You have not won," Gilifan said.

The dying kobold laughed and coughed. "Neither have you," he promised. Then he exhaled for the last time and his head slumped back against the wall.

Gilifan quickly marched out of the room, searching for any sign of the second kobold. The halls were silent. There was no trace of the other creature. "Curse you," Gilifan growled. He spun around and went back to the dead kobold. He began to utter his spell to raise the dead creature. Out of habit, his left hand went to his neck to pull the amulet that was no longer there. The necromancer closed his eyes and stood silently fuming. He looked to a small box on his desk and a hollow, gnawing feeling tore into the pit of his stomach.

In two strides he was at his desk, hands reaching down to open the silver encrusted onyx box. Instead of the old parchment, he saw only the smooth, bare stone bottom. He dropped the box, letting it clash down on the desk. "He has the spell," he muttered. He turned and looked back to the kobold. How had he been able to get the amulet? Gilifan never removed the jewel from his neck except to summon its power. Now that it was gone…

The necromancer summoned forth his portal and set his destination for Lokton Manor. He was not about to let some upstart warlock steal his power from him. A great, oval shaped light appeared. A silver mist covered the portal's surface as small bolts of green and purple light sparked across the oval. The image of the field came into the portal. The warlock had made camp for the night, and Lokton Manor still stood. "Time to pay you a visit," Gilifan snarled. He stepped forward into the portal. The cool, tingling feeling washed over him as usual, but then he stopped abruptly, as if a wall of invisible stone had been erected. A wave of searing heat poured over the wizard and ultimately ejected him from the portal with the force of a great gale.

Gilifan landed on his desk and tumbled over it to slam onto the floor. A column of fire shot out from the portal, scorching the wall behind the wizard and then the portal itself shattered. Broken images of the field fell to the floor as though they had been dashed from a large mirror. Rays of purple and green light arced through the room, hissing and sizzling wildly as they bounced around the walls. The necromancer pushed himself up to his knees and waved the portal's remains away.

"Very clever," Gilifan said. "But it will not save you." He rose to his feet and brushed himself off. Then he left the room to gather his forces.

*****

"If you keep guzzling that stuff down, it will be the end of you," Marlin said.

Lady Dimwater sniggered and pushed the glass goblet away from her. "I told you, it helps me clear my head."

"Still, even for you that can't be healthy. A glass of that could put down even the toughest men."

"I am not a man," Lady Dimwater said coyly.

Marlin ceded the point with a nod and held out a folded letter to her. "I think this will be somewhat better for giving you hope than a glass of absinthe."

Lady Dimwater took the letter and opened it. Her eyes went wide and a smile appeared on her face as she devoured the message. "Al sits upon the throne of Roegudok Hall!" she exclaimed. "He has the scale!"

Marlin nodded. "It would appear that the gods have not forsaken us," Marlin commented. "He will need to march back to Drakei Glazei, but at least the scale is coming here."

"It is good to see he can send forces to help Erik as well," she said. "Now if only Lepkin would wake up, has there been any progress?"

"He has mumbled a few times, but nothing coherent yet. He is still deep in the sleep."

Her smile diminished and she blinked a couple times. "Well, one step at a time I suppose," she said.

"At least things are moving in a positive direction now," Marlin offered. He opened his mouth to speak but was interrupted as the door to the library flew open and a huffing guard stumbled in.

"Blacktongues," he shouted in between breaths. "A lot of them."

Lady Dimwater slammed her palm on the table. "I am tired of them," she grumbled.

"How many?" Marlin asked.

"We count maybe two score," the guard said. "A couple of their scouts advanced on the wall but we stopped them."

"Why has no one sounded the gong?" Marlin asked. As the last word fell from his lips the gong rang out loud and true like a crashing wave of brass. Marlin sighed.

"Let's go," Dimwater said as she pushed the heavy-breathing guard aside. Marlin struggled to keep up with her. He could see the anger writhing within the sorceress. Her determined, quick pace and the stoic expression on her face caused even the guards at the door to scramble out of her way as she stepped out into the night.

A whirlwind formed beneath her, fluttering her dress up above her ankles as it picked her up and gently carried her above the outer wall. A slew of arrows sailed toward her, but she sent a wave of flame to devour the shafts before they could reach her. A white orb of light appeared in her left hand and she cast it out over the field. It grew to the size of a great boulder and dispelled the night's blanket of darkness from the area. A group of Blacktongues directly beneath the orb covered their eyes and shrank away from the brightness and others scattered from the field.

"Run, you infernal roaches," she growled. "Silverfang, it is time to return." She pointed her right hand to the field and a column of golden light beamed down from the night sky. A tremendous howl tore through the air and the great wolf stood snarling in the field. It tore off after the nearest Blacktongue, taking him down to the ground effortlessly before launching at a group of four enemies.

Another arrow sliced through the air at her, but the whirlwind under Lady Dimwater grew and covered her entirely, tearing the arrow from its trajectory and protecting Dimwater. She held her left hand up in the air above her and called forth a hail of yellow and white fireballs. They streaked through the air, trailing thick smoke and sizzling as they crashed down into the fleeing forces. Then she reached out with her right hand and summoned the soul flame.

From her peripheral she saw a group of temple warriors coming around the wall to engage the enemy and she held off casting the soul flame. "Get back!" she yelled. Her voice boomed out across the field with an other-wordly quality that made the men shrink away from her in fear. As soon as they disappeared behind the wall she threw the soul flame. The barely visible fire descended down and ripped into the nearest Blacktongue. He cried out in pain and fell to the ground. The fire grew in size and spread to the next enemy, burning his soul out from his body before moving on to devour many more enemies before the entire Blacktongue force was destroyed.

Lady Dimwater turned back to the courtyard in front of the temple and the whirlwind gently set her down. Marlin stood there watching her.

"You are tired," he said.

She eyed him, but said nothing. As the last support from the whirlwind dissipated, she slumped slightly under the full weight of her body. She groaned and struggled to straighten up all the way.

"You should not have expended yourself so," Marlin said. "It wasn't necessary."

"I didn't just want to win," Lady Dimwater said coolly. "I wanted to send a message." She walked past Marlin and into the temple. Silverfang howled in the distance. Dimwater paused and turned back to the doorway. "Go to Erik," she whispered to the wolf. She didn't hear the wolf, or see anything, but she could feel his departure. A smile crept over her weary face and she nodded happily to herself.

*****

Eldrik looked to his left at Silvi. She smiled at him, but it was not as warm and playful as it had been before. Her eyes seemed colder, and distant. He glanced over his shoulder and took heart at the sight of his father's men riding with him.

"There are the others," Silvi said, pointing to a group of men coming out from the forest. Merriam led them atop a great chestnut colored horse.

"I see them," Eldrik said with a nod. The two groups joined unceremoniously, and without more than a wave from Eldrik. Merriam brought her horse in along Silvi's left side and the warlocks, dressed in leather armor, fell in line with Eldrik's warriors.

"Nice to see you again, Eldrik," Merriam said.

Eldrik kept his eyes forward. His mother's last words kept ringing in his ears.

"You are with the witches, aren't you?" she had shouted when he came to the house. "You have to put away this foolishness, they mean only to harm you!" He had tried to convince her that he knew no witches, but she would not listen. He had never been good at lying to his mother. She always seemed to know the truth behind his words. Yet, she had let him go, and she allowed every warrior to go with him who chose to. Now, with the warlocks embedded with his own warriors there were about one hundred and fifty altogether. A sizeable army for any lad in his late teens. Eldrik wondered whether his mother had been right. Would the witches turn on him, as she insisted? Silvi had reassured him that they were loyal allies, that they were sworn to serve him as he was now their patriarch.

A couple days ago he would have listened unquestioningly, but now he was not so sure. Still, he was in too deep to turn back now. Senator Bracken expected him. They emerged from the forest road to find a grassy hill before them. A pair of sentries waved white and purple banners and motioned for them to come forward. Eldrik led the company up, keeping his eye to the vast smoke rising up into the purple and pink sky as the sun descended below the horizon to the west. His mouth dropped open when he crested the hill.

Before him he saw a vast field of burning brush, littered with corpses and smothered in a thick smoke that stung his eyes and burned his lungs. A ring of hot fire encircled the manor, and a hill of bodies lay in an open area between two ditches alight with orange flames. The groans and shouts of dying men filled his ears and sent a chill down his spine. He might have turned back and rode away were it not for the push of the throng behind him.

"Come," Merriam said. "The senator expects us."

A scout ran up to him and saluted. "Master Eldrik, Senator Bracken awaits you in his tent. The others may find food and rest at the rear of the camp." The scout pointed to a ring of wooden spikes hastily planted in the dirt near the western edge of the field. "Come, I will show you to Senator Bracken."

"I will take the men to make camp," Merriam said as she waved to the warlocks. "Follow me," she commanded. The warlocks obeyed instantly, but the warriors from House Cedreau waited. Eldrik eyed Merriam warily, making a point of withholding his consent for a few moments before finally gesturing for his men to go with her. Merriam arched a brow at him, but she kept her mouth shut.

"It is not wise to taunt bears," Silvi commented quietly after Merriam was far enough away.

"A bear is no threat to the hunter once it has been treed," Eldrik replied callously.

Silvi pursed her lips and looked at him keenly. "You have changed," she said.

Eldrik regarded her coolly. "I am here to restore my father's honor, and to exact justice for the blood shed by House Lokton. I have no use for her, or for Hairen."

"They gave you a great gift," Silvi reminded him.

Eldrik shrugged. "Let's go." He said nothing else to her as they dismounted and followed the scout through the camp. Many soldiers wore full helmets covering their faces, but the faces that he could see hardly paid him any mind. Many were injured, with scorch marks or blood smudged across their armor. Some had great gashes in their arms and were being sewn up as he walked by. None of them greeted him. None of them even seemed to register his arrival.

A pair of heavy-set pikemen stood in front of a large, round canvas tent. The flaps were down, blocking any view of what was inside. The guards lowered their weapons, crossing them over the entrance. "State your name and business," one of them said.

Eldrik produced Bracken's letter. "I am Eldrik Cedreau, here at Senator Bracken's request."

Barely had the words left his lips when the tent flaps flew open and a man dressed in white robes with purple stripes around the sleeves came bursting out from the tent. "Here is the hero of the senate!" he said with arms flung out wide. He brushed the guards aside roughly and came forward to embrace Eldrik, kissing him once on each cheek. "The hero who brought down the escaped lion. How was your journey?"

Eldrik was taken aback by the greeting, and unsure how to answer. He stammered and stuttered through a garbled reply and then Silvi put her hand on the small of his back and stepped forward to speak for him.

"We had no troubles," she said.

Bracken looked to her and smiled. "Good, good," he said. "Come inside the tent, let us speak in private." He turned on his heels and motioned for them to follow as he ducked under the opening again. Silvi gently pushed Eldrik forward and the tent flaps slapped down after they were inside.

Eldrik looked around and saw a crude, yet sturdy, wooden table in the middle of the tent, near the single upright support, and covered with a map of the kingdom. A cot was situated near the far edge of the tent, littered with straw and a fur blanket. A pair of leather boots sat by the foot of the bed and a sword rested over the toes of the boots. Otherwise the tent was empty, not at all what he expected for a senator.

"I apologize," Bracken said with a gesture to the space around him. "The haste and rigor of war have forced me to forego the pleasures and comforts I would normally be able to offer to my guests."

Eldrik nodded and went to the map. He looked down and traced his finger from Drakei Glazei to Lokton Manor. "You were at the senate hall when Lepkin attacked?" he asked.

"I was," Bracken said as he instinctively moved a hand up to hover over one of the great scars on his chest from the assault. "He almost killed me, in fact," he said grimly. "That is why the senate could not delay in responding to the threat." He came forward to the table and leaned on his palms, towering over the map.

"How is it that you are attacking from the west?" Eldrik asked. "If you came directly here from Drakei Glazei, then you should be attacking from the northeast."

Bracken offered a half smile and pointed at Eldrik. "An astute observation," he said. Bracken straightened and looked evenly into

Eldrik's eyes for a moment. "I am not without magic tricks of my own," he said.

Eldrik returned the gaze and took in a deep breath as he thought about it. "You are a warlock," he said after a few moments.

Bracken smiled and gave a single nod.

Eldrik glanced to Silvi and then back to Bracken. "That is your connection with Hairen, and the coven, isn't it?" The young man shook his head, feeling stupid for not seeing it before now. "So I am a pawn," he muttered.

"No," Bracken said flatly. "You are no pawn."

"You sent Merriam to find me, didn't you?" Eldrik asked.

Silvi started to step forward but Bracken held his hand up and shook his head. "The truth is that you and I have a common enemy. We both wish to see House Lokton razed to the ground. You want justice for the wrongs Erik and his father committed, and I need them removed in order to see my own goals fulfilled." The senator folded his arms across his chest and studied the young man intently.

"What are your goals?" Eldrik demanded. "I would know your intent before I commit my house to your service."

"Oh, it is a bit too late for that," Bracken sniggered. "Your warriors are here and when the sun rises we will launch an offensive, and your men will be alongside mine."

"No," Eldrik said. "I want no more of this. My mother was right. You have no love for House Cedreau, you have only treachery for me!" He turned to leave but a sudden, unseen force knocked him to the ground and pinned him flat, squeezing the air from his lungs. His eyes watered and burned as he struggled against the spell.

"Gondok'hr, that is enough!" Silvi shouted. She rushed in to help Eldrik up, but she could not counter the spell.

"You have grown fond of him," the warlock noted. He flicked his wrist and the spell evaporated. Eldrik bolted upright, coughing and gasping for air as he clutched his throat and wiped his eyes. Silvi helped him back to his feet and whispered into his ear. The young man nodded and turned back to Gondok'hr.

"So, your name is not Bracken," he noted.

The warlock scoffed and shook his head. "I am no senator,"

he said. "The men around you are also not the king's army. They are a mix of guards, soldiers, and brigands, reanimated with magic by a master necromancer."

"You can raise the dead?" Eldrik asked with sudden interest.

Gondok'hr shook his head. "I cannot, but the one I serve can," he said cryptically. He stepped in close. "I know your pain," he said. His breath was hot and smelled of garlic, but despite that Eldrik didn't turn away. There was something in the way the warlock looked at him that held his interest. "My family was taken from me, a long time ago," he said. "I serve in order to bring them back, to make my family whole again. If you serve with me, you will not only be able to grow in magical power and restore your family's former glory, you can ask the one we serve to repair the rift in your heart." Gondok'hr poked Eldrik in the chest.

"How can he?" Eldrik asked. "My father and brother lie deep in the dirt."

"The one we serve desires Erik's head. Accomplish that, and all shall be restored."

Eldrik felt torn. His heart begged him to rush out and lay waste to Lokton Manor. Even as extraordinary as it sounded, a chance of bringing his father and brother back from the realm of the dead was enough to stoke the fires in his soul. His mother's warning voice was still there, echoing in the back of his mind, but its influence was waning. "How do I know I can trust you?" he asked.

Gondok'hr smiled. "I am the patriarch of the coven to which you have been brought into," he said. "The other warlocks have pledged loyalty to you, but they are not your true followers until I make them so."

Eldrik was confused. He decided it must be some sort of trick. "No, there was a ceremony where they all pledged their lives to me," Eldrik said defiantly.

"But did they tell you their names?" Gondok'hr asked with a finger in the air. "In order to be the patriarch, you must be able to summon any member of the coven at any time."

Eldrik took a step back. "Do you know their names?" he asked.

Gondok'hr smiled. "Alrek De'nezir, I summon thee!"

A flash of smoke and light appeared on Gondok'hr's right and one of the warlocks appeared, kneeling subserviently to Gondok'hr. Eldrik recognized the warlock from the coven, but had been told the man's name was Alerik, not Alrek. Eldrik watched closely the interaction between the two.

"Master, what is thy wish?" the warlock asked.

Gondok'hr pointed to Eldrik. "This is your new master now. He is to be revered and served as patriarch of the coven. He knows your name and can summon you at will."

The warlock looked up to Eldrik and nodded. "Very well," he said.

Gondok'hr stepped forward. "Command him to disappear," he told Eldrik.

Eldrik glanced between the two and nodded. "You are free to return to where you were, Alrek De'nezir," he said.

Alrek nodded and disappeared in a puff of smoke.

"Now," Gondok'hr began with a hand pointing to the spot where Alrek had just been. "I can show you the power of knowing their names." He placed a thumb on Eldrik's forehead and leaned his own head back, closing his eyes.

A stream of images flooded into Eldrik's mind. All at once he saw every instance when Gondok'hr had summoned another member of the coven. Each image flashed simultaneously, and yet was distinct enough for him to clearly understand every memory as it transferred to him. In a mere matter of seconds, Eldrik's knowledge seemed to gain the experience of several decades. Then the connection broke and he was left to himself. He stumbled backward and reached out for Silvi, who quickly caught him and steadied him.

"Easy now," she said. "You could have warned him," she said, turning an angry glare to Gondok'hr.

The warlock shrugged. "We have little time," he said. "Now there is one more thing I wish to show you." He stepped up to Eldrik again. The young man flinched and pulled his head away. "Very well, I can show you in a different way," he said. "There is a principle that governs the darker arts," he said. "A matriarch is necessary to give life to the coven. That is, a witch of sufficient power can imbue a new initiate with the power and gift of magic if he does not already possess it. She has to use rites and rituals, of course, but that is their function in the coven. Without a matriarch, a coven is dead and barren." He looked to Silvi and then smiled. "Whatever you do, Silvi should stay with you. You will be stronger with her near, than without her."

"But I am not the matriarch," Silvi interjected. "Hairen is."

Gondok'hr's lips curled wickedly. "Her time is at an end." He said."

"What do you mean?" a voice came from the front of the tent. The three of them turned to see Merriam standing there. "Have you seen her death?"

"I have," Gondok'hr replied evenly. "She dies tonight."

Merriam shuddered and shook her head. "No, come Silvi, we must go and protect her."

"It will do no good, I have foreseen her death," Gondok'hr said.

Merriam wouldn't listen. "We must try!" she shouted back. She summoned forth a portal and jumped through it. Silvi started to follow after her but Gondok'hr grabbed her arm. The vice-like grip held her in place while he wove a spell and closed the portal.

"What have you done?" she asked.

Gondok'hr laughed. "I have done nothing," he said. "Hairen's fate is sealed. I saw it in vision long ago."

"Then why did you let Merriam leave?" she pressed.

"As I was saying, there must be a matriarch for the coven to survive." He turned back to Eldrik. "Merriam does not have your trust, and she never would. So, she has been sent to join Hairen's fate."

Silvi blanched, but remained tight-lipped.

"So what does the patriarch do, if the matriarch is to give life?" Eldrik asked.

"The patriarch has two roles," Gondok'hr said. "The first is to protect life, which he does through glimpses into the future. The second is to take life, which he can do in a variety of ways. You told your true name to Silvi, yes?" Gondok'hr asked. Eldrik squirmed inside and fear gripped his heart. "You don't have to answer, I know you did. It is natural and the proper way for beings like us. You cannot progress without it. However, you need not fear her. She can only summon your presence. As matriarch, it would be unnatural for her to do anything other than give life to the coven, so she is unable to use your true name against you.

However, you have the ability to use it against others."

"What do you mean?" Eldrik asked.

"Summon our friend, the warlock we just saw. He has been a weak member of the group and is undeserving of his gift. You can use his name to absorb his power, thus becoming stronger."

"But I thought the patriarch was to protect the coven?" Eldrik said cynically.

"To cull the weak from the fold is to make the whole stronger, thus protecting our order. This particular warlock has already revealed his true nature to his home village. He did it to impress a young girl, but nonetheless, his indiscretion poses a risk to the entire order. If he is not removed from the group, his carelessness will grow until the day that he will betray the order for the sake of a large payment of gold from a powerful witch hunter." Gondok'hr folded his arms and gave a stern nod. "Summon him forth, and then command him to surrender his gift to you."

"How do I do that?" Eldrik asked. "I don't know any spells."

Gondok'hr tapped his foot impatiently. "I know you are a shadowfiend. Take your true form, summon him, and then stretch your hand out toward him and then you have to but only think of absorbing his power. As you are the patriarch now and he has just been sworn to your service, he will be unable to fight against you."

"Alrek De'nezir, I summon thee!" Eldrik said in a shaky voice. The same puff of smoke appeared, but this time the warlock knelt next to Eldrik.

"What is your wish master?" the warlock said.

Eldrik looked to him with trembling hands and a quivering voice. He tried to muster his most authoritative posture. "You revealed your identity as a warlock to someone outside the order," he said.

The warlock's eyes went wide and he quickly bowed his head. "Forgive my indiscretion, master. I swear it will never happen again!"

Eldrik looked to Gondok'hr. The former patriarch shook his head and drew a line across his neck. Eldrik thought of his own true name and his body stretched and ripped into his darker, beast-like form. The kneeling warlock cowered before him and held his hands over his head.

"Mercy, I beg for mercy!"

In his beast-form, Eldrik felt no pity as he had only a moment ago. Instead of a shivering man he saw only a quaking worm, unworthy of the gift inside of him. Eldrik stretched out his clawed hand over the warlock and envisioned drawing forth the man's life energy. No sooner did the image appear in his mind than a terrible, thunderous crack rent the air around him and a ball of mist and light ripped free of the trembling warlock and entered into Eldrik's mouth. He felt the warmth and power grow inside him as he consumed the energy. A hunger was born inside of him in that instant. It grew even as he fed on the magical energy, awakening something deep within him that lusted for raw, unfettered power.

When he was done he instinctively wiped his mouth with the back of his long, leathery arm. He stretched his wings out wide and roared mightily, blowing the flaps of the tent as if he had sent a great wind from the depths of his throat. He turned and looked to Gondok'hr. The man stood smiling, clapping softly. Silvi stepped forward and placed a hand on the tuft of hair on his chest.

"Your men will not follow you in this form," she reminded him.

His mind turned back to the warriors from his home. He agreed and returned to his human form. The change wearied him, but Silvi held him fast.

"Well done," Gondok'hr said. "Now, so that you may know you can trust me, I will grant you the knowledge of the coven. Here is every member's true name, use the knowledge as you see fit." Gondok'hr rushed forward and placed his thumb against Eldrik's forehead again. In rushed a steady stream of names, faces, and images. All at once Eldrik saw each warlock, understood their abilities and magical strength, and knew of their past deeds and accomplishments for the coven. Then the flow stopped and Gondok'hr pulled away.

"Only one patriarch can exist," Silvi said. "By giving you the knowledge, he has relinquished his right to be our patriarch, and he remembers our names no more. The next time the warlocks see you, they will feel the shift in your power, and will become your servants."

"What of you?" Eldrik asked weakly as he turned to face Gondok'hr.

"I still retain my magical abilities," he said. "But now I am a warlock without a coven. I am close enough to my goals, that I no longer have use for the coven. Take it, do what you will with it. I have given you the strongest start I can. If that doesn't prove to you that I can be trusted, then nothing else could. Help me burn Lokton manor to the ground, and our master will reward you."

"Who is the master you speak of?" Eldrik asked.

Gondok'hr shrugged and walked for the tent flaps. "You will meet him soon enough," he said as he held one of the flaps open. "Now go and get some rest. In the morning we strike. Also, keep your men at the rear of the camp, we don't want them mixing with my army prematurely. I doubt they would like the idea of working with warlocks and the undead."

Silvi assisted Eldrik to leave the tent and Gondok'hr closed the flap behind him.

"A most impressive display," Djekk said from the shadows.

"I thought it a nice touch," Gondok'hr replied. "Now I have finished with the coven, and the fight against Erik will be stronger. Have you been successful?"

Djekk stepped forward and shook off his invisibility spell. "I have the amulet," he said with a crooked, toothy grin. He held out the emerald necklace for Gondok'hr to see.

"Your brother?" the warlock asked.

"He fell, but his sacrifice gave me the distraction I needed to lift the amulet. I sliced the necklace and took it without so much as tickling Gilifan's neck."

"Kobolds are the best thieves," Gondok'hr commented.

"You remember our bargain?" Djekk asked.

"Give me the amulet, and your debt is paid in full." The kobold's smile grew so large Gondok'hr thought the creature's teeth might leap from his mouth. He bounded forward and placed the amulet into Gondok'hr's hands. "Was there anything else?" Gondok'hr asked.

Djekk reached into his pocket and gingerly removed an old, yellowed parchment with worn, cracked edges. He carefully unfolded it. "I believe this is the original inscription for the correct spell."

"Excellent," Gondok'hr said. He laid a hand on the kobold's shoulder. "You are free to return to your people. You are in service to me no longer, your debt is paid."

"What will happen to you?" the kobold asked.

"I will put the boy's head on a platter and leave it here for the dragon as a parting gift. Then I will disappear, much like you, my friend."

The kobold nodded and a distant look came over his eyes for a moment. Then he looked back to Gondok'hr. "May your feet be silent and steady, your knife sharp and quick, and may your enemies never see you coming."

"Same to you," Gondok'hr said.

Djekk grinned and winked out of the tent like a star disappearing in the morning light.

Gondok'hr turned the jewel over in his hand. "Now I can return home," he said. "Just kill the boy in the morning and then I can leave this all behind me."

CHAPTER FOURTEEN

Lady Cedreau crept through the tunnel's opening and peered into the dark chamber before her. The water glowed with the familiar silvery green hues dancing in the mist hovering above the surface. A pair of dragonflies swirled around each other as they flew over a patch of blue cave lilies and disappeared out of sight.

"I have been expecting you," an old familiar voice called out.

Lady Cedreau stepped into the chamber, looking toward the cauldron where she finally spied Hairen. "As well you should have," she replied bitterly. "I warned you to leave my son alone."

"But he is not your son, and he never was," Hairen cackled. "Now he belongs to our coven."

"No," she spat. "I warned you." She reached into her robes and pulled an old wand made of hickory wood. She pointed it at the old witch and a bolt of blue lightning leapt from the wand to devour Hairen.

Hairen laughed and quickly cast a shielding spell. The blue lightning glanced off of an opaque, red sphere around her and the cauldron. "It will take more than a wand to defeat me, Leanor."

Lady Cedreau heard a snarl from her left and turned to aim her wand at the new threat emerging from the pool. A great, two-legged monster slowly raised itself before her, extending its webbed, claw-tipped hands out for her and shrieking horribly. She blasted the beast with a ball of fire and sent it hurtling through the air to crash back into the pool. Without another word she drew a rune in the air with her wand and blew it toward the water. Instantly the surface froze tight, cracking and sizzling as the magical ice captured everything it touched and held it solid.

"I see you have not lost your touch," Hairen commented. The old witch dissolved her shield and overturned the cauldron. A plume of purple smoke rose up from the viscous pinkish black goo oozing out. The smoke formed a veil between them and a great serpent squirmed in the ooze, hissing and spitting venom and fire as it slowly emerged from the liquid.

Lady Cedreau walked forward across the ice, undaunted by the demonic serpent. "Face me, witch!" she growled. The snake loomed forward, slithering side to side and bearing its needle-like fangs. Lady Cedreau summoned a great eagle with a flick of her wand and the bird streaked down, piercing the snake's side with its dagger sized talons. The snake hissed and squealed horridly, lashing up to bite the eagle, but the bird's thick scales protected its legs as it flew off with its prey and let out a high pitched shriek of victory.

The smoke crackled and lightning rippled over its surface, but still Lady Cedreau came forward. She sent three blasts of fire into the smoke wall and then she summoned a great sphere of energy to blow the smoke apart. The smoke groaned as it was rent in twain. Lady Cedreau saw Hairen only for a moment through the clearing. The old witch had her black wand out and was quick to repair the magical barrier. The smoke slammed together with the force of a great thunder, shaking the chamber violently. Lady Cedreau poured her rage into every spell she threw at the wall. "Face me!" she yelled out. "I will not let you sit behind your magic after what you have done. You killed my husband, you slew my innocent little boy, and now you have entrapped my eldest son in your coven. You will answer for what you have done."

"It was not me who killed them!" Hairen called from behind the wall.

Lady Cedreau summoned a bull made of fire and sent the beast at the wall. Its hooves sparked as it tore the stone floor apart and gained speed. Flames trailed behind it and it lowered its head with a mighty bellow. It slammed into the wall and the spell finally gave way. The smoke crackled and groaned as the great, red bull broke through and trampled the spot where Hairen had stood only moments before.

"You could have used your magic to save your husband," Hairen chided. "You could have gone with him to the battlefield." The old witch appeared far off to the side, next to a great desk made of stone. She summoned a massive ball of water and dropped it onto the bull. The animal hissed and dissipated into a thin cloud of steam and smoke as the water overcame the magic that brought him into existence.

"I swore to him I would not use magic again as long as he lived," Lady Cedreau snarled back. She turned her wand to point at the ceiling and sent bolt after bolt of lightning into the stone overhead. The stone split and cracked, dropping large hunks down.

The great boulders slammed into the ice over the pool and the stone floor around the two witches. The cavern shook and trembled.

"What are you doing? Do you want to kill us both?" Hairen shouted. The old witch threw a stabilizing spell up to the ceiling, strengthening it with magical columns of energy that arched underneath and spread over the surface of the ceiling.

That was exactly the opening Lady Cedreau had been looking for. She rushed forward, flashed a dagger, and stabbed Hairen through the heart. "Not both of us," she replied. "I will pay for my sins, of that I am sure, but not until after all three of you lay at my feet."

Hairen's mouth gaped open and she slowly turned her eyes to look at her. The old, gray orbs lost the spark of life then and Hairen's neck twitched. The witch was no more. Lady Cedreau removed the dagger and let the old witch fall to the floor.

"What have you done?!" a familiar voice shouted from the far side of the chamber.

Lady Cedreau turned to see Merriam standing just inside the chamber with her hands up to her temples. "How convenient," Lady Cedreau whispered to herself. She backed away from Hairen and prepared her wand. She knew that Hairen's stabilizing spell would soon lose its power now that the witch was gone, and the ceiling would become vulnerable again. She had only to bring Merriam far enough inside to prevent her escape. "I put a dagger through the old hag's heart. Apparently it isn't made of stone after all," she said as she proudly displayed the bloody dagger.

"I'll kill you for this!" Merriam promised. She rushed in, sending fireballs with her left hand while her right hand threw thin bolts of lightning. Lady Cedreau quickly cast a ward spell, summoning a golden shield of energy between her and Merriam's assaults. She strengthened the shield with her left hand and turned her wand to the ceiling.

As soon as the golden columns and arches winked out she dropped her shield, absorbing a couple of Merriam's lightning bolts in the chest as she sent one final spell up to the ceiling. A boulder of blue energy slammed into the stone ceiling, rending it asunder and dropping the entire chamber down.

"Kus-em-ia," Lady Cedreau said as she called a rush of wind

to aid her. The wind propelled her forward, toward the exit. She blew past Merriam and zapped the witch with a stun spell as she whirled by her. Merriam's ensuing screams were cut short as a cacophony of boulders slammed down to the ground and the chamber caved in upon itself.

Lady Cedreau's hip and back were caught by falling shards of stone, but with the help of her spell she managed to exit the cave just as a great wall of dust, dirt, and small bits of stone exploded out from the magical tree that served as the entrance. She flew out and landed on the ground, rolling until she slammed into a small tree a few yards away. Her body ached, and her mind was bleary and exhausted from the attack, but she had done what she had wanted to do.

She looked back to the magical tree and watched it shrivel like a great slug baking in the sun. The wood warped and cracked as the magical force which gave it life dissolved and disappeared. She pushed herself up to her feet and brushed herself off. She then sent one final fireball to the pedestal that granted entrance into the tunnel. Her spell exploded the final vestige of the coven, showering the shriveled tree in bits of stone and pottery.

"No more will this den give birth to such spiders," she said. Then she turned and started the walk back to her home. It was time to find Silvi.

*****

Erik lay awake in his bed. His mind raced through the recent events too quickly for him to find peace. Only a short time ago, he had been in this very bed lying awake and wondering about Tukai's prophecy. Now, with his father murdered, he was even more confused than ever. He was sure his father had no other children, so who killed him? Or, perhaps the prophecy was about the tribunal. Perhaps Erik inadvertently caused his father's death by trying to save him? He sat up in his bed and looked out his window.

The half-moon beamed silvery rays into his room. He rose and stood in the soft light, looking down at the smoldering ground around the manor. The fire in the moat had long died out, only a few stubborn, dying coals glowed in the night. Periodically a flame would jump up, perhaps caused by a midnight breeze, but the roaring fire was gone. Pockets of black and gray ashes littered the ground. The dead that belonged to House Lokton had been removed from the field, so he knew the bodies that lay about now were those of his enemies. At least he could take heart in the fact that the battle was decisively won in his favor. The reports had marked only a couple score of casualties for his men. There were at least seven dead enemies for each of House Lokton's fallen, based on Braun's calculations.

Erik stepped to the window and ran his hand along the sill. He remembered the last time he was in his room. It was the night the Blacktongues had come for him. A raven had lighted upon his window and woken him up with a warning. He looked up to the night sky and imagined he saw a raven now, soaring over to his window. He watched the imaginary bird descend down, its stark feathers shining in the moonlight as it effortlessly approached. It grew bigger as it came near. It cackled "ca-caw!" as it swooped down.

It was then that Erik realized it was not his imagination. The large bird landed on the window sill and stared at him with its golden eye, twitching its head up to look at him before hopping over to the glass. Erik drew in a breath, too afraid to move.

The bird took one look at the glass and then tapped the window three times. It hopped back and looked at Erik again. "ca-caw!" it squawked. Then it tapped three times again and flew off into the night, disappearing silently into the darkness.

Erik stood there, mouth agape and hardly breathing. What was he supposed to do now? What did three taps mean again? Why had a raven returned? Erik shook his head and rushed for his door. He yanked the knob and pulled the door open. A guard startled and snorted awake on the other side as Erik stumbled into him.

"Get up!" Erik commanded. He crossed the hall and threw the door open to a guest room where Wendal and Orres were sleeping. "Master Orres!" Erik said. "I need you to wake up."

Orres' eyes opened and he slowly struggled to sit upright, shaking the sleep off with a yawn and a quick stretch. "What is it?" he asked.

Wendal sat up also and he knocked on the wall next to him. A few seconds later Lady Arkyn walked into the room.

"I heard your knock," she said. "What's the matter?"

"We can't wait for the sun," Erik said. "We need to strike tonight, now."

Orres regarded him with a wary eye. "What are you about?" he asked. "We won't be able to see out there. If we lead a charge our men are as likely to slice into each other as they are to hit the enemy."

"No," Erik said with a quick wave of his hand. "Not a full charge, just us."

Wendal scrunched his brow together. "Just us?" he asked. Erik nodded.

The big man shook his head. "No," he said. "I know your legendary feats as well as anybody else, but this would be disastrous. I am barely able to walk without ripping open my sutures from the battle at Kuldiga Academy, and Wendal needs to rest before he will be able to wield any significant spells."

"But if we attack now, the warlock's forces won't be recovered either. We would have the element of surprise."

"He has a point," Lady Arkyn said, agreeing with Erik.

Orres shot her a sour look. "I heard about your lucky shot to the firedrake's eye, but don't let it go to your head," he cautioned. "We need the daylight, and we need our full force if we are to have a chance."

Erik crossed his arms and let out an exasperated sigh. "That is what the enemy expects," he said. "But they wouldn't expect a few of us to attack tonight."

Orres shook his head and laid back down. "Go back to bed," he said. "You almost got yourself killed today, I am not going to follow you to my death tonight."

Lady Arkyn crossed the room in three steps and slapped Orres' feet off the bed so they thunked on the floor and made him awkwardly arch his back as he clasped a hand to his side and grimaced.

"What's gotten into you?" he bellowed.

"Since when has the mighty Orres been afraid of a fight?" she retorted.

Erik stepped forward and put himself between them. "A raven was at my window just a moment ago. It tapped a warning. I know it sounds crazy, but if we don't do something tonight, then we are all doomed."

"A raven?" Orres grumbled as he sat back up in his bed.

"How many times did it tap?" Lady Arkyn asked.

"Three," Erik said. "It tapped three times, then crowed at me, and then it tapped three times again."

"Lepkin is right, we have no choice but to act. The raven has warned that death comes for him, but can yet be avoided."

Orres rubbed the bridge of his nose between his thumb and forefinger. "The fact remains that we cannot see in the dark," he said.

"*You can't*," Lady Arkyn said. "I can." Orres looked to her for a moment and then back to Erik.

"Do you have a plan?"

Erik shrugged. "Find the warlock and kill him."

All four of them remained silent for a few moments.

"Is that all?" Orres questioned. "You wake me up and tell me that we should pick our way in the dark, through the enemy camp to locate and kill the warlock as if it is that simple. This is madness."

"It could work," Wendal said. The others looked at him. "I mean, at least we would have the element of surprise like he said. The dark will conceal us as well."

"I know these lands," Erik said.

"I know you have come here a few times to visit Erik, but have you walked Lokton lands while they lay burned and scattered with corpses, broken bits of weapons, and sentries ready to kill you for coming close?" Orres asked pointedly.

"We could create a diversion," Wendal said to Orres. "You and I could distract the enemy. Lady Arkyn and Master Lepkin could go through the camp."

"What's going on?" Braun's voice demanded from the doorway.

Erik turned around and only briefly met Braun's stern stare before looking to the floor. "Were you awake?" he asked.

"Your door guard summoned me," he answered. "I told him to wake me if you left your room."

"We are going to kill the warlock," Erik said with as much courage as he could muster. Braun frowned and folded his arms. "A raven tapped three times on my window tonight, just like what happened to Erik the night the Blacktongues came for him." He watched the words sink in as Braun let out a heavy sigh. Erik shook his head. "I am not going to sit and wait here. I am going to end this now."

Braun stepped forward and placed a hand on Erik's shoulder. "Tell me what you want me to do."

Erik paused, thinking about each of the others in the room. Then he smiled. "Can you and Demetrius work the catapults by yourselves?"

"I can take a few of the others with me," Braun said.

Erik nodded. "Wendal, can you cover the moon?"

"I can summon clouds," he said. "If I do anything else it might be obvious to the warlock if he is watching."

"Orres, you help with the catapults," Erik said.

Orres nodded slowly.

"And me?" Lady Arkyn asked.

"You will come with me through the forest," Erik said. "Can you see even without the moonlight?"

"I have elf eyes," she said with a smile. "I can see as well as an owl in the night."

"Then, once we find his tent, you will perch with your bow and cover me. I will pick my way through to the warlock."

"And then you will use your flaming sword to battle a warlock?" Orres scoffed. "This is hardly a foolproof strategy."

"Are you offering to go in his stead?" Braun asked harshly. Orres bristled, but said nothing in response. "What do you want us to do with the catapults?" Braun asked Erik.

"Fill them with tar pots. Lady Arkyn will fire a flaming arrow once I am clear and the warlock is dead. Then you will fire the catapults at the enemy position."

"I can also rouse the mages," Wendal offered. "We can add our magic to the catapults."

Erik thought for a moment and then nodded. "Ok, but they have to wait for Lady Arkyn's signal."

"What if something goes wrong?" Lady Arkyn asked. "I can cover you well, but I will not likely be able to protect you should you cause alarm or if the warlock catches you coming."

"That is a chance I will have to take," Erik said.

"Gallantry is good in poems," Orres said. "But it hardly serves any other purpose."

"If you have a better idea I am open to hearing it," Erik said.

Orres snorted and rose to his feet. "I do," he said. "Why not go with Wendal's notion of causing a distraction? We could fire the catapults first, cause the enemy to scramble about in chaos and then while they mount a counter offensive you could slip in and take the warlock."

"No," Braun argued. "Rousing the enemy too early could destroy our chances of catching him. We need him to be completely unaware."

Orres shrugged. "It's your funeral," he said. "Just don't make me come in after you."

Erik gave a half smile and walked to the door. "I'll try to keep that in mind." Lady Arkyn was quick to follow him as he went back to his room, grabbed Lepkin's sword and put his boots on. He left his armor lying on the floor, he didn't want to be bogged down with the noisy metal. Lady Arkyn retrieved her bow and a full quiver of arrows. Then the two left and made their way around the back of the house. They crouched near the wall until a thick, dark cloud covered the moon.

"Are you ready?" Lady Arkyn asked.

Erik nodded and he led the way to the forest south of the house. They slowly picked their way through the trees, pausing periodically to listen to the night sounds and ensure they hadn't made too much noise. As they got closer to the enemy, Lady Arkyn took the lead. She pulled an arrow from her quiver. She held her hand up and motioned for Erik to hide near a large oak tree.

Lady Arkyn knelt and put the arrow to her string and quietly pulled the arrow back. A single guard patrolled the forest about sixty yards in front of her. He held a spear in one hand and a bugle in the other. The ranger watched him as his body passed behind trees and then stopped in a small clearing filled with ferns. The soldier stopped and stuck his spear in the ground, then he hooked the bugle strap back over his neck and pushed the bugle behind him. His hands went down to undo his trousers and he shuffled closer to the ferns. Lady Arkyn waited for just a moment, until she heard the pittering stream of urine striking the ground.

She took in a breath and let her arrow fly. The missile flew straight and true, piercing the soldier's neck in the gap between his leather hauberk and helmet. He slumped down to the ground with a soft *thud*. The ranger put another arrow to the string and waited for several moments, scanning the area nearby for any sign of others. When she was sure that there were no witnesses, she snapped her fingers and Erik came away from the tree.

"Let's go," she said.

They carefully traversed the forest until Lady Arkyn spied a large, round topped canvas tent. "There," she said pointing in the tent's direction. "It's a round topped tent, like the kind commanders use on the battlefield. That has to be his."

Erik nodded and took and a deep breath. "Alright," he said.

She put her hand on his shoulder. "You don't have to do this," she said. "I could go."

"No," Erik said. "I will go."

Lady Arkyn nodded. "Good luck," she said. Then she leapt up into the tree above and took a perch from where she could see the field.

Erik stood motionless for a few moments, scanning the camp. His heart was pounding and his stomach was churning into knots. He crept out from the cover of the trees, keeping low to the ground. He went slowly, trying to discern his path in the darkness. He spied a large mound straight ahead of him and made his way to it. The live grass bent under his weight, but he made no sound as he crawled. When he neared the mound, he smelled a sour, metallic odor. At first he thought it might be the ground, as it was burned and scorched in some areas nearby, but when he pressed up against the mound he realized how wrong he was. The mound gave under the pressure of his weight and he felt matted fur under his fingers. He didn't recognize the beast, but at least it wasn't breathing anymore. Judging by its size and shape, it was something he would not care to meet. He quickly skirted around a hooked arm and pressed forward.

He stopped when he heard laughter coming from one of the small fires off to his left. He slowly raised his head and spied a trio of men laughing and making obscene gestures amongst themselves. They did not wear the same kind of armor as the men he had fought earlier in the day. His heart sank when he realized that somehow the warlock had been able to get reinforcements. He watched them for a few seconds, deciding whether they might catch him if he moved forward. He noticed that each of them held a tin cup in their hands and there were several bottles around them on the ground.

Likely too drunk to notice me as long as I stay low.

Forward he crawled until he reached the side of a small tent. He pulled himself up into a crouch and gauged the distance to the warlock's tent. There were a few tents in between, but there was no movement. It appeared that the soldiers in this section of the camp were asleep. Slowly he rose up and peered around the side of the tent. Suddenly the flap opened and a large man came out wearing nothing but an old pair of ragged leggings. Erik ducked back around the tent. Something whizzed by, just a hand's breadth away from Erik's head and then the man groaned low. Erik heard something slump onto the ground. He knew then that Lady Arkyn had seen the man too. He stepped around the tent and found the man lying on his back with an arrow embedded deeply in his chest. Erik grabbed his ankles and pulled his body into the tent. Then he waited for what seemed like an eternity as he strained his ears, listening for any sign of commotion outside.

He felt his father's ring against his chest and he whispered a silent prayer. "Guide my blade," he asked his father. Then he emerged from the tent and went as quickly as he dared to the round topped tent. He checked around the front and spied a pair of guards standing there. Silently he backed away and snuck around to the back of the tent. He knelt down and grabbed the bottom of the canvas and sucked in a breath. From inside he heard a slow, rhythmic snore. He tugged the canvas up and slithered underneath.

The inside of the tent was darker than Erik expected. He sat on the dirt, completely motionless, almost afraid to breathe until his eyes adjusted well enough for him to see the snoring lump on a cot just a few paces away. Erik rose to his feet and slowly walked to the warlock. He drew his sword slowly, careful not to let the metal scrape against the scabbard and wake his foe. He gripped the sword so that he could bring the point straight down. He raised it up in front of him with both hands. Thoughts of his father in chains came to his mind then. The anger inside poured into the blade and the sword burst into white flames. The warlock opened his eyes, but Erik brought the blade down before the man could move. It pierced him through the chest and the fire engulfed the warlock.

"No!" the warlock screamed out. Erik removed the blade and backed away. His adrenaline surged through him, causing him to tremble slightly as his heart raced in his chest. To his horror, the warlock tried to stand. Erik rushed forward again and slashed down diagonally, severing the man in twain. An emerald amulet fell from the warlock's hand and bounced along the ground. The flames grew brighter and hotter, turning blue and then green. The canvas tent all at once burst into flame and suddenly Erik found himself surrounded by blinding flames. He turned for the front flaps just as the guards outside parted the burning flaps with their halberds.

Erik somersaulted between them and ran for all he was worth toward the forest. A flaming arrow went up into the sky. Shouts and bugles sounded through the air and all at once the camp came alive like a trampled ant-mound. Erik heard arrows zing by him and *thunk* into anyone foolish enough to chase him. A few moments later the ground shook as the tar-pots slammed into the camp, exploding furiously and wreaking havoc in the camp.

He almost made it to the forest when a sudden gust of wind knocked him to the ground. A maelstrom of green fireballs rained down from the sky above him. Erik looked on, petrified and breathless. He squirmed out of the way and did his best to dodge the magic missiles. One of them landed near enough that the explosion tossed him into the air, spinning him round as if he were cart-wheeling above the ground. He landed hard and felt a sting in his head. He struggled to move, but his eyelids grew heavy and then everything became dark.

*****

"Fire again!" Orres bellowed from atop the horse. From his vantage point, and with the added help of the tar-pots, he could see Lepkin running from the camp. He felt a surge of elation swell within him as the camp began to burn. "Well done," he said. Then his glee turned sour as he watched green fireballs streak down from the sky. "What is that?" he shouted to Wendal.

"Either the warlock lives, or they have others that can wield magic!" Wendal shouted. "We'll try to shield him!" Wendal and the other mages quickly weaved wards and shields around Lepkin as he jumped up and ran for the forest. Most of the green balls were deflected, but one managed to explode near him, sending him flying through the air.

"The enemy is upon him!" Orres shouted. He could see a throng of what looked to be at least fifty swordsmen running for Lepkin. He drew his sword and spurred his horse forward.

"Wait!" Wendal shouted, but Orres would not.

The large man galloped his horse over the dead corpses, weaving through the newly lit fires, and directly into the enemy group. He trampled several men under hoof and then leapt from the horse. Two more men fell down under his weight and he finished them with his sword. Orres grunted against his recent injuries, ignoring the tearing sutures and concentrating on the task at hand. He lashed out with his sword and took down another man with one blow, then flipped his sword around and stabbed into a man charging at him from behind. He tried to retrieve his sword, but it was stuck. He let go and grappled with the next foe by hand, wrestling an axe from the warrior and head butting him until he fell backward to the ground. He ducked under a quick slice and lashed out with a sideways chop of his axe. The swordsman yelled in agony and fell to the ground.

The group now fully encircled him. A trio of men cut down his horse and the throng pressed in close. Everyone stopped momentarily. Orres looked around at the faces before him. The nearby flames reflecting off their helmets and dirty, bloodstained armor. Then he let out a feral yell and charged to his right. With each swing of his axe another foe dropped. He could feel the sting of blades striking him, but he did not slow. Occasionally a fireball or arrow would drop someone around him, but he paid no mind to it. He just gave in to his rage. Like a bull he plowed through a dozen men before a spear pierced his side. He fell to his knees, still swinging his weapon and dropping those foolish enough to attack him from the front. Then another blow came to the back of his neck. As he fell down to the dirt the enemies trampled over him.

Orres grinned when he saw Lepkin duck into the forest. "You won't catch him now," he said.

"No," someone said from above him. "But I have you as a consolation." A sharp point pierced Orres' back and his grin froze on his face as he expired.

CHAPTER FIFTEEN

Erik ran through the woods. Sticks and twigs snapped under foot and the bushes and lower limbs of trees rustled and scraped against him as he forced his way through. Lady Arkyn ran above him in the trees, leaping from branch to branch with the grace of a squirrel. A mounted soldier entered the forest, charging straight for Erik. As the ranger launched from one tree to a new one she spun in midair and let loose a deadly arrow that pierced the rider through the neck and dropped him to the ground below in a gurgling heap. Lady Arkyn maneuvered back around just before landing on a thick branch and continuing after Erik.

Swordsmen crashed through the forest, stomping about heavily as they sprinted in. Lady Arkyn worked her bow furiously, dropping an enemy every couple of paces as she nimbly kept up with Erik below her. She had plenty of arrows, but there were simply too many foes to stop them all. Erik was starting to stumble, obviously still recovering from the magical blast that had exploded near to him.

A flash of light appeared then between the group and Erik. A mighty, bloodthirsty howl rent the air and a great, silver beast launched out from the light and tore into the nearest opponent. Lady Arkyn stopped on one foot, perching the other up on her straight leg for balance as she seized the moment to pick off several foes.

Arrows rained down, each one a shaft of whistling death that dropped a foe with ease. On the forest floor below, Silverfang did his work. Those men near enough to see the beast froze in place, staring at the snarling, bloody snout. A couple of the men squealed like children, but none of them moved. The wolf's spell had them petrified. Fangs flashed and tore the enemies down quickly, allowing Erik to finally put distance between himself and the enemy.

Erik stumbled out of the forest, breathing heavily and shaking his head. His toe slipped into a hole in the ground and he almost fell to his face, but a strong arm caught him and hoisted him up. He looked up to see Braun

"Is it done?" he asked.

Erik nodded. "The warlock is dead."

Braun steadied Erik on his feet and bent over to look into his face. "Are you certain?"

Erik shrugged. "Unless the man has a spell that can put him back together, he is finished."

"Back together?" Braun repeated curiously, then he leaned back. "Is he in pieces?"

Erik nodded slowly. "Split in two diagonally from shoulder to opposing hip," Erik replied. After a breath he added, "He was also on fire, from the sword."

"Well," Braun muttered. "I would wager that should do it." The tone in his voice was one of bewilderment, but Erik could sense the underlying pride in Braun's words as well. "Are you hurt badly?" he asked. "We saw the magical assault and feared the worst when you got hit."

"I'm alright," Erik said. "A little dazed, but I'll live."

Braun pulled him along to the other side of the house. Torches fully illuminated the scene before the manor. Gorin and several guards worked the catapults as quickly as they could. Demetrius was there also. Wendal and a few other mages were busy weaving spells and counteracting the enemy's magic. Several men from House Lokton's retinue were rushing about, hefting carts of clay pots filled with tar from the storage shed near the forge to the creaking catapults.

"The warlock is dead!" Braun shouted.

Everyone stopped just long enough to look back and hail Erik with a chorus of congratulatory shouts and cheers. Then a series of bells and gongs sounded around the manor and they all went back to their work.

"The warlock is dead, but the battle will be heavy tonight," Braun said.

A long faced man approached from the front of the manor and took Erik's chin in his hand, turning his head to the side. "You have a nasty gash here," the man said. "I can take care of that. Look into the torchlight for me." Erik did as he was told and the light made his eyes ache. He blinked against it, but the long faced man held him firm in the light. "Slight concussion too," he said. "Pupils are not reacting to the light evenly."

"Anything serious?" Braun asked.

The man shook his head. "No, I'll have him back on the field in a few minutes." Then he took Erik's arm and laid it around his shoulders. "Come with me, Master Lepkin," he said.

"I'm back to the battle," Braun announced. "See you when you are ready."

Erik offered a slight wave as the long faced man pulled him toward the house. They pushed through the doors and turned down the hall to the dining room. Erik looked around the room and noted that instead of food, the tables were covered with wounded men from the day's fighting. Many of them were asleep, but some were writhing in discomfort and moaning. The sight made Erik's heart heavy with sadness. He sighed deeply and turned to sit in a chair that the long faced man slid behind him.

A short, plump woman came forward. Erik could tell by her clothes that she was not from the academy, but he didn't know who she was exactly. Probably the wife of one of the men who served House Lokton, but that was only a guess.

"I thought we were done fightin' for the night," she scolded the long faced man. "Now I hear the alarms and you are bringing me more heads to sew together."

"War does not function on a convenient schedule," the long faced man said dryly. "Just bring me a bowl of water and some gauze."

The woman gave a hefty *harumpf!* and stormed off to fetch the supplies. She returned not a minute later with a small soup bowl and a blood crusted goblet stuffed with gauze and rags. "Here," she huffed as she shoved the items into Erik's hands. "I have more serious wounds to tend to." Then she turned and went back to a groaning man on a table nearby.

Erik leaned around the long faced man and watched the woman work, changing the blood soaked bandages for new ones. A rivulet of blood streamed out over the edge of the table and dripped onto the floor below. The plump woman cursed under her breath and furiously went to work applying pressure and shouting to another pair of women to come and help.

"Shouldn't you help him?" Erik asked the long faced man.

The man sighed and turned away to look. Then he summarily shook his head and went back to cleaning Erik's face. "No, he is already dead. He is just too stubborn to give up his ghost yet."

Erik jerked his head back and looked at the cold hearted man angrily. "Shouldn't you try?"

The man frowned. "I have seen more than a few battles, Master Lepkin. Obviously that bump on your head knocked your senses loose, otherwise you would see the logic of my words. In war you must be able to properly recognize those you can save from those who are too far gone. A proper triage center doesn't waste efforts on those who will expire."

"That's cruel," Erik whispered.

"War is cruel," the man repeated flatly. He then used a wet rag to wipe the last bit of blood from Erik's head before cupping his left hand over the wound. The man's eyes rolled back into his head slightly and his eyelids flittered as he mumbled words that Erik didn't understand. A warm, tingling sensation poured into his gash and he felt the skin sealing itself together. The fogginess in his head cleared away and he felt revitalized. A moment later the man pulled his hand away and dropped the dirty rags into the soup bowl. "You should be fit to return to the front," he declared.

"Why not use your magic on the others?" Erik insisted.

The man turned a crooked smile on him, the first sign of emotion that he had shown since Erik first saw him. "Surely you did take a heavy shot to the old noodle, didn't you?" he jested. "If my magic was powerful enough for the wounds these men bear, I would have helped them hours ago."

Erik stood up and left the room, barely pausing long enough to thank the man for helping him. He pushed out through the main door, his right hand sliding down for the hilt of his sword. Men ran back and forth in front of him, some carrying rocks and more tar-pots for the catapults, others rushing forward to the front lines. Captains shouted orders and soldiers grunted as they were quick to obey.

"Master Lepkin, we could use you at the front," Gorin bellowed above the din.

Erik nodded and broke into a run. He slid his sword out from the scabbard and called forth its fire. The night hung dark and heavy over the field. The few blazing fires served only to prevent his eyes from adjusting properly. It was hard for him to distinguish friend from foe, then he remembered his power. He summoned it forth, allowing his gift to highlight his enemies for him. A confident smile crossed his face and he rushed into the fray. He kept his breathing rhythmic and steady, calculating each swing of his flaming sword as the warriors closed in around him.

Gorin fought a few yards away, breaking down the enemy with his mighty hammer and working his way through, while Erik sliced and cut his way through the first wave of enemies. Thanks to his power, each enemy had a faint red glow about them, making it easy to spot them in the darkness. Flames hissed and roared, trailing behind each swing of his sword. Someone charged in with a high arching swing at Erik, but he quickly brought his sword up, catching the attack and flinging it to the side. Then he flicked his wrists, aiming the blade's point at his foe's chest and driving it through as easily as a hot knife through butter. The man's eyes went wide and he fell back to the ground.

Erik pressed on, sequestering his fear with each breath farther and farther to the back of his mind. He allowed only enough of it to remain so as to keep himself alert, otherwise he was in the moment, as Master Lepkin had taught him.

*****

Silvi ran to the burning tent and let out a horrified scream when she saw Gondok'hr's charred remains. As she surveyed the scene in unbelieving shock, her eye was caught by an emerald amulet reflecting the dying flames where the tent had stood. Sensing a subtle pulse of power, she went in quickly to retrieve it. Then she ran toward the rear to find Eldrik. Many of the warlocks were already engaging the enemy, but the sight of magic being used was causing more than a few of Eldrik's men to balk. When she finally found Eldrik, he was being confronted by several of his men.

"What evil is this?" one of the men shouted at Eldrik. "Where did these wizards come from?"

Silvi stepped forward, shouting over the men. "They are Senator Bracken's allies. That is all you need to know!"

"Horse-apples!" another shouted. "I am not throwing myself in with this lot. They aren't wizards, they're warlocks!

A third man added, "The mindless warriors and now the

wizards. It's unnatural."

Eldrik pushed Silvi behind him. "A battle rages behind us," he shouted. "We have come here to put down enemies of the crown, enemies of House Cedreau. Will you now abandon the oath you swore to me, to my father?"

"I promised you my blade, not my soul," the first man shouted back. Others joined in with him.

A large man broke through the throng. "Master Eldrik is the leader of House Cedreau now," he boomed. "I say any man willing to fight with him is a friend. We could use magic if we are to fight against the likes of Lepkin and others from Kuldiga Academy." A few of the men agreed with him.

"No," said the first. "I watched these other soldiers butcher Master Orres not more than a few minutes ago. This is not the fight I believed it to be."

"Master Orres fought against Senator Bracken," Silvi pointed out. "You saw him fall this day because he was a traitor."

The man spat on the ground. "I went through Kuldiga Academy during Orres' first year as headmaster. He was always a stubborn, proud man, but never a traitor. I am done here." The man turned and left.

"You can't let them leave," Silvi said.

Eldrik shrugged. "What should I do, turn on my own men? No, let them go." Then he turned to the men. "Those who wish to go may go, but you are no longer in the employ of House Cedreau. Gather your belongings and leave. You have no more place with me. The rest of you, those of you who honor your word, you are my brothers. Fight with me this night, and let us lay waste to Lokton Manor."

"For the honor of House Cedreau!" the large man shouted. Several others repeated the chorus. Some of the men went toward the back, obviously on their way out, but the majority of the group stayed true and moved forward. "Shall we march to the front?" the large man asked.

Eldrik glanced to Silvi and then turned to survey the battle. Occasional blasts of fire exploded on the ground just fifty yards away, obliterating man, tent, and horse alike. Some two hundred yards beyond that the rest of Bracken's forces were engaging the enemy. In the dark it was impossible to know who was winning.

He knew that Bracken's forces outnumbered House Lokton, and with the addition of his own army plus the warlocks it should be even more tipped in his favor, but he didn't know strategy very well.

Silvi approached him from the side. "If your men are good with bows, they could skirt around the forest edge to the north, and flank House Lokton's mages. They don't have many, just a handful of left over mages from the academy."

"The warlocks are already engaging the mages," Eldrik replied. Even as the words left his mouth, he could see the wisdom in her idea. He nodded and changed his mind. "Yes, that is a good plan." He turned back to his men. "Grab bows, sneak along the edge of the forest to the north and take out their mages. Afterward, make for the catapults. Destroy their ability to launch long ranged assaults."

The men cheered and sprinted off to accomplish their orders. Eldrik started to walk after them, but Silvi stopped him. "A general does not fight with the men," she said. "Leave the blood to them, yours is to observe and command."

"It would be better if Bracken were still alive," Eldrik admitted. "I have never commanded others in battle."

"I will be with you," she assured him. "Also, I thought you should have this." She pulled a great jewel from her robes.

"What is it?" Eldrik asked as he took the stone from her. He turned it over in his hands. The deep, vibrant green gem felt warm to the touch and had a glow about it. It was half as large as his hand, but it was not exceedingly heavy. The chain it hung from was severed in the back, but it appeared easy enough to exchange for a new one.

"I am not certain what it is," she said. "When I ran to Gondok'hr's tent, it was the only thing not consumed by the fire. I can feel magic inside of it. Strong magic."

Eldrik tucked it into his pocket. He looked up to the battle. Green, purple, and blue fireballs rained down from the night sky. Some dissipated as they struck invisible shields, others exploded in the air, but a few managed to wreak havoc on the men below. Both armies took heavy casualties from the magical missiles. He marveled at the power the mages and warlocks controlled. "I wish I could do something like that," he said.

"I will teach you," Silvi promised. "After this we will have time to train you properly."

"Can you cast any spells?" he asked. She looked at him curiously. "I mean, can you summon a great fireball to hit the house?"

"The house?" she echoed.

"If Erik's family is still inside, then striking the house may divert the enemy's attention."

Silvi took three steps forward and held both of her hands up to the sky. She muttered words in a tongue that Eldrik couldn't understand. Her head fell back and she shouted into the night, repeating the words over and over in a cadence.

A great light flashed high in the sky, up above the clouds. The ground shook as a wave of thunder rumbled down over the battle and a mass of churning, yellow flames tore through the clouds, descending toward the house. Frantic shouts filled the night and men scurried out of the way as the fire struck the far corner of the manor. Tile, stone and wood splintered apart, cracking and popping loud enough to be heard even where Eldrik stood. A thick wall of flames spread out around the area of impact until a third of the manor was ablaze. Shouts and agonized yells went up from the enemy and brought a great smile to Eldrik's face.

*****

Erik felt a wave of heat pass over him as a large fiery sphere devoured a portion of his home. Archers too slow to scramble out of the way vanished in an instant and others leapt from the roof out of desperation. Wood and shards of stone flew into the battlefield, ripping through several men and laying them low. One particularly large hunk of rock blasted through one of the catapults as it was in mid-launch. The tar pot shot up a few feet and then dropped back onto the catapult, drenching it and the crew around it in liquid fire.

"Go!" Gorin shouted from nearby. "We'll hold them off while you get everyone out!"

Erik nodded and sprinted for the house. A pair of axmen were foolish enough to try and stop him. Erik made quick work of them and continued on his way without losing a step. He ran as fast as he could, but Braun was already leaping up the steps to the front door, followed by a handful of footmen.

"Braun, use the tunnel!" Erik shouted. Braun turned and gave Erik a single nod.

"I'll get them out," he promised. "I'll meet you at the stables."

Erik shook his head. "No, stay in the tunnel," he shouted. "In the last chamber where you have a few weapons and armor, just before the exit to the stables. Stay down there and wait until it is over."

"I'm not leaving you to fight them by yourself," Braun replied hotly.

"Do it," Erik said.

Braun frowned, nodded, and then disappeared into the burning house. An arrow *zinged* by Erik's ear and he turned, expecting to see Lady Arkyn, but instead he saw an enemy soldier reloading his bow for another shot at him.

"They're coming from the north!" Erik shouted. He ran forward, somersaulting under the soldier's next shot and stabbing the man through the gut. Erik stood and surveyed the scene quickly. To the west Gorin was leading the defense. He was heavily outnumbered, but managing to hold the front. To the north, Demetrius and his catapult crew were busy defending themselves from a group of twenty while the mages from the academy were caught between the enemy warlocks and a large force pouring out of the forest to the north. Erik made a split decision to attack the enemy warlocks.

He ran forward as quickly as his legs would propel him. Arrows flew by him, but this time they came from the direction of the house and bit into the enemy. He guessed Lady Arkyn had seen him and was lending her support. A warlock turned to face Erik. A swirling green snake of fire coiled before the man. Just as he moved to send the spell, an arrow sunk into his forehead. The spell fizzled and the warlock fell backward.

The next warlock threw a large spike of ice, but Erik sliced through it with his flaming sword, instantly melting the spell. The water harmlessly splashed onto his chest as he ran forward and drove his sword into the warlock's chest. The warlock dropped to his knees, snarling and cursing as he fell. Erik pulled his sword free just in time to block a warrior's axe as he came in with a diagonal chop aimed for Erik's neck. Erik stepped back and swung horizontally, catching the axman's hip with the top third of his flaming blade. The man lurched forward and twisted, trying to close his wound. Erik then reversed and brought his sword back to finish the man with a quick slice through the neck. Then armor and bodies slammed together as House Lokton warriors rushed around Erik to engage the warlocks and enemy warriors with him.

The battle raged furiously for hours. Arrows flew into both armies, cutting them down considerably, but neither force gave any ground. Blades rang out until the dawn light broke in the east and sent the first golden rays down to the field.

Bodies and limbs covered the ground like thick leaves dropped in an autumn forest. The blood painted the ground scarlet and the last wisps of smoke from the previous day's fires gasped their dying breaths up into the early morning breeze.

Erik's muscles ached and begged for respite. His eyes stung, pierced by the bright rays of the early sun mixed with the salty sweat from his brow. His right shoulder was almost numb now, and he had to fight gripping the sword with two hands for his waning strength. The others around him were equally as tired. The shouts and grunts were no less savage, but the pace with which the soldiers swung at each other had lessened considerably. Even the mages who still stood now went several minutes between spells. Many of them had even resorted to using daggers and short swords as they grew too weary to cast their spells. Arrows overhead were scarce now. The archers had joined the main fighting sometime in the night. Erik had seen Lady Arkyn fighting her way toward Gorin, but that had been a long time ago.

Erik forced himself to concentrate on the pocket of warriors in front of him. He staggered forward, picking each swing and strike of his sword carefully to ensure each expenditure of energy either took a foe, or prevented a strike from killing him. The men at his side pounded forward with him, beating the remainder of the group before them back until they broke ranks and ran for the forest.

His men gave a shout and waved their swords triumphantly. Erik gave a weak half-hearted smile and watched the seven swordsmen tucking tail and sprinting for the forest. Then he turned back to survey the rest of the battle. The men to the west were still engaged in combat. He watched for a few moments until he spied Gorin, still at the front of the line and still powering through the enemy ranks. Lady Arkyn was nearby, flashing bright crimson scimitars and dropping enemies as effortlessly as if she had started fighting only a minute before. Eventually the enemy broke on the west as well and ran back for their camp.

The men near Erik let out another chorus of triumphant shouts. This time the men on the field echoed the shouts and banged their swords against their shields. A hand fell on Erik's shoulder and he turned to see Demetrius standing near him. The man had blood oozing from under the sleeve on his right arm, but he didn't appear to be bothered by it.

"We did our best, but the catapults have been destroyed," he said.

Erik looked back and saw that all of the machines were broken and torn down. Heaps of bodies piled around each one. "I'm sure you did your best," Erik said. "What of the wind-lance?"

Demetrius shook his head. "They got to it too."

Erik nodded and looked back to the west. "Then let us hope there are no dragons in our future," he said under his breath.

"From what I can tell," Demetrius continued. "We have no more knights. I believe we are down to footmen only, so we cannot give chase to the enemy without risking our men."

Erik nodded and looked back to the manor. "We need to find Braun," he said. He stood, watching the flames eat through the last portions of the once great manor. "I have failed," Erik said.

Demetrius slapped Erik's back. "A house is but stone and wood," he said. "We can rebuild that easily enough. We fight to protect lives." The big man turned and walked away after that, leaving Erik staring at the wasted house.

"Go, get some rest," Erik told the others.

"Shouldn't we set a perimeter?" one of the men asked.

Erik nodded. "We are going to fall back to the stables, we can set lookouts in the trees to the north of the stables, and some more to the south."

"We will do it," another said.

"You all fought well," Erik said. "You have earned your rest."

They all protested. "No, we'll rest when the fight is over."

Erik nodded and made his way out to find Gorin and Lady

Arkyn. Men hailed him and clapped him on the back as he passed. Some shouted adulations, others simply smiled, but Erik could not share in their revelry. His hand went up to touch the ring hanging around his neck. *I did my best, father.* He recalled his father's smile as he had shared an orange with him in the solarium. Erik looked to the spot where that room had been. Now only a few beams and smoldering piles of ash remained. He could hardly imagine his father smiling now.

Lady Arkyn appeared before him and pulled him from his thoughts. "I asked if you were alright?" she said with a hint of impatience in her voice.

"What?" Erik asked. He hadn't noticed her approach. Erik looked to her with a long face. "I am fine," he said flatly. "Could you and Gorin make the casualty report? I need to find Braun and make sure they made it out of the manor."

"They are alright," Lady Arkyn assured him. She gently grabbed his shoulder and turned him toward the stable. "There is Braun, and Lady Lokton is a few steps behind him."

Erik turned and a wave a relief washed over him when he saw them. He fell to his knees and tears filled his eyes. He clutched the ring through his shirt and let out a long sigh as he tried to choke back his emotion.

Lady Arkyn glanced to Gorin who only shrugged.

"Not exactly what I expected from the great living legend," Gorin jabbed.

Erik paid him no heed. He wiped his eyes and put his left hand to the ground next to him. He thought to explain himself, but chose not to. He wasn't sure he would know what words to say anyway. How could he explain what he had been through over the last few weeks?

"Gorin, go and make the casualty report," Lady Arkyn said firmly. Gorin marched away dutifully without another word. Then Lady Arkyn bent down and placed her scimitar on the ground before her. "You are different," she said tenderly. "If I didn't know better, I would say you were not Master Lepkin."

Erik looked up and smiled in spite of everything. "Who else should I be?" A tear slid down his left cheek.

Lady Arkyn looked to the burnt manor, then back to Erik. "I wonder what Master Lepkin's pupil would feel like now, at this moment?"

Erik remained silent, trying to understand whether she had guessed who he was.

She offered him a smile and patted his shoulder. "I would imagine it would be a bit overwhelming."

Erik nodded. "It is," he admitted.

"Still," she said as she rose to her feet, grabbing her scimitar and swirling it back into its scabbard. "I think *if* he were here, he would have fought like a lion." She reached down and offered him a hand.

Erik took it and she helped him to his feet. "Like a lion?" he echoed with a hint of a grin on his face.

Lady Arkyn shrugged. "Maybe like a dragon." She poked his chest. "You have a strong heart," she said.

Erik opened his mouth to speak, but Braun came up and interrupted.

"You alright?" he asked hastily.

Erik nodded. "I will be," he said. Erik looked back to his adoptive mother. "Is she alright?"

Braun shrugged. "Honestly, I am not sure. She hasn't said much of anything since we went into the tunnel."

"Come with me, Braun, there is something I want to tell her."

"I'll go and find Maser Wendal," Lady Arkyn said.

Erik was already walking toward the stable. He saw his adoptive mother standing, leaning on the entrance in a long black dress. The bottom of the skirt was smudged with dirt and a couple shafts of straw clung to the cloth. Her face was stoic, but Erik could almost feel her heavy heart as if it beat in his own chest.

"Are you sure this is wise?" Braun asked. "You haven't told anyone else, what if…"

"It may not be wise, but it feels right," Erik said with a quick shrug. "I only hope she won't hate me."

Braun gripped Erik's shoulder tight and spun him around. "None of this is your fault. Not your father's death, not this battle, none of it."

"All of it is my fault," Erik replied bitterly. "Unless you know of another son born to my father, I am the curse. The warlock was right." Braun stepped back and Erik walked away, leaving the man standing baffled. As he approached the stable a pair of footmen came out to greet him. One held a water skin and the other held a loaf of bread. He waved them off and went straight to his adoptive mother.

"It was a great house," she told him as he came close.

Erik turned and looked once more at the charred remains of his home. "Yes it was," he agreed. He turned back to her and stammered through an apology.

"What have you to be sorry for?" she asked.

"I have failed to protect us," Erik said. His hand went for his necklace and pulled his father's ring from under his shirt. He brought it up over his head and held the ornament in his right palm. "I took a vow to serve the family, but I have repaid you only with blood."

Lady Lokton stepped forward and took the ring from him. She slipped it onto her thumb. "This ring was given to him by his father, who received it from his father before him," she said. "My husband was a strong believer in family." She looked up with the first smile on her face that Erik had seen since arriving. "That's why we chose to adopt," she said. "He felt like a failure for not being able to produce his own heir, but eventually he warmed to the idea of adopting another as our own."

Erik stared at the ring while he tried to formulate his next sentence. How could he ask for her forgiveness? How could he face her now?

She stepped forward and placed the ring back into his hand. "You make sure this gets back to my son," she instructed him. "He should know how proud we are of him."

"Even now?" Erik ask, bewildered.

She nodded. "Even now," she said. "He was the only one we felt connected to. My husband loved him as much if not more than he could have ever loved another child. I do too."

"But, everything is destroyed," Erik protested.

"No," Lady Lokton reassured him. "Everything is not lost. You make sure my son fulfills his destiny. I will see my husband again in the halls of his fathers in Volganor, of that I am sure. Just as the sun brought victory to us this morning, there will be a new dawn to chase away the night from my heart, in time."

Erik stood speechless. He slowly put the ring back around his neck and tucked it under his shirt.

"I'm sure Master Lepkin will pass your message along," Braun said as he came up from behind.

"Yes," Erik said with a nod. "I will see he gets it."

Lady Lokton's smile faded and she looked past them to the house. "Braun, I am sorry I didn't listen to you before. I should have gone with the caravan from here."

"It's not too late," Braun said.

Erik placed a hand on Braun's shoulder. "Braun, go and lead the caravan out. Go as quickly as you can to Drakei Glazei. I am sure the king will provide shelter."

"I should stay with you," Braun protested.

"No," Erik replied. "Your place is with Lady Lokton and the others of the house. Go, and take enough men to make sure you reach Drakei Glazei."

"What about you?" Lady Lokton asked.

Erik looked out behind him. "I have a feeling the enemy will make another run at us. I and the other masters will stand here and finish the fight." A vein in Braun's forehead popped out and throbbed as he stared hard at Erik, but Erik shrugged and offered a smile. "We'll be alright," he assured him.

"Come, Braun, let's not waste time. There are many other women here who should go with us."

"Very well, milady," Braun said. He stayed a moment longer, making sure his disagreement registered with Erik, and then he followed after Lady Lokton, bellowing out orders for preparations to be made.

Erik crouched down and leaned back against the stable wall, watching the field to the west. A footman came and plopped some food and drink before him without a word, and then continued on with whatever he had been doing. Erik slowly ate the bread as he scanned the skies. "If only I could turn back into a dragon," he said between bites. "Then I could end this fight."

He closed his eyes and went inside his mind, accessing his power and trying to call forth the power of the dragon form. Nothing happened. He continued to meditate for several minutes, but instead of assuming the form of a dragon, sleep overtook him as exhaustion finally was allowed to surface and his muscles submitted to the battle fatigue.

"This is a disaster!" Eldrik shouted. "The men are routing!"

"Not to worry," Silvi assured him. "We still have our last hundred in reserve. Have them form up behind the crest of the hill. When our men see them, I will cast a spell to give them courage. We will let them rest for a time, allowing the enemy to think they won. Then, we shall strike at midday when our men are fresh."

Eldrik threw his hands up. "Or perhaps I should take my true form and show them the sharpness of my fangs!" he growled.

Silvi rubbed his arm with her left hand and looked into his eyes. "You are strong," she said. "But you are still green. You are not ready for such a task."

Eldrik pulled away from her. "Fine. Cast your courage spell and bring the men back to the camp." He stormed off through the camp passing by groups of mindless soldiers that hardly acknowledged him. "What good are these men to me?" he grumbled.

"My lord!" someone shouted from afar off. Eldrik turned to see one of his warriors running for him. "We have suffered heavy losses," the man shouted.

Eldrik stopped and waited for the man to approach. He recognized his face, but he couldn't quite remember the man's name. Eldrik thought perhaps it was Mendael, or Maebel, but he couldn't be certain. "What is the report?" Eldrik asked.

"The mages that joined us, only seven of them remain. Of our numbers, we lost seventy."

"So we are down to fifty-seven?" Eldrik calculated.

The man shook his head. "No, there were twenty who abandoned the fight when they saw the mages. We have only thirty-seven left."

"There is another hundred in reserve," Eldrik said.

The man's head snapped back in shock. "Why didn't you send them in to the fight?"

Eldrik didn't want to admit that the men would not listen to him. So he ignored his warrior's question. "We also have the remainder of the men from the front. Go and count our total numbers and come and report back to me."

The man nodded crookedly and turned on his heels.

Eldrik returned to his tent and threw himself face-down on his cot. The thin boards creaked and groaned under his weight, but the bed held. A moment later he heard the tent flap open and someone walked in. He turned to see Silvi smiling at him.

"What do you want?" he asked.

"I thought you might need the company," she said as she coyly stalked up to the side of his bed and knelt beside him. She stroked his hair to the side and bit her lower lip. "Many great men face setbacks in the time before their rise." She took in a deep breath. "Have you heard of Gokal the Blooded? He suffered thirty military defeats before he was able to found his mighty empire in the south."

"And then one hundred years later his empire was overrun with orcs," Eldrik countered.

Silvi laughed. "Well, Lucien the First suffered from the shaking disease. That's why he held court behind closed doors, and commanded battles from inside a great tent. His was a mighty empire. It lasted centuries, and many of its traditions permeated even the farthest corners of our world."

"Bracken is dead," Eldrik said suddenly, cutting off the conversation. "I do not have the experience to command a battle."

"But the enemy is weak now," Silvi said. "We still outnumber them, but now they are worn down and we can crush them with our fresh reserves. As soon as our other warriors have rested, we can run them down. I have finished my spell on the reserve as well. They will listen to you now."

Eldrik shook his head. "We shall see," he said. "I thought this would be much easier, especially with our warlocks, but they lack the strength to fight and their spells are not as wonderful as I had believed."

"We live in an imperfect world," Silvi noted. "As such, magic is as prone to faults as is any endeavor of the flesh, but I assure you that we still have great strength. We have crippled the enemy."

The tent flap opened and in walked a stone-faced lieutenant. Eldrik raised his head from the bed and noted that it was not one of his men, but one of Bracken's.

"You are the commander now?" the man asked.

Eldrik pushed himself up and turned to face the lieutenant. "I am," he said.

"We have eighty-nine men who survived the skirmish," he said. "Add this to the thirty-seven men remaining from your army and the hundred in reserve and we have a total of two hundred twenty six men."

"I don't suppose you know how many warriors the enemy has?" Eldrik chided.

"Seventy three, except they are preparing a caravan and several soldiers are departing with them. Our scouts will have the exact count soon."

"Who is in the caravan?" Eldrik demanded.

"The womenfolk, and a few guards as escorts. Masters Lepkin, Gorin, and Wendal remain with Lady Arkyn and the main body of the army."

"Are those the only masters left?" Silvi asked.

The man nodded grimly. "Shall I have the reserves prepare?" he asked Eldrik.

Eldrik nodded. "That would be helpful."

CHAPTER SIXTEEN

Erik woke to the frantic shouts above him. People ran to and fro before him, scrambling to man the crude picket line they had apparently erected during his nap. Clanking armor and bandaged bodies filed out of the stable. For all of the shuffling about, Erik's view was completely blocked, but judging from everyone's grim faces, something was very wrong.

His first thoughts went to the dragon he had seen in the warlock's house. He jumped to his feet and involuntarily let out a sigh of relief when he failed to spy anything more than a couple of buzzards circling the area.

"Lepkin, up here," Lady Arkyn called out. Erik turned and went up a ladder that she dropped for him from the stable's roof. As he neared the top rung he turned and his mouth dropped. A man bearing the colors of House Cedreau rode at the front of an army easily more than four times the size of what he had left. "We have fifty men," Lady Arkyn said as if reading his thoughts. "Braun led twenty others out with the caravan about an hour ago." She squinted her eyes for a moment and scanned the oncoming army. "They have more than two hundred."

"I thought killing the warlock would give us a better advantage," Erik admitted.

"We are not dead yet," Gorin gruffed from below.

"Nor shall we be," Lady Arkyn said. She put an arrow to her bow string and aimed high into the sky.

"Can you hit the man in front?" Erik said.

"I can try," she said. She stood up to her full height and set the arrow loose. The missile flew high into the midday clouds and disappeared only to arc down and stick in the ground well short of its mark. "Too far," Lady Arkyn said.

Erik hooked his feet around the outer edges of the ladder and used the leather around his forearms to buffer his skin as he slid down the ladder. He straightened his sword belt and gave Gorin a nod. "Let's finish this."

Gorin nodded and the two walked to the front of the line. Erik looked to his right and left. Thin, hastily carved pikes jutted out from the ground like jagged fangs of some wild beast, but Erik knew they would not deter the enemy.

"We slaughtered them," Gorin commented. "For every one of ours that fell we dropped at least five of theirs, yet they still come at us."

"They are determined," Erik replied.

"You know, Lepkin, I heard about what you did at Valtuu Temple." Gorin turned and looked into Erik's eyes. "I also heard Lady Arkyn's account of what happened at the senate hall." He paused and looked back to the approaching army. "If there was ever a time to use your dragon form, now would be it."

"It is not so simple," Erik said. He completely agreed, but he had no idea how he had unlocked Lepkin's power before, nor did he have the time now to fumble around with it. The marching feet pounded the earth before them. They moved as one being, each of them in lockstep with the other. As they neared they started to beat their swords, axes, and spears against their shields. The terrible rhythm sent chills down Erik's spine, yet he stood firm and drew his sword. He unleashed the sword's magical flame and held his weapon at the ready.

"They look to be in range now," Gorin said. Erik nodded. Gorin turned and gave a sharp gesture with his left arm. Lady Arkyn and three others, for that was all the archers the army had left, drew their bows back and let their arrows fly. Two men in the front fell as the shafts beat down upon them. The enemy army marched on, paying the archers almost no mind at all. As Lady Arkyn and the others continued to fire, the enemy was able to defend themselves easily enough for the most part. Only a handful of men had fallen by the time the army came within fifty yards of Erik and his men.

A mighty wave of shouts and roars rippled forth from the enemy and they charged in. Erik held his sword up in a high guard, preparing for his final battle.

Gorin stepped forward and yanked the pike nearest him out of the ground and heaved it with all of his strength. The point drove through several men and pinned them to the ground like writhing rabbits on a spit. Gorin smiled, pleased with his work. "That will put a damper in their spirits!" A chorus of cheers went up from Erik's men. Gorin pulled his mighty hammer from its harness and went back to Erik's side.

Then the enemy was upon them like a tidal wave crashing onto a beach of stone. Bodies flew every which way as swords and axes found their marks, men rammed into each other using shields or their own armored shoulders as they ripped into one another. Erik managed to drop a couple of soldiers before being pushed back by the sheer force and momentum of the opposing group. The wooden pikes snapped and splintered, some of them catching an enemy warrior like a stuck pig, others being cleaved down by axes or swords.

The enemy force fanned out, spreading around Erik and his men, closing them in and grinding them down. Comrades fell around Erik, but others quickly stepped in to take their places and fill the gaps. House Lokton's men fought gallantly that day, but it was not enough. Slowly, the fifty men became thirty, and then twenty. Finally, there were twelve, including Erik, Masters Gorin and Wendal, and Lady Arkyn. They all fought near each other, helping to guard each other's backs when danger struck close.

Wendal weaved lightning in and around their circle, frying scores of men who came too near. Any that managed to slip through the spells were quickly squashed by Gorin's hammer or cut down by Lady Arkyn's flashing scimitar. Erik also racked up a number of fallen foes as his flaming sword devoured many warriors.

A whirlwind tore through the enemy army and blasted the group of twelve apart, flinging each off separately. Erik caught a glimpse of Master Wendal throwing a counter spell at the enemy warlocks, but a sword pierced Wendal's chest before he could finish and he fell to the ground. A group of seven jumped on Gorin, pounding on the giant man furiously so that Erik was sure he was also dead. He couldn't see anyone else. He struggled to his feet just in time to see a spear flying for his chest. Reflexively he flipped his sword around and managed to catch the spear's tip. While he evaded the deadly part, the tail end of the spear whipped around and split his upper lip open.

A warrior rushed in, and was a breath away from finishing Erik with a mighty chop of his axe when a dwarf appeared out of nowhere and drove a war hammer into the man's chest. Erik stumbled back a few feet with eyes wide and his mouth hanging open. The dwarf was riding some kind of large lizard!

A bugle blast made Erik turn around and he saw an entire army of dwarves slithering through the field around him to tear into the enemy. He spun back around and watched as the dwarves cut the enemies down left and right. One dwarf even rode his lizard under a horse and struck up into the horse's belly with a spear while the lizard tore one of the horse's legs clean off in its jaws. The rider was flung to the ground and barely managed to scream before another lizard bit into his neck and the dwarf rider thrust a spear into his chest.

"What in the…" Erik muttered as he staggered back. He wasn't sure whether to run or join in the fight. He had never seen anything so gruesome and brutal in his life. The lizards moved as quickly as any horse he had ever seen, and they were as vicious as their riders, eager to tear into anything near enough to its jaws.

"Cavedogs!" Gorin shouted as he threw off the last warrior from his back. He pumped a large fist into the air and gave a sharp whistle. "The dwarves have come for you!" he taunted the enemy.

Erik was happy to see Gorin was still alive, if a little worse for wear. A streak of blood covered the left side of his head and he was obviously limping as he moved to fetch his hammer. Erik looked around for Lady Arkyn, but he saw something else first.

One of the dwarves carried a strange, yet familiar banner over his head. The banner's field was golden yellow with the simple, yet exquisite image of a dragon in full roar emblazoned in black. Red flames flew forth from its mouth and a series of runes were written beneath. As his eyes took in the runes, a fire grew within his breast. Somehow he knew this image, and he understood the words.

"Sharukan em nah'kunah," he said. The fire in his chest expanded and grew into the deepest parts of his soul before exploding out into his limbs. Bones stretched and skin covered itself in scales as it stretched over new muscles. A pair of wings poked through his back and spread wide over the field. His mouth elongated and grew enormous fangs while his fingers became sharp talons and claws.

Erik let out a deafening roar that forced all but the dwarves to cover their ears and shy away. As before, his senses were heightened, and he was able to see the battle clearly. In an instant he slashed down with his mighty talons and took seven men to their doom. Then he leapt forward, beating his great wings twice to fly beyond the dwarves and cut off the enemy's retreat. His hot breath spewed death over the last of the enemy warlocks and took several warriors down with them. Something poked his hind leg so he turned and swatted the spearman down with his tail, crushing the man like a dry twig. The cave dogs rushed in, weaving around and under him as he continued to terrorize the battlefield and eradicate the enemy.

With his keen sight, he saw the man on horseback bearing House Cedreau's colors turn and leave, along with a woman at his side. He thought to devour them as well, but like his senses, his power of discernment was increased as well and when he looked at the fleeing pair, he saw something that compelled his mercy. So he turned his attention to the warriors underfoot and let the retreating pair escape to the forest on the western side of the field.

All around him the dwarves whooped and hollered as they cut through the enemy ranks. Erik crushed opponents by the dozen, swatting others into oblivion with his tail or disintegrating scores of helpless men before him. Lady Arkyn and Gorin were standing at the back of the field, near the stable with mouths agape and wide eyes, but Erik paid them little mind other than to see that they were safely away from the last of the fight.

Axes and spears broke against his thick scales, as though each one was a shield of the best steel backed by muscles of iron and bones of granite. The enemy soon broke rank and tried to escape, but those who were lucky enough to escape Erik's wrath lived only long enough to be run down by the dwarves and their savage cavedogs.

As the fighting wound down and the last of the enemy lay on the ground, Erik turned about to scan the field. His heart was still heavy as he looked over the remains of his house and the many who had died in his defense, but it was not the same as before. In his dragon form it was easier for him to distance himself from the emotions and accept the events as they had transpired. He turned and started to walk back toward the stable, but stopped when a dwarf approached.

It was the dwarf who held the golden banner of the dragon. The dwarf's long, white beard was stained with blood, but the banner he held was still clean, flapping in the morning wind. The dwarf looked up to Erik with wise, deep blue eyes and smiled.

"My name is Alferug," the dwarf said telepathically. "I am Al's friend, and he has told me about your plight."

Erik nodded and a tendril of smoke slithered out from his nostrils. "How is Al?" Erik asked in his mind, hoping he was communicating correctly.

Alferug smiled, showing that he had heard Erik's thoughts. "Al now sits upon the throne of Roegudok Hall. The dwarf folk have their proper leader."

Erik's leathery lips tightened over his fangs in what could only be recognized as a smile. "That is good. So he has the scale?"

Alferug shook his head. "I have the scale with me, and I wait to go to Valtuu Temple with you to end your plight."

Erik hardly scanned the dwarf for more than a second before he knew he could trust him. His dragon form easily saw into the dwarf's soul. Erik turned his eye back to the banner. "What is that you carry?"

Alferug smiled. "It is the symbol of the Ancients, a sacred flag that was given to us after the founding of Roegudok Hall."

"The runes below, they are familiar to me," Erik said. "But I do not remember what they mean."

Alferug's smile widened. "From the flames I am born, on the wings of eternity I fly," Alferug said. "That is what they mean. It is an ancient phrase passed to us from the Ancients."

Erik nodded his massive head. "It is time to return to the temple," he said.

Alferug nodded. "When Lepkin is in dragon form, Nagar's Secret is able to control him. How is it with you?" he asked.

"I feel nothing, other than peace and confidence with my strength," Erik said.

"There is no evil entering into your mind?" Alferug pressed.

Erik shook his great head. "I am the same in this form as I am when in my normal form."

Alferug nodded and looked to the others with him "They will follow you," he said. "Al has sent us to escort you."

Erik looked off to the east, extending his neck to its full height and peering out over the vast carpet of green trees to the horizon. "Why should we walk, when I can fly?" he asked.

"You could fly for a short while, I am sure, but it is not wise,"

Alferug cautioned. "Until you have passed through the Exalted Test of Arophim, you should take care not to over extend yourself."

Erik looked to the scale. "When you use your magic, I will no longer be able to use this form." He sighed and a bit of flame spat from his mouth to dissipate in the air. "There is something familiar about this, and I do not want to give it up just yet."

Alferug shrugged, but did not answer.

Erik looked down to the dwarf's eyes and saw that the creature was holding something back. "What is it that you know that I do not?" Erik asked.

"Do not ask me now," Alferug begged. "Trust me a little while longer, and I will tell you in due time."

With his heightened perception, Erik knew that Alferug was not hiding it out of spite or malice, so he relented and did not press the subject further. "Give me a few minutes then," Erik said. "Often I have gazed at the birds and wondered what it was like to fly. I would fly now, and feel it for myself."

"I do not think that would be…" Alferug stopped his protest. Erik wasn't listening anyway.

The great dragon sat back on his hind legs and leapt up into the air. A powerful rush of air flattened the grass and bent the nearby trees. Dust and small rocks kicked up into the air and the dwarves all covered their eyes until Erik was high enough that his wings did not disturb them.

The circling buzzards scattered away as Erik climbed up into the sky. Each beat of his massive wings propelled him up fifty yards. He smiled wide and let out a mighty roar, relishing the rush of the wind on his face and the utter feeling of power and control he felt as the world fell away underneath him. Soon he was parallel with, and then far above the mountaintops in the distance. The clouds became his playground and he looped and soared through them.

Despite his altitude, he could clearly see the impatient dwarves below him, waiting for him to return and continue on with his duties. He understood their urgency, but he felt he deserved this reprieve. He streaked through the sky, out to the west. His keen eyes spotted rabbits and deer below through clearings in the canopy of trees. Then he circled back toward the north and let himself glide on the wind. He closed his eyes and let the experience completely envelope him.

Then something else came over him. He couldn't identify the feeling exactly. It was heavy, foreboding. It reminded him of the nights when he had to go into the basement. The feeling he would get as he blew out the last lantern below and only the light from the door above lit his way. The same hair-raising feeling of darkness encroaching on him from behind nagged him now. He opened his eyes, but the world was a bright as it had been only a moment before, yet the feeling remained.

Was this the power of the book? Was Nagar's Secret reaching out to snare him as well? He wasn't sure, but he knew it was time to change back. He dropped down suddenly, turning his wings up at the last moment so that he landed as gracefully as a sparrow upon a tree branch.

He then spied Alferug. "How do I change back?" he asked him with his thoughts.

Alferug frowned. "Think of the runes I will show you," he replied. The next mental image that came was a series of golden runes. As had happened before, they were familiar, and Erik was able to understand their sounds even without comprehending their meaning. As soon as he pictured them in his mind again, a warm, tingling sensation overcame him and he found himself standing on the ground, back in Lepkin's human form.

"We should get moving," Alferug said.

"We will go with you," Lady Arkyn said as she and Gorin approached.

"No, for now we should part ways," he said. "Go and catch up with Braun. Take any survivors we have left with you. I must go to the temple alone."

"We will be with him," Alferug said quickly.

Lady Arkyn nodded. "I have heard of you, Alferug," she said respectfully. "I was saddened when the dwarves turned away from their traditions."

Alferug grinned wide and folded his thick arms. "I am pleased to report that a new king sits on the throne, and the dwarves have returned to their traditions," he said emphatically.

"Who is king of the dwarves?" Gorin asked.

"Al, my friend," Erik answered quickly.

Alferug nodded. "Aldehenkaru'hktanah Sit'marihu, the rightful heir has taken the throne and now Roegudok Hall has pledged its support to King Mathias in this time of great need."

Gorin smiled and held out his hand to Erik. "Until we meet again, Master Lepkin," he said.

Erik took the hand in his and gave it a hearty shake. "We will see each other soon, I am sure of it."

Lady Arkyn then stepped forward and looked into Erik's eyes. "I wish you luck," she said. The tone in her voice clued Erik in to the fact that she had something else on her mind, but he did not press her to discover what it was.

"And I wish you the best," Erik replied.

"Come," said a red-bearded dwarf hotly. "We have a long road, and I would wager there will be more enemies between us and the temple."

"Faengoril is right," Alferug said. "We should be off."

*****

Gilifan emerged from the forest and surveyed the scene before him. Crows, buzzards, and eagles squabbled with each other over carcasses in the late afternoon sun. Burnt tents and bits of wood and metal lay scattered over what must have been a camp the day before. Gilifan strode through the mess, carefully picking his way through so as to avoid dirtying the bottom of his robes. A pack of wolves chased the vultures away from a horse carcass and began to feast upon the fallen. Beyond them, wisps of smoke lingered in the air above the razed manor.

The wizard barely recognized Gondok'hr's body when he found it. The two halves were horribly charred and mangled, but he knew it was him. He could still feel the remnants of his last breath lingering in the area around his body.

"Pity," Gilifan said coolly. "I would not have let you off so easily had I found you first," he said. The necromancer conjured forth a large, wooden staff and used it to overturn the burnt rubble around him. "Where did your little kobold friend put my amulet?" he asked as he searched the area. After several minutes he even used his staff to turn over Gondok'hr's remains and peer underneath, but the amulet was nowhere to be found.

Frustrated, Gilifan slammed his staff in the ground and a mighty ring coursed out through the field as though he had struck a great gong. The ring echoed off a few areas on the field, including Gondok'hr's body. Gilifan went quickly and searched each area where the sound had reverted back to him, but he found only the corpse of mages and warlocks. He struck the ground again, sending out his locator spell, but it only bounced off the bodies he had already searched. There was no other magical presence to be found.

"Who took it?" he grumbled. "Who would dare steal from Gilifan?" He turned about, scanning the area around the manor once more. Seeing that the stable was still intact, he went inside and located a stall near the back where he felt secluded.

He drew a circle around himself on the ground and tapped it three times. "Tu'luh, master of the night, and the great commander of death, hear me," Gilifan said. He tapped the ground once more and a hiss of black fire rose from the circle to enclose him, but the flames were not hot. They were as cold as ice and they damaged not a thing around him. As the cylinder rose up over his head he felt the ground sink beneath him and give way, revealing a vast, empty void of darkness. Into the darkness his body descended slowly, like a leaf falling gently from a tree.

A voice rumbled through the darkness. "I trust you have a good reason for disturbing me."

Gilifan bowed his head reverently and respectfully put his staff behind him. "Gondok'hr has failed to slay the boy," he said.

"Mmm," the voice hissed. "And he has betrayed you, has he not?"

"Yes, Master Tu'luh, he stole my amulet from me."

"No matter now," Tu'luh replied. "His shortcomings have already been rewarded."

"Master, I cannot raise the army without the amulet," Gilifan said.

Tu'luh sighed slowly, shaking the void with the thunderous roll of his breath. "Get yourself out of the Middle Kingdom," Tu'luh commanded.

"Shall I return to Kuressar?" Gilifan asked.

"No," the dragon replied directly. "Abandon the island and go to our friends in the south. There you will find refuge, and we shall meet in my home in due time."

"What of the boy?" Gilifan asked. "Shouldn't I try to finish this?"

"I will see to him myself. I am almost ready to make my move."

"And what of Kuressar, I was amassing forces there," Gilifan said.

"Leave your puppets there to watch over the island if you must, but do not send them anywhere else. Gondok'hr has exposed our northern position too much with his failures. Let the humans scramble to hold the kingdom while we come up from the south with our other allies."

"By your command," Gilifan pledged. "I will go to them straightaway."

"Good," Tu'luh said. "See that they prepare to march on Ten Forts before the last sun of the summer sets."

"It will be done," Gilifan promised.

A great *whoosh* of air sucked him back upward and within an instant he was again standing on solid ground. The black flames around him shrank back to the dirt and faded without sound. The necromancer took in a deep breath to clear his head, and then he exited the stable. He was anxious to obey, but he was not keen on letting the boy escape so easily.

His mouth turned up into a wicked grin at the corners when his eyes once again fell upon the wolves. He brought forth his staff and uttered an ancient, dark spell to transform them. Each animal grew four times larger in size. The fangs elongated and the claws grew sharper, like daggers. A pair of leathery wings burst from their backs and they howled in hungry delight. They turned their depraved eyes on Gilifan and charged him in unison. The wizard held forth his staff and a blinding light shot out and seared each of the beasts on their foreheads, directly above their snouts.

"I am you master," Gilifan said confidently.

The beasts slowed to a walk and stopped before him, staring at him as a dog might look to its owner just before a hunt.

Gilifan moved forward and stretched his staff to touch each of the winged monsters on the head. As he did so, his knowledge of Erik transferred to each beast, so that they knew the smell of his very soul. The animals snarled and gnashed their teeth after discovering their target, eager to begin the hunt.

"Go," Gilifan commanded. "Go and kill the Champion of Truth."

CHAPTER SEVENTEEN

Al sat at the front of the wagon, next to the driver, listening to the men behind him talk about how interesting the forests were. Al smiled to himself at their talk. To him, this was now the normal way to live, but for his soldiers, this was the first time many of them had ever left the tunnels of their home. That was probably why he wasn't wearing his royal armor. It didn't feel natural to him. He knew he would likely readjust to living in Roegudok Hall, but he doubted if the armor or the crown would ever become normal for him. Despite everything, he still couldn't help but look at the crown as a fancy version of a ball-and-chain. True, he might wear the crown on his head, but it felt as though it weighed him down every step he took.

"We are almost there," the driver announced. The wagon lurched around a copse of trees and was suddenly thrust into the midst of a great field, lined with a couple of farmhouses where workers tended to budding crops of corn and wheat. Beyond the field, stood the high, thick walls of Drakei Glazei.

"Wow, would you look at that!" someone exclaimed from the back.

"I didn't know the humans could build anything like this," someone else said.

"Not as impressive as our hall," another put in.

Al started to turn around and add his comments, but he stopped when he spotted a wagon on a parallel road emerging from the forest. The driver was frantically snapping the reins and his shouts were just audible enough for Al to note the tension in his voice. The dwarf king stood on the bench and put a hand over his eyes.

"What is it?" the driver asked.

"Hard to tell from here," Al replied. "Why don't we speed up and see if we can't catch them before they get to the gate."

The driver sent a mighty crack of his reins and the wagon lurched forward as the stout ponies broke into a run. Al nearly fell back to where his soldiers sat, but he managed to catch himself with his left hand and sit down again. As they raced down the road another carriage emerged from the forest parallel with them. Al couldn't be sure, but he thought he recognized it from Lokton Manor, or at least he had seen one very similar during his time there.

He motioned for the driver to speed up and the dwarf grunted and snapped the reins again. The ponies pulled with all of their might, but they simply weren't fast enough to keep up with the long-legged horses. By the time the two roads converged into one, the horse-drawn carriage was a couple hundred yards ahead of them and it showed no signs of slowing as it sped for the gates.

"We'll catch them at the gate," the driver said. "They'll have to stop and check in with the guards."

Al huffed. He had wanted to get to them *before* they all got to the gate. If they were from Lokton manor, he wanted to hear an update without additional ears nearby. He would just have to content himself with catching up with them at the gate. There wasn't anything else to be done.

As his driver pulled the wagon in to the guard house on the right side of the gate's exterior Al leapt from his seat and sauntered up to the other carriage. A pair of guards started coming out to him from the guard house, but he let his driver deal with them. He wanted to discover who was in the carriage.

"Hello to the carriage," Al called out.

A scrawny old man peered over from the driver's bench. "What do you want?" he shouted out.

The door to the carriage burst open and out jumped Braun. "Wouldn't have guessed to meet you here," he said. The big man eyed the wagons filled with dwarf soldiers in shining armor. "Could have used them back at the manor," Braun said.

"I was unable to come personally," Al explained. "But, I did send some of our best warriors as quickly as I could."

A woman dressed in black descended from the carriage and slowly moved around Braun. "And what of Roegudok Hall?" she asked. "Is there a new king upon the throne?"

Braun glanced from Al to Lady Lokton and the confusion was written all over his face. Al chuckled.

"She and I had a long chat before I left the manor," Al explained to Braun. Then he moved forward and gently took Lady Lokton's hand in his and kissed it. "I wish with all of my soul that we had succeeded in bringing your husband back to you. I don't often fail to fulfill my promises." A tear slid down Lady Lokton's cheek, but the woman smiled and nodded.

"I know you did everything you could," she said.

"My liege," the dwarf driver called out as he bounded up to them. "We have been asked to assemble in front of the gate and go into the town on foot."

"King Al?" Braun asked.

Al shot the big man a quick scolding glare and then turned back to his driver. "So stable the ponies then and have the others assemble as we have been asked."

The driver nodded and went back to the others without another word.

"I guess that answers my question," Lady Lokton said. "Well, perhaps now that the dwarves stand with us, we shall have a good chance."

"I hope so," Al said. He looked beyond to the gate. It was shut and a line of soldiers stood before it. He couldn't see into the city, but it was obvious that things were not as tranquil as they had been before their last visit. As he looked at the guards, a smaller door opened off to the side and out walked Senator Mickelson. Instead of walking with the pomp of a senator, the man ran out to greet them. His mouth turned up in a broad smile and his arms out wide in greeting.

"My friends!" he greeted warmly. "I did not think to see you again so soon. Come, what news do you have?" His smile faded somewhat when he gave Braun a good looking over. "You have seen trouble," Mickelson noted.

Braun nodded. "Lokton Manor is no more, and our house has been devastated. We humbly ask for shelter here, and of course pledge whatever service we can to King Mathias in return."

"You have already served him more than any house ever should," Mickelson was quick to reply. "We have space for you, and for all that belong to your house."

"What news from here?" Al cut in, pointing to the row of guards along the gate. "Things have not been static here I suppose."

Mickelson shook his head. "The Lievonian Order arrived and helped restore order to the streets," he said. "Together with the regular guard we have rounded up the more serious insurgents. There are no more riots in the streets, but there is still a curfew." Mickelson looked back to the guards. "Of course, we have to enforce much stricter scrutiny of all travelers now as well, so we have more than tripled each watch."

Al nodded and pointed over his shoulder at his waiting dwarves. "As is the custom, I brought a few of my own to pay tribute with."

Mickelson's face scrunched up as he looked at the dwarves. "A few of your own?" he repeated.

"I am now king of Roegudok Hall," Al said flatly.

Senator Mickelson watched him for a moment, looking into his eyes with a knit brow and a slight frown on his face. Then his expression lightened and he clapped his hands together. "Well, then there shall be great rejoicing in the palace today!" he exclaimed. "I would be happy to escort you to King Mathias myself."

Al gestured to Lady Lokton. "First you should see that the lady is settled. My kinfolk and I can wait until then."

Mickelson nodded. "Of course." The senator walked over to the guards and took a roll of parchment from them. "Good sir," he called out to the driver. "I shall help you navigate the streets." He climbed up to sit on the bench and waited for the scrawny old driver to clamber up and take the reins. Lady Lokton offered Al one last smile before returning to the carriage.

"Come and find me when you have a moment," Braun said to Al.

"How does Lepkin fare?" Al asked.

Braun smiled and leaned in close. "Erik is fine."

Al bristled, but softened quickly when he saw Braun's smiling eyes and happy demeanor. "How did you know?" Al asked.

"I didn't, not at first. But I figured it out," he said. "Don't worry though, the secret is safe and so is he, as far as I know."

Al nodded and then went back to his comrades. He watched the carriage drive through the heavy gate and then the doors closed like massive jaws around a morsel of food. The guards returned to their stations and no one else went in or out for the space of an hour.

In the interim time, Al went into the guard house to change

into his royal armor. It wasn't as functional a suit as one he would make for himself. It was meant for occasions such as this, where the show and perception of power was more important than the armor's actual strength. A silver encrusted breastplate with gold inlay around the engraved edges shone brightly in the torchlight of Roegudok Hall, but in the daylight above ground it was radiant beyond compare. Each masterfully carved rune was traced with a line of gold. Each rivet that attached the layering plates was covered with a cap of ruby or emerald stone. The suit was polished to such a high sheen that Al dared not look at it long for fear of burning his eyes. The greaves were equally as stunning. They were made from black Telarian steel. Sharp contrasting lines of silver and gold were braided down the outer sides of the greaves, weaving around each other in such a way as to dazzle any onlooker when the armor walked past.

One of Al's footmen came in to help him with his boots. The insides were made of leather lined with thin rabbit fur to keep the sharp, rigid plates of steel from cutting into his shins. He barely managed to stuff his feet down inside without falling over, but they eventually managed to get them on and hitch them to the greaves with the clasps just below the knee. Al picked up his right leg and gave a practice swing. He found his range of motion drastically reduced. He would have to walk slowly. The footman grabbed Al's left arm and clasped the plated gauntlets around his hand. Rubies and sapphires studded the wrist, while a great diamond was set in the middle of the forearm so as to look like an eye, outlined in gold. The final piece was the helmet. It was an open faced helmet with a crown fused to the top. As if the rest of the ensemble wasn't gaudy enough, the crown featured a diamond directly in the center, flanked by two rectangular cut amethysts, which were followed around the rim by a pattern of emeralds, sapphires, rubies, and onyx.

"All that's missing is a great horn sticking out of my forehead," Al quipped.

The footman looked up, but didn't laugh.

"What, they didn't issue you a sense of humor?" Al asked.

"No," the dwarf said flatly. Then he checked the fit and exited the guardhouse.

Al started to follow after him, but stopped when he caught a glimpse of his reflection in the window. "I look like an overdressed peacock," he grumbled. He could almost hear Alferug lecturing him about what a great honor it was to wear the royal armor.

"It was fashioned for the first dwarf king by the Ancients themselves," Alferug would say.

"Doesn't help me feel any less like a bird in a gilded cage," Al replied to the imaginary scolding. "Let's get on with it so I can put this back in the glass case where it belongs."

He walked out of the guardhouse and instantly all of his warriors fell to a knee. The moment caught him by surprise, and was a bit humbling. "You've already seen me," Al said. "Get up."

"This is the first time we have seen you in the royal armor," one of his lieutenants said. "It is tradition to kneel before the king whenever he wears the suit."

"Well, you can't march on your knees, so get up and let's assemble in front of the gate." Al tried to walk quickly, but was painfully reminded by his rigid suit that he would have to walk slowly. He swore he could hear his father laughing at him, but he just growled to himself and set his jaw while everyone else around him stared and gawked.

When at last the gates opened again, Mickelson had returned and stood in the opening motioning for Al to bring his group forward. Even the senator was taken aback by Al's suit of armor, but one glance at Al's face was enough to keep him silent about it.

Only a few yards into the city a man approached from the street ahead of them. He wore black trousers, a maroon tunic with a golden dragon emblazoned above the breast, and a simple black cape. A long sword hung from his belt. The runes on the scabbard were old dwarvish symbols that Al recognized.

"Grand Master Penthal," Al said. "An honor to see you again."

Grand Master Penthal stopped and waited for Al to walk up to him, and then he turned to walk with the group on their way to the palace. "It has been a long time since I have seen you, King Sit'marihu." He glanced over his shoulder at the other dwarves. "Longer still since I have seen the dwarves come to Drakei Glazei."

"Is the entire Lievonian Order here?" Al asked.

Grand Master Penthal nodded. "King Mathias summoned us

shortly after Master Lepkin destroyed the senate hall. We all responded as quickly as we could."

"What is the situation now?" Al asked.

"I am sure Senator Mickelson has already informed you that we had to deal with a few insurgents, but it was nothing that we couldn't handle together with the regular guard. We do maintain a curfew though, just to make sure things do not get out of hand again."

"Yes, he did tell me," Al admitted.

"I would be interested to know the situation outside of Drakei Glazei," Grand Master Penthal said. "I cannot say for certain, but I think within a month we may have the situation well enough in hand here that we can come out to the field. We would be wont to lend our assistance wherever the Keeper of Secrets says we are needed."

Al nodded thoughtfully. "I can't speak for him," Al said. "But I believe he is on his way to Valtuu Temple at this moment."

"He aims to complete the boy's training then?"

Al nodded.

"What of the Warlocks of the Order of the All Seeing Eye?" he asked.

"Tukai was the first to fall," Al said. "Lady Dimwater and Master Lepkin slew him. Master Lepkin then killed another one of the warlocks after he left your palace for Valtuu Temple." Al stopped for a moment and the chorus of marching feet behind him stopped an instant later. Al looked up to Grand Master Penthal. "Janik, was the third warlock."

"You mean Master Orres' brother?" Grand Master Penthal asked with an arched brow.

Al sighed and nodded. "Best I can figure, he befriended Erik in order to get close to him. I was there when he attacked him though, and we managed to come through it alright."

"That makes three," Grand Master Penthal said. "I heard of the encounter in Buktah recently. Folk from there say you not only slew a group of Blacktongues, but Master Lepkin killed a corrupt city guard captain and the both of you managed to take down another warlock. Is that true?"

"It is," Al said. "And I am waiting for word now, but we believe the man masquerading as Senator Bracken was actually another warlock of the same order. Master Lepkin sent word to me about the battle with him asking for reinforcements, I sent my cavedogs in response but I have not heard the outcome of the battle as of yet."

"Cavedogs," Grand Master Penthal repeated. "I would not want to find myself on the wrong side of those beasts." Grand Master Penthal stroked his chin and nodded thoughtfully. "I spoke with Braun, House Lokton's man-at-arms, just a short while ago as they got situated in a house nearby. He gave me an accounting that the warlock is, in fact, dead. He said the man was cleaved in two by Master Lepkin himself."

"Then you know more than I," Al admitted.

"It would appear as though the Oder of the All Seeing Eye has been eradicated," Grand Master Penthal said with a short, pointed nod.

"There are others," Al pointed out.

"Yes I know," Grand Master Penthal replied. "Master Lepkin told me of the Wyrms of Khaltoun." His voice was grim. "I was happy to learn that one of their kind was slain at Valtuu Temple, a wizard by the name of Erthor, but he was not alone."

"Do we know where the others are?" Al asked.

Grand Master Penthal shook his head. "We know neither where they are nor exactly how many there are."

Al began walking again and the chorus of footsteps resumed behind him. "So that is why you are anxious to join us out in the field."

"Quite right," Grand Master Penthal confirmed. "Our place is beside the Keeper of Secrets, hunting down any devious enough to pursue the wretched arts of necromancy."

"I suspect you will get your chance," Al said. "I will be sure to check in with you before I leave," he promised.

"Be sure that you do, King Sit'marihu," Grand Master Penthal replied. "And, if I may, I am happy to see the rightful heir on the throne of Roegudok Hall. I am certain your father would be proud."

Al took the compliment in silence and Grand Master Penthal broke away from the group, heading back to where they had met. Al marched on to the great tower, observing the city as he walked. It felt much different from the last time. There were no crowds of people on the streets, only a few scattered individuals who would stop momentarily and gawk at the dwarves before hurrying on with their own business. There were no horses, no carriages, and no merchants selling any wares of any kind. Knights of the Lievonian Order dotted the streets, and they were augmented by the regular guard and king's guard.

As they turned down the wide avenue to the great tower, he was pleasantly surprised to see King Mathias standing before the steps waiting for him. He was flanked by a handful of senators and a healthy compliment of the king's guards.

"He has made a point of appearing outside the tower as of late," Mickelson commented. "He believes it will help settle the citizens to see their king at this time."

Al nodded.

King Mathias lifted his arms and let his flowing yellow robe sway gently in the breeze. "King Sit'marihu, welcome to Drakei Glazei," King Mathias announced as loud as his voice would permit.

Al stopped several paces before the king and bowed his head. "Thank you for receiving us, King Mathias," Al said. "I have brought a contingent of my finest warriors as tribute." Al waved his hand behind him, gesturing to the others. "So that all may know that the dwarves of Roegudok Hall do stand with you at this time."

King Mathias smiled appreciatively and surveyed the warriors. "What, may I ask, is the fate of the former king?"

Al frowned. He had already informed King Mathias of his brother's fate in a letter carried by falcon after he took the throne. The dwarf was unsure if the question was merely a formality, or a sign that Mathias' memory was fading. In either case, he did not withhold the answer. "After defeating him in honorable challenge, I sent him to live in the mountains. He is banished form Roegudok Hall and henceforth no longer counted among our folk."

"Ah," Mathias said. "A merciful solution."

The expression on the king's face proved to Al that it was a lapse in the man's memory that had prompted the question. He had hoped that was not the case. "As is our tradition upon crowning a new king," Al continued. "I have come with the tribute of sixty-five dwarf warriors. They are among our best, and will serve you well."

Mathias nodded. "I will put them with my personal guard," he said.

Al frowned. Normally the tribute was returned to the giver. Tradition held that the king of the humans would only ever accept the gift of tribute from the dwarves for a period of three nights, after which he would return the warriors to their rightful king. It was symbolic, calling to memory the three days and nights that the dwarves and humans fought together to drive out the orcish hordes centuries before. The tradition served as a kind of renewal of the alliance between the two races. King Mathias knew all of this, or at least he had before. Now he had apparently forgotten.

A tall senator leaned in close to the king and whispered into his ear. Then King Mathias was quick to throw a hand out toward Al. "Of course, I only mean they shall stay with my personal guard for three days, as is our custom," King Mathias said.

Al could see the look on the senator's face, as well as the embarrassment on King Mathias' slightly blushing cheeks. The dwarf king played into it well, allowing King Mathias to save face. "Of course, King Mathias, I understood that to be your intention." Then Al bowed again and motioned for his warriors to join with King Mathias. Out of the corner of his eye he saw the senator lean in again, but Mathias waved the man away.

"Come, let us feast together in my hall," King Mathias said. "We shall have much merriment tonight."

Everyone filed into the great tower but Al remained with Mickelson and waited. "When were you going to tell me?" Al asked.

Mickelson sighed. "His mind has become extremely weak over the last couple of days," he said.

"I can see that for myself," Al quipped. "What I want to know is whether he remembers anything from the last time I was here, does he know what happened in the senate hall?"

"Oh yes," Mickelson assured him. "He remembers that very well. He still holds you and Lepkin in the highest esteem. It is just that he has not been able to retain new things as of late. We have had to remind him several times of different things."

"He appears to have forgotten old things as well," Al said.

"Yes well, it has been a long time since he has made any effort to come down from his room," Mickelson explained. "He has not had to act so formerly in recent times." Mickelson clapped a hand to Al's back. "Come, let us go in and eat. Don't worry about King Mathias, the senators who remain here are all good and honest men. We will help him."

"A mind is usually the last thing to go before the spirit," Al said pointedly. "You may want to think on that."

Senator Mickelson stopped and frowned down at the dwarf. "I know he is old..." his sentence trailed off and he relented with a nod. "You are right, of course, but what are we to do? We have only just barely restored order to the streets. None of the senators want to think about who will take the throne if the king passes away."

"Not *if*, but *when*," Al pointed out. "My guess is within a few months at the latest, but I wouldn't be surprised if it was much earlier." The dwarf poked a stout finger in Mickelson's side. "As for the question of *who*, that has already been settled. Master Lepkin should assume the throne."

"It is not so easy," Mickelson replied. "After what he did in the senate hall, the other senators are afraid of him. The people are afraid of him."

"I wouldn't have thought you one to succumb to political games, Mickelson," Al chided.

Mickelson shook his head. "It isn't that, it's just that Lepkin sitting on the throne might cause another division among the people."

"As your friend, I would advise you not to play games. The fact that Lepkin should be the heir is already decided. To make a deal in a back room for anything else would do more to undermine the peoples' confidence than to have Lepkin on the throne." Al snorted. "And as a king, I say it is good for the senators to fear him. Perhaps that will help them avoid the corruption their fallen colleagues gave themselves to."

Mickelson shrugged and offered a weak half-smile. "Perhaps you are right," he said. "But let us hope the king lives so that the change will not be soon."

Al nodded heartily. "I agree with that completely."

*****

"What do we do now?" Eldrik asked. "The other warlocks are slain, Senator Bracken and his army are dead, and those who served House Cedreau faithfully now lie on the dirt as well."

Silvi looked back through the trees and shook her head. "If not for the dwarves, we would have succeeded," she said.

"Was Bracken right about Hairen and Merriam?" Eldrik asked.

Silvi nodded quietly. "I felt their life force when they expired," she said.

"How?" Eldrik pressed.

"There was a bond between us," she said. "Now that bond is severed and I am alone."

Eldrik regarded her curiously and then kicked a small stone through the bushes. "We can't go back to my house either," he said. "I can't go back to my mother like this. The other men would come for me in the night for leading so many of our house to their deaths." He spun on her. "I thought this was going to restore us!" he yelled.

"You are not the only person who has lost," Silvi said with tears in her longing eyes. She looked to him and leaned back against a tall oak tree. For the first time, Eldrik saw her as the vulnerable one. She was scared, and unsure.

He folded his arms and stared at her for a few moments. "So what do we do?" he asked in a softer tone.

Silvi shrugged.

"Is there no one else?"

The black haired witch nodded slowly. "There is someone," she said. "But, I am not sure we could trust him."

"Who is he?" Eldrik asked.

"He is a member of the Black Fang Council," she replied.

"What is that?" Eldrik pressed.

"It is a select order of Shadowfiends."

"Shadowfiends, you mean they are like me?" Eldrik repeated.

Silvi blinked slowly and looked off to the side, away from Eldrik's intense stare. "They are." The witch rubbed her arms as if a sudden chill wrapped around her. "But they are different too. Instead of going through a matriarch and gaining the power through our ritual, like you did, they received it with even darker magic. Some have been known to enlist the help of demons, while others have uncovered the forbidden rites that allow them to absorb the power from others and claim it for their own."

"That doesn't sound so different from what we did," Eldrik pointed out. "I absorbed the power of another warlock in the coven, which then turned me into what I am. Then I slew another in front of you and Bracken and devoured his power as well."

"It may be hard for you to see the difference," she agreed. "But within the coven there is order. A matriarch follows specific rules when transferring power from one to another. For most other shadowfiends, there is no order. Their growth comes only through murder and absorbing the life energy of others. They devour the magical and mundane alike. Each kill boosts their power."

"So they are unpredictable," Eldrik guessed.

Silvi nodded. "And extremely dangerous," she added. "The Black Fang Council is the only order of shadowfiends, as most prefer solitude and would rather kill each other to absorb the other's power. The Black Fang Council is different. Its members seek a common goal."

"What is that?" Eldrik asked.

"They seek immortality," she said flatly. "While most shadowfiends are content with their existence, the members of the Black Fang Council seek to prolong their lives indefinitely, at the cost of any who stand in their way."

"How do you know of them?" Eldrik asked.

"Because the man you know as Senator Bracken, the previous patriarch of our order, was familiar with them. He even spoke with a couple of them over the years."

"If these shadowfiends are so unpredictable, why would he talk to them?"

Silvi shrugged. "I don't know all of the details. I only know that he had a question for them. He sought them out for years before finally finding one. Hairen said once that he traded the souls of ten men for the answer he desired. Then, from that point on he would periodically deal with them, always taking more sacrifices to them in exchange for whatever wisdom they gave him."

"What would be so important to Bracken?" Eldrik mused aloud. "What did they have that he wanted?"

"I suppose he also sought the secret of immortality," Silvi

said. "It is the only reason I have ever been able to come up with."

"Well, if that is true, then they obviously didn't give him the right answer," Eldrik said.

"Perhaps," Silvi agreed. "I guess there is no way to know now," she said.

Eldrik nodded. "Yes there is," he said. "We will go to them."

Silvi's eyes opened wide. "Eldrik, we can't go to them, they will kill us."

"They didn't kill Bracken," Eldrik replied.

"Bracken was a lot stronger than both you and I put together," she pointed out. "And even he needed to bring them something in return."

"You just said you know of one that we could turn to," Eldrik pointed out.

Silvi nodded. "We could try, but it will be a long journey. Beyond the sea."

Eldrik frowned. "I have nowhere else to go," he said.

"We could start a new coven here," she reminded him.

Eldrik shook his head. "No, let us go find this shadowfiend."

"Alright Eldrik," she relented.

"No, the battle is over and everyone here will assume that Eldrik has died," he said. "From now on I wish to be called Aparen."

"What of your mother?"

He shrugged. "Aparen has no mother," he said callously.

CHAPTER EIGHTEEN

Erik stepped around his horse, keeping a wary eye on the cavedog nearby. The lizard was enormous, like a wingless, fireless dragon. A long snout filled with razor sharp fangs situated on a stout, thick neck. The back was broad and muscular, affording ample space for each dwarf to affix a saddle to. The forelegs were strong and tipped with heavy, black claws. The back legs were similar, except almost double the size. The tail stretched out mightily behind the beast, about three feet in length. It looked up at him with angry yellow eyes and flicked its forked tongue out into the air.

"Don't let it bother you," Alferug said. "He won't strike."

Erik kept watching the lizard. "How do you know?" he asked. "And for that matter, why don't they attack all of you? Each lizard is about seven feet long," Erik said.

"Most are closer to eight or nine feet long, actually," Alferug corrected. "They are a savage beast in war, but to the dwarf folk they are as kind and loyal as a sheepdog might be to its master. That's why they are called 'cavedogs' in fact. They have many endearing traits." Alferug bent down and stroked the back of the lizards shoulder and it lifted its head and closed its eyes, emitting a low, throaty sound that almost resembled a purr.

"I don't know," Erik said. "It seems like saying a snake could be a good friend."

Alferug turned sharply and frowned. "The comparison is not apt at all," he said. "A cavedog is a distant cousin of the dragon. As such, we are actually able to communicate with them the same way that I can communicate with you while you are in dragon form."

Erik shrugged. "If you say so."

"Come put your hand on its snout," Alferug said.

Erik shook his head. "No, that's alright."

"I'm not asking," Alferug said tersely. "Come over here and put your hand right here." Alferug jabbed a finger down on the beast's snout.

Erik sighed and slowly approached. He reached his hand out but stopped suddenly when the lizard opened its big yellow eye and looked right at him.

"Go on," Alferug urged. "Put your hand on him." Erik barely inched forward with his fingers. His eyes were locked on the cavedog's eye. Alferug reached out and grabbed Erik by the wrist and yanked him the rest of the way until his hand was on the cavedog. "What do you feel?" Alferug asked.

"It's rough," Erik said noting the thick, bumpy scales.

Alferug shook his head. "No, not that," he said. "What do you feel in here?" He jabbed a finger into Erik's chest.

Erik shrugged. "Nothing," he said.

"Bah," Alferug gruffed. The dwarf stood up and scratched the back of his neck. "We'll try again some other time then," he said.

A loud howl pierced through the forest.

"What was that?" Erik asked.

"Not sure," Alferug admitted. "But it is still a ways off yet. Come, let's see if we can stay ahead of it." He turned quickly and shouted out, "Faengoril, time to move!"

"Already ahead of you," Faengoril shouted back from across the camp. Erik looked over and saw the dwarf was already atop his cavedog as were several others. "They'll be on us by nightfall," he added.

Alferug nodded. "If not sooner."

"We can make Buktah by then," Erik put in.

Alferug turned back with a wicked grin on his face. "Oh yes, you mean the town where you severed the captain of the guard in half?" he chided. He quickly shook his head. "We will find no rest there. Besides, the beast that tracks us is not one we should take to a city."

"So where do we go?" Erik asked.

"We stick to the forest south of Buktah, like we planned originally." Alferug threw his leather saddle onto his cavedog and tightened the strap before hopping on.

Erik went back to his horse and jumped into his own saddle. Faengoril led the pack with a sharp shout and the cavedogs tore off through the forest, darting through the trees and bushes with blinding speed. Erik spurred his horse into a gallop, but had to stick to wider paths as he followed the cavedogs. His horse nickered and snorted any time one of the great lizards ran close to it. Erik patted his horse as he leaned forward.

"They make me nervous too," he confided.

The group charged through the forest, trampling over sticks and leaves, churning up dust and breaking ferns and bushes back as they rolled through. Occasionally a howl would sound from somewhere behind them. Each time, Erik would look back, but he never saw their stalker. Still, the hairs on the back of his neck started to prickle and raise as the howls seemed to grow closer to them.

Erik was careful to keep his head low to avoid branches as they departed from the main road and went deeper into the forest itself. The trees in this part grew close enough together that Erik could not keep up with the cavedogs. The dwarves pulled ahead of him as their animals were much nimbler and easily able to navigate the tight turns. Erik almost shouted out to the group but a loud, piercing howl made him turn back. His horse snorted and increased its speed, carelessly bolting through the trees and through a patch of brambles and briars that ripped and pulled at Erik's legs.

He grit his teeth and tried to pull the horse off to the side but it was no use. The animal was spooked and running any way it thought it could go to escape from the howling. A deafening growl ripped through the trees and a great beast broke through the forest canopy snapping large branches like dry twigs. The horse whinnied and turned off to head due south.

The beast landed hard on the forest floor, just a few inches short of the horse's rump as it got a mouthful of hair from the animal's tail. The horse jumped forward tearing off for all it was worth. Erik looked back. The great beast folded its wings close to its massive body and sped forward after them, nipping at the horse's heels. Erik had no idea what to do. He tried to reach for his sword but had to lay flat against the horse's back in order to avoid a thick, low hanging branch.

A great shout sounded from his left and a cavedog burst through a holly bush. It snatched the beast by the left foreleg and dragged it to the ground as the dwarf warrior jumped up from the cavedog's back and bore down with his axe on the beast's spine. The beast howled and twitched, but it was no match for the surprise attack.

"This way!" Alferug shouted.

Erik nodded and tried to pull the reins, but the horse was not soothed by the sight of the great lizards. It turned slightly toward the east, jumping over a small brook and out from the trees into a rocky clearing of black sand and pink, porous rocks.

"No, not that way!" Alferug shouted. "Come back!"

Erik tried, but his horse would not obey. Above circled several more of the horrid winged beasts. They howled and swooped down, snapping their great maws at him. Erik pulled his sword and was able to slice one of the beasts across the chest. It fell to the ground behind him, but it was not dead.

A great hole loomed before him and the horse tried to jump across. It didn't make it. Its forelegs fell short of the opposite rim and the horse flipped over, flinging Erik to the ground beyond while the horse slid into the large, funnel-shaped pit.

Erik rolled and slammed into a large rock, spitting the black sand from his mouth. He rose quickly and kept his eye on the beasts above. Arrows zinged up from the edge of the forest and Erik saw dwarves furiously working short recurve bows from the back of their mounts.

"Don't move!" Alferug shouted.

"What?" Erik yelled back.

His horse started to get up and Erik went to move to help the beast, but something moved in the bottom of the funnel that caught his eye. He stopped and watched as what appeared to be a black, furry snake stretched out.

"What is that?" Erik asked.

The horse saw the thing too and started to run up the side of the funnel. As it did so it churned the black sand, tearing down the loose side of the pit and gaining no traction. A flash of black erupted from the bottom of the pit and a great spider seized the horse. Massive fangs bore down and Erik heard a resounding *crack* as the animal's spine snapped in two and blood showered the black sand of the pit.

Erik blanched and took a few steps backward until he felt nothing below his left foot. He turned around and narrowly avoided falling into a similar pit. His mouth dropped open and he surveyed the area about him. He was in the middle of a field full of such pits. He looked back to his dead horse and the spider dragged the limp corpse under the sand.

Then Erik saw the bloody chest of the winged beast he had

wounded on the opposite side of the pit. The winged monster growled, pulling its lips back to reveal blood red gums over gleaming, sharp fangs. It launched toward him, extending its wings to glide across. Erik dove to the side, slamming into the ground and letting the beast sail into the pit behind him. By the time the monster realized its mistake it was too late. It beat its wings furiously, but its heavy tail dragged along the side of the pit and awoke the spider inside. A great, brown spider lunged out with scary accuracy, wrapping its fore legs around the beast's wings and biting into the back of its neck. The beast howled and snarled, slinging a string of foamy slobber, but it was no match for the giant spider.

"Come on, try to stay atop the rocks," Alferug shouted. Erik pushed himself up and sprinted as quickly as he could while still picking his steps carefully. When he was able he jumped from rock to rock. The remaining winged wolves circled above, kept at bay by the dwarves' arrows.

One of the wolves howled and fell from the sky to land in a pit, arrows protruding from its chest. No sooner did it touch the sand than a great spider leapt out and pounced on it. Erik couldn't help but watch the hairy spider, but he should have been watching where he was running. He tripped on a large stone and tumbled forward, barely stopping before falling into a pit himself. His heart pounded in his chest as he gingerly lifted his foot and pulled it back from the rim of the funnel. A couple of pebbles jiggled and skitted down a few inches and he held his breath, too afraid to move, staring at the bottom of the funnel.

Nothing moved.

He exhaled and slowly rose to his feet.

"Behind you!" Alferug bellowed.

Erik wheeled around and barely caught sight of a mass of fur and teeth before a monster plowed into him. The two of them went down into the funnel, tumbling and lashing out at each other. Erik fumbled for his sword and barely pulled it out in time to catch the massive wolf in the jaw and prevent the beast from tearing out his throat. The wolf snarled and growled, ripping at him with its front paws and snapping down with its great maw. Erik furiously worked the sword, but he couldn't get the right angle for a killing thrust.

The sand below his back shifted and heaved under him. Then a great flurry of sand and pebbles exploded out around him and a pair of hairy, thick legs planted themselves in the sand on either side. The wolf above him howled horridly and lurched down, nearly crushing Erik. A sharp pain stabbed Erik in the stomach and then the wolf was yanked back, away from him. The beast twitched and gnashed its fangs until it disappeared below the sand with the spider. Erik slowly, delicately pointed the tip of his sword at the bottom of the funnel.

With his left hand he picked up a sizable rock and threw it at the opposite side of the funnel. It splashed into the sand and then tumbled down the side, creating a small slide of sand and pebbles. Nothing happened. Erik picked up another rock and threw it. This time the rock only rolled half way down the funnel when the spider emerged.

However, it didn't pounce like it had before, it came up slowly, letting the sand fall from its hairy, black body as it pushed up from below. Erik's heart jumped into his throat and his breathing became fast and shallow. His hands trembled and he had to struggle to keep the sword steady.

The beast turned on him and looked down with eight, beady black eyes. A pair of pedipalps spread apart slowly, revealing bloody fangs dripping with green venom. Erik held his breath, hoping beyond hope that the beast would be satisfied with its previously caught meal. The spider pulled its legs free of the sand and stretched to its full height, towering over him. It leaned to the left and then broke to the right before pouncing. Erik called forth the sword's magic and the blade encased itself in white-hot flames and sunk deep into the spider's body through its mouth.

The pair of bloody fangs stopped just inches from Erik's hands and the spider twitched and quaked wretchedly until its strength expired and its legs collapsed. Erik barely managed to roll the spider off to the side and retrieve his sword before being crushed. As he pulled the blade back, the flames were gone, replaced by a hissing, steaming sheath of green ooze that dripped slowly to the ground.

Erik backed away and scrambled up the edge of the funnel with more than a little difficulty. Sand and rocks fell away from under him as he clawed his way up. When he finally made it to the top he pulled himself onto a flat rock big enough for him to lay his upper body on and he hugged the stone.

"Come on," Alferug said gently as he bent down and grabbed Erik's arm. "You did well, but we aren't safe yet."

Erik stood with Alferug's help and followed the dwarf back through the dangerous pits to the forest. He barely noticed when the last of the winged wolves fell to the ground, and may not have noticed it at all had the other dwarves not let out a chorus of victory shouts and cheers.

"Nasty beasts," Faengoril noted when Erik finally was back in the safety of the trees.

Erik looked back to the field and doubled over, sick to his stomach. Faengoril slapped him on the back and then motioned for the others to move back. Alferug stayed with Erik while the boy regrouped.

"I have never in my life even heard of those," Erik said. "How is it that I can live so close to something so awful and yet have no idea it is nearby?"

Alferug spat on the black sand. "Humans have a way of not talking about things that displease or scare them," he said. "Sometimes they ignore evil for long enough that they forget about its very existence."

Erik shook his head and went down to his knees. "I need a few minutes," he said.

Alferug knelt down and put a hand on the boy's shoulder. "Are you..." his words trailed off and Alferug looked down to Erik's stomach. "Lean back," he said.

Erik gave the dwarf a curious look, but Alferug was not patient enough to repeat his request. He roughly pushed Erik down to lie on his back and awkwardly pulled his legs out to set him straight. His hands went down for the bottom of Erik's chainmail shirt and lifted it up.

"You have been bitten," he said grimly.

Erik lifted his head, trying to look past his clothes and armor to where Alferug was looking. "No, it bit the wolf," Erik said. "That is just a scratch."

"Stonebubbles," Alferug said. "I know a bite when I see one. He may have only hit you with one fang, but he got you. Probably bit through the wolf and got you as well."

Erik tried to sit, but he found the strength in his arms was waning. Alferug's face became blurry, as if covered with a thick sheet of water. The boy opened his mouth to speak, but barely more than a whisper of air came out.

"Faengoril!" Alferug shouted. The stocky dwarf bounded through the brush quicker than a rabbit, axe drawn and ready. Alferug shook his head and gestured with a nod of his chin to Erik's stomach.

"By the Ancients," Faengoril muttered. "I don't have anything for him," he said.

"Me neither," Alferug admitted. "Pick him up and let's get him strapped to a cavedog." Faengoril reached down and plucked the boy up with one hand, slinging him over his shoulder and ran back to the main group.

"Klefil, I need your cavedog, now!" Faengoril yelled.

"Yes sir," the dwarf warrior shouted as he hopped off the cavedog.

Faengoril put Erik on the lizard and lashed him to it so that he would neither fall nor have any dragging limbs as the beast moved.

"Will he live?" someone else asked. Faengoril shrugged.

"We have no remedy for him," he said.

"There is someone who might help us," Alferug put in as he jumped atop his cavedog.

Faengoril spun around. "He is not fond of dwarves," he said.

"What other choice do we have?" Alferug asked.

Faengoril looked to Erik and saw the blood draining from the boy's pale face as the area around the puncture in his stomach started to turn purple and blue. He shook his head. "There is no other choice," Faengoril agreed.

Alferug gave the signal and charged out. Klefil jumped onto a cavedog behind another dwarf and all tore off after Alferug. The cavedogs slithered and skittered through the woods farther to the south, but careful to stay away from the funnel spiders.

Erik's body bounced and shook as the lizard he was lashed to darted under a fallen oak and then leapt up onto an outcropping of boulders that allowed it to cross a brook without getting wet. The dwarves traveled at a grueling pace for the space of two hours before they finally came to a green knoll in the middle of a small clearing. Marigolds and poppy flowers caught the last light of dusk as the dwarves dismounted and walked through the knee-high grass up to a wooden hut at the top of the hill.

"Hatatuk," Alferug called out. "Hatatuk, are you home?"

The door opened and a two foot tall gnome with a long, hooked nose and wispy gray whiskers dangling from his angular chin emerged. He rubbed a bony hand over his liver-spotted bald head and stared up at Alferug through a pair of thick spectacles.

"What do you want, eh?" Hatatuk inquired.

"We need a healer," Alferug replied.

"Can't help you," Hatatuk snipped. "Go north to Buktah."

"You don't understand," Alferug said as he stuck his hand out and stopped the gnome from closing the door to the hut.

The gnome snapped his fingers and out from hidden holes in the ground popped a small army of young gnomes, most holding spears leveled at the dwarves, some holding short crossbows. "You must truly be desperate to come here," Hatatuk said. "Everyone knows I have no love for the dwarves." His beady, blue eyes looked Alferug up and down and then he glanced out to the others. "I suggest you leave, you are trying my patience."

"It isn't for a dwarf," Faengoril bellowed as he stepped forward. A pair of gnomes pressed the tips of their spears into his chest just enough to force the dwarf to stop walking. He glowered at them for a moment and swept the spears away abruptly. "It's for him," he insisted as he stepped to the side and revealed Erik laying upon a cavedog's back.

"Can't help you," Hatatuk repeated.

"He is the Champion of Truth," Alferug said.

Hatatuk stopped and turned back around slowly. "That is the Keeper of Secrets," Hatatuk said. "I can see for myself that it is Master Lepkin."

"Still you won't help?" Faengoril growled. "Why?"

Hatatuk reached up and pulled his spectacles down to clean them with an old brown cloth he pulled from his green trouser pocket. "Where was he when the Wyrms of Khaltoun first arrived in the Middle Kingdom?" he asked. "Where were any of you?" He slipped his spectacles back over his nose and wrinkled his forehead. "We were the first to see them, in the islands in the west. We tried to warn you, but none came to our aid. You let us die by the hundreds. When we escaped and sought refuge, no one would take us in. We had to come here." Hatatuk gestured around the field with a sweep of his arm. "We had to come out and live deep in the forest past the funnel spiders and next to the old giants who roamed these parts at that time."

Alferug looked to the ground. "Neither I, nor my father lived during that time," he said.

"True, a gnome's life is much longer than that of a dwarf, to say nothing of a human's lifespan, but I was there, and I remember the way your grandfathers treated us. Now you come to me as though I should owe you anything. I suggest you leave."

"To punish us for the wrongs our ancestors did to your people only perpetuates the bad blood between our people."

"You perpetuate it yourself," Hatatuk said. "I have not seen you come to us before with offers to help us find a new home, and certainly no one has come forward to help us reclaim our homelands."

"What is done is done," Alferug said firmly. He pointed to Erik. "This may be Lepkin's body, but inside is the spirit of a boy who is the Champion of Truth," he said. "He has been stuck by a funnel spider's fang, and we do not have the time to go to Buktah."

"If you fail to help him, you will not only condemn the dwarves and humans to death, but yourselves as well. How does that sit with your sense of justice?" Faengoril asked.

Hatatuk stepped forward and extended his hand out over Erik, letting it hover over the wound in his stomach. "Jaleal, Mecarrel, go inside and fetch me the tincture of glory-root, the jar of ground bitter-finger leaves, and the salve of lurevan root."

Two gnomes nodded and disappeared down the holes they had popped up from.

"Thank you," Alferug said. He started to step forward but Hatatuk reached out and stopped him.

"I'll treat him, but none of you are going inside. Have your warriors go back into the trees, you may stay here with me while I work."

Faengoril looked at Alferug and shook his head disapprovingly, but Alferug held up a hand and pointed to the trees. "Please do as our host requests," Alferug said. He could tell by Faengoril's reddening face that the dwarf was anything but happy about the situation, but to his credit he kept his mouth closed and moved the others back.

Hatatuk began removing the rope from around Erik. "Command your foul beast to go with them," the gnome said.

Alferug helped lay Erik's body on the grass and then mentally commanded the cavedog to join the others. Just as the beast disappeared through a bush of brambles and briars, the other gnomes emerged from the hut's doorway holding several colored jars and bottles.

"We also brought this for the pain," Jaleal said as he handed a pink bottle to Hatatuk.

"And this for the fever," Mecarrel added as he held out a green bottle.

Alferug could see that Hatatuk was not well pleased, but he took the extra medicines anyway and began administering to Erik. "Give me the tincture," he said as he knelt over Erik and pulled the clothing away. Jaleal handed him a dark brown bottle and Hatatuk popped the cork and generously poured the pungent liquid directly into the wound. Bubbles and foam rose out of the hole and Erik convulsed and babbled nonsensically.

Jaleal stepped forward and poured some of the caramel liquid from the pink bottle into Erik's mouth. He followed that with a chaser from the green bottle. Hatatuk took the bottle from him and set it on the ground.

"That is more than enough to fix an ox," he grumbled.

Jaleal backed away and let Hatatuk work. The gnome leaned over and sniffed the wound. The putrid, fizzing hole seethed with a sickly gray liquid. Hatatuk pressed his bony fingers into Erik's abdomen and applied just enough pressure to force more of the liquid out, then he reached his hand back to Jaleal and took a thick cloth from him and sopped up the goop from Erik's skin.

"Pour more of the tincture in after this next purge," Hatatuk instructed. His beady little blue eyes never looked away from the hole in Erik's stomach as he massaged Erik's abdomen and worked more of the bubbling liquid out. Then he pressed in deep and copious amounts of the liquid flowed out, followed by a spurt of curdled purple blood clots. Hatatuk pinched around the wound with his right hand as he wiped the area clean with his left.

Jaleal deftly moved in over Hatatuk's hand and poured the liquid into the gaping hole. White bubbles foamed up as before and

Erik writhed, moaning and groaning.

"Come hold his legs, dwarf," Hatatuk said.

Alferug jumped to and seized Erik's legs, pinning them solidly to the ground so the gnomes could finish their work.

"Give me the salve of lurevan," Hatatuk said. Jaleal handed him the jar and Hatatuk drew a generous amount out with his index and middle fingers. The salve was thick, like yogurt, and he drizzled it from his fingers to the wound below, carefully aiming so that it dropped in as far as possible. When the last bits had fallen from his finger he snapped his fingers and muttered something to the grass behind him. A blade of grass stretched wide, shifting into a large, soft leaf instead of a thin, grainy blade. Hatatuk plucked the leaf from the ground and wiped his fingers on the underside of it. Then he folded the leaf into a bowl shape. "Pour the ground bitter-finger root inside."

Jaleal unscrewed the top and poured half of the contents into the leaf.

Hatatuk folded the sides of the leaf over the top and started to squish and crush the poultice just until a slight amount of moisture from the leaf broke through its skin. He then held the poultice out over the grass and two blades stretched up to wrap themselves around the bundle and tie it together. Then he stuck the poultice directly over the hole and pressed it in so that roughly a third of it was in the wound.

"This will draw the rest of the poison back and clean the blood," Jaleal explained.

"He'll make it, then?" Alferug asked.

Jaleal nodded. "Most likely he should be fine by the morning."

Hatatuk rose to his feet. "Just remember that this doesn't engender any love between me and your kind," he said. "I did it only because the Champion of Truth is the only being capable of stopping what is coming."

"You could join us," Alferug said.

Hatatuk shook his head and folded his bony arms. "My part is done," he said. "As you left me and my kind to our fate, so shall I leave you to yours."

"You just said you understand how serious this is, why not come with us and help us fight?"

"No," Hatatuk said.

Alferug stood and watched the gnomes disappear into the hut
as the last rays of daylight faded and the shadow of night swept in.
Alferug turned to face the woods and motioned for Faengoril to
come and help. The stout dwarf rushed back up the hill, a cavedog
on his heels and the rope in his hands. The two of them picked
Erik up and laid him on the lizard's back, being careful not to
disturb the poultice as they lashed him in place.

"Alferug, look," Faengoril whispered.

Alferug turned and saw numerous glowing, blue flowers
emerging from the ground. The soft petals opened slowly and
ejected glowing pollen into the air. The golden dust swirled around
on the twilight breeze until the whole hill was covered as though by
a fog of gold dust. The aroma was sweeter than that of a newly
blooming rose, almost intoxicating.

"It is called a starbowl," a voice said from behind them. The
two dwarves turned and saw Jaleal standing there. He was every bit
as thin as Hatatuk, but not bony. His skin was still firm and held
the vibrancy of youth. His bright, green eyes looked to them much
kinder than Hatatuk's, and his hair was closer to silver than white,
with a healthy shine upon it that reflected the glowing pollen above
them. "These flowers are what saved us from the funnel spiders,"
he said. "Something about the pollen repels the predators in the
forest."

"But not other animals," Faengoril said as he pointed out to
the far side of the clearing. Alferug turned and breathed a hushed
sigh when he caught sight of a great deer emerging from the trees
to graze upon the tender grass in the clearing.

"The other animals come here often, to escape the predators,"
Jaleal said.

"It is a marvelous place," Alferug commented. "I thank you
again for your help."

Jaleal smiled and smoothed his silver mustache down to meld
with his beard. "I was hoping I could join you," Jaleal said.

"You want to join *us?*" Faengoril said skeptically. He looked
to the hut beyond.

Jaleal nodded knowingly. "Hatatuk would not approve, but it
is my choice," he said flatly. "I am good with herbs, and I have a
good knowledge of the plants and forests." He then moved back
into the blades of grass and disappeared before them despite the

glowing flowers and pollen. He reappeared a moment later on their other side with a silver spear in hand. "I am also a great scout," he said. "I can move among the grass as a shadow in the night."

Faengoril smiled wickedly. "I like him," he said to Alferug.

Alferug nodded. "Are you averse to riding a cavedog? We have a long way to travel yet, and we need to make good time."

Jaleal nodded. "I will stay to the trees, but I promise I will remain ahead of you."

Alferug frowned. "I don't think you know how fast our cavedogs are," he said.

Jaleal grinned and motioned for them to follow him. "We gnomes are endowed with a unique kind of magic," he said. "We can walk and run quickly enough, but we have easier methods of travel at our disposal." He walked to a fir tree and ducked under the lowest branches. He turned back to them and put a finger to his lips. Then he touched the tree trunk and vanished.

A moment later he whistled from a high branch in a tree on the other side of the clearing.

"How did he do that?" Alferug whispered.

"I don't know," Faengoril smirked, "but I really like this guy."

An instant later he was back at the base of the fir tree with his arms folded and a big, proud smile on his face. "Like I said, I can keep pace."

Alferug nodded. "Let's be on our way."

The dwarves all mounted up and the cavedogs darted through the forest once again. The beasts zipped through the trees at an alarming rate, almost keeping up with Jaleal as he travelled over and through the trees ahead of the group. Alferug and the other dwarves loosened their grips on their reins, as good as their dwarf eyes were in the darkness, the cavedogs were better, so they let the beasts travel as they wished through the thick forest.

The night air grew cold and damp, like the deeper reaches of Roegudok Hall. The moon and stars peeked through the leaves above and cast their silvery light in streaks on the forest floor. Alferug kept Erik between him and Faengoril, just in case the group encountered anything else, but his worry proved to be unwarranted. Aside from the occasional mouse or deer, the horde saw neither tail nor claw of anything for the rest of the journey. As the sun broke over the jagged peaks far to the east, the dwarves emerged from the forest to see Valtuu Temple standing tall in all of its glory.

Alferug halted the group and the dwarves all stopped to gaze upon the temple.

Great, thick walls of white stone rose up topped with battlements enclosed by a green tile roof. At each corner a square tower rose up from the ground, half again as tall as the wall, with red and gold flags flying over them. Each corner of the roof on each tower was fashioned into the head of a dragon.

Jaleal dropped down from a leaning magnolia tree, silver spear in hand. "It's as magnificent as the stories say," he commented. "The tower must be at least seventy feet tall."

"Magnificent indeed," Alferug agreed. "We won't be able to take the cavedogs in beyond the gate. We'll have to stable them outside."

"Stable them?" Faengoril replied as he arched a brow and frowned. "Good luck with that."

Alferug shrugged. "The alternative is that you and the others make camp out here while I go ahead with Erik."

Faengoril sighed and looked back at the group. "I think that will work better than trying to box these beasts in with horses."

Jaleal cut in. "Can I go inside?" he asked. "I would very much like to go."

Alferug nodded. "The prelate will decide that, but you are welcome to come and ask." He then dismounted from his cavedog and grabbed the reins of Erik's mount, pulling the beast along slowly.

Faengoril turned around and started barking orders to establish camp and break out the cooking pots. "I want to smell bacon and coffee before I see the sun standing two fingers above the mountains," he shouted. The others snapped into action.

Alferug walked on, listening to the chatter and ruckus of the others setting up camp. The cool morning air filled him with a joy he had long forgotten existed outside the tunnels of his home. Erik moaned and stirred atop his cavedog and Jaleal reached out to steady him.

"His fever has broken, and his color is returning," Jaleal stated.

"Thanks to you and Hatatuk," Alferug replied. "I shudder to

think what would have happened had we not found you."

"He may have made the journey," Jaleal said simply. "The cavedogs are extremely fast."

Alferug nodded, but he doubted that Erik would have lasted through the night, and he knew that Jaleal knew that as well. The gnome was simply being polite, and trying to add what little hope he could to the situation.

As they came closer Jaleal could see more detail built into the walls and the tower. The outside walls were not plain white, but made of yellow, white, gray, and even some black stones placed in a weaving pattern. The effect of the sunlight reflecting off the wall was dazzling, almost blinding in fact. The large green double doors matched the color of the tile roof above, made of some kind of metal. The doors were studded with round protrusions, like the round tops of black helmets.

"Stop here," Alferug said as they approached the gate.

The door creaked open, slowly at first, then a little faster as the dust fell from its surface and it gained momentum. A pair of men in white robes, carrying great spears appeared and waved to them.

"Al told us you would be coming," one of them said. Then they looked to Erik and glanced at each other. "Bring him in, quickly," the guard added.

The dwarf pointed to the beast. "What about him?" he asked. "I know that horses are forbidden."

The guard shrugged. "That is obviously not a horse, and I imagine it is easier to let the beast carry him," he said as he pointed to Erik.

Alferug and Jaleal led the cavedog in through the gate and the gnome couldn't help but gawk at the temple's main tower. The base was made of gray granite, reaching up a third of the way until it gave way to darker stones. Windows were evenly spaced along the tower in a vertical column. The top third of the tower was wider than the base of the tower, with wooden porches protruding out and encircling the structure

"Magnificent," Jaleal said again.

"Wait here, we will fetch the prelate," the guard said as they drew near to the front steps.

Alferug reached over and patted Erik's chest. "Alright, my

boy, we are here." The dwarf smiled to Jaleal and let out a great sigh as though a thousand pounds had been lifted from his shoulders.

CHAPTER NINETEEN

Marlin opened the door to the temple and felt a mix of emotion when he saw Erik lying atop the back of a great lizard. He had never seen a cavedog before, but he was knowledgeable enough to know what it was when he saw it and it didn't surprise him as much as it did some of the others nearby.

He saw Alferug standing next to Erik, and noted a curious aura next to him. It was green, as deep and lush as any forest he had seen before he lost his natural sight. Strings of yellow swirled through it. "And who is this?" Marlin asked.

Alferug put a hand on the gnome's shoulder. "This is Jaleal, he is one of the gnomes responsible for healing Erik."

Jaleal bowed with a great flourish of his right hand. "Jaleal, at your service," he said confidently.

Lady Dimwater stepped out past Marlin and descended the steps to Erik's side. "He was hurt badly?" she asked.

"Not in the battle," Alferug said. "But on our way here he was stuck with a funnel spider's fang."

The sorceress arched back and reflexively jerked her hand away from touching Erik.

"He's alright now," Jaleal assured her. "Or, he will be soon."

Marlin clapped his hands and whispered to the guards to go and fetch the healers. Then he turned back to the gnome. "You have our thanks for your assistance," he said.

Jaleal wrung his hands before him and looked up to Lady Dimwater. "I was hoping to join with you," he said.

Dimwater looked down to the two foot tall gnome and folded her arms. "You would join with us?" she asked.

Jaleal nodded. "I am the son of Borleal, the son of Flealor who forged the great spear known as Aeolbani." Jaleal produced the spear and held it horizontally before him for her to see. "Aeolbani has passed from father to son since the times the Wyrms of Khaltoun first descended on us. It is said that the spirit within the weapon thirsts for the blood of those who devoured our homeland. I am not saying I am the best warrior, but I promise I will serve as loyally as any other."

Marlin came down the steps and examined the diminutive creature's aura. He almost felt the strength and power radiating out as he scanned Jaleal's soul. He nodded after a minute and held his hand out for the spear. Jaleal gave him the silver shaft and watched as Marlin turned the weapon over in his hands.

"It has incredible balance," Marlin said.

Jaleal beamed with pride. "It was forged in the light of a new moon, crafted from mithril and overlaid with silver and enchanted by my grandfather Flealor."

"Enchanted how?" Marlin asked.

Jaleal took the weapon back and looked off to the right. He saw a man watering a shrub near the inside of the far wall. Jaleal whistled and told the man to put the bucket down. The man looked to Marlin, who nodded his consent and then he put the bucket down and stepped away from it.

The gnome flipped the weapon around his hand effortlessly and threw it quick and straight to the bucket. The point split through the bucket easily, spraying water all around.

"Impressive throw," Alferug commented.

Jaleal then held out his hand and the spear vanished, reappearing in his hand a moment later. "Aeolbani is bound to me, and answers to my call." He spun the weapon around and then posted the back end atop his boot. "That isn't the only enchantment, of course," he said. "But to show you the rest I would need to actually be in combat."

"He has other skills as well," Alferug commented.

"Do you have the scale?" Lady Dimwater asked.

Alferug reached under the back of his shirt and pulled out a gleaming, golden scale. "I have it," he replied with a smile.

Lady Dimwater took it gently and looked into the reflection. "I thought it would have been larger."

"It came from a young dragon." He took the scale back and gently wiped the fingerprints off the surface. "Where is he?"

"He is inside the temple," Marlin replied. Just then a group of four men in white robes emerged from the temple and went to Erik, picking him up gently and carrying him back inside. "Take him up and lay him next to Lepkin," Marlin said.

"What will you need for the ceremony?" Lady Dimwater asked Alferug.

The dwarf shrugged and started in after the healers. "Actually I just need some water."

"Water?" Dimwater echoed. "That's all you need?"

Alferug nodded. "Essentially, yes. If someone brings me enough water to fill the inside of the scale that will be all I need."

Dimwater looked to Marlin and scrunched her face into a frown. "Well then let's begin."

Jaleal waited until the others entered the temple and then he scurried in silently behind them. He took in the extravagant murals as he crossed through the first couple of chambers, but he made sure not to fall out of step with the group. Even when they ascended the seemingly endless stairs the gnome was able to keep up just a few paces behind the others. When they reached the room where Lepkin was, Marlin motioned for Dimwater and Jaleal to stay in the hall.

"Can't I go in?" Lady Dimwater asked.

"I am sorry," Marlin replied. "But I want to be as safe as possible."

She sighed and fell back to sit on a bench in front of the door. Jaleal sat next to her, his feet dangling off the bench as he kicked them back and forth.

Marlin and Alferug walked into the room just as the other healers laid Erik down on a bed and slid it closer to Lepkin.

"Incredible," Alferug said. He stepped forward and pulled a small, round end table between the two beds. He set the scale on the table and held his left hand out expectantly. One of the healers brought him a blue and white ceramic pitcher of water and the dwarf poured the liquid into the hollow of the concave scale. As the water trickled down into the scale it took on a golden hue and light bounced out in several different colors as if a rainbow was sprouting out from the scale.

Alferug placed a hand on either side of the scale and looked into the water. He spoke in an old, almost forgotten tongue, speaking to the water inside. The many colors streaming out from the scale merged into a single column of pure, white light that ascended up to the ceiling. Alferug knelt before the scale and uttered a prayer, then he rose and took the scale carefully in his hands and walked to Lepkin. With his left hand he opened Lepkin's mouth and poured some of the liquid down into his throat. Then he turned and did the same to Erik.

The same white light shined forth from their mouths and Alferug stepped back, holding the scale up above his head between them. "As the darkness yields before the light, let the sacred scale correct that which is wrong, and restore it right."

The light from their mouths bent, connecting their columns to the scale and the scale began to float up out of Alferug's hands. The light flashed and changed hues from white to green, to red, and then to blue. The room itself vibrated, as if the ground beneath the temple shook, but only subtly. The scale spun slowly and the water remaining inside rose up in a column, joining with the light and creating a brilliant golden prism that bathed the entire room in its radiance.

Lepkin and Erik both convulsed then and a great, blinding orb came out from each to pass through the golden water and then into the other body. As the orbs disappeared, the light dimmed and the scale floated down to return to Alferug's waiting hands.

Everyone was still, almost afraid to breath. Even Alferug stood motionless, staring at the bodies before him. All at once Erik's body began to move and the boy sat upright and looked down at his hands. A large smile flashed across his face and he turned to face Marlin and Alferug.

"I am me again!" he shouted. He went to kick his legs over the side of the bed but stopped suddenly and cried out in pain. The healers rushed forward to catch him before he fell out of the bed.

"Be careful," Marlin said. "Remember, your leg was broken during the battle with Erthor. We have done much to mend your body, but there is still some healing left to be done."

"Can I walk?" Erik asked.

Marlin nodded. "Your bone is set, and the fracture has been set back together, but your bone will be tender for some time yet. Your deeper tissue will also be in pain, but we have done our best to speed the recovery."

Erik nodded and leaned back on his elbows. Then he looked over to Lepkin. "Why doesn't he wake?" he asked.

Marlin sighed. "I don't know," he replied. "We will continue to work with him, but for now at least we have set things back as they should be."

Alferug stepped forward and stuck out a stout hand. "It is

nice to finally meet the Champion of Truth," he said with a smile.

Erik returned the gesture and shook his hand.

"Come, we will let them rest and then we can come back tomorrow," Marlin said as he put a hand to Alferug's shoulder.

"I don't want to wait," Erik said. "I want to resume my training."

Alferug smirked. "I have something for you," he said as he reached into his satchel and retrieved an old, leather bound book. The edges were well worn and it smelled of old paper and dust. "I believe Al had you read portions of this book. You should read the last chapter."

"Do you think it wise for him to read that now?" Marlin asked. "He has not progressed that far in his training."

Alferug winked to Erik and then turned to Marlin. "From what I have seen, the boy is ready."

The two of them then walked out, leaving Erik to flip through the pages to the back of the book.

No sooner did Marlin close the door behind him than Lady Dimwater jumped up and grabbed his arm.

"Did it work?" she asked.

Marlin nodded. "It did," he replied evenly.

"Is he awake, can I go to him?" she asked.

"He didn't wake yet," Marlin said. "Our healers will continue to work with him until he does."

Lady Dimwater let her hands fall limply to her sides and her shoulders slumped over. Jaleal moved to her side and looked up to Alferug.

"Is there anything I can do?" he asked.

"No," Marlin answered for the dwarf. "We will handle it. It just takes time."

"We don't likely have much of that," Alferug butted in. "Based on what happened at Lokton manor I would say the enemy will be upon us very soon."

The door opened and they all turned to see Erik, his weight shifted to his good leg and his hand on the door for additional support.

"You should be resting," Marlin said.

Erik nodded and looked to Lady Dimwater. "I wanted to tell you something, and I didn't want to wait until tomorrow."

"What is it?" Lady Dimwater asked.

"Master Orres relinquished his claim to your hand," Erik said with a half-smile.

Lady Dimwater arched a brow and looked at him curiously.

"Braun was there, he can vouch for it," Erik put in quickly.

"I would rather hear it from Orres himself," Lady Dimwater said.

Erik looked to the floor. "He, didn't make it," he said quietly.

A long, uncomfortable silence ensued. Each of them looked away from each other, off in their own thoughts until at last Alferug broke the silence.

"The good news is that Senator Bracken is dead, along with the army he brought to sack Lokton manor."

Marlin let out a sigh of relief. "That is good."

The dwarf frowned. "The bad news is that we lost many good men in the battle."

They all looked to Erik and the boy nodded, acknowledging that the duty fell to him to account for the slain. "Braun and my mother were able to escape," he said. "They, and a few of House Lokton along with them. The rest of House Lokton perished in the battle, along with Master Peren, Master Wendal, Master Orres, and several others from the Academy."

Lady Dimwater nodded slowly and walked away. Marlin stepped forward and put a hand on Erik's shoulder.

"You should go back in and rest."

"I will come for you in the morning," Alferug promised.

Erik nodded and they all parted ways.

*****

"Marlin, your countenance is heavy," the dragon said in his deep, throaty voice.

Marlin bowed reverently before the great, golden dragon. "Erik has returned."

"I know," the dragon said. "I could feel his presence when he arrived." The dragon reared his head back slightly and blinked lazily as he stared down at Marlin. "That is why I summoned you." Marlin nodded.

"I am at your service," Marlin said. "What would you have me do?"

A deep, low rumbling sigh emitted from the beast along with a plume of smoke. "Your predecessor asked me that same question, when Erik first arrived," he said. "I will tell you what I told him then." The dragon pushed himself up on his forelegs, the horns on his head nearly scraping the highest reaches of the vaulted ceiling. "You must quicken his training, and have him take the test as soon as possible."

Marlin looked up, with a frowning face. "You would have me force him to take the test?" The prelate thought for a moment and then shook his head. "I cannot do that, I promised him I would not."

The dragon bent his neck low and brought his snout directly in front of Marlin. "I did not say that," he corrected. "I said only to hasten it. Your predecessor was over zealous in his willingness to please me when I asked the same of him." The dragon pulled back a few feet. "I am sure that you will find Erik more than willing to expedite the process as well."

"That may be true, but he isn't ready for the test yet. He hasn't had nearly enough time to prepare."

The dragon tapped his thick claw on the stone floor. "I think you will find he has made great leaps in his abilities, even without the proper tutelage." The beast looked upward, as if he could see through the ceiling up to where Erik lay. "There is a change in his power, in his spirit. I can feel it. Surely you have noticed a shift in his aura as well?"

The prelate nodded reluctantly. "I saw it," he said. "I will do what I can, but I will need some time to ensure he is ready for the test. You know as well as I that the test itself could rend him asunder if he isn't properly prepared."

The dragon bent back low and let his hot breath wash over the prelate. "If Erik is not ready within two weeks, it will no longer matter whether he is the boy of prophecy or not. The enemy grows strong, and is preparing to strike."

The words shook Marlin to his very core. The hairs on his neck stood on end and shivers ran along his spine. "What aren't you telling me?" Marlin asked nervously.

"There is one in the temple that seeks to undo all that Erik has accomplished."

"Who?" Marlin asked. "I have the gift of sight, and I see no malice in the auras in the temple."

The dragon shook his head. "Someone has deceived you," he said. "I can feel their force in the temple."

"Can't you give me more than that?" Marlin pressed.

The dragon slowly laid back on the stone floor. "I grow weary," he said. "You will have to find the deceiver on your own. Should I emerge to reveal myself now, all would be lost."

"There was a gnome who came recently, with the dwarves," Marlin said.

"Hmmmm." The dragon drew in a deep, slow breath. "Gnomes have a reputation for being tricksters," he said. "Or perhaps it is one of the dwarves," he added. "Their folk have turned away from the ways of the Ancients."

Marlin started away and then stopped suddenly. "If I cannot see the treachery in the deceiver's aura, how do I know who it is?" he asked.

A long sigh was the only response he received. The dragon was back in its sleep.

Marlin left the chamber, less sure of himself now more than he had ever before been.

CHAPTER TWENTY

"I see you are eating well," Alferug said as he walked into the library. A plate sat before Erik with only a few egg shells and strawberry stems left of the food that had once been on it.

Erik looked up from the book. "Is this true?" he asked.

Alferug smiled warmly and sat in a chair opposite him. "It is," he answered.

"You are telling me that this is how I was able to change into a dragon?" he asked.

"In a way, yes," Alferug said. He reached across and turned the book around to face him. "You see here in this paragraph it talks about the sacred runes that enable the Champion of Truth to shift into his alternate form?"

"Yes," Erik said.

"The runes it speaks of are the runes upon the sacred banner that I carried with me to battle. When you saw it, you recognized the symbols didn't you?"

Erik sat back in his chair. "I felt they were familiar, but I wouldn't say I recognized them."

"Your spirit recognized them, and that enabled you to use them."

"I thought I was accessing Lepkin's power," Erik said.

"You were," Alferug said. The dwarf laughed to himself when Erik looked up quizzically. He patted the air with one of his hands. "Let me explain," he said. "The Champion of Truth is imbued with the same power that the Keeper of Secrets has, but yours comes from birth." Alferug picked up the book and closed it gently. "However, because the spell would tear your adolescent body apart, your gift is sealed until you reach maturity."

"So, I was able to unlock Lepkin's power because I was in an adult body?"

Alferug nodded. "Essentially," he said. "You also needed a bit of help. The first time, from what Al told me, you were motivated by your desire to save your father and root out the corruption in the senate." He paused. "That is why Al gave me the banner. He figured that seeing the symbols in a time of great need might help you shift again and tip the balance of the battle in our favor."

Erik folded his arms and smiled for a moment as he thought of his friend. "He always has clever ideas," Erik said.

"That he does," Alferug agreed. "However, you should know that your power is growing. He told me that in the valley north of Buktah, near a brook, you were able to summon a great amount of power and use it to blind a Blacktongue."

Erik recalled the moment Alferug was talking about. "She was about to kill me," Erik said simply.

"No," Alferug corrected. "There was more to it than that. The Champion of Truth is motivated by pure desires, and abhors chaos and debauchery. You saw something in that Blacktongue's soul that angered you all the way down to your very core. True though it may be you were reacting at first to save your own life that was not what called forth the power. You reacted on a visceral level, determined to expel the evil you were confronted with."

Erik looked at him with a knit brow. "Aren't all Blacktongues evil?" Erik countered. "Why didn't I react like that before?"

Alferug shook his head. "There are beings who allow themselves to give in to evil impulses, and then there are those who are driven by their evil desires. Think, how did you feel at that time?"

Erik thought again and remembered how he had felt. "I summoned my power, hoping I could use it somehow," Erik said. "I looked into her eyes and I could feel her intentions. She had no compassion, no sympathy, nothing good. Her soul was as hollow and dead as her black eyes." Erik closed his mouth and his chest began to burn again, as if she were before him even now.

"Your anger then became a hot fire. It seemed to want to consume her cold, barren soul," Alferug said.

"She pressed the dagger into my cheek and wanted me to tell her where the book was. When I said 'no' a great light erupted from my mouth, blinding the Blacktongue and throwing her to back as she covered her eyes."

"And then that is the first time you were able to light Lepkin's sword with white flames," Alferug finished.

Erik sat and pondered for a moment and then he shook his head. "No, it isn't," he said.

Alferug looked at him with puzzled eyes. "It isn't?" he repeated.

Erik shook his head again. "No, the first time the white flames came was when I battled with Erthor."

"Al didn't tell me about that," he said.

"Al didn't know," Erik replied. "He was at my home resting from battle when I fought with Erthor."

"Still," a third voice said from the doorway. The two of them turned to see Marlin approaching. "The concept is the same. The first time you used the white flame was in response to the darkest evil."

Erik nodded his head. "I knew that if I didn't stop Erthor, then he would get the book, and everything I loved would be taken away."

Alferug leaned forward. "The white flame is a sign of the Champion of Truth," he said.

"Where is that written?" Marlin asked.

Alferug offered him his book. "It is in the final part of the last chapter."

Marlin shook his head. "I can't read that," he said. "I can only read books inscribed with…"

The dwarf opened the book and Marlin fell silent. "This is the original manuscript, written personally by Al's grandfather, and I believe you will find it has enough magic in its words that you can read it," Alferug said confidently.

Marlin eagerly snatched the book and flipped to the last page. "The last time I read this book was many ages ago, before I lost my natural sight," he said. "But I don't recall this part being in the version I read."

"That is because we withheld it," Alferug said. "By our king's order we kept the final passage hidden when we copied the book for others."

"Why did you do that?" Erik asked.

"To protect you," Alferug said. "If everyone knew how to identify the Champion of Truth, then it would be easy for the enemy to find you, or worse still, perhaps they could have found a way to impersonate the Champion of Truth by using spells of deceit."

"What do you mean?" Erik asked.

Marlin nodded and set the book down. "Because everyone knows that the Champion of Truth has to be proven through the Exalted Test of Arophim, no one dares try to step forward falsely, but if they knew that all they had to do is fashion a black sword and make white flames appear on it, then any half-witted mage could try to come forward and claim to be the Champion of Truth."

"Exactly," the dwarf said. "So we kept that part back from the rest of the kingdom. We wanted to avoid the chaos of having multiple false champions coming forward to try and get the book."

"Clever," Marlin said. "How is it that *you* have the original copy?" he asked.

Alferug beamed with pride. "By virtue of my office in the court, I am entrusted to keep the book safe, and to offer advice to the king when needed to help the Champion of Truth."

"So, when will I be able to use my dragon power?" Erik asked.

Marlin cut in. "There is some debate about that," he said. "Some believe that The Champion of Truth will automatically change into a dragon upon reaching the age of adulthood, and others believe it is a power that he can use at will once his training is complete."

"Which is it?" Erik asked. Marlin shrugged.

"I can see the merits of both theories, but I have not run across any texts that decide the matter definitively." The prelate then turned a keen eye on Alferug. "The dwarves wouldn't have kept that secret as well, would they?"

Alferug scoffed. "No," he said. "We have the same debates in our hall about the meaning of the word 'maturity' that is written in the passage." He sighed and looked back to Erik. "One thing most of us do agree with is that it is likely extremely dangerous to try and force the change. Al and I took the risk only because you had already been able to change from Lepkin's form into the dragon."

"But to do so now could be disastrous," Marlin interjected. "Not only is your power raw, but unlike Lepkin's body, yours has not reached maturity and would likely not survive the change."

Erik looked to the floor. "So what *do* we do?" he asked.

"We train," Marlin said. "And as soon as you are ready, you will take the test and advance to the next stage."

"I am ready now," Erik said confidently.

Alferug leaned back in his chair and looked at Erik hard for a moment. "You have been through a lot," he said. "But I don't think you are quite ready yet."

"Why not?" Erik argued. "I have already changed into a dragon, twice! I have called forth the white flames many times now, and I have been able to use my power in all sorts of ways. I used it to dispel the warlock's spell and reveal his true form in the senate hall, I used it to discern which senators were evil and corrupt, and I even used it to find magical traps in the warlock's home. What more do I have to prove before I can take the test?"

"There is a lot more," Marlin said softly.

"And in the meantime how many more of my friends will die?" Erik spurted out. His face was flush red and he was breathing heavily. "I don't want to wait anymore."

Marlin knelt down next to him. "I understand," he said. "I can see the anger and the hurt in you. Do you remember when I said I would never force you to take the Exalted Test of Arophim?"

Erik nodded once.

"I also can't allow you to take it too early. To do so would be carelessly risking your life."

"I have already been risking my life," Erik replied.

Marlin smiled. "That you have," he said. "I promise I won't delay your test one second longer than I have to in order to prepare you."

"What else do you want me to do?" Erik asked.

"Come with me," Marlin said. "Let's go back up to the training room."

*****

Marlin moved quietly through the halls and up the stone steps. As he slipped out from the stairwell and into the hall where Lepkin lay, he looked both ways. One of the temple priests stood at the far end, leaning on the window sill and looking outside. No one else was in the hall. The prelate walked to the door and opened it just enough to slip inside the room.

Inside only a few torches were lit, but it was more than enough light to see clearly. Four priests stood around Lepkin with their hands on his upper body. They chanted healing spells and Marlin could see the energy flowing from them to Lepkin. The priests' eyes were closed, and none seem to notice him as he moved behind one of the pillars closer to where Lepkin lay.

His mind was heavy, still replaying the warning he had received earlier. Who could the traitor be? He scanned the healers' auras briefly, just to double check his own men. He saw no fault in any of them. He thought about the dragon's words and knew that it had to be one of the people who came with Erik to the temple. He found it hard to believe that either Alferug or Jaleal could be the traitors the dragon spoke of.

Perhaps it was one of the dwarves outside the walls? That would be the only thing that made sense, since he hadn't been able to scan any of their auras. Except, he was told that it was someone *inside* the temple. He sighed and put the thoughts out of his head.

Marlin stepped forward, scanning Lepkin's aura as the healers finished and began to break their connection with him. "Any change?" he asked.

"None," one of the healers said.

Marlin walked in and placed a hand over Lepkin's forehead. "We are running out of time," he said. The hairs on the back of his neck began to rise, as they had in the sacred chamber below. It was as if a pair of eyes were upon him. Marlin used his peripheral vision to scan the room, but saw no hint of any other life force. Suddenly Marlin looked up, and saw an aura hiding up on top of one of the large beams, in the crook of a joist, high up on the ceiling. Marlin squinted and recognized the aura almost instantly. "You can come down," Marlin said with a hard edge to his tone.

The aura didn't move.

"Come down, Jaleal," Marlin said. His tone was sharper this time.

Jaleal descended and bowed before him. "I only came to help," the gnome said.

"By hiding in the shadows with a spear?" Marlin questioned.

"It isn't what it looks like," Jaleal said. "Trust me, I can help him."

"How?" Marlin said. His white eyes bored into the gnome's swirling aura, looking for the truth behind the creature's words. Jaleal started to fidget and squirm.

"Just…" the gnome stammered. "Just watch." He moved to Lepkin's bed, jumped up and raised his spear overhead.

Marlin launched into action and struck Jaleal with a psionic blast that sent the little creature sprawling through the air to land on the far side of the room. "Hold fast!" Marlin commanded. "Move and we will send you to Hammenfein!"

Jaleal shook his head and scanned the room. He sprinted for the nearest shadow and called forth his cloaking spell, but it proved useless. Every man in the room came charging straight for him. "Stop," Jaleal said. "It isn't what it looks like."

"Take him!" Marlin commanded.

Several hands gripped Jaleal's arms and legs, wrenching the spear from him and holding him in the air above the floor.

"I was warned," Marlin grumbled.

"Warned about what?" Jaleal asked with trembling voice. "I just want to help!"

"You just tried to kill Lepkin," Marlin countered.

"No, I can wake him," Jaleal insisted. "I knew how it would look to you, so I was going to wait until the others left before I did it."

"You expect me to believe that?" Marlin asked.

"Prelate, I see no lie in the gnome's words," one of the healers said. "His aura is clean."

"See?" Jaleal squealed with a nod toward the healer. "Listen to him, let me show you."

Marlin paused and looked intensely at the gnome. He too saw no hint of falsehood in the gnome's aura, but he also knew what he had just seen, as well as what the dragon had said. Finally he gave a shake of his head. "No, I can't risk it," he said.

"What do we do?" one of the healers asked.

"Give me his spear and then expel him from the temple." One of the healers handed him the mithril spear and then Marlin watched the others struggle to hold the writhing creature as they quickly hefted him out of the room. The prelate looked down to the spear. "What else can I do?" he asked himself.

*****

"So, how was the training session?" Alferug asked.

Erik looked up from the round cushion he sat on in the middle of the room and saw the dwarf walking into the room, book in hand. "We just did a review," Erik said impatiently.

"Oh?"

"Just dispelling fake images and guessing which warrior wants to bash my head in with a rattan sword, things like that," Erik explained.

Alferug drew his mouth to the left corner and wrinkled his nose. "Ah, I see," he commented. "Well, a review is the proper place to start, I suppose."

Erik shrugged and drew an imaginary line on the floor with his index finger. "I don't really feel like reading," he said.

The dwarf sat in front of Erik and opened the book to the final page. "That's alright with me," he said as he turned the book around for Erik to see. "I wanted to concentrate on writing." He took a piece of chalk from his satchel and held it out for Erik. "Come on," Alferug insisted when Erik hesitated. "I saw how much you enjoyed the wind on your face and the power of your wings. If you want to feel that again, then we should learn how to write this."

Erik took the chalk and his mood improved noticeably. "Writing the rune will help me change?" he asked.

"No," Alferug said with a frown. "Not by itself, anyway. But it will help you commit the runes to memory, and you will need to be able to do that before you can use them."

Erik nodded and looked down at the book. Alferug placed his pointer finger just above the first rune. Erik started from the left and drew the top line to the right. Alferug reached out and wiped the line away. "What are you doing?" Erik asked.

"These are not written from left to right, like the common tongue," Alferug explained. "You must start each line from the right and go to the left. Begin with the top stroke and work your way down, but always from the right to the left."

"What difference does it make, as long as it looks the same?" Erik asked. He didn't mean to sound rude, but he could tell by Alferug's stern expression that he had struck a small nerve.

"You aren't drawing a picture," Alferug said. "You are writing an ancient, magical language. It must be exact, or else it will have no power."

Erik nodded and started over. He placed his chalk farther to the right and drew a mostly-straight line to the left.

"It may feel strange at first," Alferug said. "But that is why we practice, to get it right." Alferug erased the line with his sleeve. "Do it again, as straight and exact as possible."

Erik sighed and leaned forward, concentrating to hold the chalk just so. He slowly, purposefully drew the line to the left and once he finished he pulled the chalk away and looked to Alferug for confirmation before continuing. The dwarf nodded and gestured for him to continue. Next, Erik started a curved line, like a 'C' which was easy enough. Then he connected a third line to the bottom of the curve and drew it up to the opposite line, but he pressed too hard and the chalk broke and his line ended with a jagged hook.

Alferug leaned forward, erased the whole rune, and said, "Try again."

In the space of three hours Erik had only drawn two of the symbols to Alferug's satisfaction. Erik leaned back from the floor and stretched his back. His leg ached too, and it was highly uncomfortable to sit on the cushion.

"We can continue tomorrow," Alferug said.

"No, I can continue," Erik said. "Just, maybe let's write on the wall instead of the floor."

The dwarf smiled and nodded his agreement. "Alright." He walked over to a clear space on the wall and drew the first two runes for Erik. Each stroke was quick and exact, like the precision of a master swordsman. As each symbol was completed it began to glow slightly. The first was green, and the second was yellow.

"They glow when you write them," Erik commented.

Alferug nodded. "I have learned the magic behind the symbols," he said.

"When I learn the magic, will the symbols glow like yours?" Erik asked.

Alferug shook his head with a big smile. "No, your symbols will be much brighter than mine," he said. The two spent the rest of the day writing the runes on the wall until the bell chimed for dinner and Lady Dimwater came up to get them both.

When the three of them entered the dining hall, Erik noticed that Jaleal was not at the table, nor anywhere in the room. "Where is Jaleal?" Erik asked.

"He is no longer a guest of the temple," Marlin said.

Erik frowned. "Why not?"

Marlin tapped his fingers on the table in front of him.

Lady Dimwater came to his rescue. "Jaleal tried to stab Lepkin with his spear," she said coldly. She turned an eye on Marlin. "So the Prelate expelled him from the temple."

"Why save me only to try to kill Lepkin?" Erik asked.

"The boy's right, that doesn't make much sense," Alferug added.

"I saw it with my own eyes," Marlin said. "The healers in the room saw it also."

"I would have fried the little pygmy," Lady Dimwater growled.

Marlin pushed his plate away. "I agree with Erik and Alferug," he told her. "I don't think it makes sense either."

"Then why expel him?" Alferug pressed.

"Because I received a warning," Marlin said simply.

Alferug started to ask a question but Lady Dimwater shook her head and he stopped. Erik glanced between the three of them, trying to decide what the unspoken message was. When none of them offered a more detailed explanation, he gave up and took a bite of his roast chicken. They ate their meal in silence and each went their separate ways at the end of the meal. Erik felt a rift in the harmony that had once been so prevalent in the temple. He found himself longing for Lepkin to wake, or at least for Al to return.

He went off to bed feeling more alone than he did during his early training days at Kuldiga Academy when Lepkin hardly spoke to him and the other boys teased him. As he laid his head on his pillow he found his mind going back to his time at the academy. He recalled the tournament where he had beaten so many of the other apprentices. He thought about his first glimpse of Lady Dimwater's study. A slight chill ran down his spine as he remembered the ghost that had chased him through the hall.

Then his mind drifted back to the tournament and he remembered Hal, the asthmatic apprentice. He wondered where he was now. All of the other masters were either dead or in Drakei Glazei at the moment. Had they been able to send all of the students home, or had something happened to them? He briefly thought of Orres and the others who had fallen, and then he raised his hand up to his chest. His eyes shot open wide when he realized he didn't have his father's ring.

He jumped down from his bed, stopping and grabbing his leg as the pain reminded him he had to move slower at the moment. The burning knot gradually lessened enough for him to climb the stairs up to where Lepkin was. He found a pair of temple guards flanking the door.

"The prelate has ordered that no one go in," one of them said.

"Even me?" Erik asked.

The guards looked to each other briefly. "I doubt he meant him," the other said.

"Be quick," the first said.

Erik nodded and went in. Six healers stood around Lepkin, about to begin their spells. They stopped and looked at him curiously. "I came because I forgot something," Erik said. "When I was in his body, I had a ring around my neck on a leather thong. I need it back." One of the healers gently lifted Lepkin's shirts and pulled the necklace out. Erik sighed with relief when he saw the emerald ring and he rushed forward to take it. He quickly slipped the leather thong around his neck and tucked the ring under his shirt. "Thanks," he said. Then he slowly made his way, limping down the stairs back to his bedroom.

Once on his bed he fell asleep within minutes, clutching the ring through his shirt.

CHAPTER TWENTYONE

Erik stood in the center of the training room. His lungs burned and his head ached. His throat was dry and begging for a drink. Sweat dripped from the back of his neck and the front of his brow.

"Let's try once again," Marlin said.

"It has been almost two weeks," Erik said. "I can't do this."

"If you want to take the test, you will have to be able to do this."

"Did you have to master this before *your* test?" Erik asked.

Marlin bristled. "Mine was not the *exalted* test," he said coolly. "But, yes, I did have to demonstrate this power as well."

Erik jerked his head to the left and cracked his neck. He picked his hands up and held them both in front of him, palms out as if about to push someone. He focused, concentrating on the air between his hands. He nodded when he was ready.

Marlin moved to a lever on the wall and pulled it. Oil rushed into a trough along the wall. Then the prelate set a match to the oil and flames *whooshed* through the room, filling it with a thick smoke. "Light banishes the darkness," Marlin called out as he disappeared behind the film of smoke. "Your gift allows you to control physical elements as well as magical ones. Now, concentrate and banish the smoke."

Erik took in a couple of shallow breaths, reflexively coughing as the thick, hot smoke seeped into his lungs. He called upon his power, focusing on the smoke. It started as a tingle at first, and then felt like a rush of heat inside his chest. For a moment he thought it was the smoke, or perhaps the heat from the burning oil, but this time it was different. He was generating the heat. He concentrated, letting his inner fire build to a peak before opening his mouth. In his mind's eye he envisioned a blinding light bursting out of him, like it had with the Blacktongue by the brook, but the reality was much less impressive.

A small, almost indiscernible flash sputtered out from him. Instead of banishing the smoke, it only made it swirl in front of him slightly under the force of his yell. Then it closed in and he succumbed to the stinging heat of the smoke. As he feel to his knees, coughing and sputtering he heard a click somewhere behind the smoke and a few seconds later the smoke dispersed out through the open windows above them, as it had many times before over the last week.

"That was good," Marlin said with a huge smile on his face.

"Good?" Erik coughed.

"I saw the spark that time," he said enthusiastically.

"A spark?" Erik laughed and fell back on the floor, exhausted. "I would be more effective if I lit a match and threw it at the smoke."

"No," Marlin said. "I have seen many students unable to produce a spark that bright," he said. "And for most, myself included, it takes at least a year to become this good. Your progress is astounding!"

Erik lifted a tired hand and twirled a finger in the air. "Woo-hoo," he said.

Marlin came to sit next to him. "Enough for today. Go and practice your writing with Alferug. We will continue this tomorrow."

"I can't wait," Erik said as he lurched up, struggling to get his elbows under himself. "Couldn't we just practice this at night so I don't have to breathe in all this smoke?" Erik asked.

Marlin rustled his hair and stood back up. "Then what would the distraction be?" he asked. "This test was designed to be passed under physical duress."

"Who thought of this stuff?" Erik asked as Marlin helped the boy up to his feet.

"It is meant to help you prepare for the challenge ahead," Marlin said flatly.

"It feels like someone with a lot of time on their hands sat around thinking of horrible ways to torture people," Erik shot back. "Remember that gauntlet test you put me through the first time I came to the temple, you can't tell me that a normal person thought of that, and now you are trying to suffocate me."

Marlin chuckled. "The Champion of Truth is destined to dispel Nagar's Blight. You, Erik, are the only person capable of destroying the magic that the enemy would use to enslave us all. It is a magic that can't be beaten by the sword. It is itself a shadow, a thick fog of darkness, and we need to train you to use the light in order to banish it forever."

Erik nodded. "Why not just take the book and throw it into a volcano, wouldn't that destroy it?"

Marlin paused for a moment and stroked his chin. Erik could see that the man was thinking very carefully before answering. "The book is only one aspect," Marlin said. "The first time the book was used, it unlocked Nagar's Blight on the Middle Kingdom. Even if we could destroy the book, which we can't, without banishing the magic it unlocked, the threat will still remain. The Ancients cannot return until the curse is lifted from this land. To do that, we must destroy the magic itself, those who seek it, and find a way to dispel the book."

"And throwing the book, made of paper, into a volcano wouldn't destroy it?" Erik asked skeptically.

"It is not a simple book. It is a very powerful magical artifact. No physical element, even a volcano, can destroy it. Do you remember that Allun'rha was able to counter the magic during the Battle of Hamath Valley?"

"Yes, I read about that with Al," Erik said.

"You will have to find that book and finish unlocking its magic in order to finally dispel Nagar's Secret and destroy the book."

"Well, if he already had the spell, why didn't he destroy Nagar's Secret?"

"He wasn't strong enough," Marlin replied. "He was a powerful wizard, but even he was not able to finish the battle."

"What happened to him?" Erik asked.

Marlin was silent for a moment. "Most think he died, but no one knows for sure," he said after a moment. "Come, let's go see Alferug in the library. I am sure he is getting anxious."

The two of them walked down a couple of levels and went into the library to find the dwarf pacing in front of a large easel filled with blank parchment. A small jar of black paint rested on a round table nearby, along with a paintbrush. When he saw the two of them he smiled and pointed to the easel.

"Are you ready?" he asked Erik.

Erik sighed and nodded slowly. He went to the easel and took the paintbrush in hand. "From the beginning?" he asked.

"Of course," Alferug said.

Erik nodded and dipped the paintbrush into the jar of paint. He made the first stroke, perfect and exact. Then he made the curve, the next stroke, and finished with the last three strokes and stepped away from the easel.

"Good," Alferug said. "Now, take that one down, set it on the floor." Erik did as he was asked and went to paint the next rune, but Alferug held a hand up and stopped him. "This time, I want you to imagine the meaning as you draw the rune. It isn't enough to just slosh paint around. You have to feel it." The dwarf cupped a hand to his heart for emphasis.

Erik sighed and closed his eyes to clear his mind. Then he opened his eyes and focused on the meaning of the rune as he redrew it. This time, as he finished the last stroke the paint changed from black to green and the rune glowed and hummed. Erik smiled and looked to Alferug. The dwarf was almost as excited as he was.

"Do the next one!" Alferug said as he churned his finger in the air. Erik ripped the paper down and quickly drew the next rune, focusing on the meaning and letting his hand flow with the symbol. As with the first, the paint changed color. The symbol glowed bright yellow, almost hurting Erik's eyes.

He took the paper down and drew the third. As he finished each rune, it would glow a different color. Once he finished the last one the room began to hum and Erik felt a rush of wind around him. He looked to see Alferug's beard floating up in the whirlwind and laughing giddily.

"Well done!" Alferug shouted. "Can you feel it, boy?" he asked.

Erik felt the wind rush into him and for a brief moment it was as if he was in the sky again, soaring on great, powerful wings with the cool breeze caressing his face. Then it faded and the runes stopped glowing.

"I could feel it," Erik said.

Alferug stepped in and poked him in the chest. "Right here," he said as he drilled his finger into Erik's heart. "This is where the magic comes from. Keep at it, and you will be back in the sky soon enough!" Alferug clapped his hands. "Ha ha!" he shouted. "This is wonderful!"

Erik laughed out as well and went back to the easel. "Again!"

he shouted.

"Yes, yes, do it again, boy!" Alferug agreed. "Let's see if we can take some books off the shelves!"

*****

Erik woke to the sudden sound of his door bursting open. He sat up in his bed to see who was invading his sleep, but all he saw was a wall of flames closing in. He rolled off his bed and ducked under the rush of flames. Thick smoke filled the room, making it impossible to see. His heart raced in his chest and his eyes stung from the smoke. He coughed the bitter, harsh smoke out of his lungs as he gasped for air. The roar of the flames was almost deafening. The smoke grew so thick that he could almost feel it closing in around him, choking the clean air out of him.

He wasn't sure what was going on. In his half-awake state he was disoriented, and couldn't think clearly. All he knew for sure was that if he did nothing, he was going to be burned alive.

Instinctively he called upon his training over the last week and rose to his feet. He put his hands in front of him and called upon his power again. The spark appeared inside his chest and grew until its intensity matched the fire around him. Then, he closed his eyes and opened his mouth.

A great light burst out from him and dispelled the smoke as the day chases the night. The flames rolled back, shrinking away from his power and then the room was still. Despite the fact that it was still dark outside, the inside of his room was bright, as though the sun was shining directly above him.

There, in the doorway, stood a very pleased Marlin. The man was smiling and clapping softly. "Well done," he said. "Well done indeed."

Erik's heart started to slow and he looked around him. None of the furniture in the room showed any sign of the fire, nor were there any scorch marks on the wall, or any wisps of smoke left. "This was a test?" Erik asked incredulously.

"You are the one who said we should do it at night," Marlin pointed out.

"I meant *without* fire and smoke!" Erik said.

Marlin patted the air and stifled a chuckle. "Relax, this is the final phase of the training," he said. "Once a student is able to show the spark, no matter how small, the next phase is to catch them while sleeping."

"I'll ask again," Erik started. "Who thought of this stuff?"

Marlin couldn't help but laugh now and he stepped into the room and closed the door. "I'm sorry, I really am, but over the years we have learned that a student never progresses beyond a simple spark unless they are put into a situation where they actually think the danger is real." Marlin calmed himself and took a moment to straighten his face before continuing. "Given the fact that all of our training is about how to discern truth from error, we also discovered that we could never fool a student once they had progressed to this stage unless we waited until they were deep asleep." Marlin walked forward and put a reassuring hand on Erik's shoulder. "Do forgive me," he pleaded. "But it is the way we administer the final test."

"The final test?" Erik echoed skeptically.

Marlin nodded. "Well, there is *one* more for you."

Erik looked at Marlin's white eyes for a moment and then a smile crept across his face. "You mean?"

Marlin nodded. "Tomorrow I will take you downstairs. There you will go through the Exalted Test of Arophim, if you believe you are ready."

Erik smiled and hugged Marlin. "Thank you!" he said. Marlin hugged the boy back for a moment and then pushed him away.

"Get some sleep," he said. "You will need it."

CHAPTER TWENTY TWO

Marlin led Erik through the hall and gestured for him to stop next to a simple iron crossed door at the end of the hall. Marlin produced a long, slender claw from a pocket and slid it into the opening under the knob. Golden rays snaked out from the brass key plate, reaching and stretching across the iron bands over the door. The metal glowed and vibrated against the wood.

Marlin stood back and looked to Erik. "Go on," he said. "Open it."

Erik hesitated momentarily and then turned the knob. The latch clicked and the door gently fell open.

Marlin reached forward and removed the claw. "Hang on to this," he said as he offered it to Erik.

Erik took the claw and then stepped through the doorway. Marlin followed and pushed the door closed behind him. The steps steeply descended down a tight spiral. Small, goat horn sconces adorned the wall every seven feet to illuminate the tunnel and caused the gold inlay between the red bricks to shimmer and dance.

At the bottom of the stairs the brick opened up into a green marble tunnel. Torches hung silently halfway down the smooth, hard walls. Erik put his hand on the wall and gently stroked the surface. As he walked deeper into the tunnel a golden radiance appeared, growing brighter and brighter until he stood in a large antechamber made entirely of gold with glowing crystals hanging from the ceiling.

A small golden dragon head protruded from the left wall. The eyes were open, made of jade, and staring at him.

"Wait for one moment," Marlin told Erik as he walked up to the dragon's head. "As we told you before, the other initiates of the temple go through the Test of Arophim. It is not the same as the test you are about to experience. The Test of Arophim is administered by the prelate, and it usually is held in the training room, or in the council chamber at the top of the temple. However, you are going to go through the *Exalted* Test of Arophim. This has never been done before." Marlin paused and smiled at Erik. "I want you to know that it has been an honor to work with you," he said.

Erik nodded, he fumbled for the appropriate thing to say but all that came out of his mouth was, "Thank you."

Marlin smiled and slid his index finger over the dragon's head. A small hole opened in the top and Marlin pointed to Erik's hand. "Now you will insert the claw into this hole."

Erik moved forward and went to put the claw in. The jade eyes began to glow. Green light exuded from the dragon's eyes until it enveloped Erik and Marlin entirely. After a few moments, the light died down and then the golden mouth opened, revealing a key on the dragon's tongue.

A door materialized in the wall at the end of the hall. The bricks cracked and crumbled as golden light ripped through the green marble, revealing the golden door. A large golden eye opened on the door.

"What's inside?" Erik asked.

"That is the test for you to find out," Marlin said with a smile. He placed his hands on Erik's shoulders. "I wish you all the luck in the world," he said. "Now take the key and slide it into the keyhole in the eye." Marlin then backed away.

"You aren't coming in with me?" Erik asked.

"No," Marlin said. "No one is permitted into this test except those who claim to be the Champion of Truth."

Erik nodded and watched Marlin disappear back through the tunnel. Then he turned and looked at the key on the dragon's tongue for a long time, occasionally glancing up to the keyhole in the door nervously.

"Come on," Erik said to himself. "This is what you wanted." He reached forward with a trembling hand and took the key from the statue. He moved to the door and slid the key into the pupil and turned it. The tumblers inside clicked and snapped. The door slid back three inches and then sank into the floor below.

Erik took a deep breath and held it for a moment. The stark darkness beyond the open doorway gave him more than a little reason to pause. There seemed to be nothing beyond the doorway. Finally a faint red glow appeared and Erik heard a voice.

"Enter, Champion," the deep, thunderous voice said. There was a strength and vibrance in the voice that unsettled Erik.

Erik stepped into the darkness and pushed forward, aiming to go to the red glowing light. A few yards into the next chamber the door behind him rose up from the floor and sealed the way back. Chills ran through Erik's spine and his feet halted in mid step for a moment. After a couple of seconds he continued going forward. He made no more than four steps before the red light winked out and he was left in total darkness.

"Is the Champion afraid of the dark?" the voice bellowed. "Can't you banish the darkness?"

Erik felt uneasy, sick to his stomach. He thought to turn around and go back, but he pressed forward a couple more steps. Then he stopped and concentrated hard on his power. "Shall I use the spark?" Erik asked.

"If you can," the voice echoed.

Erik nodded to himself and slowly raised his hands before him. He felt the cold, icy fingers of fear swiping at his back from the shadows, but he put the feeling out of his mind and concentrated on summoning the light from within himself. Unlike before, he found it almost easy to conjure the spark within himself. It started as a fuzzy tingling behind his sternum, and then it grew until his whole upper torso felt hot. He barely opened his mouth to shout when the darkness evaporated and he found himself standing in a great hall of blue stone.

Great, thick columns held up the high, vaulted ceiling. Statues of human warriors were carved into the walls behind the pillars and the floor was polished to such a high shine that Erik could almost see himself in the stone beneath his feet.

It took him several minutes to reach the large stone pedestal in the center of the chamber. Next to it a fist-sized garnet sat upon a golden candlestick with smaller jasper stones placed into the base of the stick. Erik resisted the urge to reach out and touch the jewels. He brought his attention to the pedestal and searched it. Its surface was covered in ancient runes, most of which he had never seen before. Each of them glowed just enough to be seen, but not as bright as a candle burns.

"That was impressive," the voice echoed through the hall.

Erik wheeled around, but saw no one there. He reached into his power again, seeking to find the source of the voice. When he turned back and looked beyond the pedestal, his mouth fell open and he nearly staggered backward in shock. His power had found the source of the voice, but it was not anything he had expected to see.

A great, golden leg rested before him. He stared at the shield-sized scales briefly before following the leg up to the shoulder, glancing nervously at the long spikes protruding from the dragon's spine. He then looked to the great, angular jaws filled with teeth the size of spears protruding through the thin, leathery lips. The eyes opened slowly, revealing great green orbs flecked with gold and red specks. The long, angled pupil shrank quickly and then widened slightly as the eye shifted to focus on the boy.

"Impressive indeed," the dragon said in its deep, throaty voice. "You have blossomed very quickly," he said.

"How can you be here?" Erik asked. "I thought all the dragons left a long time ago."

"The temple protects me from the power of Nagar's Blight," the dragon replied. "So long as I do not stay awake for too long."

"And you are here to find the Champion of Truth?" Erik asked.

"I am," the dragon said. Its large, penetrating eyes locked with Erik's and the boy felt a chill run through him. The dragon's stare was more intense than any Marlin had ever given. "Are you ready to begin the test?"

Erik looked behind him and replied innocently, "I thought it already began."

The dragon chuckled and plumes of smoke spurted out through its nostrils. "That was only a warm up."

Erik nodded. "So what do I need to do?" he asked. His voice cracked in the middle of the question, but he stood still and tried to display confidence.

The dragon reached forward and placed a claw over the pedestal. A large, brown book appeared before him. "Open the book," the dragon commanded. "We shall see if you can resist its power."

Erik stepped close and stared at it. "Is this…" He couldn't bring himself to finish the question. He could feel the darkness inside, and he had his answer. "If I open it, won't it affect you?"

"Why would you say that?" the dragon asked.

"A book I read says that the mere presence of the book Nagar's Secret would warp dragons," Erik replied. "If the book is here, and I open it, it could destroy you."

"You worry about me?" the dragon laughed. "If you want to pass the test, you will have to open the book."

Erik slowly reached forward and placed a hand on the bottom corner of the large tome. The leather felt cold to the touch. He thought to open it, but then he pulled his hand back and stepped away from the pedestal. "I can't open this," he said. "I am to destroy the book."

The dragon leaned down close and its hot breath washed over Erik as it spoke. "You would destroy it?" the dragon asked. "Why would you do that?"

"Because it would enslave everyone," Erik replied. "It would take away our will and destroy us."

"Hmm," the dragon said. "You are wise, for such a young boy."

Erik then looked at the book and had a strange thought. He reached into himself and used his power on the book. Then he grinned. "That isn't the book," he said.

The dragon smiled, drawing its leathery lips tight over its sharp teeth. "I never said it was Nagar's Blight," he said. "You only assumed."

Erik then looked to the large book. "But it is evil," he said. "I can feel that much."

The dragon nodded. "It is indeed," he confirmed. Then he placed a claw under the cover and flipped it open. "It is called the Chronicles of the Spurned," the dragon said. A ghastly screech erupted from the book and Erik was wrapped in a cold, silver mist. "You must witness its contents."

Erik's very soul froze in horror as he watched the pages before him. Instead of words, they held pictures. As the pages turned, the pictures began to move as if a scene was unveiling itself before him. Demons and warlocks appeared, ravaging the countryside and laying waste to entire villages and towns. Behind them came another, clothed in black robes and holding a large jewel with which he raised the dead corpses and bound them to his will. The army washed over the land like a plague of locusts until it reached Valtuu Temple.

"This is what is coming," the dragon roared above the din of the magical book.

Erik's eyes grew wide as Valtuu Temple was engulfed in flames and collapsed to the ground. The man with the jewel then pulled a black book from the rubble and opened it. A great red flare erupted from the pages as though it contained a massive volcano and demons and monsters poured out from the pages of the book.

"Now look!" the dragon bellowed.

Erik watched as the pages turned again and a great dragon flew in from the south on wings of fire. His great breath spewed black fire and lightning over the kingdom and all melted away before him until he stood alone atop a glossy black granite mountain.

"He is Tu'luh the Red," the dragon said. "And he comes to claim this land."

The boy couldn't move. His eyes were transfixed on the dragon in the book. At the base of the mountain laid an ocean of corpses. Then the dragon roared and a great crackle of lightning struck the ground. Those who were dead were given their lives back, though now they were all twisted and disfigured, like the demons that had come with the man to the temple.

"He will rule over all in the Middle Kingdom," the dragon hissed. "Unless the Champion of Truth stops him."

Erik felt a hot wave as the dragon in the book roared again and its eyes locked onto Erik. Somehow, Tu'luh the Red could see him. At that moment, Erik recognized the dragon's eyes. It was the same pair of glowing eyes that he had seen in Bracken's house, in the warlock's secret chamber.

The boy's fear melted away, replaced in an instant by a visceral anger that welled up inside of him until he yelled in anger. The power of his spark shook the room and the light blasted into the evil book and burned it to ashes. The silver mist dissipated and Erik was left kneeling on the floor, gasping for breath.

He looked up to see the golden dragon smiling and looking into his eyes. "You are strong indeed," he said. "Perhaps you do have the power to change what is coming."

Erik huffed and sucked in a couple of breaths before nodding. "That cannot be our future," he said.

"There is another way," the dragon said.

Erik pushed himself up and looked to the dragon.

"Let me show you the alternative." The dragon waved his massive claws before Erik's face and Erik was swept back. The temple fell away around him and he found himself on a green mountain looking down at the temple. The ground shook beside him and he turned to see the golden dragon standing next to him. "The power of Nagar's Blight is not necessarily evil," he said. "It can be used for good."

"What do you mean?" Erik asked.

"Look down," the dragon said.

Erik looked and a great army came out of the forest. Their gleaming armor reflecting the sunlight as they marched to the temple. From the temple emerged ranks of priests and warriors, as well as a sizable army of dwarves. The two forces clashed together and within a matter of moments the green valley was stained red.

"You have seen this kind of scene before," the dragon said. "I know of the battles you suffered." The dragon snaked his neck around to look at Erik. "Even if you destroy Nagar's Blight, this kind of war will continue. Mankind has never been a race of peace. They are, and ever have been, petty, jealous creatures that take by force what they cannot earn by virtue."

"What are you saying?" Erik asked.

"Isnt it obvious?" the dragon replied. "I am showing you the true nature of mankind. You would risk everything you are, everyone you love, to destroy a book that has the power to prevent this."

Erik shook his head. "But there would be no choice," he said. "I cannot abandon everyone to become what I saw in that first book you showed me."

The dragon sighed. "There is more to this," he said. "Watch the sky."

Erik looked up and saw four pillars of fire descending quickly. One went to the far east, another went to the west, one streaked overhead, fire roaring and sparks trailing behind. The fourth dropped far to the south. A moment after it disappeared beyond the southern horizon a great plume of smoke rose up and a wall of fire grew like a tidal wave.

"Are they dragons?" Erik asked.

The dragon shook his head. "They are worse than dragons," he said. "They are worse than anything this world has ever seen."

Erik watched wide-eyed as the wave of flame rushed toward them, devouring everything in its path. A moment before the fire crashed into them, they were back in the temple. Erik was still standing in front of the pedestal, and the dragon was behind it, looking at him intently.

"What you saw, is the end of Terramyr. If the world continues as it is, it will be destroyed by powers greater than anything that has ever walked this plane." The dragon hung its head low and a single tear emerged from its right eye. The great, sparkling droplet fell and crashed to the floor.

Erik looked down at the small puddle and then back up to the dragon's eyes. "So, you are saying it is better for the world to be overrun by demons?" Erik asked.

The dragon shook his head. "No," he said. "But the power of Nagar's Blight can be used for good as well. Someone with a pure heart can alter it, and use it to create peace." The dragon leaned in. "An everlasting peace that will save the Middle Kingdom, and the world, from both of the fates you have just witnessed."

Erik thought for a moment, trying to understand everything he had just seen. "But I thought the Champion of Truth was meant to destroy Nagar's Blight."

The dragon nodded. "That is true," he said. "But I have had many years, centuries actually, to meditate upon our future." The dragon turned his head so that his right eye was only a few inches away from Erik. "What would the Champion of Truth do?" he asked. "Would he save the kingdom only to condemn the world? Or would he rise above them all to save everyone from a doomed future?"

*****

Jaleal used the shadows of the giant clouds above to cover his tracks. It proved useful in evading the dwarves, but he knew that it would provide little protection against the temple guards. As he neared the southern wall he glanced around. He didn't see any guards nearby. He slipped his tiny, agile fingers into the spaces between the rocks and went up and over the temple's outer wall as skillfully as a lizard. He dropped down into a soft fern and flattened himself against the ground. A pair of guards came around the western corner and started walking near him.

The gnome used his magic to expand the leaves, effectively shielding himself from their sight. After the guards passed he sprinted for the temple and ascended up. Occasionally he would glance back, ensuring there were no guards looking his way, but he doubted anyone would be looking for a gnome climbing the outside of the temple.

Just in case, he hurried up the side as quickly as he could, pausing underneath awnings or behind window shutters as guards passed by below. After a few minutes, he reached the second floor from the top. He moved to a window and slowly poked his head around to look inside. Seeing the room was empty he put his hand to the glass and gently slid the pane up just enough to slip inside. He crept to the door and bent low to look through the space underneath. He couldn't see anything, so he put his ear to the door and listened for footsteps. He heard nothing. He softly turned the knob and pulled the door open enough to peer down one side of the hall.

He spied the room where Lepkin was laying, but there were a pair of guards standing in front of the door. Jaleal jerked his head back and pushed the door closed. He scrambled back to the window and went back outside. He quickly worked his way around the temple building until he was on the north side. His hands moved quickly, finding grooves just big enough for him to dangle from as he climbed sideways to the window where he supposed Lepkin's room was.

The gnome climbed above the window, then turned himself upside down and slowly lowered his eyes down to look through the window. He saw a pair of men standing over Lepkin, with their backs turned to him. He moved one hand down and tested the window. It was locked.

He pulled himself back up. "You made it before," Jaleal told himself. "There are only two of them this time." He climbed up and grabbed hold of the beams in the awning above him and thought of a plan. He positioned his feet against one beam with his back against the opposite beam to let his arms rest. Then he pulled a small flute from a pouch around his neck and wet his lips. He put the instrument to his mouth and worked his fingers as he blew into it, but no sound came out. He continued to play vigorously, as though he was playing for a royal court, but no music emitted from the end of the bone flute.

A few minutes later a red-headed woodpecker flew up and lighted on his knee.

"Hello there," Jaleal said as he took a short break. "I have a task for you." He cupped a hand to the bird's head and whispered to it. Then he went back to playing the bone flute. The bird flew down to the window sill and began tapping on the wood below the window.

Tap tap tap. Tap-tap. Tappity-tap-tap.

Jaleal grinned and played the flute while the woodpecker continued his rhythm below. A minute later the window flew open and a man shouted at the bird.

"Be gone, pest!" Jaleal saw the man sweep his arm at the bird. That was his opening. The gnome dropped down from his hiding spot, landing on the man's forearm. He sent a deft kick to the man's jaw, knocking his head back. Then he came in with a series of quick strikes to the man's temple. The healer lost consciousness and fell backward.

Jaleal sprinted forward, fast as the wind. The woodpecker flew in above him, landing on the other healer's head and pounding the man's skull for all he was worth.

"Argh!" the healer cried out as the bird pulled out bits of hair.

The door flew open and in rushed the two guards. They ran in toward the healer, but never saw the gnome coming. Jaleal mentally called out for his spear and it magically appeared back in his hand. He spun the weapon around and cracked the first guard's nose. Then he spun it back around and jabbed the blunt end into the base of the man's neck. He grunted and fell to the side. The gnome then flicked the spear and whacked the guard across the back of the man's head and he fell to the floor.

The second guard had caught on and was now running toward Jaleal, leaving the other healer to fend off the angry bird. The gnome slid on his knees under a sweeping halberd and then lashed out stabbing the guard's right wrist with the tip of his spear. The gnome then jumped up and kicked the guard in the groin as hard as he could. As the guard fell, face twisted in agony, Jaleal slammed the side of his head with the blunt end of the spear.

After the second guard fell the gnome went to the healer. He agilely ran up the man's backside and reached around his face to cover his mouth while he used his left arm to pinch a nerve in the man's neck. The healer twitched and convulsed, but ultimately he too fell to the floor.

Seeing that his obstacles were now out of the way, Jaleal saluted the bird and then closed and locked the doors to the room. The bird flew away without another sound, leaving Jaleal to his task.

The gnome bounded atop the bed where Lepkin lay and crouched in close, placing his left hand on Lepkin's chest, exactly over the man's sternum. Then, he pointed the tip of his spear into Lepkin's skin just between where Jaleal's thumb and forefinger rested.

"Forgive me," he whispered to Lepkin. Jaleal raised the spear high as his hand would go and then closed his eyes. A moment later he brought the spear down to Lepkin's chest. At the exact moment the tip pierced Lepkin's skin a bolt of lightning coursed in from the window and struck the end of the spear. Jaleal and Lepkin were bathed in silver, shimmering light for a blinding instant and then a crack of thunder ripped the two apart from each other. Jaleal careened through the room, crashing to the floor with his spear tumbling after him.

The gnome struggled to lift his eyes and looked at Lepkin. A blue, silvery flame rose up from Lepkin's chest for just a moment and then it flickered and died. Lepkin's body convulsed and his back arched up as he gasped and choked. Then his eyes opened and he slowly turned to his side, moaning. The man coughed and sputtered for a few seconds and then his eyes met Jaleal's.

Jaleal smiled. "Nice to meet you, Keeper," he said.

Lepkin shook his head and pushed himself up, looking around the room. "What happened? Who are you?"

The gnome chuckled through gasps for breath and then nodded. "We'll have time for introductions later. We need to get to Erik."

CHAPTER TWENTY THREE

Erik stood in front of the dragon. He could see the merit in the dragon's words, but he couldn't believe that everything he had been through, all of his training, and the suffering that the others went through, would lead him to this.

"You hesitate," the dragon said, breaking the silence. "Do you not understand what I have said?"

"I understand," Erik said.

The dragon breathed in deeply and let out a small spark of fire with his next sentence. "You have the power to use Nagar's Blight for good. You can prevent this world from perishing in a lake of fire."

"The book is evil," Erik countered. "It can't be used for good."

"You misjudge," the dragon said. "Think of a sword." The dragon waved his claw and a great, shining sword appeared on the pedestal. "Is a sword good or evil?"

Erik thought for a moment. "It is neither. It is only a tool," he said.

The dragon nodded. "As a sword may either hew down the weak if wielded by an evil hand, so to it might protect the same if wielded by an honorable hand."

Erik shook his head. "There is no honor in this magic," he said.

"Not so," the dragon said. "Even the wizard Allun'rha saw this. How do you think he stopped the power of Nagar's Secret during the battle of Hamath?" The dragon paused for effect. "He turned the spell against itself. Just as those who seek the book would use it to warp men's souls, it can be used to perfect them. By so doing, you can create an everlasting peace and end all suffering on this world. It would become a paradise."

"Paradise?" Erik echoed. He thought for a minute and then the conjured sword before him vanished. He looked up to the dragon. "If that is true, then why didn't Allun'rha do that at the battle of Hamath?"

"He did not understand the full potential of the power he

had," the dragon replied simply. "But I do, and now I present the opportunity to you." The dragon reached forward with a single claw and gently pressed it to Erik's heart. "You are pure," he said. "You have the power to use this for the right reasons. You will be hailed as the greatest of kings for all generations to come. All will know that it was Erik, the Champion of Truth, who finally dispelled all evil from Terramyr."

The dragon then backed away and looked down to Erik with a smile.

Erik smiled as he thought about it. "Can you show me?" Erik asked.

The dragon nodded and blew a gentle breath on Erik. As with the previous magic, the temple fell away and Erik found himself on the same green mountain overlooking the valley. The dragon came and stood next to him, causing the ground to tremble under his weight.

"Look to the forest now," the dragon said.

A horde of men, women, and children marched out from the forest. They wore plain clothes and pulled carts behind them filled with various goods and food supplies. Then, from the temple issued a great throng of priests, but instead of holding weapons, they went out with open arms to the people and when the groups met they embraced and sang songs.

"Look," the dragon said as it raised a claw to point to the temple.

Erik looked up and saw himself standing on the balcony of the temple, wearing a crown of gold and jewels and dressed in a robe of red and white. Marlin stood next to him, and the golden dragon circled above with a triumphant roar as it landed atop the temple.

"What are they doing?" Erik asked.

"The people of the Middle Kingdom have come to pay tribute, and to establish a new order wherein no one suffers. No one goes hungry. No sons kiss their mothers as they depart for war, and no more fathers will bury their sons. Order will be restored." The dragon then leaned down close to Erik's ear and whispered, "And there will never be another orphan, lost and forgotten by the world."

"Paradise," Erik said as he listened to the joyful singing below.

Then he turned and looked to the dragon. "What of the four pillars of fire?" he asked.

The dragon shook his head. "They will never come," he said.

Erik looked back to the scene and started to walk a few steps down the mountain. Then, just as he was about to agree, something nagged at the back of his soul, tugging at his gut. He couldn't quite put his finger on it at first, and then he realized what it was. It was there before him as clearly as a pile of manure dropped by a careless dog on its master's bedroom floor.

The boy turned back to the dragon. "But, to do this is not really any better than what Tu'luh would do," he said. "Either way it robs people of their will to choose. The world would be a hollow paradise, void of virtue or real honor."

The dragon hissed and nodded its great head. "You are a wise boy indeed," it said solemnly.

The spell faded away and they were back in the temple as before.

"So that is the test, then?" Erik asked. "To see whether I would allow myself to fall prey to the temptation of the book?"

The dragon stood motionless, peering into his soul. "You would rather let the world burn?" he asked.

"Life without choice would be empty, and meaningless," Erik replied. "Why trade Tu'luh's tyranny for a different version of the same?" Erik then realized why the dragon was trying to persuade him. He called forth his power one more time and scanned the dragon.

The dragon scraped its claws along the stone, gouging the blue granite and causing Erik to shudder at the sound. "I had hoped to convince you otherwise," he said. His golden scales melted away like dirt being washed from a porcelain statue and revealed fierce, red scales beneath. The horns and spikes along his spine lost their shine and instead glowed from within as though fire was inside. The two massive horns on his head curved down around his snout and the green eyes changed to the color of molten lava.

"You are a nightwing?" Erik gasped.

"No," the dragon hissed. "I am Tu'luh the Red!" he bellowed. Then he reared up and stretched his mighty wings out beside him.

Erik stumbled over backwards and gasped. "No, how could

you be *here*?" he shrieked.

Tu'luh stepped forward, crushing the pedestal underfoot and leaned down with his massive head. "There was a dragon left behind by the Ancients," he said. "One that was to give the Exalted Test of Arophim. But he could not withstand the power of Nagar's Blight. Not even here in this... temple."

"Where did he go?" Erik asked.

Tu'luh stepped aside and revealed a ragged tunnel clawed through the granite in the back of the chamber. "He tore his way out," he said. "There was a fountain there, for the dragon to sustain himself during his long sleep. But this chamber could not protect him. After the blight drove him mad he came to me. He was twisted, warped. He was no longer a dragon, but a nightwing, as you call them." Tu'luh growled low. "You met him when the wizard Erthor came to the temple."

"Lepkin killed him," Erik said.

Tu'luh nodded.

"If you were here, why not attack me when I first arrived?" Erik asked.

"The battle of Hamath nearly killed me," Tu'luh explained. "I needed to recover my strength. So when the other vacated the temple, I came here. It was the perfect place for me to convalesce while simultaneously keeping an eye on the temple."

"You were the one who told the other prelate to force me to take the test," Erik guessed.

Tu'luh nodded. "If I could have gotten to you then, I think you would have seen things differently." The dragon slammed his tail into one of the massive columns, breaking it apart and causing the chamber to quake. "Last chance, boy," the beast hissed. "Join with me and we can still make the world a paradise."

"And if I refuse?" Erik asked with trembling voice.

"Then the future you saw in the Chronicle of the Spurned will come to pass. Either way, I will rule."

"You're a monster!" Erik shouted.

Tu'luh slammed his great foreleg down, a claw landing on either side of Erik and pinning him to the floor. "I am a savior!" Tu'luh roared. "I want to save this world from its end. I thought you would understand that!" The beast coiled its neck back and angled its snout down toward Erik. "However, I am willing to rule over a kingdom of demons and monsters if that accomplishes the same end. The world of men may end, but the dragons will be able to live on." A great rumble sounded deep within the beast's body and an orange glow shone through the scales of its underbelly. Tu'luh then opened his mouth and a great light shined forth.

Erik squirmed and wiggled, but he was pinned. The light in the back of Tu'luh's throat grew more intense and Erik could hear the roaring fire welling up the beast's neck. He kicked furiously, but he couldn't free himself.

Just before the fire spewed out of Tu'luh's mouth, a flash of silver flew through the air and slammed into the dragon's snout. The dragon snarled and recoiled away, misdirecting its fire to a wall. Next came a flourish of flame near the back of the beast's foreleg and the dragon launched itself forward between the pillars and crashed almost one hundred yards away, sliding into a column and shattering the stone. A hand reached down and Erik's eyes went wide when he saw Lepkin pull him up by his shirt collar.

"Behind me!" Lepkin shouted.

"Fool!" Tu'luh growled. "Not even you can defeat me!" The dragon spewed roiling, red flames at them.

Erik and Lepkin took shelter behind the remains of a column as the fire wrapped around them. Lepkin held Erik in close to the stone until the flames subsided and the dragon snarled again.

"Where are you?" the beast roared.

Erik drew his brow together, but Lepkin held a finger to his mouth. Then the same flash of silver spun back through the air. Erik looked around Lepkin to see Jaleal, the gnome, holding the gleaming spear in hand.

"I am here, foul beast," Jaleal shouted in a voice that should have come from a much larger creature. "Come and feel the sting of Aeolbani's wrath!"

Tu'luh hissed. "I know the gnome who forged that spear" he growled. "I thought I destroyed his line long ago."

Jaleal stood in the center of the chamber, in full view of the dragon.

"We should help him," Erik said.

Lepkin nodded and motioned for Erik to remain quiet. "When the time is right." He then reached behind him and retrieved a second sword. He handed the blade to Erik. "This won't do much more than anger the beast, so wait until I give the signal."

Erik nodded. Then a chill went up his spine as he heard the rumbling sound of the fire building in the dragon's throat again. Tu'luh rushed forward, shaking the chamber with each step. Then a rush of fire washed over them again. Lepkin pressed harder into Erik this time, and Erik could feel the heat of the flames much more intensely. He was sure the gnome was caught this time, but an angry snarl and hiss from Tu'luh was quickly followed by Jaleal's cackling laugh.

"Never were good at catching gnomes, were you wyrm?" Jaleal taunted the beast from somewhere down deeper in the chamber. A sudden crack, like the sound of bursting thunder rumbled through the chamber and shards of rock flew overhead.

"Now," Lepkin said. "Stay with me." Erik got up and tried to keep pace with Lepkin, but with his leg still knotting up in the middle, he found it difficult to do. Lepkin stopped behind another column and motioned for Erik to take cover.

Erik ducked down just as Tu'luh's head poked through an opening between two pillars. Erik's mouth fell open when he noticed the pair of deep gashes in the dragon's snout.

"He's bleeding," Erik whispered to himself.

The dragon turned and his big red eye looked down and saw Erik. "Champion!" he growled. The beast opened its mouth but Lepkin rushed forward with his flaming sword and sliced diagonally across the beast's snout. Tu'luh recoiled and his head bent low enough for Lepkin to jump onto the back of his head. Lepkin raised his sword to strike down at Tu'luh's eye, but the beast snapped its neck back and jerked its body to the side. Lepkin connected with the side of Tu'luh's snout, but missed the dragon's eye as he toppled off and crashed to the ground.

Tu'luh snarled again and disappeared from view. Erik scooted around the other side of the column and saw Jaleal quickly working his spear on the back of Tu'luh's left hind leg. The scales were thicker there, but there was still one line of blood from where the gnome was able to slip his spear up under one of the scales.

The dragon snapped down at the gnome with its teeth, but Jaleal dodged out of the way and ducked behind a column as a fireball sailed by him. Tu'luh then shattered the column with his tail and lunged forward with his claws to get at the gnome.

A fog filled the room then, covering all but the bottom six feet of the chamber. Erik watched as Lepkin rushed out into the middle of the chamber and gave a mighty swing of his blade to Tu'luh's foreleg again. The blade connected hard, showering sparks around Lepkin and a scale broke in half. The dragon roared and Erik saw a great light above the smoke as a wave of fire rolled across the ceiling. Lepkin then ran across the chamber and hid behind another pillar just as the flames turned down and descended on the spot he had been standing in.

Lightning struck out from the thick fog, stinging the great beast and causing him to spin around wildly, swinging his tail and snapping his maw at everything the way a dog might fight off a swarm of bees.

Then Erik heard a thunderous ruckus from behind. He turned to see the cavedogs pouring in from the cavern. Their riders whooping and hollering madly as they brandished their axes. Faengoril led the charge, winking at Erik as he sped past.

Shortly after, the chamber filled with the sound of steel ringing against the dragon's scales. Erik took heart and stood out from behind the column, awestruck by the sight before him. Lightning continued to blast the dragon from above, while the cavedogs and their riders worked feverishly under the fog. The boy smiled to himself, amazed that the end of Tu'luh was at hand.

Then a great quake shook the chamber and shards of stone flew into the dwarves, knocking several of them from their mounts. The dragon dropped his sharp claws down, tearing many more dwarves apart. Then the dragon spun around and the column Erik was standing near burst asunder as if struck by the gods themselves. Erik ducked and somehow managed to avoid being crushed by flying stone, but he soon realized that none were safe. A crack appeared in the floor a few yards away from him and a great snap echoed from above as hunks of granite fell to crush any slow enough to be caught in its path.

"You shall all burn!" Tu'luh swore. His fire engulfed several dwarves and turned them to ash in the blink of an eye.

Erik felt his heart sink. They were so close! Now to have the dragon snatch victory from them was unthinkable. His mind recalled the images that Tu'luh had shown him. As he thought of the red dragon sitting upon the black mountain with an ocean of dead below him, he couldn't stomach the thought anymore. His inner courage rose to the surface and he ran forward. He leapt over the widening crack in the floor, dodged a fiery hunk of stone from above, and sidestepped Tu'luh's massive tail as it swatted down a pair of rider-less cavedogs. Then he jumped on the tail and ran up. It was hard to keep his footing, as the dragon was moving and in the throes of battle, but somehow he managed to move in between the spikes along the beast's spine and make his way to the beast's shoulder.

The boy let out a feral yell, and sent his spark of power with it, dispelling the thick smoke so he could see his target easily. Everything around him seemed to slow, as if each second was an entire minute. He saw the dragon spread its left wing and he lashed out with his sword, tearing a small gash in the leathery wing and forcing the beast to turn and look at him. Then Erik launched himself forward, sword high above his head as the dragon's mouth came in for him, opening wide.

A flash of silver came up from below and slashed the beast across the snout. The dragon turned at the last minute, giving Erik the opening he needed. He brought his sword down, slicing through the dragon's left eye as the steel shattered in a storm of sparks. The beast reeled back in agony, roaring and hissing fire all over the ceiling as it fumbled backward.

Erik let go of the broken sword and fell down. He looked up to the ceiling and the flames above him seemed to pass peacefully over the stone, as if they were nothing more than orange and red waves of water. The air beneath him felt cool as he descended and he closed his eyes, remembering the feeling of flight when he had been in dragon form. Then he slowed in what felt like thick air.

He opened his eyes and saw Lady Dimwater standing before him, holding her hand out. "Get up," she scolded. "We aren't done yet!"

Erik fell the last two feet to the ground and jumped up to his feet. He looked up and saw the mighty beast still convulsing and writhing in pain, slamming its head and tail into anything nearby, including the wall.

The entire chamber shook violently and then the dragon tore through the ceiling with its claws and ejected a column of fire up through the hole. Erik could hear gasps and screams from above and then the whole earth around them began to tremble.

Tu'luh then flipped from his back and beat his wings, launching himself toward the tunnel at the far end of the chamber. As he exited, he took down the last three remaining pillars with his tail for good measure and disappeared through the tunnel faster than a rabbit fleeing a pack of dogs.

"Come on!" Faengoril shouted from nearby. "This place is coming down, everyone out!" he bellowed.

Erik and Lepkin ran for the tunnel, following after the cavedogs and their riders. Lady Dimwater rode upon a cloud, using her magic to steady the ceiling as best she could until everyone was well into the tunnel. Then she flew out after them.

A great plume of smoke and dust erupted from the tunnel, carrying shards of stone and rock through the air. Erik shielded his face from the debris and then waited for it to clear so he could survey the scene.

As the dust settled, he barely saw Tu'luh flying toward the south. He was already so far away that he looked no bigger than a falcon in the sky.

"He won't be coming back for a while," Lepkin said assuredly. "You gave him quite the sting."

Erik turned and saw Lepkin sitting near him, breathing heavily. Marlin was coughing and shaking dust from his hair. Faengoril was counting his troops, and Alferug was tending to one of the wounded dwarves. Lady Dimwater was standing a few yards off, tending to a hole in her sleeve and mumbling something about exacting revenge on the dragon for tearing her favorite gown. Then the dark haired woman whirled around and pointed an accusing finger.

"And you!" she shouted angrily.

Erik's heart jumped into his throat and he nearly squeaked like a mouse until he realized that she was marching up to Lepkin, and not him.

Lepkin jumped to his feet and started to open his mouth but no words came out. Dimwater jabbed him in the chest with her finger.

"Why have you been asleep this *whoooole* time?!" she shouted. Everyone shifted nervously away from her except for Lepkin. He was too dumbfounded to react. The woman then grabbed a fistful of Lepkin's shirt and pulled him in for a long, hard kiss that made Erik blush and look away. When he looked back, he saw that Lepkin's face was red as well.

"I—er—" Lepkin stammered as she pushed him away from her again.

She poked him again, hard enough to push him back a couple inches. "Don't *ever* do that again!" she scolded.

"Awww," Faengoril smirked. A couple of dwarves laughed, but they all quickly looked away when Dimwater turned a glaring eye at them.

"Alright," Lepkin said sheepishly.

Dimwater then pulled him close again and buried her face in his neck as she squeezed him close to her. The two held each other for a few moments and then Lady Dimwater let go and moved to Lepkin's side, holding his left hand with both of hers and leaning her head on his shoulder with a tear falling down her cheek.

Erik smiled and turned away, trying to give the two of them what little privacy he could. He looked up to the right and saw Jaleal, standing proudly on top of a boulder, spear in hand and shouting at Tu'luh in a foreign tongue.

"See," Lepkin said as he nudged Erik in the back with his foot. "Heroes come in all sizes."

Erik nodded and Jaleal turned around, spinning his spear and smiling as he bounded down to stand next to Erik.

"As I said," Jaleal started. "I am here to help."

"How did you know I would be in trouble?" Erik asked. Marlin came in close as well, obviously eager to hear the story.

Jaleal blushed. "Well, after I was expelled from the temple, I was looking for a way to get back in." He pointed to Lepkin. "I was trying to wake him up."

"Sorry about that," Marlin said.

"Don't be," Jaleal said quickly. "If you hadn't expelled me, I never would have found this tunnel." Jaleal gestured to the opening where dust was still rolling out from the collapsed chamber. "The opening wasn't as obvious as it is now. It was overgrown and hard to see, but we gnomes can talk with the plants, so I was able to find it easily enough. I went in, hoping to find a secret way back up to Lepkin. Instead I stumbled on the dragon's lair."

"But how did you know it was Tu'luh?" Marlin asked. "The dragon who was first there was a golden dragon named Hiasyntar'Kulai."

Jaleal held a finger up in the air. "I heard two voices," he said. "One was the dragon's, and the other was a man's. So I went in to investigate. When I did, I saw the apparition of a man dressed in black robes. I could tell it was magic, and not really an audience in any physical sense, so I crept in closer to see what I could see." Jaleal's smile faded then and he brandished his spear. "It was the same man I saw as a young child," he said. "He torched my villages and murdered my grandfather."

"Who was it?" Erik asked.

"It is a powerful necromancer. He goes by the name of Gilifan, and has unnaturally prolonged his life with the use of the darkest magic." Jaleal propped his spear on his foot and wrinkled his nose. "Once I saw who it was, I knew the dragon had to be an imposter. So I came to Lepkin as soon as I could."

"Then, after he woke me, he told me what he just told you and he rushed out to get the dwarves while I went and told Marlin," Lepkin added.

"And I went to fetch Lady Dimwater," Marlin added.

Jaleal nodded. "Then we came for you as soon as we could," Jaleal told Erik. The gnome then twirled his toe, digging it into the dirt and looked up to Marlin. "I should apologize for the two healers and the guards," he said.

"Perhaps I should have listened to you," Marlin replied.

"Perhaps?" Jaleal retorted sarcastically before he quickly covered his mouth and blushed a bit behind his silver beard.

Faengoril came up and slapped the gnome on the back. "I really like this guy," he said with a big grin.

CHAPTER TWENTY FOUR

Gilifan surveyed his room once more. All of the artifacts he no longer needed were piled in the room, each stored in a wooden box and sealed shut. He weaved a spell over the items to prevent them from being tampered with. Then he set a cohort of ten soldiers in front of the door and gave them the order to kill any who approached until he returned.

Next he sent a rider to Spiekery with a message for the village people there that they could come to the keep if there were any problems. What he didn't tell the villagers was that the rest of his mindless army would be waiting in the keep's courtyard with orders to kill everyone that showed up. He was meticulous like that. No reason to allow loose ends to dangle freely in the wind.

A dead mouth tells no secrets, that was his philosophy. Besides, he could always bring them back anyway.

At that moment he remembered he didn't have the amulet anymore. He exhaled angrily and silently berated himself for letting a kobold get the better of him. Then he shook the thought away and focused on the task at hand.

He finished the final preparations. He packed the lockbox with the treasure and sent it to the ship at the dock with his two best warriors. He also sent a coin purse with them to pay the ship's captain the prearranged fare for his voyage south. Then he went to the dining hall for his last meal in the keep before heading out to the ship and watching the men load the master's cargo.

As Gilifan stood on the ship, watching the men load the large crate onto the deck he couldn't help but chew his lower lip nervously. They pushed the crate up the gangplank and nearly slammed it into the deck railing. "Be careful with that," he warned. "The master will not be pleased if anything should happen to it."

The mindless servants nodded blankly and carefully slid the crate into place. Then they finished securing the pulley ropes around the crate. A series of short whistles sounded and then a group of men pulled on several different ropes, all attached to pulleys that hung from above to hoist the crate up and then lower it into the cargo hold below through an opening in the deck.

A heavy set man with dark skin came out from the captain's cabin and approached Gilifan. "Will we be taking the men as well?" the captain asked.

Gilifan shook his head. "No," he replied. "Except for the two down below, I will go alone this time."

The captain rubbed the back of his neck and looked up from the dock to the long road winding up a green hill to the back of the great keep that had once belonged to Lord Hischurn. "Seems a pity to leave such a great home."

The necromancer offered a polite smile and then walked over as the men closed the grate over the hold where the crate had been loaded. After they locked the grate in place he sent the men back to the keep. "Maintain order until I return," he told them.

"Obedient lot," the captain commented. "Where did you find them?"

"Why do you ask?" Gilifan questioned.

The captain shrugged and looked around his deck at his crew. "I wouldn't mind having men like that in my employ," he said.

Gilifan sniggered to himself and then went below deck. He had arranged for a cot to be set up in the hold, next to the crate, and had purchased the use of the entire cargo hold as his personal quarters for the duration of the trip south. When he entered the hold, he found his two best men standing guard.

The necromancer gestured for the men to turn away from the crate. They did so and he went up to the wooden box and slid a hand over the front. The crate was as tall as his chest, and each side was four feet long. He slid a key into the lock and unhooked the latch. The necromancer gently pushed the lid up on its hinges to peer inside and check the contents. With his left hand he brushed away some loose straw to reveal the top of a massive, golden egg with red spots.

"Master Tu'luh will be happy to have you home, young prince," Gilifan said to the dragon egg.

ABOUT THE AUTHOR

I like to call myself a well-traveled story teller of Irish and Cherokee heritage. Currently I live near a Stone Bridge on Eagle Mountain, however, I count seven U.S. states as home. I have spent several years abroad, first as a missionary in the Baltic States and currently as a Diplomat in the U.S. Foreign Service. When I'm not wrestling with my sons or hefting iron in the gym I can be found at home relaxing with my wife or setting pen to paper, bringing stories to life.

www.ingramcontent.com/pod-product-compliance
Lightning Source LLC
Chambersburg PA
CBHW050016180626
46810CB00002B/442